"Twenty-year-old Jonas Weaver can't resist fighting the evil of slavery by joining the War Between the States. Off to the army he goes, despite strong objections by his family, his Amish church, and his sweetheart, Katie Stuckey. When Jonas's letters stop coming, Katie has to face something from her past she has tried to ignore. Jan Drexler's *The Sound of Distant Thunder* combines historical research with compelling characters to create a memorable story of love in the time of war."

**Suzanne Woods Fisher,** bestselling author
of *Anna's Crossing*

"In *The Sound of Distant Thunder,* the sweetness of young love, the conflict and sorrow of the War Between the States, the wisdom of couples long married, and the cost of making a stand for what one believes are blended into a story that kept me turning pages. The way Jan Drexler's Amish characters spring to life off the page will leave readers wanting to know more about the people in this Amish community. For sure and certain."

**Ann H. Gabhart,** bestselling author
of *These Healing Hills*

"Faith, family, and freedom are tested by the crucible of war in this haunting love story of a gentle people whose lives—and hearts—are disrupted by the sound of distant thunder. Historically rich and rare, this is a unique glimpse into a nation divided that both captures the mind and nourishes the soul."

**Julie Lessman,** award-winning author of The Daughters
of Boston, Winds of Change, and Isle of Hope series

"In a beautifully woven story, Jan Drexler once again gives her readers a true look at the struggles of faith, hope, and love facing families, churches, communities, and a nation during a time of turbulence . . . and love."

**Ruth Logan Herne,** award-winning author

## Other books by Jan Drexler

THE AMISH *of* WEAVER'S CREEK #1

# *The*
# SOUND
# *of* DISTANT
# THUNDER

## JAN DREXLER

Revell

a division of *Baker Publishing Group*
Grand Rapids, Michigan

© 2018 by Jan Drexler

Published by Revell
a division of Baker Publishing Group
PO Box 6287, Grand Rapids, MI 49516-6287
www.revellbooks.com

Printed in the United States of America

Library of Congress Cataloging-in-Publication Data
Names: Drexler, Jan, author.
Title: The sound of distant thunder / Jan Drexler.
Description: Grand Rapids, MI : Revell, a division of Baker Publishing Group,
    [2018] | Series: The Amish of Weaver's Creek ; 1
Identifiers: LCCN 2018014428 | ISBN 9780800729318 (softcover : acid-free paper)
Subjects: LCSH: Amish—Fiction. | GSAFD: Christian fiction. | Love stories.
Classification: LCC PS3604.R496 S68 2018 | DDC 813/.6—dc23
LC record available at https://lccn.loc.gov/2018014428

ISBN 978-0-8007-3549-4 (casebound)

18  19  20  21  22  23  24      7  6  5  4  3  2  1

For John Tomlonson, my dad, whose love of history
has done much to shape my life.

*Soli Deo Gloria*

And it came to pass, when Joshua was by Jericho, that he lifted up his eyes and looked, and, behold, there stood a man over against him with his sword drawn in his hand: and Joshua went unto him, and said unto him, Art thou for us, or for our adversaries? And he said, Nay; but as captain of the host of the LORD am I now come.

Joshua 5:13–14

# 1

"Jonas! Pay attention! You're going to drop that sack!"

Jonas Weaver barely heard his brother Samuel's warning above the tumult of the crowd down the street. As he had come out of the feed store, balancing the fifty-pound bag of seed on his shoulders, the shouts had drawn him. He stared into the crowd gathered in front of the office of the *Holmes County Gazette*. Among the raised voices, the only clear word was "War!"

Samuel grabbed the sack of seed corn off Jonas's shoulders and tossed it onto the wagon bed. "What are you doing? I thought you were going to wander off with that seed. You need to keep your mind on your work, not on Katie Stuckey."

Jonas glanced at his older brother's stormy face, then back at the crowd that commanded his attention. Katie was never far from his thoughts, but Samuel was wrong this time. Something big must have happened in the war. A big battle, maybe. The Federals needed a big win to end this war and bring peace to the country.

"Don't you hear what they're saying?" Jonas followed Samuel as he turned to walk back into the store. He caught up with him at the freight door, next to the rest of their sacks of seed corn. "They're talking about the war, Samuel."

His brother ignored him as he hefted the next sack of grain onto his shoulders and headed toward the wagon again. Jonas grabbed a sack off the pile and hurried after him.

"What do you think it means?" Jonas tilted his sack onto the wagon bed.

Samuel pushed the sack into place against the others, then he leaned one hand on the tailgate and frowned at Jonas. "What does it mean? It means more evil, and more fighting. Bloodshed and violence. Homes destroyed, men killed, farms torn in pieces so there's no possibility of crops. It means terrible things. It's been going on for a year now with no end in sight, and I'm sick of hearing about it."

Samuel stalked back to the freight dock. He was right. Jonas glanced across the street again, where the crowd was getting larger. But where there was war, there might also be change. Change that could bring the freedom to the slaves in the South that the abolitionist preachers had been urging.

"Jonas!" Samuel's impatient voice strode ahead of him as he came back with another load. He heaved the grain onto the wagon. "I need to get some things for Anna at Wilson's Dry Goods. When you're done loading the grain, drive down and meet me there."

"For sure, I will."

At thirty-four years old, and married with four children, his brother acted as if Jonas was still a young child. But Jonas was twenty years old, old enough to know his own mind. Old enough to make his own way in the world.

As Samuel walked off, Jonas quickly loaded the last two sacks and closed the tailgate.

And war or no war, he was old enough to know who he wanted to marry. After all, Samuel had been nineteen when he married Anna. There was no reason why Jonas couldn't marry his Katie and start farming his own land. Tonight, after storing the seed and before the hard work of planting began tomorrow, would be the time to talk to *Datt*.

Years ago, when Samuel and Anna had set up housekeeping on the north section of the farm, Datt had let Jonas choose a quarter section of land for his own, and Jonas had chosen the woods in the east section. If he wanted to marry Katie in the fall, it was time for him to start building a house for the two of them, but he had to convince Datt to give him the time off to do it. He had been rehearsing what he would say ever since the idea had come to him.

Climbing onto the wagon seat, Jonas picked up the reins. As he drove closer to the newspaper office, he was drawn by the excitement of the crowd. He wished he had the money to buy a copy of today's edition, but he'd have to make do with gleaning what he could from the crowd.

Not that he read the newspaper often. The Amish didn't involve themselves in politics, as Datt always said. Not just Datt, but all of his family. All of the church community. But Jonas wanted to know what was happening in the world around him, especially during an exciting time like this. Ever since last spring, when the Southern states fired on Fort Sumter, Jonas had found himself held captive by the events.

As he came closer to the newspaper office, the large crowd

forced the wagon to the far edge of the street. Everyone was focused on a man standing on a box in front of the *Gazette*'s office, reading aloud from the paper that must be fresh off the press. Jonas only caught snatches of what he was reading, but the meaning was clear. A battle had been fought in a place called Pittsburg Landing in Tennessee. He had nearly reached the far edge of the crowd when the speaker came to the end of the reading, listing the number of casualties. Then he read that the Confederates had been defeated, and a roar of dismay went up from the crowd that startled Jonas and spooked the horses.

Jonas stood on the wagon box, leaning back on the reins to hold the horses in as well as he could, speaking to them in a low tone that he hoped would carry to the frightened team. The horses jostled the men at the edge of the crowd, and one of them looked around, annoyed. Jonas met his eyes before turning his attention back to his team. It was Ned Hamlin. Ned and his father weren't farmers but lived off the land in the wild, swampy area on the other side of Weaver's Creek, east of the Weavers' farm.

Ned spat in the dirt next to the wagon wheel, then grinned at Jonas. "One Federal victory ain't gonna win this war, right?"

Jonas clenched his teeth to keep from entering into an argument with Ned. "I need to move on."

Ned stepped back. "Sure you do. You and all your cowardly family. Amish don't fight? I say Amish can't fight. They're too busy running scared with their tails between their legs."

Jonas tightened sweaty fingers around the reins as one of Ned's companions noticed them. He clapped Ned on the shoulder. "Them Amish are all Lincoln's lackeys, ain't they? Doin' whatever he wants."

Clucking to the team, Jonas drove away from the boisterous crowd, toward the block past the courthouse where Samuel would be waiting. A different kind of crowd gathered along the boardwalk, keeping their distance from Ned Hamlin and his like. These men were quieter, grouped in twos and threes, reading the paper to themselves. John Cabot, the publisher of the paper, stepped up next to the wagon and handed Jonas a copy.

"I don't have the money to buy a paper today, Mr. Cabot." Jonas knew the man from the abolitionist meetings he had attended during the winter.

Mr. Cabot's smile was genuine. "No charge today, Jonas. In celebration of the Union victory." He folded the paper up and tucked it under the seat, keeping pace with the wagon. "Look at the notice on page 3. There's a meeting for volunteers in Brownsville on Tuesday. We need every able-bodied man we can get."

Jonas glanced toward Wilson's store, where Samuel waited for him on the boardwalk in front. "I don't know, Mr. Cabot. I support abolition, but joining the fighting—"

Mr. Cabot waved his protest away. "I know, I know. You Plain folk won't enter into war, and I won't push you." He turned to head back to his office, where more people had congregated, and threw a last comment over his shoulder. "But think on it, boy. It could be the Lord has a place for you in the Cause."

Drawing the team up in front of Wilson's store, Jonas handed the reins to Samuel as his brother climbed into the driver's seat.

"What was that all about?"

Jonas refrained from glancing toward the newspaper office. "What?"

"I saw that newspaperman talking to you. Did he want the Amish perspective on the price of corn?" Samuel started the horses off, turning the corner to avoid the crowds on Jackson Street.

"You know what they're talking about." Jonas leaned over and drew out the newspaper. He opened it to page 2, where the news of the war started. "Do you want me to read to you about the battle in Tennessee?"

Samuel hunched in his seat, his eyes on the near horse's ears. "I have no interest in what is happening in the world. It has nothing to do with us. It's foolishness. God calls us to live separate from the world, and that's what we do." He shot a meaningful glance in Jonas's direction. "It's what you should do too."

"You forget," Jonas said, crossing one leg over the other knee, "I'm not baptized yet."

A growling sound came from Samuel's side of the seat, but Jonas ignored it. He folded the paper so he could focus on the third page. Between an advertisement for men's clothing and one for prickly plasters was the notice Mr. Cabot had mentioned. "The time is now for all men of good conscience to act . . ."

Jonas glanced at Samuel, then back to the notice. Did a man of good conscience live as if this conflict didn't exist?

⟵~~~⟶

"Katie!" Mama's tired voice drifted up the stairway from the kitchen. "Where have you gotten to?"

Sitting on her bed, where she could see the road and the turn into the Weavers' farm through the fence row, Katie glanced toward the stairway, then out the window again. Jonas and Samuel should be coming home from Millersburg any time now. He must come home before sunset, because Papa wouldn't let her walk out after dark.

Mama's foot sounded on the bottom step. "Probably dreaming again." Mama was muttering to herself again. "Head in the clouds, that one."

Two more steps. One more, and Mama would be able to see her. Margaretta Stuckey wasn't one to condone daydreaming. Katie stood and untied her apron strings, tying them again just as Mama's frowning face appeared at the top of the stairway.

"I'm coming, Mama. I just needed to retie my apron."

Mama leaned back as Katie slipped by her on her way down the steps. "Those supper dishes won't wash themselves."

"*Ja, ja, ja,* Mama. I know."

Katie grabbed the tin washbasin off its nail on the wall, leaning over to look out the kitchen window. She couldn't see past their own barnyard from here, the bushes were too thick. The spring growth already covered the opening she had been able to peer through all winter, blocking her view of the road and the neighboring farm in the distance. She had to hurry, in case he did come in time.

She ladled hot water from the pot Mama kept on the back of the stove into the basin and set it on the counter. A few quick shavings of soap, and Katie stirred the water with her fingers, trying to get the soap to dissolve.

"I have to say you aren't wasting any time." Mama came up behind her with the plates she had gathered from the table.

"You always say that tasks are already halfway done when you start them." Katie put the plates in the dishwater and started scrubbing while Mama took the second washbasin and filled it with clean water for rinsing.

"Why are you in such a hurry?" Mama asked as Katie put the first plate in the rinse water.

"Jonas should be home at any time, and I expect he'll come over."

Mama wiped off the table, clicking her tongue. "Don't put all your eggs in one basket. There is more than one boy interested in you."

Katie knew who Mama was thinking of and suppressed a laugh. "Levi Beiler might be interested in me, but I'm not interested in him."

"You shouldn't dismiss him. He's a good worker, and not too bad looking."

"But I like Jonas." Katie kept her voice firm. She had always liked Jonas, and always would. Levi was a friendly boy, and he would make someone else a fine husband, but not her. Jonas was the only man she would marry.

"Where has Jonas been today?"

"He went to Millersburg with his brother to buy seed."

"That's a far piece to travel. He'll be late coming home." Mama fetched the broom and swept under the table.

"Not too late. And if he comes after sunset, we could sit on the porch, ja?"

She gave Mama the smile neither of her parents could resist.

"If you must." Mama turned her eyes toward the ceiling. "*Ach*, these young ones! How did I ever survive until your sisters all married?"

Katie grinned at her. "You were much younger, then."

Katie's sisters were all older than her own seventeen years. Susanna, the next youngest, was nine years older, and Katie hardly remembered when she went through her courting years. Her brothers and sisters, from twenty-six-year-old Susanna to Hans, who was approaching forty, had all been born in Germany, before the family had emigrated to Ohio in 1840. Mama always said that Katie had been a surprise, born four years after they had arrived in their new home. Katie often wondered if she had been a good surprise or a bad one. Mama had always seemed to make her feel like her arrival created a lot more work.

As soon as the dishes were done and the floor swept, Katie plucked her shawl off the hook by the back door and took the kitchen towels to the clothesline to dry as well as they could before dark. The sun was low enough in the sky that it no longer gave the warmth it had earlier in the day, but there were more than two hours until dark. Papa had gone out after supper to finish plowing the east field, and the home place was quiet. No sound of a wagon coming down the road.

She glanced back at the quiet house, then slipped into the washing porch to fetch her fishing pole and bait bucket. Mama opened the kitchen door just as she was on her way out again.

"I thought I heard your papa coming in."

"He's still working."

Mama shook her head. "He works too hard, that one. It's time he slowed down some."

"You know Papa, he's never happy when there isn't work to do."

"Ja, ja, ja. But I wish he'd let one of the boys take over more of the farm." Mama turned to go back into the house. "You're going fishing, then?"

"They should be biting well this evening."

Mama frowned. "And the best fishing spot happens to be where you can see up the road and watch for Jonas to come home."

"I'll be back before dark." Katie jumped down the step and started running along the lane to the road, until she remembered that she was a grown woman. Only little girls ran everywhere.

The road followed Weaver's Creek, winding through the Weavers' land toward the town of Berlin, then beyond to the bigger city of Millersburg twelve miles away. Papa had purchased a quarter section from Jonas's grandfather when the family had arrived from Europe and, in the process, had ensured they had good neighbors. The Weavers owned more land than Papa could have imagined back in Germany, he often said. But Katie didn't care. She only cared that Jonas would always live close by. This quarter section, across the road from Papa's land, would belong to Jonas one day. His father had already set it aside as part of Jonas's inheritance, and he would receive it next year when he turned twenty-one.

Mama was right about her favorite fishing spot, but for the wrong reason. Katie turned off the road to follow the worn trail to the creek's edge. Ja, she could see up the road from here, to the bend where it turned away from the creek and went up the hill at Samuel Weaver's place, across the road from Jonas's parents. But this spot was her favorite because it was across the creek from where Jonas had chosen to build his own house someday. Their house.

Baiting her hook, Katie threw it into the slow-moving water, then settled down on the log to wait. And dream. Fishing was an excuse to gaze into the forest in front of her. She had built countless houses in her head, planted hundreds of gardens, hung a thousand shirts on the imaginary clothesline. Someday, she would live here. Someday, Jonas would say it was time for them to get married. Someday, her life would begin.

Then came the sound she had been waiting for, the rumble of a loaded wagon and the jingle of the harness as the horses came down the hill and around the curve a few hundred yards away. She leaned her fishing pole against a tree and gathered her skirts, peering around the tree closest to the road. If Samuel spied her, Jonas would have to endure all manner of teasing, but at this distance, only Jonas knew where to look for her. As the wagon turned into the Weaver farm lane and across the short bridge over the creek, Jonas looked in her direction. Even from this far away, his smile melted her heart. She went back to her fishing, satisfied that he would come to find her as soon as he could.

On the ride home from Millersburg, Samuel had driven in stoic silence for the entire twelve miles. Silence was normal for Samuel, but this one was punctuated by sighs and growls every time Jonas shifted his newspaper.

The war news was unbelievable, with reporters' eyewitness accounts of the two-day battle that had taken place at the little spot called Pittsburg Landing along the Tennessee River. Some of the reporters were calling it the Battle of Shiloh. Jonas read of the first attack of the rebels on the

Union forces at two o'clock in the morning, and the resulting slaughter. According to the article, one hundred thousand men had been engaged in the battle, a number Jonas couldn't begin to imagine. But with every account, a longing in his breast to be part of something bigger than working a farm along a creek in Ohio was fanned by the images the words produced. There must be something he could do to help abolish slavery.

He glanced at Samuel's profile. With the set jaw and his beard jutting forward, Jonas knew his brother was in no mood to discuss the news with him. Samuel was rarely in a mood to discuss anything with him, considering him too young to have an opinion that warranted attention.

Turning the paper to page 3 resulted in a heavy sigh from his brother. Jonas ignored him and focused again on the notice Mr. Cabot had mentioned. The headline of the notice pulled him in. "The Hour! The Peril! The Duty!" Jonas shifted in his seat and glanced at his brother again. If Samuel had read the newspaper, he would understand the peril their country faced. Didn't they have a duty to help their country in this crisis, even if they were Amish? He wished Samuel would discuss the issue with him rather than bury himself in the traditions of their faith.

Jonas turned back to the notice. A meeting was being held in Brownsville, a little town near Millersburg, next Tuesday for the recruitment of volunteers. Someone, identified only as "A Volunteer," was urging all true men to turn out in support of the president and the Constitution of the country. His fists gripped the paper so tightly it tore at the edges. He lowered it with shaking hands, folding it with careful motions and tucking it into the back waistband of his trousers.

A volunteer militia. They would join with the other volunteers from across the North who had marched toward Charleston, or toward the Southern capital of Richmond all through the spring and summer last year. They had tried to stop the rebellion before it turned into a full-scale war. But they weren't successful. Every schoolboy knew that a fight never stopped with one blow. The South had thrown the first punch a year ago, and the North had returned the attack. The South had defended itself and the war was on. A bitter taste rose in Jonas's throat. Samuel was right. At the end, there would be no clear winner, only loss and devastation on both sides. But still, that pull to action called to him.

As the wagon crested the hill before descending into the little valley of Weaver's Creek, Jonas's mood lifted. There may be rumors of war in the distant east, but here, in this valley, peace reigned. They rumbled past their brother-in-law Reuben's place, then down the gentle slope as the road ran alongside Samuel's farm, meeting up with the creek at the bottom of the broad valley. Samuel turned off the road here and went over the stone bridge to the home farm. Jonas looked down the road toward the land Datt had set aside for him and caught the glimpse of Katie he had been hoping for. She had heard them coming and was waiting for him.

Stacking the sacks of corn on the barn floor only took a few minutes, and Jonas was soon on his way down the road. Supper could wait.

The sun touched the top branches of the western trees by the time he reached the path leading to their favorite spot, away from the road and curious eyes. Katie was sitting on the log by the creek with her fishing pole idle beside her, but she sprang up when she saw Jonas.

"I thought you'd never come."

Her smile struck at that place deep inside him, like a spark hitting tinder, setting off a glow that pulsed and grew until it became a burning flame. Katie's smile was all light and brightness, and the promise of their future together.

"It's a long trip to Millersburg and back. You knew we wouldn't be home until evening."

She stepped closer and he reached out for her, bringing her into his embrace. He leaned his nose next to her *kapp*, breathing in the scent that was all Katie, and the day's events melted away like snow in a spring rain. The world might be falling apart in this war, but here, with Katie in his arms, his foundation was secure.

He released her and took her hand, walking with her back to the log and sat beside her. "Have you caught any fish?"

"Enough to have for breakfast in the morning." Her brown eyes were nearly black in the fading light. "Did you get the seed for planting?"

"Enough for both farms." Samuel, Datt, and Jonas worked together on the cleared acres on either side of Weaver's Creek. "We start planting tomorrow."

Katie leaned against his shoulder. "I've been thinking about your house."

Jonas smiled to himself. This was Katie's favorite subject.

She went on. "I think it should have glass windows, right from the start. It's easier to put them in that way, rather than adding them later."

"Where did you get that idea?"

She shrugged, snuggling closer to him. "I thought of it myself. And the kitchen should face east, so the morning sun can shine in."

His future took on form and substance as Katie talked. "And the fireplace?" he asked, knowing her answer.

"The kitchen will have a stove, not a fireplace. If you want a fire in the front room, that will be all right. But I think it should have stoves. They're cleaner and easier to care for. They provide better heat too."

"You've put a lot of thought into this house of mine."

She slipped her arm around his back. "For sure and certain I have. You're only going to build one house, and it should be perfect."

As she tightened her hug, the newspaper in his waistband crinkled. She pulled it out and unfolded it. "What is this?"

Jonas took it from her. The smell of the ink brought the woes of the world back with a cold chill as he turned to page 2, where the war news was emblazoned with headlines on every column. "There was a big battle in Tennessee last week."

"Why did you bring this paper home? It has nothing to do with us."

"But maybe it should."

Katie laced her fingers around one knee, a puzzled frown on her face. "I don't know why. We live here, not wherever Tennessee is."

"Our country is at war, Katie. A war that could change everything. This could be the end of the United States."

She shook her head. "It still doesn't have anything to do with us. We aren't involved, and we won't be."

Ja, he knew that. The Amish only concerned themselves with the things of God, not worldly affairs. At least most didn't. Some men kept up with worldly things that would affect the Amish communities, and he was glad they did.

They needed to be prepared to meet whatever the world sent their way, including wars.

Jonas glanced up at the violet sky above them and folded the newspaper again. "The sun has set and it's getting dark. You should be getting home."

"Not until you give me a good-night kiss." She stood, pulling his hands until he stood with her, facing her.

Jonas captured her cheeks between his hands and ducked his head to give her a quick, gentle kiss. He knew from experience that if he let the kiss linger, his thoughts would drift toward a deeper kiss, a closer embrace. But that time would come. He and Katie had their whole future to look forward to sweet kisses.

## May 2

Two weeks had passed, but Katie still smiled when she remembered that sweet kiss by the creek. Jonas's kisses were always gentle, without asking for more than was appropriate. When she was with Jonas, she could forget about the past and look forward to a wonderful future with him.

She finished tying her apron and picked up her comb, walking over to the window as she unbraided her hair. The early morning sun shone on the leaves that covered the maple trees in the sugar bush, making the light green turn to bright gold.

"Katie!"

Mama's call charged up the stairway before Katie had run the comb through her hair even once.

"Ja, Mama, I'm coming."

"Hurry up, then. I need you to go to Lena's to see when she wants to plant the gardens, and then to ask Esther and Mary the same. May is upon us already, and we only have the lettuce and peas in."

"Ja, Mama." Katie gathered her long hair in one hand, then twisted it in a bun, securing it with a few hairpins before setting her kapp over the whole thing. It felt lumpy this morning, and anyone who looked closely would be able to tell she had done it in a hurry. But she wouldn't be seeing anyone except her brothers' families, and her sisters-in-law were too busy to notice a little thing like messy hair.

Lena was her first stop. She and Hans had seven children, three boys and four girls. The girls were a blessing, for sure, especially thirteen-year-old Margaret. Katie suspected another baby was on the way, and she sent a quick prayer to the Lord that this one would be another girl. Three boys were enough for any family.

As Katie approached their kitchen door, she saw one-year-old Ruth sitting in a dishpan of water, with three-year-old Gus on one side of her, and five-year-old Marta on the other side. All three children were soaked from head to toe. They watched her come toward them, Gus with a grin on his face.

Katie stopped when she reached them. Ruth's clothes were strewn in the muddy grass between the house and the dishpan.

"Are you supposed to be giving the baby a bath?" Katie tried not to laugh at Marta's red face.

"She was dirty as a pig," Marta said. "She can't go in the house like that."

"Pigs are dirty, for sure and certain." Katie smiled at Ruth, who was happily chewing on a rock.

"I'm dirty too." Gus lifted his hands to show Katie. "But Marta won't let me take a bath."

"Not yet," Marta said, her voice sounding just like Lena's. "Your bath will come after the baby is done."

Gus tried to grab Katie's apron, but she moved away from his muddy hand just in time. "You can take a bath too, Katie. You can go after me."

"I'll take my baths at home, Gus." Katie shook her head as she picked her way around the muddy spots in the yard and continued to the house. Lena certainly had her hands full. All three of those children would need a real bath before dinnertime.

"Come in, Katie!" Lena called when she saw her through the open door. "Come and sit down. We're just ready to rest for a few minutes."

"Those cookies smell delicious." Katie smiled at Margaret, who was taking a pan out of the oven. "Did you make them?"

Her niece, only a few years younger than Katie, blushed as Lena sat at the table with a sigh. "Ja, for sure. Margaret does all the baking now, and I'm so glad. She bakes softer bread than I do." Lena shook her head as she laughed at herself. "I never could make bread as well as your mother."

Katie sat at the table as Margaret brought a plate of cookies over and sat next to her mother. Margaret had always been shy, even as a baby. But Lena talked enough for both of them. Katie had been like Margaret as a girl, but now she wanted to be more like Lena. Always happy, smiling, taking life as it came. Her joy was infectious.

"Tell me all the news." Lena brushed some crumbs off the table and leaned toward Katie. "Have you been to Esther's and Mary's yet?"

"You're the first."

"Good. Now I can find out all about what you and Jonas are up to."

Katie felt her face heat up, but tried to keep her voice even. "What do you mean?"

"Ach, Katie, everyone knows you two will be getting married someday. Has he mentioned it? Have you talked about it?"

"Not yet." Unless one counted planning a house together.

A cry sounded from the yard outside, and Lena glanced out the door. Satisfied that the children weren't hurt, she turned her attention back to Katie. "He might be waiting until you're a bit older, although some girls get married as young as sixteen."

"That didn't work out so well for Jonas's sister, Elizabeth," Margaret said, sounding like her mother.

Lena nodded her agreement. Elizabeth had married Reuben Kaufman when she was sixteen, without even joining the church first. And if she had been a church member, she never could have married Reuben. He was an outsider who had bought the farm north of the Weavers when he was newly arrived from Germany. According to the gossip Katie had heard, he had taken one look at Elizabeth and hauled her off to the Lutheran church to be married. The whole event had seemed terribly romantic when Katie was a young girl, but now the thought was a bit frightening. After eight years there were no children, and whenever Katie saw Elizabeth, she seemed quiet and sad. Katie wasn't surprised. Reuben reminded her too much of another man she had known.

Lena broke the silence with a sigh as she took another cookie. "At least she still lives close to her family."

The little children's voices grew louder in the front yard, reminding Katie that she was on an errand.

"Mama sent me to see when you wanted to plant the garden. Wilhelm is planning to plow it tomorrow, so we can do it any time after that."

"The next day, Saturday, will be a good day for me. Margaret can care for the little ones, and I'll bring Naomi and the older boys to help."

"I'll tell Mama and let the others know." Katie brushed crumbs off her fingers and stood up. "Do you want me to help you clean up the little ones before I go?"

Lena's laugh rippled. "They'll only get dirty again. Let them play and have fun. They're only little once."

Katie waved to Margaret and left, taking the worn path through the woodlot to Wilhelm and Esther's house, where they lived with their four boys.

By the time she had made the rounds to the other two homes, the family's garden plans had been made. It was the same every year, so Katie wasn't sure why they had to discuss it, anyway. Wilhelm would plow the big garden near Mama and Papa's house tomorrow, and then on Saturday the other women would come over, bringing the seeds they had saved from last year's garden. Meanwhile, Mama would plan where to plant the cucumbers, beans, potatoes, carrots, turnips, and cabbages. Every family had their own kitchen garden for salad greens and herbs, but this big garden was to grow the vegetables they would store for the coming winter. Even though the plans never varied from one year to the next, Katie still made these visits every spring so that Mama could be sure everyone knew what to expect.

Katie turned her face to the midmorning sun as she walked

home. It was too early in the spring to be thinking of storing vegetables for the winter. From the pasture on Karl's farm, the lane led through the woodlot. Pine trees grew along either side of the lane, shading the way and blocking out sights and sounds from the farms. On windy days, the pines whispered above her, but today was still. She couldn't even hear her footsteps on the carpet of pine needles.

As she brushed by a stand of small trees that crowded the lane, a hand reached out to grasp her arm and Katie shrieked, but her voice was swallowed by the pines. Ned Hamlin held her arm in an easy grip that tightened when she tried to pull away.

"Don't be scared."

Sweat beaded on Katie's lip. Ned's face was friendly enough, but her insides quivered. "What are you doing here? Let me go."

"Been out hunting this morning and taking a shortcut home. Didn't expect to find such a pretty thing in the woods, though." He smiled. "I've seen you with Jonas Weaver, by the fishing hole." His dark eyes narrowed. "I've seen him kiss you."

Katie tugged at her arm. "Let go of me."

Her voice shook, but not as much as her knees. She flinched as Ned set his rifle against a tree and reached for her with his other arm. She swallowed the bitter taste of panic.

"Don't . . . don't do this."

"I thought maybe you'd let me have a kiss too."

He pulled her closer, and she thrashed, pulling one arm and then the other, but he only laughed and then pushed her away. She stumbled and fell back, her vision clouded. She wouldn't faint. She couldn't.

"You weren't so squeamish with Jonas." Ned leaned over her, still laughing. "But I promise, you'd like me better than him."

Her sight cleared, and she scooted away from him. He picked up his rifle again, watching her with a leering grin just like Teacher Robinson's.

"Leave me alone." Katie's ears roared. "Go away and leave me alone."

He leaned near again, brushing her cheek with a filthy finger. His eyes smoldered. "I'll go. But maybe I'll run across you when I'm hunting again. And maybe you'll come find me sometime."

Ned left her then, disappearing into the trees. Katie sat, drawing her knees up.

"He didn't do anything," she told herself, taking a deep breath. "He didn't hurt you. He was only teasing you. Nothing happened."

She stared at the opening where Ned had disappeared.

It had happened again. As careful as she had been, she hadn't expected this. Ned had appeared out of nowhere and she had panicked. She folded her arms on her knees, resting her forehead against them, slowing her breathing. She was cursed, and because of the curse, a man had died.

She drew a deep breath and let it out slowly.

But Ned hadn't hurt her, not like Teacher had. Maybe he wouldn't die.

# 2

**MAY 2**

Abraham Weaver stopped the horses at the end of the upper field for a rest. Harrowing the oat field wasn't a hard task for the team, but he still gave them a breather after every acre or so. It was good for the horses and, as a result, good for the farm.

From here, he could see the fields falling away toward Weaver's Creek at the bottom of the little valley, and the familiar feeling of gratitude filled him as he took in the view. Gratitude for the choice his father had made when he pioneered this land more than fifty years ago. Gratitude to God for the blessing of such rich, fertile farmland. Gratitude for sons who cared for the land as much as he did, and would carry on for another generation. Gratitude for grandsons who would carry on the family name.

He chuckled to himself at that thought. His Lydia always reminded him that granddaughters were just as precious as grandsons, and he agreed. Ach, the blessing of grandchildren! He and Lydia had nine of them so far. They were blessed. Truly blessed.

The only shadow on their family was the fate of dear Elizabeth. He tried to ignore the anger that still rose after eight years, but he had to admit it was there. Forgiveness for the pain that Reuben Kaufman had caused their family had been slow in coming. Abraham could say that he had forgiven the man for stealing their young daughter and making her his wife at such an early age. But forgetting was another matter. The pain of a child living outside the faith was like no other. And as the years rolled by and no children came, Abraham wondered about God's providence. Children were a blessing, but God had not yet chosen to bless the couple.

Shaking his head to scatter his thoughts to the wind, he rubbed Boss's nose. The horse was breathing easily and widened his nostrils to take in the scent of Abraham's shirt. The horses were rested, and it was time to finish this field and head home for dinner.

After reaching the end of the oat field, Abraham drove the harrow to the edge of the forty acres where he and his sons had planted barley and unhitched the team. The barn and house were nearly a mile from these far fields, and the walk was a pleasant one in the spring air. As he drew near, following the team, he saw Samuel making his way to the same destination. He had been cultivating the cornfield, planted in the eighty acres along the creek in the lower field. His team looked worn and ready for the hour rest they always took at noon. The soil near the creek was heavier than on the upland and taxed the horses' strength.

He called to Samuel as soon as he was close enough to be heard. "The corn is done, then?"

"Not yet. Still a few more acres to go." Samuel halted his team outside the barn and dropped the traces as Abraham's team stopped next to him. "I'll finish it up this afternoon. But as I passed the near end of the field, I saw that I'll need to start a second round." He unbuckled the harness as he talked. "Five days since I started cultivating that field, and the weeds are coming back already."

"Ja, ja, ja." Abraham started unharnessing Boss. "That's the way it is this time of year."

"Where is Jonas this morning?"

"Helping your mamm with the garden. She wanted him to plow and harrow it so she could get to work with the planting."

"Then he can finish the corn after dinner. Anna has been after me to plow her garden too."

"Jonas could plow the garden for you." He put Boss in the pasture and started unfastening Nell's harness.

Samuel shook his head. "I'll do it. Anna wants to expand the garden space this year, and I don't have the new edges marked. Besides, Jonas has been too flighty lately. Can't keep his mind on his work."

Abraham chuckled. "You were the same when you were his age. It's the age of dreamers, ja?"

A snort came from Samuel's direction. "I was never this bad. His mind is on worldly things."

"Ja, ja, ja. And Katie."

Samuel started unharnessing Nan, leaving his own team to stand in the shade of the elm tree. "You're not worried about him?"

"I've learned to give my worries to the Good Lord and keep my head bowed in prayer." Abraham turned Rocky and

Nan into the pasture with the other horses and leaned one hand on the top fence rail next to his son. "You'll learn that with your own children soon enough."

Samuel's four children, from Bram, his oldest son, to little Dorcas, were growing faster than the weeds in the cornfield.

"I'm already learning that with Bram. That boy thinks it's time that he strikes out on his own already."

"He's thirteen. That's a hard age, caught between childhood and manhood."

"Some days he reminds me of a half-trained colt, fighting the harness at every turn."

Abraham kept his smile to himself. Samuel had been the same at thirteen, causing grief to his family and everyone around him.

"You'll figure out how to handle him. Loosen the reins a bit. As long as you treat him like a child, he'll act like one."

"As long as he acts like a child, I need to discipline him like a child. That's what a father's job is." Samuel shot a glance in his direction. "I remember your discipline quite well when I was his age and older."

"When you needed it." Abraham remembered those times too. "Give Bram some responsibilities. Have him plow the garden for Anna this afternoon."

Samuel shook his head. "I'd have to do it all over again." He started toward his team, ready to go home to his dinner. "But I'll try. Maybe he'll surprise me."

Abraham's stomach growled in anticipation of his own dinner. He washed up and went into the house, where Lydia was just setting a dish of mashed potatoes on the table. As he sat, she brushed his shoulder with her hand. He smiled at her as she sat at her place. Jonas sat at the third place, his face still wet from washing.

"Ruby isn't joining us today?" Abraham asked.

Lydia shook her head. "She is spending the day with Elizabeth."

Abraham bowed his head for the silent prayer, starting with a petition for Ruby. The daughter who didn't seem to care if she married or not. Even at the age of twenty-six, she seemed content to live at home, helping Lydia or one of her married sisters with the housekeeping or child care. As his prayer moved from one child and their family to the next, he ended with Jonas, his thoughts pausing as he remembered Samuel's comment. Was Jonas caught up in the affairs of the world? Leaving that worry to God once more, he lifted his head, clearing his throat to signal the end of the prayer.

"Is the garden ready to plant?" Abraham speared a slice of ham from the platter in front of him.

Jonas reached for his own slice and put it on his plate. "All plowed and harrowed."

Abraham glanced at Lydia for her confirming nod. "Good. Then this afternoon you can finish cultivating the corn in the lower field."

Jonas paused, his fork in midair. "Can that wait? I had hoped to get started clearing my land this afternoon."

Buttering his bread, Abraham felt the surprise of Jonas's words wash over him. "Your land?"

"The land you're planning to give me next year, when I reach legal age. You remember, don't you? We talked about it a couple weeks ago, before we started planting."

Abraham chewed the delicious bread, fresh from the oven that morning. Ja, he remembered. The quarter section to the east. Jonas had chosen the only part of the farm that hadn't been cleared yet, agreeing with Abraham that the bulk of it would remain wooded so they would always have a source of timber and firewood.

"It isn't yours yet, Son."

"Ja, ja, ja, I know. But I want to clear an acre or so." Jonas paused, looking him in the eye. "I want to start building a house."

"A house?" Abraham let this information settle as he piled mashed potatoes on a forkful of ham. "It's gone that far, has it?"

"By the time I am twenty-one, I want to live on my own."

Abraham considered the boy sitting across the table from him. His youngest. Strong, able, smart. But was he responsible enough, mature enough, to live alone? He was only in his teens . . . no, Jonas was twenty.

Sitting back in his chair, Abraham whooshed out a breath. Jonas had grown up, and he had missed it. He wasn't a boy any longer. Twenty years had gone like a wisp of smoke driven before a strong wind.

His words to Samuel came back to him. As long as he treated Jonas like a child, that's what he would remain. He couldn't keep Jonas from manhood any more than he could keep an acorn from growing into an oak tree.

"Before marriage, you need to join the church. You know that, ja?"

Jonas turned red and stared at his plate. "I'm not talking about getting married. I only said I wanted to build my house."

"But marriage will soon follow, won't it?"

The back of Jonas's neck turned even redder.

"Do you want me to talk to Bishop about it?"

"I'll do it. It's my responsibility."

Abraham took a second piece of ham from the platter and dared to look in Lydia's direction. Her eyes shone as she smiled at Jonas, then met Abraham's gaze. She nodded, and he knew she was right. It was time for their boy to grow up.

———

After Datt's reaction at dinner, Jonas wasn't surprised when he didn't give permission for him to start clearing the land today. And he had to admit that Datt was right. Cultivating the corn had to be done before the weeds took over the field, but Jonas's hands itched to start felling the trees on the rise just south of the creek. He could feel the felling axe in his hands, and the solid *thunk* of the blade cutting into an oak or maple.

He let his thoughts wander as the horses pulled the cultivator through the heavy soil, between the rows of tiny green shoots of corn. The trees he felled would be used to build the house. He would haul them to Stevenson's sawmill and have them made into beams and boards. The figuring of how many beams he would need for the house he envisioned took all afternoon. By the time he was done, the cultivating was finished; the horses unharnessed, fed, and watered; and the evening chores done.

As Jonas left the barn, on his way to the house for supper, a distant sound from the east caught his attention. He stopped, listening. Snatches of music drifted on the early evening breeze, and underneath was a low rumble, as if a swamp full of bullfrogs were muttering their spring chorus.

Datt joined him. "What is it?"

"Nothing I've heard before."

"I'll tell your mother to hold supper for us while we investigate this."

Samuel joined them on the road, and when they reached the Stuckeys' house, Gustav, Katie's father, came out his front door, pulling on his coat.

"Ja, then, you heard it too?" His breath puffed as he hurried to catch up with them.

The sound was clearer from here, where the Stuckeys' house sat on a rise before the road went down toward the creek again and on toward the Hyattsville Pike. The bullfrog rumble was more distinct, and Jonas heard men's voices filtering out of the background of rolling drums and fifes.

"It's men," he said, and the others nodded in agreement.

"Many of them," Datt said. "Traveling along the pike, from the sounds of it. They must have stopped to make camp along the creek."

"I've seen enough," Samuel said. "We know it's a group of men, and they aren't likely to come up this way."

"Aren't you curious about who they are and where they're going?" Jonas asked.

Datt and Gustav turned to go back with Samuel.

"Your brother is right," Gustav said. "These men don't concern us. It's best to leave them be."

The three men walked away, Gustav turning toward his house when he reached his farm lane at the top of the hill. Jonas listened to the rise and fall of the humming conversations in the valley behind him. Hatchet strokes punctuated the drone, and the occasional whinny of a horse. How could Datt and the others just walk away without knowing more?

He would find out, even if the others didn't care. Setting out, he covered the half mile to the crossroads in a few minutes. As he drew closer, he saw men erecting tents in the meadow that spread on either side of the pike, along the north side of Weaver's Creek. Campfires dotted the meadow and glowed in the mist that rose from the creek as the sun's warmth disappeared from the land. He counted more than twenty of the campfires on this side of the pike alone. Wagons had been parked along the road, and horses had been put out in a rope corral a few yards downstream from the camp.

A man came toward the tent closest to Jonas, carrying a steaming pail from the campfire.

"Hey, brother." He grinned and waved at Jonas. "Where did you come from? Are you with the Company?"

Jonas shook his head, walking toward the man. "I'm Jonas Weaver. We heard the commotion and I came to see what was going on. I never thought I'd see so many men at our crossroads at one time."

"Tom Porter." The man's mustache was bushy and black, but the face behind it was young, no older than Jonas himself. "You live up that way?" He gestured up the road with his chin as he took a seat on an upturned log.

"Our farm is up the road a bit, along Weaver's Creek."

Tom regarded him with a frank gaze, taking in his Plain clothes. "You're Amish? We have a lot of you folk up in Wayne County."

"That's where you're from? All of you?"

"Most of us. Some from Holmesville area, in Holmes County. We're Company K." He waved his arm behind him, to the campfires on the other side of the pike. "Company H is from up by the Black Swamp, and we joined with them as they came by our camp on the way to the rail station in

Hyattsville. I'm from Wooster, myself." He set the steaming pail on the ground at his feet and pulled a spoon from his back pocket. Polishing the spoon on his trouser leg, he nodded at the container. "Want some stew? I'd be glad to share."

Jonas waved the offer away. "Thanks, but my supper is waiting for me at home." He sat on one heel, next to Tom. "Where are you going?"

Tom leaned forward, his face lit with excitement. "There's a whole regiment gathering in Hyattsville. A thousand men, under Colonel Westcott from Columbus. We're meeting up with Wilson's Brigade in Baltimore, and then on to the next battle."

"In Tennessee?"

Tom shrugged, his mouth full of stew. He swallowed. "Or Virginia. We're gonna whip those rebels and end this war for good." His spoon scraped the side of the can. "You should join up. The more soldiers we've got, the sooner this war will be over." His spoonful of stew paused in midair. "But you Amish don't fight, do you? At least, that's what I heard."

Jonas shook his head. "Not usually." Not ever. But as a rat-a-tat of drums sounded, Jonas's heart beat faster. It must be exciting to be part of a regiment.

"Do you think you'll see any fighting?"

Tom made a face that pulled his mustache to one side. "It could all be over by the time we get there, but I hope I get to do my part. Some of us have been drilling for weeks, up in Wooster, waiting to get enough volunteers to form a company. But I'm sick of pretending. I want to get in the real thing. Be in a real battle."

Jonas pulled at a stalk of grass. A battle. He had read about the battles King David had been part of. The stories in the Bible pulled him in as he read them by candlelight in his bedroom at night. Datt said those battles were part of the past, and that God's people lived under a new law, the law of love that Christ taught. But perhaps God still worked through wars. Wars like this one, where the result could be freedom for the slaves. But men also were killed and wounded in battles.

"Are you scared?" He searched Tom's eyes.

The other man grinned. "Naw. None of us are scared. Those rebels will take one look at us and turn tail."

But Jonas saw a flicker of something in Tom's eyes. "How about shooting another man? Are you scared of that?"

Tom shook his head, but some of his confidence had fallen away. He looked at the neighboring tents, then lowered his voice. "I'm not scared of that, either. At least, not much I ain't." He leaned closer to Jonas. "But some of the boys, well, I heard that in battle some will get so scared that they forget to fire their guns. Can't kill the enemy that way, can you?"

Jonas swallowed, his throat dry. If he was in Tom's place, he wasn't sure he'd be able to pull the trigger either. Killing an animal while hunting was bad enough. He couldn't imagine shooting another man.

He stood. "I had better be getting on home. They'll be wondering where I am."

Tom stuck out a hand and Jonas shook it. "You take care now. And think about joining us. It's a glorious cause."

Jonas headed home, up the long road toward the lowering sun. A glorious cause? That might be reason enough for Tom to join in the fight, but not for him. The roll of drums might be exciting, but war wasn't any place for a coward.

## MAY 3

Saturday morning was fine and sunny, perfect for planting the big garden the four families shared on the Stuckeys' land. In the twenty years that Mama and Papa had lived here, the garden had expanded with the growing families. This year Wilhelm had plowed a full acre in the area behind the barn that had once been pasture, while Papa's team had been moved to a different pasture in a newly cleared part of the woodlot.

Katie worked with Lena's three older children, Naomi, Ben, and Josef. Margaret, being the oldest, was watching the little ones at home while the four of them planted hills of potatoes. Katie and Mama had marked out the rows early in the morning, before the others had arrived, by dragging a log with spikes two feet apart through the potato field one way, marking little furrows, and then crossways. In each place where the furrows crossed, Naomi and Ben dropped a piece of potato, then Katie and Josef followed behind them with their hoes, covering up the potato pieces. All through the spring, Katie and the others would hoe around the growing potato plants, keeping weeds from choking the baby plants until they were large enough to cover the ground.

Next to the potato field, Mary and Esther worked together planting long rows of turnips. They had their heads together as they worked, pausing often to discuss something at length before getting back to their work. It was a good thing Mama was working by herself with her back to the two younger women. Mama didn't like gossiping, and it looked like that was exactly what Mary and Esther were doing.

Eleven-year-old Josef was a good worker, keeping his hoe moving with a rhythm that would keep him from getting tired. It didn't keep him from talking, though.

"Katie, Datt was at the Weavers' yesterday, and he said he saw Jonas sharpening his felling axe."

His felling axe? Men only used that kind of axe to chop down trees.

"Is that so?" She kept her voice steady. Josef didn't need to know how interested she was in what Jonas was doing.

"Ja, for sure. Mamm said that could only mean one thing."

He went ahead to the next hill, following eight-year-old Ben, while Katie waited for seven-year-old Naomi to straighten the potato she had just dropped.

"It doesn't have to be perfect, Naomi. Just drop it in the middle of the cross."

"But Mamm said the eye should be up."

Naomi stooped down to dust a bit of dirt off the potato she had just straightened while Katie held back a sigh. As Naomi moved on to the next cross, Katie pulled dirt over the potato and hurried to catch up with Josef. That boy could be such a tease, making a comment like that and then waiting until she was bursting to hear the rest of what Lena had said.

She came abreast of Josef, pulling dirt over the next potato as soon as Naomi dropped it. "What did your mamm say it meant?"

Josef grinned. He had her undivided attention and he knew it. He let her stew while he covered two more potatoes.

"She said Jonas must be clearing some land. Then Datt said—"

He broke off as he moved to the next hill and Katie followed him, passing Naomi.

"Datt said that Jonas was building a house on the land his datt is going to give him when he turns twenty-one." Josef stopped, leaning on his hoe and grinning at Katie. "Then Mamm said she wondered if Katie knew he was building a house." Josef stretched his cheeks down with two fingers and rolled his eyes up. "Jonas is in love," he said in a falsetto voice. Then he doubled over with laughter.

"Ach, you are a pest!" Katie lobbed a clump of dirt in his direction with her toe and went back to covering potatoes.

But she couldn't stay upset at Josef because his news made her smile so. Jonas was finally starting his house.

The rest of the day couldn't pass quickly enough, but by late afternoon, the entire garden had been planted and Katie's sisters-in-law had taken their families home.

"I think we'll have a cold supper tonight," Mama said as they went into the house. "Some of that roast sliced thin will make a good sandwich. And we'll make a salad out of the leftover potatoes from yesterday's dinner."

"I think I'll pack a picnic for Jonas and me for this evening."

"Ja, you do that. I'm going to rest for a bit." Mama moved stiffly through the kitchen to her bedroom beyond. "You'll make the potato salad before you go, ja?"

"For sure, Mama."

Katie loved having the kitchen to herself. She fetched the leftover beef and potatoes from the springhouse and set to work. She packed her basket with sandwiches, a container of potato salad, and a jar of the little dill pickles Jonas loved. She put the rest of the potato salad and the sliced beef back in the springhouse to keep cool for Mama and Papa's supper, then took her basket and went down the road to Jonas's land.

As she drew close, she could hear the axe echoing through the woods, and each time the blade bit into the tree, it brought her closer to her dream. She hurried down the road to the path, watching for Ned or anyone else who might be hiding among the trees, but didn't see anyone. She went along the shady path, relieved that she was alone but angry at herself for giving in to her fear.

"You have to get over this," she whispered to herself. "Be strong, like Lena. She would have kicked Ned Hamlin in the shin, and that's what you should do the next time." She walked faster, as if she could avoid another meeting with Ned by hurrying.

Jonas had laid a log, peeled and hewn into a flat bridge, across the creek. Katie crossed to where Jonas was working and stopped near a new stump. He was cutting a small maple tree a few yards away from the first stump. His back was toward her as he concentrated on his task. With each swing, his entire body moved in an arc, shuddering a little as the axe bit into the tree. Then he loosened the axe and swung again. Katie watched him until the tree fell, crashing into the underbrush.

"That's the second one you've felled?" Katie called to Jonas, and he turned with a grin, wiping sweat off his brow with his forearm.

"Ja, for sure. You came across the bridge I made from the first one."

"And it's a fine bridge."

Jonas hadn't only cut two trees, but he had cut the underbrush and grasses between the trees to give him more room to work. Katie could imagine the house he would build in the little clearing.

"How many more trees do you need to cut down?"

Jonas leaned the axe against the stump and walked toward her. "Enough to build the house, and then a barn. We'll want a chicken house and garden space too. Datt recommended an acre."

Katie's hopes fell. "An acre? That will take a long time."

"Long enough." Jonas lifted the towel Katie had used to cover the basket. "And what's in here?"

"I thought we'd have a picnic supper."

He grabbed her free hand. "To celebrate the beginning of my house?"

"It's something to celebrate, isn't it?"

His face grew serious, watching her. She set the basket on the ground and stepped closer. The silent forest embraced them, folding them into itself. Cool air rising from the creek swirled around Katie's bare legs and feet, drawing her even closer to Jonas. This was where she belonged, gazing into the depths of Jonas's indigo blue eyes. This is where she was safe.

"This could be our house." Jonas lifted her hand to his lips and gave it a quick kiss. "If you would marry me."

Katie took a deep breath, letting this moment sink into her memory. The moment she had been waiting for. All of her hopes centered on this space in time, like a door on a hinge. She only had to answer him, agree to marry him, and that barrier would swing open. Like a flood, all of her being rushed against the door, swinging it wide to the bright future ahead.

"I'll marry you," she said, unable to stop a smile that threatened to disrupt this solemn moment.

But why be solemn? She laughed as Jonas's eyes lit up at her words.

He caught her in his arms, swinging her around in a circle, then kissed her.

As she clung to him, resting in his embrace, she laid her cheek on his broad chest. This was where she belonged, for sure and for certain. Now she could lay the past to rest.

# 3

**MAY 28**

By the end of May, after almost four weeks of felling and trimming trees, Jonas finally had enough logs to take to the sawmill. Samuel had helped him load the logs onto the chassis of the big farm wagon and then he was on his way.

It was drawing close to summer and the days were long and productive. Jonas had been able to spend many evenings in the growing clearing in the woods, and often shared a cold supper with Katie as they made plans for their home together. Katie was anxious to share the news of the coming marriage with her family, but they both agreed to wait until closer to autumn, when the bishop would hold a membership class. They could marry as soon as they both were baptized and joined the church.

Until then, the families would be curious about their plans, but no one would ask outright. Smiling, he remembered when one of the couples at church finally announced their coming marriage. Everyone had known what was going on, but part of the fun was pretending to be surprised when they shared the news.

Jonas kept the team going at a steady rate on the narrow road. Six miles lay between Weaver's Creek and the sawmill at Stevenson, and he had no desire to spend his time reloading the logs because he was in too much of a hurry.

But driving only required part of his attention. The rest was wrestling with a problem. When he took the vows of baptism, he would never be able to go back on them. Just like marriage, joining the church was a lifetime commitment. And he could easily promise everything that was required of him, except one. Confessing his faith in the Lord Jesus Christ and vowing to submit to the fellowship of the church were easily done. He already lived that way, and would continue to. But he would also have to vow to support the teaching of the church in all things, including nonresistance.

Up until he attended the abolitionist meeting last February, he had never questioned the teaching that God had dealt with his people one way in the Old Testament and a different way in the New Testament. Wars were part of the Old Testament. The church taught that, at that time, God used men like King David to deal out his justice, but in these days, God was a God of mercy.

But Jonas had trouble accepting that people had changed very much between David's time and the present. Couldn't God still call some men to war when the cause was just? The abolition of slavery seemed like a just cause to him.

He remembered his conversation with Tom Porter as he was on his way to war earlier in the month. Tom had mentioned a glorious cause. Glorious? He shook his head at himself. No cause was glorious, unless the Lord himself had established it. At least, that's what he thought. And he still felt the way he did then—he didn't want to fight. He didn't want to kill another man. But if it became necessary? If he was in a situation where killing a man would save the life of another, what would he do? A chill ran down his back at the thought of the possibility.

The problem came back to that vow he would need to take at his baptism. He couldn't see taking a vow to support all the teachings of the church when questions like this still swirled in his head. But without taking that vow, he wouldn't be able to marry Katie.

Reaching the sawmill before noon, Jonas was surprised to see a dozen or so men outside the mill. As he drew close, he saw that they were listening to a man reading a newspaper tacked on the wall next to the mill's door. Stopping the team at the watering trough, Jonas leaned forward to listen.

"Cabot says that Congress should pass the confiscation law." The man's voice was clear as he read the editorial, and it carried to the edges of the group. "With that law, as currently proposed, the civil authorities would be able to set the slaves of rebel masters at liberty and appropriate the property of Confederate officials to help defray the cost of the war."

A thrill ran through Jonas at hearing Mr. Cabot's words. Set the slaves free? But at the same time, the idea was unsettling. Perhaps that was something the government shouldn't have the power to do. The rising murmurs among the gathered men told him he wasn't the only one who wondered about this idea.

After a pause, the reader continued, "The rebel forces continue to advance in the Shenandoah Valley, and the citizens of

Washington City are very concerned." Another pause while the man scanned the columns. "The president says he needs two hundred thousand more men."

"Where's he going to get them?" A stout man with a bushy black beard turned to his neighbors, his voice loud enough to be heard by all. "Every man who would volunteer has already gone."

"He'll have to squeeze them out of the woods," another man said, and the crowd laughed.

"Any local news?" A man standing a few feet away from Jonas shouted this.

"Yep. It seems those rebels in our midst are at it again." The man proceeded to read an account of a flag, made and raised by schoolchildren, being destroyed during the night by anonymous Southern sympathizers.

"A cowardly action, that," said a man to Jonas's left. He turned and saw Jonas and the loaded wagon. "Well, it looks like I have a customer." He extended his hand. "The name's Stevenson."

"Jonas Weaver." Jonas shook the man's hand. "I have some logs I need cut into lumber for a house."

"Sure thing." Mr. Stevenson walked around the wagon, briefly inspecting the logs Jonas had brought. "Recently felled?"

"Over the past few weeks."

"We can do it for you, but I have other orders ahead of yours."

"Whenever you can get to them is fine, as long as it isn't too long of a wait."

Following the mill owner, Jonas passed through the gathered crowd and into the dark interior of the building. To the right, a door opened into a tiny office with light filtering into it through a small, dusty window.

"Interested in the war news?" the man asked as he sat at a desk covered with ledgers, loose papers, and bits of wood.

"For sure I am. I like to keep up with what is going on."

The man perched a pair of wire-rimmed glasses on his nose and peered over them. "That's unusual for an Amish man, isn't it?"

Jonas shrugged. "Probably. But the war affects all of us in one way or another."

"You're right about that." The man opened a book and turned to a blank page. "How do you want the lumber cut?"

Jonas gave him the order he had figured in his head and the man copied it down along with his name.

"Right. I should be able to start working on this in a few days." He closed the book, laid his glasses on top of it, and leaned back in his chair. "You live out by Weaver's Creek?"

"Our farms are in the valley there, just west of the Hyattsville Pike."

"I thought so. I passed by that way a few months back. There's quite a nice stand of trees along there. An entire section of virgin forest."

Jonas nodded. "That's my land."

Mr. Stevenson leaned forward, his forearms resting on the desk. "I'd like to buy that timber from you. I'll give you top dollar for it."

Jonas shook his head. Datt had been clear when he proposed giving that section to Jonas. The forest there was for the use of the entire family. With good management, it would provide firewood and lumber for generations. Jonas might own the land, but the trees belonged to the family.

"The trees aren't for sale. And what use would you have for them?"

"The war, Mr. Weaver. With any war comes the need for raw materials. Wood, iron ore, wool, corn . . . anything we can produce can be used to help our troops and the war effort."

"Sorry. They aren't mine to sell."

"Who can make that decision?"

"My father, but I can tell you his answer. He'll say no."

Mr. Stevenson smiled. "It won't hurt to ask him. I'll deliver your lumber when it's ready, and I'll talk to him then."

When Jonas left, the men were still standing outside the mill, listening to another account of what was happening in Virginia and Tennessee. Datt and Samuel might want to ignore what was going on in the world, but they would have to face it eventually. And Datt might change his mind about selling some of the lumber if the man offered a high enough price.

~~~~~

Abraham dropped his fork on the table and stared at Jonas. "Stevenson wants to buy our timber? Why?"

Jonas sopped up some gravy with a crust of bread. "He said that he could sell it to the army. He said they'd need all kinds of raw materials, including wool. Maybe we should think about raising sheep."

"I think sheep would be a good idea," Ruby said. As tall and angular as a man, his daughter could never keep quiet during discussions about the farm. She buttered a piece of bread as she spoke. "Wool is always useful, even if we don't sell it."

"They could graze in the meadow by the creek." Jonas grinned at his sister. "We could be shepherds, like King David."

"Maybe *you* could be like David," Ruby said. "I'd rather be like his wife, Abigail."

Abraham pushed his plate away and leaned back in his chair. "Does Mr. Stevenson think the war will last long enough for him to get a return on his investment?"

Jonas leaned his forearms on the table. "Folks thought the war would be over last summer, but it just continues. Men are dying on battlefields all over the South."

Even Ruby had nothing to say to that, but lowered her bread to her plate, uneaten. War. Abraham propped his elbows on the table and leaned his head in his hands. Would men ever learn to live in peace?

He ran his hands over his face, glancing at Lydia. She hadn't said anything, but her forehead creased with worry as she glanced from him to Jonas. She rose and gathered the few plates from their supper to take to the sink. Ruby joined her, but Abraham knew the women were still listening.

"I'll not be part of anything that supports war."

"I thought that," Jonas said. "I told him you weren't interested in selling."

"And yet he's coming here?"

"He's delivering the lumber for my house in a week or so and wants to talk to you then."

Jonas paused, watching him, his eyes lit with . . . what? Excitement? Only an inexperienced youth would be excited about war.

"You should consider it, Datt. We could make a lot of money selling timber and such."

An icy knot formed with that statement. How could Jonas suggest such a thing? "Money? I'll not be part of any blood money. I refuse to make a profit off other men's suffering."

"But Mr. Stevenson will buy the lumber he needs from someone. Why shouldn't it be us? What does it matter?"

Abraham sighed, tired of the talk of war already. And to have this discussion with his own son was breaking his heart. A sudden fear of the future gripped him, a fear that no matter how hard he tried, he wouldn't be able to stand apart from this war. A fear that it would reach insidious tentacles into his own home.

"It matters because of principle. I won't participate in anything that will help the war, whether I could profit from it or not. I won't support a war in any form."

"But doesn't the church only teach against a man's participating in fighting? It doesn't say anything else about war, does it?"

"The church teaches that any involvement in war is sinful, Jonas. War is cruel and brutal and doesn't solve anything."

"What about the slaves? Isn't it right that the North should fight this war if it could lead to freedom for thousands of people?"

Abraham rubbed his forehead. "Fighting one evil with another won't solve anything. I agree that slavery is wrong and should end. But war isn't the way to do it."

Jonas ran a finger along the edge of the table. "I understand what you're saying." Then he grinned. "When I told Mr. Stevenson you wouldn't be interested in selling, I don't think he believed me. I wonder how high his price will go as he tries to convince you?"

"It doesn't matter what he offers, we're not selling that timber."

Jonas rose from the table. "I'm going to visit Katie before it gets dark."

"Don't be out too late, Son."

He paused at the door. "I still think it would be a good idea to raise sheep, though. With cotton nearly impossible to buy, we could supply wool cloth to the entire county." He winked at Ruby. "We could be a family of weavers, right?"

Abraham waved him out the door, finally smiling at the boy's teasing. What he wouldn't give to be young and care-free again.

Lydia set a cup of tea in front of him and sat down at the table while Ruby brought pieces of pie for the three of them.

"Jonas is missing out on his pie again," she said.

"If I know him, he'll have his share when he comes back from visiting Katie." Lydia cut the pointed end of her piece.

"I've noticed that he spends nearly every evening with her." Ruby picked at her pie, breaking off a piece of crust and popping it in her mouth. "Should we start making a wedding quilt for them?"

Abraham let the women's conversation fade to the background as he stared at the doorway where Jonas had disappeared. The boy's questions disturbed him more than he wanted to admit, and he was glad when Lydia and Ruby moved from talking about Jonas to discussing tomorrow's work. He cut through his pie with the edge of his fork. Cherry pie, made with the first cherries from this year's harvest. Their lives were so blessed, and yet the world still intruded.

He couldn't remember Samuel ever having such questions

as the ones Jonas brought up. Samuel was like his mother. He accepted things as they were and never tried to change them. If something wasn't the way he wanted, he worked around it or waited for the situation to change.

Jonas, though. Abraham smiled to himself, remembering Jonas as a four-year-old, rescuing a runt piglet from the sty. Anyone else would have let nature run its course, and the piglet would have died. But Jonas had fought for that little pig, feeding it cow's milk from a rag soaked in the pail until the pig learned to drink on his own. He fed it table scraps and sour milk until the pig grew to be as large as its littermates. Jonas never worked around a problem, he worked through it.

And now he was trying to work through this problem of the war. Jonas would wrestle with it until he came to a decision. But Abraham had no idea what that decision would be.

Abraham speared another bite of the pie but left it on his plate and laid his fork down. If Jonas had already joined the church and been baptized, then they'd have a better idea of where his thoughts were leading him. But as long as he was outside the church, he was free to test new ideas. Once he found that those new ideas didn't satisfy the way belonging to the Lord did, then Jonas would welcome becoming a member of the church body.

But that was the worry and the focus of Abraham's daily prayers for his son, that he would see joining the church as a privilege rather than a means to an end. More than one young man had joined the church only so they could be eligible to marry, and he prayed that none of his children would be guilty of that.

## JUNE 1

Levi Beiler rose from the fellowship meal on Sunday, thinking that he needed to ask Mother to let his trousers waistband out a little. Katie Stuckey had made the cream pie he had eaten for dessert, and she was the best baker among the girls, no question about that.

As some of the younger girls cleared off the soiled dishes so the women could take their turn at the table, Levi wandered over to the barn. Church was at the Lehmans' farm today, and Caleb had already gathered their crowd at the pasture gate.

"Look at that colt," he said as Levi joined them. "Isn't he a beauty?"

Jonas Weaver leaned on the top fence rail. "He has a lot of potential. Is your father going to train him?"

"Datt and I are working with him together."

Levi slid into an empty spot along the fence next to Jonas. Peter Lehman was the best horse trainer around, and Caleb had inherited his skill.

"What did you name him?" Levi watched the foal. The bay colt, a perfect copy of his mother, looked over his shoulder at the five young men along the fence, switched his tail, and broke into a sudden run to the far side of the pasture.

"We named him Blitz, because he's as fast as lightning."

"He won't need that speed when he's pulling a plow," said Ben Fischer.

The others laughed, and Caleb joined in. "It's a good quality, though, Datt says. He's spirited and lively, and once he's trained, he won't balk at doing anything we ask him."

Some girlish laughter rose from the yard next to the house,

where the tables and benches had been set up under a shade tree. Levi wasn't the only one who turned his attention away from the colt. The girls were all dressed in identical black dresses with white aprons, but each face was different. Levi let his gaze linger on Katie's joyful expression before seeking out Rosie Keck. But she wasn't with the other girls.

"Henry, where's your sister today?"

"She went to Smithville to visit our cousins. Someone in the family had a baby and she went up there to help the family for a couple weeks."

Levi leaned back against the fence. Rosie was supposed to be his girl, but he couldn't get her to pay much attention to him. He figured she wasn't ready to settle down, even though he was.

His gaze drifted over the group of girls and found himself watching Katie again. She was Jonas's girl.

They had all decided a couple years ago which of the five of them would marry each of the girls. There were only four girls to choose from, but Henry had already been interested in a girl from Berlin. Ben had said they should choose while they were young, so they wouldn't have to ruin friendships by competing for the same girl. But Jonas had picked Katie before Levi even knew it was time to stake his claim. So he had chosen Rosie. A pretty enough girl, but not as pretty as Katie. On top of that, he had this uncomfortable feeling that whenever Rosie laughed, it was at his expense.

Jonas nudged him with his elbow. "Are you going to that ministers' meeting next week? That's the only thing the men are talking about today."

"For sure, I'm going. I wouldn't miss it."

Ben, the youngest of them, laughed. "You're going to

spend three or four days sitting on hard benches, listening to a bunch of old men talk? I'm glad I'm not going."

Levi pushed at Ben's shoulder as he laughed even louder. "This is an important meeting. What is talked about and decided here will affect all of us. This could decide the future of our church, and I want to be there."

Ben stopped laughing as Jonas agreed in his quiet voice. "I'm going too. My datt and Gustav are driving up to Smithville, and I'm going along."

Henry grinned. "If I didn't know better, I'd think both of you were lining yourselves up to be ministers."

"Not me," Jonas said. He leaned his elbows on the top rail, his back against the pasture fence. "Levi is your man, though. He has everything it takes to be a minister. Even a bishop."

As the others laughed, Levi felt the familiar feeling of pride wash over him and turned his thoughts away from it.

"We all know that no one aspires to an office like minister or bishop," he said. "The ministers are chosen by lot."

Jonas laid an arm around Levi's shoulders. "That may be. But don't you think the Good Lord prepares the ones he chooses? I wouldn't be surprised to see your name on the list the next time they call for nominations."

Levi let Jonas's words sink in and tamped down that flash of pride. The others went on to talk about the new wagon Ben's datt was building, but Levi didn't join in. Jonas was right, that God prepared the ones he chose ahead of time, but Levi thought it was prideful to look for that preparation in his own life. Perhaps that was why he loved to read the Good Book when none of his friends except Jonas did. And why his thoughts never wandered during the long sermons at church meetings. If God was preparing him for a call to be a minister, then well and good. He would do his best to be worthy of that call, as Paul urged in Ephesians.

He found himself watching the group of girls again. When he married, he would need to choose a wife who would be the perfect minister's wife. Rosie was too flighty. Too taken with things of the world. He needed to find someone more like Katie. She wasn't only pretty, she also had the kind of personality that made everyone else like her. Even now, she sat in the center of the group, holding the attention of all the other girls. Ja, for sure and certain, she would make a fine minister's wife.

Jonas started telling about the house he was building in the woodlot along Weaver's Creek.

"Is it a log house, or are you building with boards?" Henry asked.

"I wasn't sure, until Katie told me what kind of house she wanted." Jonas's face turned red as he realized what he had said.

"So Katie is choosing what kind of house to build?" Caleb said, jabbing Jonas in the ribs. "I think there will be a wedding soon."

Jonas laughed. "Not very soon, but eventually." He grinned, no longer embarrassed. "You fellows should think about doing the same. We're not getting any younger, you know."

Levi shifted his gaze over to Katie again, surprised at how Jonas's words had felt like a cow had kicked him in the belly. He knew they were getting married someday, but things seemed to have gotten more serious lately. He needed to concentrate on finding his own wife. Maybe he would visit some of the other churches in the county to meet some new people. New girls.

Anything to help him forget about Katie Stuckey.

# 4

**JUNE 6**

Abraham gave the horses a day of rest on Friday, the first week of June. He spent the morning giving Rocky and Nan a good grooming, since he was planning to drive them to Smithville in the morning to attend this gathering of Amish ministers from almost every community in the country, from Iowa to Pennsylvania. The ministers had gathered before to discuss issues that faced the church, but this time the organizers were planning annual meetings. That was new. That and this disturbing change-minded undercurrent within the church, even here in Holmes County, drew Abraham to attend this meeting. Rocky stepped aside as Abraham brushed the horse's flank harder than he intended.

"Sorry," he said, addressing the bay horse. "I'm worried about tomorrow." Rocky turned his head. If Abraham didn't know better, he'd think his horse was listening. "You know I don't like new things." Rocky nodded his head and Abraham grinned. "And I know you're only asking for a carrot."

When he finished brushing both horses, he turned them into the pasture with the rest of the team. He leaned against the doorframe, considering this new thing. This annual ministers' meeting. Bishop Moses Miller had been visiting from a neighboring church and had told Abraham and the other men of the church about it on Sunday. He had urged all of them to attend.

"My uncle, Bishop Lemuel Miller, is one of the men behind this." Bishop Moses was sometimes called little Moses, but there was nothing little about him. He was a large man and a strong leader, able to express his thoughts in ways that even the children in the congregation could understand. "The organizers want to find some sort of agreement between the differing factions, to make decisions about what our beliefs and practices should be as Amish in the world."

"What do you hope to gain from this meeting?" Gustav had asked.

"Peace," Bishop said, his face full of sorrow. "Peace and unity. The change-minded factions must be brought back to the narrow way of the church." He sighed deeply, then smiled. "And I also hope that the division in the Indiana churches can be healed. But most of all, that God's will would be done."

Gustav and Abraham had decided to attend the meeting together, and to Abraham's surprise, Jonas had asked to come also.

So in the morning, the three of them would start the long trek to Smithville, in Wayne County. Thirty miles would tax the team, but they would take the spring wagon and the burden wouldn't be too great for the young horses. And they would have two days of rest before they returned next week.

In the distance, the sound of a heavy wagon approaching drew him to the front of the barn. Braking as he guided his horses down the hill came the mill owner Stevenson with a load of lumber. Two men rode in the back, perched high on the stack of boards.

"Jonas!" Abraham called.

"Ja, ja, ja. I see him." Jonas came from the shop where he had been repairing a harness, pulling the leather apron off as he came. "The lumber is here. I'll help Mr. Stevenson unload it."

"Put the apron away first, Son."

By the time Abraham had crossed the stone bridge, Stevenson had pulled the team to a halt. Jonas came running to meet them.

"I have your lumber here, young man," Stevenson said. "Where do you want it delivered?"

"I'll show you," Jonas said, climbing up to the wagon seat next to the sawmill owner. He looked down at Abraham. "Are you coming too? There are plenty of boards to unload."

Abraham nearly reminded the boy to temper his pride, but he didn't blame him for his excitement. He knew the sense of accomplishment Jonas was enjoying. The fruits of weeks of hard labor were stacked in the wagon, filling the air with the aroma of freshly sawn lumber.

Stevenson drove on, following Jonas's directions until they arrived at the clearing in the woods. The boy had built a log bridge over the creek wide enough and heavy enough to support the wagon and team. Abraham nodded his head with satisfaction as they drove over it. The last time he had seen this bridge, it had been a single log. Only a footbridge. But

Jonas had planned ahead, preparing what he needed as he expanded the little clearing.

As the wagon halted, Stevenson whistled as he looked up into the towering branches over their heads. "One hundred sixty acres of virgin timber." He glanced at Jonas. "You're sure you don't want to sell it? You haven't heard my offer."

Jonas looked at Abraham, questions written in his eyes, but Abraham shook his head. "I'll not make a profit from war."

"That profit would be high," Stevenson said, trying to strengthen his argument with the powerful temptation money held. "And think of the good you could do with those resources! Your family would be very wealthy."

Abraham shook his head. "We won't sell this timber."

Stevenson shrugged as he wrapped the reins around the brake handle. "I thought I'd try to convince you. Jonas told me you wouldn't sell, and I see he was right."

With five men working, the lumber was unloaded and stacked before dinnertime. Abraham asked Stevenson and his men if they wanted to stay and eat with them, but the mill owner waved off his offer.

"We have a cold dinner with us, and I need to get back to the mill." He shook Jonas's hand, then Abraham's. "Anytime you decide to sell that timber, whether it's wartime or not, contact me."

As the wagon rumbled away, Abraham examined the lumber. "This wood needs to season before you start building with it."

"I know. I'll restack it so more air can reach the inside of the pile." Jonas ran a hand across a board. "I hope to start building by the end of September. That will give the boards nearly four months of drying time."

"We have an hour before dinner. I'll help you get started."

They laid down a foundation for the stack, using narrow logs Jonas had set aside. They laid the boards across this foundation, then laid another layer across the first one, running the opposite direction, keeping a couple inches between the boards in each layer. By the time they set the third layer in place, they had reached a rhythm in their work.

"This meeting we're going to in Smithville," Jonas said as he placed another board on the stack, "what is it going to be like? Have you ever attended one before?"

"There has never been one before, not like this. The idea has been talked about for years, ever since the Indiana congregations finally split almost ten years ago, but this is the first time one has ever been organized."

"I think it's a good idea. Instead of the ministers in Pennsylvania going one way and the ministers in Iowa going another, they can get together and decide what to do."

Abraham grunted as he pushed a board onto the growing stack. "It isn't just to make sure the churches are going the same direction, but to determine if they're going God's direction. The biggest question should be whether we are following the Scriptures or not."

Jonas stopped, resting one hand on the stack of lumber. "Do you think the Walnut Creek church is following the Scriptures?"

"There is nothing in the Good Book about Sunday schools and meetinghouses." Abraham wiped the sweat off his nose with his handkerchief.

"But isn't the biggest issue about stream baptism?"

"As I understand it, that is one of the issues. We've always had house baptism, taking place during a worship service."

"There is mention of stream baptism in the Scriptures, though. So why shouldn't we do that?"

Abraham held Jonas's gaze with his own. He didn't have an answer, because Jonas was right. The folks who objected to stream baptism could only do so on the basis of tradition, not Scripture. "That is one thing I hope will be cleared up in this meeting. The ministers will come to an agreement on whether stream baptism is allowed or not. The other issues will be discussed as well. I hope it will be a good, godly time."

"Do you think the war will come up?"

"They might discuss it, but the church's response to war is clear and has been since the beginning. The teachings of Scripture are also clear. So I don't think there will be any dissent on the matter."

Jonas continued his work in silence. Abraham shifted another board onto the next stack, considering Jonas's question. The ministers would never support the war and would probably go so far as to forbid any member's participation in the army. But the subject seemed to be on Jonas's mind, and since he wasn't yet a member of the church, he wasn't bound to what was decided at the meeting.

Abraham lifted another board, waiting for Jonas to place his on the stack. His son would make his own decision, but Abraham prayed that it would be the right one, in line with the teachings of the church.

~~~~~

## June 8

The first annual ministers' meeting was held in the large barn of one of the many Schrock families near Smithville. Most of the participants had arrived on Saturday, and Sunday morning's service was the largest one Jonas had ever attended.

With so many ministers present, the sermons were lengthy. Then each sermon was followed by many responses, where the other ministers added details in support of the sermon or correcting points of doctrine. The service dragged into the afternoon. Jonas listened to all the speakers, glad to hear the differing points of view. He had always thought Amish congregations were the same, whether the community was from Iowa or Pennsylvania, but each minister had his own style of preaching and his own slant on the Bible passages.

Datt, Gustav, and Jonas had set up their camp next to their wagon for the two or three nights they planned to be there, near Levi Beiler, his father, and the other men they knew from Holmes County. Bishop Lemuel Miller and the group from Walnut Creek were grouped together, a little bit away from the rest of them. Although Walnut Creek was one of the Holmes County congregations, their change-minded actions made them the topic of much discussion among the other churches in the county.

Gustav sat on an upturned log on Sunday evening, watching the Walnut Creek group.

"What do you think of that?" he asked Datt.

Datt followed the direction of Gustav's gaze. "What do I think of what?"

"The Walnut Creek group, keeping to themselves like that. Do you think they're conspiring to take control of the meeting?"

Chuckling at Gustav's words, Datt buttered a slice of the bread Mamm had sent for their supper. "You're seeing problems where they don't exist. You could say we're keeping to ourselves, also, here in our camp."

Jonas grinned at Gustav's frowning reaction.

"It isn't the same, and you know it. We're here with men from Millersburg, Berlin, and Holmesville," Gustav said, pointing to the wagons camped around them.

"Don't start looking for disunity where it doesn't exist," Datt said. "Let's wait and see what the meeting brings when it begins tomorrow."

On Monday morning, Jonas followed Datt into the lofty barn and took a seat next to Levi in the back row, right behind Datt and Gustav. The church benches had been arranged in a U shape, and the front rows were filled with ordained ministers from across the country. Nearly every Amish settlement was represented by the seventy-two ministers. Onlookers, like Jonas, were welcome to attend, and the crowd packed the barn. Jonas saw young boys and a few girls in the haymow, ready to watch the proceedings.

Levi rubbed his hands together, as if he expected a banquet to be served. "I'm glad you're here, Jonas."

"Why?"

Lowering his voice, Levi said, "Then you and I can discuss what goes on."

"Won't you talk it over with your father?" Amos Beiler was one of the ministers present, sitting in the second row.

"He never discusses such things with me."

Jonas caught a glimpse of Preacher Amos across the way, watching Levi with a frown. Levi had told him he wasn't close to his father, but that frown made him think that Amos didn't want Levi here at all.

Bishop Jonathan Yoder from Pennsylvania brought the

meeting to order. After an opening prayer and song, the meeting was under way. The first discussion had to do with the long-festering difficulties between the Elkhart County and LaGrange County congregations in Indiana, and Jonas's attention flagged.

He studied the faces of the men sitting in the front row of the benches facing him. Most listened intently, standing to indicate when they wanted to add their thoughts to the discussion. The deliberation lasted most of the morning, until the moderator finally assigned a committee of six bishops to examine the problem and bring a report back to the meeting later.

The reading of a letter from a Pennsylvania congregation requesting a written report of the meeting was the next item of business. Once it was read and agreed to, the meeting broke for dinner.

The women of the Smithville church had provided dinner for the ministers, but Datt and Gustav had brought food for the three of them to share near their wagon. With close to three hundred laymen and observers attending, Datt had said they shouldn't expect others to provide food for them and their horses.

So Jonas tended to the team while Datt built a fire and cooked some bacon to go with the bread and dried apples they had brought. At the end of the noon hour, a clanging bell called everyone back to the meeting.

Almost before the moderator had finished calling the afternoon session to order, Bishop Levi Yoder from a neighboring church in Holmes County stood.

"Uh-oh," Gustav said. His voice carried to the folks sitting nearest to him.

Jonas knew what he meant. Bishop Levi could be a bit tactless when he was impassioned about a subject, and from his stance and the way he regarded the men sitting around him, he was ready to dive into his subject with as much zeal as Jonas had ever seen him exhibit.

He started out by repeating the history of the calling of this meeting, beginning with the idea that had been proposed by Bishop David Beiler of Lancaster County several years before.

"I was in support of that proposal," Bishop Levi continued, but then indicated the gathered ministers with a sweep of his hand, "however, this meeting wasn't called by the majority of the churches but by a few change-minded bishops who are intent on forcing the rest of us to accept their progressive ways."

With that statement, many of the assembled ministers started talking at once, some of them shouting to make themselves heard over the tumult.

Jonas scooted forward so he could hear as Datt and Gustav leaned their heads toward each other.

"I told you there might be trouble," Gustav said, watching the scene in the center of the barn.

"This is terrible," Datt said as he shook his head. "Where is the unity of the church?"

"Thrown out the window. Those change-minded men won't stop to consider what they're doing. They would rather tear the church apart than listen to reason."

The moderator called for order, and the shouting voices quieted. Finally, the ministers settled back in their seats, and Bishop Levi continued. He went on to bring up the Walnut Creek congregation by name, listing the new things that the church had adopted, accepting such innovations as photography, lightning rods, insurance policies, and large church buildings.

"The lack of unity between the four conservative churches in Holmes County and the change-minded one isn't because of the issue of stream baptism, as some have reported," Bishop Levi continued, "but because the change-minded leaders continue to bring these new things into the church without discussion among the neighboring congregations, and we can't tolerate them."

Then Bishop Lemuel from the Walnut Creek church stood, and the gathered assembly was silent, waiting to hear what he would say. Jonas leaned forward to see him better.

"Let me say first that I am unaware of any Walnut Creek members who have had pictures made using photography."

This brought some scattered laughter from the crowd.

Levi leaned toward Jonas. "Bishop Lemuel always knows how to entertain a crowd."

Jonas smothered a chuckle as Bishop Lemuel held up his hand to silence them before he continued.

"These things that Brother Levi has mentioned played no part in the division between the Walnut Creek church and the rest of the Holmes County churches," he said, starting with a calm and clear voice. "But the division has come about because of the refusal of some conservative church leaders to even talk about the possibility of adopting new innovations that would benefit everyone."

At those words from his uncle, Bishop Moses rose, his hand raised to gain recognition from the moderator. At the nod from Bishop Jonathan Yoder, he faced the assembled ministers.

"I agree with Brother Levi. The stream baptism is no hindrance to unity among the churches, but the insistence of one church to force the rest of us to accept their progressive ways and still expect us to remain in fellowship with them is. If those who have accepted these new things will not dispense with them, I cannot be in agreement with them."

Bishop Jonathan asked, "What would satisfy you? What would bring unity and peace to Holmes County?"

Bishop Moses turned to his uncle. "I would be satisfied if all five churches would submit to the old order."

Another man rose and said, "The same thing would heal the division between LaGrange County and Elkhart County in Indiana. We have more new things that the change-minded have accepted than have been named here, and they must be given up. Only submission to the old ways will bring unity."

The response from the other bishops and ministers was drowned out in another heated exchange of words. Jonas sat back as the moderator banged a hammer on his desk. Datt had bowed his head, his lips moving in silent prayer.

As the voices quieted once again, Bishop Jonathan spoke. "I remind my fellow ministers that we must not seek to judge each other in matters of conscience. This discussion is closed. We will continue to the next item of business, the report from the committee that has been considering the Elkhart and LaGrange problem."

With that, Jonas left the barn. He had witnessed enough discord among these ministers to fill many days of meetings. If the church couldn't agree on these simple things, how would they ever achieve the peace and unity they desired?

## JUNE 10

Five days. Jonas had been gone for five days.

Katie took another cooked and cooled beet from the pan on the table. Mama had roasted the vegetables in the oven while she cooked breakfast that morning before the day grew warm. Now Katie's job was to peel and slice them so they could be pickled in the crock sitting at her feet. After roasting, the peel came off easily, but slicing the slippery red orb was tricky. As much as she tried to prevent it, her hands were stained bright red, and so was her apron. She was glad she had remembered to wear her oldest clothes this morning.

This task was as endless as waiting to see Jonas again. Once he was home, she should make him promise to never be gone for more than a day. She couldn't live without seeing him for so long.

Of course, Papa was gone to the ministers' meeting too, but Mama didn't seem to miss him at all.

She peered at Mama, who was working across the table from her. Sitting with the box shredder balanced over the biggest stoneware crock, Mama was slicing cabbages. They had picked two dozen heads of fresh cabbage early that morning, and Mama was making sauerkraut. Katie wrinkled her nose. As much as she disliked slicing beets, the process of making sauerkraut was much more tedious. Mama would shred some cabbage into the crock, then sprinkle salt on top, then shred more cabbage. Her arms ached to think of it.

Just like her arms ached to think of all the work they had done to harvest these cabbages and beets. Mama had planted the seeds in trays back in March, letting the little plants sprout and grow in the sunshine coming in the south window in the front room. They had planted the seedlings in their kitchen garden in April, and now the vegetables were ready, just in time to plant a second crop of lettuce in their place.

When Katie finally got to the end of the pan of beets, she slid the last of the red slices into her crock, and dumped the peels and stem ends into the old dishpan they used for kitchen scraps.

"Should I take the peelings to the pigs now, or do you want me to wait until you've finished the cabbages?"

Mama looked up from the cabbage shredder. "You're done already?"

"Already? I've been slicing beets since breakfast, and it is nearly dinnertime."

Rising from her chair, Mama stretched and flexed her fingers. "No wonder my hands are so stiff. Time gets away from me when I'm working." She looked out the window toward the road, just as Katie had done many times in the last five days. "I thought your papa might be home in time for dinner today, but they must have stayed in Smithville last night too."

"I thought they were coming home yesterday." Katie sliced a loaf of bread for their lettuce and bacon sandwiches. Since the weather was warm and Papa was away, they had been having light dinners that didn't take much preparation. Mama had cooked the bacon in the morning while the stove was hot, then put out the fire to keep the house cooler.

Mama put the plate of cold bacon on the table along with the lettuce they had picked and cleaned that morning. Katie missed having tomatoes in their sandwiches, but that treat would have to wait until the tomatoes ripened in a few weeks. She moved the rest of the cabbages to the side of the table, and she and Mama sat in their chairs.

When Katie opened her eyes after the prayer, she couldn't help giggling at the sight of a cabbage in Papa's place.

"Look! Papa has a green head."

Mama smiled, but at the same time her eyes filled with tears. Katie froze, staring at her. Mama never cried.

"What's wrong? Mama?"

"Nothing." Mama shook her head. "It's nothing. Just . . ." Her voice trailed off.

"What?"

Patting her hand, Mama sniffed, and the tears were gone. "Never mind. You'll understand when you're older."

"I'm not a child. I'm a grown woman." Katie blinked. "Well, nearly grown."

Mama looked at her, staring as if she had never seen her before. "You are, aren't you?" She shook her head as she leaned back. "You have always been in such a hurry to grow up, and now it's happened. Where have the years gone?"

"They've gone very slowly for me." Katie took a bite of bacon. "Are you going to tell me what's wrong?"

Mama made her sandwich in silence, as if she was considering what she should tell Katie.

"It's just that your papa is later than he should be. I keep telling myself that the gathering must have lasted longer than he thought it would, or they took a longer road home for some reason." Mama stared at her sandwich, but made no move to pick it up.

"You're worried about him?"

"I shouldn't be, should I?" She frowned at her sandwich, but then her face twisted as if she would hold her tears back by the force of her will. "But I don't know what I would do if something happened to him."

Katie grasped her hand. Mama had always been strong and unyielding. A force to push against, to set the boundaries that were so frustrating. A solid wall. But Mama's hand was thin and fragile, with age spots dotting crepe-like skin. When was the last time she had held her mother's hand?

With a start, Katie realized that she wasn't the only one who had gotten older as time had flown by. The world shifted beneath her feet. The days had been long, but the years . . . The years had gone, and no one could bring them back.

She grasped at her childhood, fluttering just beyond her sight, but it was fading. With Mama's admission of her frailty, she shrunk before Katie's eyes. No longer the unbending ruler of the household, Mama became a woman, sitting at the kitchen table with Katie. A woman with fears just like her own.

"They'll be home soon. Today or tomorrow." Katie smiled as she spoke, ignoring the growing certainty that Mama was right to be worried.

The afternoon passed slowly. Katie wanted to wait for Jonas at the cabin site, but her new realization made her reluctant to leave Mama alone. Katie finished shredding the cabbage while Mama boiled the cloth cover and cleaned the crock weights. Every day for the next two weeks, Mama would skim the brine that covered the shredded cabbage and boil the cloth again. By then the sauerkraut would be finished and ready to eat all winter long.

When the cabbage was all in the crock, a final layer of salt added, and the weights and cover set in place, Mama glanced out the window once more.

"It's still early," Katie said.

"Ja, ja, ja," Mama said with a sigh. "And there are many miles between here and Smithville."

She tried to think of something that would take Mama's mind off the empty road. Her mind too. Keeping busy was the only way to make the hours pass quickly.

"I need to start preparing to set up housekeeping." She forced a smile as Mama pulled herself from the window. "For when I get married someday."

Mama nodded, thoughtful. "You know what you will need. Bedding, kitchen towels. You use them every day."

Katie's smile became genuine as the brisk Mama returned. She counted the items off on her fingers. "For the bedding you'll need a quilt, bedsheets, and a ticking for the mattress."

"I could start on the quilt this fall."

Mama sat at the table across from her, all business. "We will ask the girls if they have scraps of fabric to use for it. I have lengths of linen that I wove last winter, and you can make sheets and kitchen towels from that. We'll have to weave some more linen this winter for your mattress ticking." Mama pursed her lips, tapping them with her forefinger. "We should plan a trip to Millersburg soon to do some trading. We can work to fill your blanket chest when our other chores aren't so pressing this winter."

"I don't have a blanket chest," Katie said.

As her sisters had grown into adulthood, Papa had made each of them a chest. She remembered spending hours in his workshop watching him as he built each box, planing and sanding the boards until they were as smooth as glass. She had been hoping that Papa would make a chest for her, but something else always came up. There was no hurry, he had always said. She had a feeling he had forgotten.

"Perhaps Papa will make one this autumn, once the field-work is done." Mama's statement sounded like she was checking another item off her list rather than fulfilling Katie's cherished desire, but Katie didn't mind. What Mama didn't know, though, is that she would need it before winter.

"What should I start making first?"

"The sheets. We have the linen, and once you've measured the lengths you need for the sheets, you can make kitchen towels from the rest. They will be easy to hem . . ."

Mama's voice trailed off at the end of her sentence, as she stopped, listening. Then Katie heard it too. Footsteps on the porch. Papa opened the door, a frown on his face.

"Gustav," Mama said, rising from her chair. "You're home."

She took his hat and coat and hung them on the hooks by the door while Papa sat in her chair with a heavy sigh.

"How did the meeting go?"

From Mama's expression, Katie would never have thought that she had been close to tears earlier. Both of her parents acted as if Papa hadn't been farther away than the oat field. But as she slipped out the door, hoping to find Jonas, she glanced back. Mama stood behind Papa, her hand resting on his shoulder, and he reached to clasp it in his.

Katie smiled, skipping down the porch steps to the path. She would never doubt that Mama and Papa loved each other.

# 5

A week after returning home from Smithville, Jonas still wasn't sure what to think about the things he had seen and heard. Even with all the talk of unity and brotherhood at the ministers' meeting, most of the Holmes County churches weren't satisfied with the decisions that had been made.

"They ignored us," Gustav had said on the trip home, sitting on the wagon seat next to Datt while Jonas had lounged on a blanket roll in the back. "It was as if our opinion counted for nothing."

Datt kept his eyes on the horses' ears and his voice mild. "Be careful not to fall into the same trap, Gustav. Labeling folks with ideas different from your own as 'them' and calling yourself 'us' is the best way to create division."

Gustav muttered, then said, "I think the division is already there, but no one will admit to it."

As Jonas made his way through the woods to his clearing, he thought about Gustav's words. The division in the country had happened the same way, with no one wanting to admit the seriousness of the break until it actually took place last year. Since the Confederate States proclaimed their separation from the rest of the country, though, things had only gotten worse.

The newspaper he had brought with him to read crinkled as he walked. Stuck in his back waistband, it folded and bent with every step. He had picked it up in Wooster on the way home last week, wanting to read a different editor's point of view, but in every paper the war news continued its unending chant of doom and death. Even the army's victories were hollow as Jonas read the lists of dead and wounded after the battles. The only good news was that one of the politicians running for state office in Ohio had promised that if a military draft happened, the Amish, Dunkers, and other nonresistant churches wouldn't be required to fight. He had proposed that they could pay a fee instead.

But Jonas wasn't sure how he felt about that. What would that money be used for? And if the military needed soldiers, they would get them from somewhere. It didn't feel right that if he was drafted, he would be able to avoid serving while someone else went instead. Someone else who might end up on the casualty list someday.

When he reached the clearing, Jonas put the paper on the bench and started in on the task of moving and turning the drying lumber. If he didn't turn the boards every couple weeks and restack the piles, the planks could warp as they dried. A well-seasoned stack of lumber would make a weathertight house, just right for Katie and their family.

He grinned at that thought, looking toward the lowering

sun. Katie had told him she'd bring supper for them both, and anticipation made his stomach growl. Not only his stomach, but the rest of him yearned for Katie's presence. They couldn't spend enough time together to satisfy him. Fifty years wouldn't be enough time, for sure, although it made him dizzy to look that far into the future.

As he moved the stack from the one he and Datt had made to a new one that mirrored it, Jonas thought about the family he and Katie might have one day. They would have a boy first, for sure and certain. Maybe two or three boys before a girl came along. That would be the best way for the family to grow. And by the time the girl came along, the boys would be big enough to sit with him in church. He would teach them to listen to the minister and to sit quietly.

With that thought, he dropped the board he was carrying onto the new pile with a slap and straightened up, stretching his back. He pulled his straw hat from his head and wiped his brow. He thought he hadn't made up his mind about joining church, but he guessed he had after all. His boys would go to church with him, and if there were going to be boys, then he and Katie would need to get married first. That meant he was joining.

He put his hat back on and reached for the next board.

But what about his doubts? After last week's meeting, he had even more. He knew where he stood on the matter of introducing new things into the church. As far as he was concerned, the Walnut Creek congregation should have conferred with the other churches before beginning to build their meetinghouse. And when the other churches in the county objected, they should have stopped the building until the matter could be resolved.

Jonas finished that stack of wood and started on the next one, laying fresh logs down for a clean foundation. As he reached for the first board, he glimpsed Katie walking across the bridge from the road, carrying her basket. He left the board where it was and met her as she reached the clearing, reaching for her basket.

He took a deep breath. "Do I smell cold fried chicken in here?"

Katie smiled, her face lighting up. "For sure. I made it for dinner at noon, and saved extra pieces in the springhouse for our supper."

She followed him to the log bench and he set the basket down.

"I have to move these boards before I stop to eat. Do you mind waiting?"

She shook her head. "You can tell me about the meeting. Every time I ask Papa, he just scowls."

"He wasn't happy with the way the meeting turned out."

"I doubt if he'll ever want to go to another one."

Jonas started shifting the boards from one pile to the other. "Next year's meeting will be in Pennsylvania. I don't think any of us will be traveling that far, except the bishops."

"Papa said something about the meetinghouse in Walnut Creek. Will they tear it down?"

"I don't think so. Bishop Lemuel didn't seem to think it was a problem."

"Then he hasn't heard Papa's opinion."

Jonas paused before moving the next board. "That's the problem. I don't think the bishop heard anyone at the meeting except the men he agreed with."

Katie sighed, resting her chin in her hand. "You could say

the same about Papa. He's so set in his ways. What's wrong with a meetinghouse?"

"I don't have anything against them, except that we have never had them." Jonas left the lumber and sat next to Katie. "Other churches have them, like the Mennonites, so it seems like the Walnut Creek folks could join them instead of insisting that the other Amish congregations accept the changes they want to make."

"But that would divide the church. At least, it would divide the Holmes County churches."

"What they are doing now is creating division." Jonas shook his head. "The meeting was filled with change-minded ministers, ones who agreed with Bishop Lemuel. But those of us from the churches that keep to the old order felt like we were shoved aside. Like our opinion didn't count. I say let the church be divided, but Datt says we still need to work and pray for unity."

"All this talk makes me worry about what will happen in the future." Katie's brown eyes were wide as she watched his face. He stroked her cheek and brushed back a lock of hair that had escaped her kapp.

"There's no need to worry. What we believe and how we worship won't change, whether the change-minded folks want us to or not."

She grinned at him. "I didn't realize you were so stubborn."

He grinned back, reaching for the basket. "I haven't even begun to be stubborn." He pulled the towel away. "Can we eat now? I can't wait until after I finish stacking the lumber."

Jonas fetched a couple clean boards to use for their plates while Katie unpacked the cold chicken and greens sprinkled with vinegar. Pickled eggs and thick slices of buttered bread came out of the basket next. After a silent prayer, Jonas picked up one of the pickled eggs. Katie had boiled it and taken the shell off. A week being pickled in beet juice turned it pink and sweet.

"I could eat pickled eggs all day."

"I only brought one for each of us, so you'll have to wait until another time."

Jonas picked up the newspaper and opened it to the second page. "Do you want me to read to you about the war?"

Katie shook her head. "I don't want to hear about it. Every time you mention it, all I can think about is how men are killing each other for no reason."

"It isn't no reason, Katie. It's to preserve the Union and to free the slaves."

"But is anything worth killing another man?"

Jonas took another bite of his egg. "You can't put a price on a man's life."

"That's what the war does, doesn't it? It says that stopping slavery is worth . . . how many lives? A hundred? A thousand?"

Jonas's eyes flitted to the list of casualties from a recent battle in Tennessee. The editor of the paper had praised the small number of soldiers killed in the skirmish, but each one of those twenty-seven men had families who loved them. Dreams of their own. Each one of their lives had been precious, but now they were gone . . . and slavery still flourished in the South.

And at the same time, each slave was a person, a life worth defending. Was it right to trade one person's life for another? He shook his head. He knew he was right. Slavery was wrong. Abolition was worth fighting for . . . but was it worth killing for?

He grasped at something to defend his opinion. "The preservation of the Union is important . . ." That phrase sounded weak, even to his own ears.

Katie crossed one leg over the other, bouncing her foot up and down. "So men are dying in order to preserve the unity of the country, but when it comes to the unity of the church, you say we should let the dissenters go their own way? Isn't the church worth fighting for just as much as the country?"

Jonas had no answer for her. The church was too close, and too dear, but the war . . . His thoughts went to a place he didn't like. Up until now, the war had been interesting to read about, but it was something that happened to other people, like Tom Porter. Or in other places, like Tennessee. The war was only words in a newspaper article. He closed the paper as he finished the egg, the treat turning bitter in his mouth. Katie was right. The war wasn't glamorous or exciting. He was sick of reading the accounts of battles, sick of skimming over the numbers of casualties. Sick of reading the conflicting opinions of the different editors as they argued over the question of slavery and the inaction or actions of Congress and the president.

His attention and his energy should be spent here, in the church, where it mattered. Where he could make a difference. In the church, he could work to build a place for Katie and their family within the bounds of the community. Any questions he might have about the doctrine were minor compared to that.

He glanced at Katie. "Before we get married, we need to join the church."

Katie nodded. "The next membership class will probably start in September. We can be baptized in time for a November wedding."

Jonas watched Katie's smile as she looked off into the trees. She loved watching the birds in the forest. He would make sure her kitchen window faced east, toward the woodlot near the creek, so she could watch them all day once they were married. That vision of the little boys sitting next to him during the church service came to mind, and he could see them as if they were a reality, playing among the tree stumps at the edge of the woods while he and Katie worked together to build their home and raise their family.

This was what he would sacrifice if he let his questions about the war prevent him from joining and being baptized. Katie's words about fighting for the church rang in his heart. He loved the church enough to fight for it and its commitment to follow the Scriptures.

"We'll go to membership class together."

She smiled at him as he took her hand in his own.

## JULY 11

July had turned hot and stifling, but Katie still had plenty of chores to keep her busy. As the green beans ripened, Katie's days were filled with long hours of stringing them to dry. When she wasn't stringing beans, she was weeding the gardens. The work never ended.

Suppers were quiet meals. Katie had been the only child at home for so long that the routine grated on her. If only she could eat supper with Jonas every evening, but Mama would only allow her to pack a picnic supper for them once or twice a week. Every night Mama and Papa would discuss the day's work, or tomorrow's plans, or what one of the grandchildren had done, and ignored her.

To them, it seemed, she was still a child when they were at the table.

On this July evening, she finished her soup in silence, listening to her parents' conversation.

"The corn has grown tall enough that we don't need to use the cultivator to control the weeds anymore. It should be a fine crop, as long as we get some rain."

Mama's hands stopped moving, her spoon halfway between her bowl and her mouth. "We haven't had any rain since a fortnight ago. We're overdue."

"Ja, ja, ja. But the rain will come in God's own time."

Katie stifled a sigh. When she and Jonas were married, the last thing they would talk about at the supper table was the weather. She must have been wrong about her parents loving each other. They certainly didn't talk as if they knew what the word even meant.

"Mary brought the children by today. That Lizzie is growing up. I've never heard a two-year-old talk as much as she does, chattering all the time."

"Are Leah and Rosie over their illness?" Papa's words were muffled as he tore off a piece of bread and stuck it in his mouth.

"Only a bit of a cough left. They're past the danger point."

Katie laid her chin in one hand. Her nieces had been quite ill for a week, and being so young, only four and five years old, the entire family had been concerned. But that was a month ago, and they had been well enough to be out and visiting for at least ten days now. Her thoughts drifted to Jonas. This week or next, he would start laying the foundation for his house. As soon as it was finished, he had promised Katie, they would be married. But they wouldn't tell anyone until autumn came. For now, their plans were their own sweet secret.

"I heard that Rosie Keck is getting married next month." Papa finally had some news. Katie sat up straight.

"To the Schrock boy from up north in Smithville?" Mama shook her head. "I know Hannah had hoped for someone better suited for her daughter."

"Ja, ja, ja. That's the one. I'm not sure what Simeon is thinking, letting his daughter keep company with a boy from a change-minded church."

Mama shook her head. "You know one can't always choose who their children marry. At least he's Amish, not like—"

Mama glanced toward Katie and pressed her lips together. But she didn't need to. Katie knew she was thinking of Elizabeth Kaufman. That's why Mama wasn't sure about her friendship with Jonas. He was from a good Amish family, and as conservative as the Stuckeys themselves. There would be no talk of Sunday schools or stream baptisms in the Weaver house, but there was still the sister who had married badly.

Papa glanced at Katie at the same time, then smiled at her. "I'm just happy that all of our children have made good choices so far. And we know Katie will make a good choice when it's her turn too."

"It's my turn now, Papa." As soon as the words were out of her mouth, Katie gasped. Her fingers flew to her lips as if she could push her announcement back in.

Mama's eyebrows raised in surprise, her head tilted to one side. "What did you say?"

Papa leaned toward her, looking at her as if she had just sprung from under the table. "I think she said it was her turn."

"Her turn for what?"

Katie wished they would stop talking about her as if she wasn't there. "I said it's my turn to think about marriage. Jonas and I are planning to be wed in the autumn."

Papa's face grew red. "You are not having a wedding so soon. You're still a child." He turned to Mama, pointing in Katie's direction. "Tell her, Mama. She's just a child."

"I'm not a child. I'm seventeen."

Papa's hand came down on the table with a slap. "Seventeen is too young to be thinking about a wedding."

"Mama was eighteen when you got married."

"That was different." Papa got up and paced around the table. "We were living in the old country, and people got married younger then."

"Rosie Keck is eighteen."

Papa turned toward her. "Ja, that's just what I mean. Rosie Keck is making a poor choice."

"Jonas is not a poor choice."

Papa ran his hand over his beard. "I have nothing against Jonas. He's a fine young man." He pointed his forefinger in her direction. "But I still say that seventeen is too young to be married."

Katie's hands trembled as she faced Papa's lowered eyebrows. "But Papa, I love him."

Mama brought her hand up to her mouth with a little cry as Papa's hands flew up in the air. "And now she thinks she knows what love is."

Katie's face grew hot. She had inherited Papa's temper, and she was close to losing it. "I am not a child." She fought to keep her voice level. "I'm going to marry Jonas in the fall and we will be very happy together."

"You will not disobey me." Papa's voice had the hard edge to it that told her he was not going to argue any longer.

"Oh, Papa!" As the words tore from her throat, she lost all control. Katie stood so quickly that her chair clattered to the floor, but she didn't care. She ran out the door and down the road toward the little clearing in the woods where her house would soon stand. She ran across the log bridge and to the bench Jonas had built at the edge of the woods.

Here, there was peace. Here she could let her tears fall with no one to tell her she was only a child and wasn't old enough to know what she wanted.

Here was where Jonas found her.

"What's wrong, Katie?" He knelt beside her and cradled her face between his hands. "Tell me why you're crying."

She closed her eyes as her mind went back to another time, years ago, when Jonas had found her in this same spot, and asked that same question. With a shudder, she closed her mind to the memory of that horrible day.

Jonas handed her his handkerchief. The cloth was wrinkled and soiled from a day of wiping his brow with it in the hot weather, but she didn't care. She blew her nose and wiped her face dry.

"I did an awful thing. Now Papa will never let us get married."

Jonas sat on the seat next to her and held her tight. "It can't be as bad as all that. What happened?"

Katie told him how the news of their coming marriage

slipped out before she could stop herself. "I wanted to wait until the time was right to tell him, but it just happened."

"We'll get him to change his mind. You'll see."

"If you think you can get Papa to change his mind, then you don't know him." Katie wiped her nose again. "Once he sets his mind to something, he won't change it."

"Perhaps my datt can talk to him."

"I suppose he could try, but I doubt if it would make a difference." Katie leaned her head against his shoulder. "Have you told your parents about our plans?"

"They know we want to get married, but I haven't told them that we've already set the time."

Katie stifled another sob. She didn't want to start crying again. "We talked about getting married in November, after we both joined the church, but now that can't be."

"Why not?"

"I can't go against Papa's wishes."

"Then we'll wait until he changes his mind."

Papa never changed his mind. The hopelessness of the situation beat against Katie's emotions. "We'll have to wait for years, maybe." She would never get married. Jonas was the only man she could trust. The only man she could be sure of.

A gust of wind stirred the treetops above them, followed by a distant roll of thunder.

Jonas's arms around her tightened. "A storm is coming. Listen."

The wind strengthened, sending a cool wind between the trees and swirling around the two of them. The fresh smell of rain accompanied it, along with another long roll of thunder.

Jonas leaned his cheek against her kapp and tightened his

hold. "I love listening to a thunderstorm, don't you? Someday we'll be cozy in the shelter of our own house, listening to the rain on the roof and the thunder crashing overhead."

Katie shivered. "I hate thunder. When I was little, I used to think the sky was going to fall in on us."

Jonas stood, her hand in his. "Then I'd better take you home before the storm comes." He smiled as he pulled her into his arms and gave her a kiss. "Don't worry, Katie. Everything will turn out fine. You'll see."

By the time they reached the Stuckeys' house, both Jonas and Katie were breathless and laughing, her worries about her father forgotten. He leaned one hand against the porch rail, watching her as the lightning cracked, followed by a boom of thunder that shook the house. She hugged herself, shivering as she moved closer to him. The rain started then, pouring as if God had turned a bucket over Weaver's Creek.

Jonas longed to pull her close, to hold her safely in his arms while the storm raged above them, but not here. Not where her parents could see them.

She turned toward him, their laughter still lingering in her smile. "I must go in. Mama and Papa will be worried about me. You should come in too. You can't walk home until the storm is over."

A movement at the window told Jonas they were being watched. Facing Gustav so soon after Katie had spilled the news of their plans sent a shiver through him that had nothing to do with the thunderstorm, but he couldn't ignore his future father-in-law. He needed to act like the man he was.

"Did you get soaked?" Margaretta asked as they opened the door.

"We reached the porch just before the rain hit," Katie said, pulling Jonas into the kitchen with her. "The storm came up so quickly that we barely made it in time."

Gustav sat at the kitchen table, reading from the ancient Bible he had brought from Germany. He stared at Jonas from under his eyebrows. "I thought you would bring Katie home as soon as you saw that a storm was coming."

Jonas cleared his throat. "Like Katie said, it was sudden. We started for home as soon as we—"

"But you nearly got our Katie drowned." Gustav shut the Bible with a thump that rivaled the thunder.

"Ach, Papa, don't be like that." Katie sat at the table.

Another thunder crash drowned out Gustav's answer, but he pointed to the chair next to him. Jonas took it as an invitation to sit down. He had known Gustav all his life and had never had an issue with the man. The families had been good friends ever since before Jonas had been born.

"Katie tells me you plan to marry her."

Thunder sounded again, but not quite as loud. The storm was moving east as quickly as it had arrived. Jonas glanced at Katie. She sat next to Margaretta with her hands clasped together, staring at the table.

"We thought this autumn would be the right time."

Gustav drummed his fingers on the table. "Neither of you have joined the church yet."

Katie leaned forward. "That's why we're waiting until autumn. We'll take the baptism class and join the church, and then we'll have the wedding as soon as we can after that."

Frowning, Gustav looked from Katie to Jonas. "Why are you in such a hurry? Katie is only seventeen."

"And I'm nearly twenty-one. We've been waiting for a long time, and we don't want to wait any longer."

"Katie's age is only one of my concerns." Gustav pulled on his beard. "I've known you since you were a little child, Jonas, and I see a trait in you that speaks of a man who doesn't have the maturity to make a lifelong commitment like this."

Jonas shifted in his chair as he felt heat rising in his breast.

"You are impetuous. You make decisions quickly, without taking the time to deliberate and seek the advice of your elders."

Jonas rose halfway from his chair, but glancing at Katie's worried expression, he sank back down again. Storming out of the house now would only prove Gustav's opinion of him.

"That may be true, but when I make a commitment, I follow through on my word. This is something I've thought long and hard about. Katie and I love each other and want to be married."

Gustav leaned back, lacing his fingers over his stomach. "Margaretta thinks you should be married—"

At this, Katie released a pent-up breath.

"But," Gustav raised a finger, "not this year. Wait until Katie turns eighteen, and we'll talk about it then. Meanwhile, both of you will have time to grow up a little. Join the church. Prepare for your lives together."

Ignoring Katie's tears, Jonas leaned toward Gustav. "An entire year? You want us to wait another whole year?"

Katie's father nodded. "When you reach my age, you'll realize that a year isn't long at all. The time will pass quickly."

Jonas couldn't look in Katie's direction, but stared at

the floor. Anger rose like a red-hot poker, ready to lash out. Ready to insist on his own way. Ready to claim his right to marry Katie anyway. But he tempered his thoughts, knowing that anger wouldn't convince Gustav to change his mind.

He leaned on his knees, matching his fingertips together to form a point. Katie continued to cry softly as her mother tried to comfort her, but the way was clear to Jonas. As much as he hated to, he must submit to Gustav's wishes if they were to continue a close relationship with Katie's family into the future. He didn't have to look any further than his own family to know the heartbreak of a girl marrying against her family's wishes. If Gustav insisted that they wait a year, they would wait.

"All right," he said, meeting his future father-in-law's gaze. "We will do as you say. But next summer, by August at the latest, we will be married."

Gustav broke into a grin and grasped Jonas's hand. "That is a wise decision, son. Very wise." He looked toward Margaretta and Katie, beaming. "Next summer, a wedding!"

Jonas rose from the table. "The storm is over, and I must be getting home."

"I'll walk you to the end of the lane," Katie said, heading for the door.

"It's after dark." Gustav nodded toward the window. "You'll go no farther than the porch."

Katie glanced at Jonas, her expression unreadable.

"No farther than the porch," Jonas repeated, and pushed her through the doorway.

"Why did you agree to that?" Katie asked as Jonas closed the door behind them.

"Because it's dark, and you need to stay near the house."

"Not that." Katie sounded as irritated with him as she was with Gustav. "Why did you agree to wait a year? Maybe we could have convinced him that waiting until December or January would be long enough."

"Because as much as I hate to admit it, your father is right."

Out of the corner of his eye, Jonas saw the kitchen door open just enough to let Katie's parents hear their conversation. He led her along the porch, away from the door.

"You know I love you," he said, keeping his voice low. "I want us to be married as soon as we can, but I don't want to cause a rift in our families."

Katie didn't respond but kept her gaze looking out on the freshly washed night.

Jonas put one finger under her chin and turned her face toward his. "You are worth waiting for." A reluctant smile lifted the corners of her mouth. "And by next summer, our house will be built and ready for us to move in. That will be better than living in a tent, or with my parents for a time, won't it?"

She nodded, then thrust her arms around his neck and drew him close. "But I wish we didn't have to wait another day."

Pulling her arms loose, Jonas held her hands together between them, mindful of the eyes that were probably watching every move he made. "So do I, Katie. So do I."

But the extra time would help him sort out his thoughts about the war and abolition, and then he could join the church with a clear conscience.

# 6

As Levi and his family approached the Weavers' place for Sunday worship, Jonas met him at the bridge.

"I have news to tell you."

Levi met Father's frown. "I need to go in and sit down. You know Father doesn't want me to fool around before church."

Jonas pulled him to the side, away from the gathering crowd. "Rosie is getting married."

"To whom?"

"Some fellow from Smithville. Katie told me about it, and I thought you would want to know before you heard folks talking about it."

Levi shrugged. "That's all right."

"I thought you wanted to marry her."

"We never got along. Not like a couple planning to marry should." He looked toward the house, where Father was just disappearing inside the door. "I have to go. Don't worry about it. I'm fine."

But he wasn't fine. Levi kept a smile on his face as he walked toward the house and nodded a greeting to Caleb and Ben. He slipped into the house and onto the second bench, right where he always sat. The big room was cool for now, but before long the air would be sweltering. Levi bowed his head, pretending to pray. No one would bother him, and he could work through what Jonas had just told him.

Rosie's face flashed in front of him. Pretty, spoiled Rosie. He fidgeted with the edge of his jacket. He didn't want to marry her. He wasn't fooling himself. But for her to marry someone else . . . It stung.

Levi closed his eyes, scrunching them shut, searching his mind, examining his thoughts. Why did it sting? Because it was embarrassing. The girl he had chosen was marrying someone else. He tried to let the tension out. It was all right for Rosie to marry that other man, whoever he was. He didn't care.

So why was his throat so tight? Why had he rushed into the house when Jonas gave him the news?

Low voices hushed as the room filled. From his seat, he couldn't see the rest of the congregation, but he knew where Katie sat. Jonas sat next to him on the bench, and Caleb beyond Jonas, like they did at every church meeting.

He lifted his head as Abraham Weaver announced the first hymn. The singing started as Father and the other ministers filed out of the room to pray during the hymns. Levi put aside his own feelings and concentrated on the song. The first one chosen was one of Abraham's favorites, about the love and brotherhood of the followers of Christ. Levi had a good voice, and often sang while doing his chores at home, letting the words ring in the rafters of the barn. But on Sunday, he worked to keep his singing blended with the others. To let it stand out would be a sign of pride, and he didn't want to be guilty of that.

It wasn't until the service ended three hours later that he was reminded of Rosie again. Henry came up to him as they waited their turn at the fellowship meal.

"Have you heard? My sister Rosie is getting married."

Levi met Jonas's eyes, giving him a nod of thanks for the early warning. "Ja, I heard. It's sudden, isn't it?"

"I should have told you she was seeing someone." Henry scuffed his shoe against a stone in the grass. "I know you chose her and all, but she met this fellow last year when she was visiting our cousins, and then I guess he proposed to her when she was there last month. I'm sorry I didn't let you know earlier."

"That's all right. I hope they'll have a good life together."

Levi smiled. The tension he had felt earlier was gone, and there was nothing between him and Rosie to make him regret losing her.

"I think they will. We met him last week when he came down here to arrange the wedding and all. Datt isn't sure he likes the change-minded church he goes to, but he's a nice fellow. One of the Schrocks from up that way."

"I probably met him while I was at the ministers' meeting. What is his first name?"

"David."

Levi nodded. "I remember him. He was interested in what was going on in Walnut Creek. His own church has already built a big meetinghouse."

"Datt isn't too happy about that part of it. He'd rather Rosie marry someone who wants to follow the old order."

Henry shrugged. "But, as he says, you can't reason with a girl in love."

Levi smiled as the others laughed at this. "Is that church near Smithville going to stay Amish?"

"As far as I know, they are. Why?"

"I heard of another church that was discussing joining the Mennonites, ministers, bishops, and all. They would call themselves Amish Mennonites."

"I suppose that's better than trying to divide the Amish church with their change-minded ways," Jonas said. "And it's a good way to bring peace to this whole issue."

"Except that they aren't Mennonites." Ben's face was growing red. "They're Amish, and should stay Amish. Forget their change-minded ways and settle down."

"You go ahead and try to tell Lemuel that." Caleb laughed as he said it and the others joined in.

Levi smiled. This conversation finally got his mind off the whole kerfuffle with Rosie.

"Before it's time to start for home, you should show us your house, Jonas," Caleb said. "Hans told me you have the foundation started."

Why did a headache suddenly start up between Levi's eyebrows?

Jonas nodded. "I'll start building once the boards are seasoned. Let's walk over there. There's a path leading that way behind the chicken coop."

The boards were stacked in two piles, six feet high. Each board was placed so that air could reach as much surface area as possible. Evidence of Jonas's work showed wherever Levi looked around the clearing. The spot was pleasant, even on a hot summer's day, with the trees shading most of the clearing. Even the bridge over the creek had been built with care, and across the road he could see the roof of the Stuckeys' house.

Katie probably loved this place.

A tight spot appeared in the middle of his back and he rolled his shoulders to loosen it. Was this tension he was feeling because of Katie, rather than Rosie?

The group crossed the bridge and started walking back to the Weavers' farm on the road. Levi lagged, glancing again at the outline of the foundation Jonas had laid out. That would be Katie's house. He looked up into the treetops. He didn't want to be jealous of his friend, but he was. No matter how many times he told himself to forget about Katie, he couldn't.

He could fall in love with her so easily if Jonas hadn't already claimed her.

⟶

### AUGUST 12

As the hot summer weeks passed, Katie made progress on sewing the things she would need to set up housekeeping, in spite of the demands of the garden. This August afternoon was sultry. Sweat trickled down her back as she sat with yards of linen covering her lap. The needle was slippery in her fingers as she sewed the long seam that would bind the two pieces of cloth together into a large sheet for the bed Jonas had not yet built.

She stopped, wiping her fingers dry on her skirt, then picked up the needle again. Katie had measured and cut the fabric with Mama's help and started the long, tedious job of sewing the pieces together in a flat seam to make them wide enough to cover the mattress of their marriage bed. Katie shivered a little at that thought. Jonas would want to do more than give her a sweet kiss after the wedding.

It would be all right. Not like Teacher Robinson. She ignored the pounding of her heart and took a deep breath. When she and Jonas were husband and wife, it would be right. What happened to Teacher would never happen to Jonas.

Katie took a few more stitches and shifted the heavy material on her lap. Her heartbeat returned to normal as she realigned the edges of the seam and stuck her needle in once more. When the sheets were done, then she would sew the huge ticking for the mattress. After that, she would go through the scraps of fabric and find some that would work for a quilt top. The garden produce was coming on, so the work putting all that food up for the winter still had to be done too.

As Mama came in from the garden, carrying an apronload of beans, Katie couldn't keep from groaning.

"Doesn't the work ever get done?"

Mama dumped the beans on the table and reached for a dishpan. "What do you mean?"

"This seam goes on forever, and when I finish it, I have another one to do. And we worked to plant those beans, and now, every day, there are more to harvest and dry. Then there is the cleaning and cooking, and everything else. Just when we finish one task, there's another one waiting."

Mama frowned at her. "That's the way life is, Katie. You must have learned that by now. Work doesn't end until we die."

Katie slouched in her chair. "It isn't fair."

"Just wait until you have a house full of children. Then you'll look back on these days with longing."

"I'll make my children do some of the work." Katie stuck her needle through the seam and jabbed her finger. She stuck it in her mouth with a scowl at the taste of blood. "At least then I might get some rest."

"Have you ever seen me rest? Or one of the girls?"

Katie inspected her stuck finger. The bleeding had stopped. Mama had always called her daughters-in-law and daughters "the girls." After her wedding, would Katie be part of that group in Mama's eyes?

"It seems like Lena enjoys her life more than the others," she said. "I often see her sitting down to rest."

The dishpan pinged as Mama snapped off the bean stems, dropping the cleaned vegetables into it. "Lena has her own way of doing things." Her voice sounded like Lena's way of doing things wasn't up to her standards.

"She's happy, though. And so are the children."

"Maybe so, but—" Mama stopped herself with a shake of her head. "I decided long ago that I would never criticize Lena or any of the girls for the way they kept house. I had enough of that with my mother-in-law." She snapped a few more beans. "But I hope you'll remember how I have taught you to keep house and run your own household in the same way."

Katie bent her head over her stitching. She liked Lena, and always felt at home when she went to visit, but she could agree with Mama. Lena's way of raising her children and keeping house were more relaxed than Mama's, and the house often reminded her of a crow's nest. Once Katie went to Lena's in the middle of the morning, and the breakfast dishes had still covered the table, crusty with dried food, while Lena had been out in the yard, playing a game with the children. Katie couldn't imagine taking time to play while there was work waiting to be done.

Steps on the porch and a rap on the door made Katie look up from her sewing. Jonas stood in the open doorway, grinning at her.

"Can you spare a few minutes? I need to ask you something."

Katie glanced at Mama, who nodded her permission. "For sure, I can. Just let me put my sewing away."

By the time Katie had folded the linen and put it away in her bedroom, Jonas was waiting for her in the lane. He grasped her hand and pulled her to his side as he started walking.

"What did you want to ask me? I thought we had everything planned already."

"It isn't very important, but I wanted to see you."

"You could have just stopped by after supper. The evenings are long now, and we would have plenty of time to spend together."

"I can't tonight. The moon is full, and Datt wants to do the fieldwork tonight instead of in the heat this afternoon, so I have a few hours to spend on the house." He squeezed her hand. "I also want you to tell me where you want the windows."

"I've already told you that. One in the kitchen, and two in the main room. And one in the bedroom."

"Ja, ja, ja. But what about the loft? And which wall of the bedroom? We could have two in there."

Katie was thinking of how nice it would be to have two windows in the bedroom when Jonas stopped.

"What is Reuben doing here?"

Reuben Kaufman stood at the side of the road, peering across the creek at the clearing, but turned to greet them as they drew near.

"Jonas." He nodded at Katie. "I heard you were building a place in the woods."

Reuben spoke German most of the time, but today he slipped English words among the German ones. Katie let Jonas step ahead of her. She had never had much to do with Reuben. He was tall, strong, and good-looking with his straight blond hair and blue eyes, but his gruff manner reminded her of a bear, snuffling among the berry bushes.

"For sure. I'm nearly of age, and it's time to prepare for my future."

"Better than a log cabin, building with boards and all." Reuben spit toward the grassy bank of the creek. "I'd build with boards, but the old log cabin seems to do all right."

Katie shuddered as she thought of the Kaufmans' cabin. It had been built by the original settlers on Reuben's land more than fifty years ago, and it showed its age. The roof hung down over the low walls, and it had no windows. Elizabeth propped the one door open, even in the winter, to let air and light into the place. It was more like a cave than a home.

"You've heard the news?" Reuben's voice held a note of excitement.

"What news?"

"There were seven days of battles near Richmond last week. The Confederates beat the Yankees in a rout. Sent them heading for cover all the way back down the peninsula. I should like to have been there to see that."

Katie covered her mouth with her fingers. She had never heard anyone speak like Reuben. War was something to be grieved over, not joyful about.

Jonas straightened his shoulders. "You're happy the Federals lost the battle?"

"Of course. They have no right to come into Virginia and tell them what to do. Virginia is a sovereign state and part of the Confederate States of America. The Federals aren't welcome there."

"You sound like Ned Hamlin."

Reuben grinned. "We're talking of joining up together." He stepped closer to Jonas while Katie moved to keep out of his sight. "You ought to come along, little brother. You're young and strong, and the South can use every fighting man it can get."

"I'm not a fighting man." Jonas's voice was low, but Katie could hear the anger rising in it. "And I'm only your brother by marriage."

Reuben stepped back. Katie peered around Jonas. The man's face grew hard at Jonas's words. "I'm still not good enough for you, am I? Even after eight years of being married to your sister."

"It isn't a question of being good enough, Reuben, you know that. We're different, you and I."

"Because I'm not Amish, and never will be."

"We see things differently. If I was going to fight in this war, I would join in the Union army."

Reuben took a step back, his eyes narrowed. "Then I'm

glad you aren't going to volunteer. I'd hate to see your face in my rifle sights someday."

"And I'd hate to see yours." Jonas's voice was weary.

Without another word, Reuben headed down the road, going east toward the crossroads beyond Katie's home.

"Do you think he really will join the army?" Katie asked, watching Reuben's jaunty step.

Jonas stared after Reuben too. "The way he was talking, he probably will."

"But he has a farm and a wife to care for."

"I'm not sure he's thinking about that right now. Some men have a lust for fighting and war."

Katie slipped her hand into Jonas's arm. "I'm glad that's not you. I'd much rather have you here, building our house."

Jonas laid his hand over hers, pulling her close to his side. "Me too."

He glanced down the road at Reuben's retreating back with a thoughtful expression that sent a shiver through Katie. The way he had spoken of joining the army showed that he had thought about it, perhaps more than once. Even though he had denied it, did he hold a desire to follow Reuben to the war? He couldn't do that. She wouldn't let him.

---

Jonas watched Reuben disappear as the road curved. He didn't understand men like his brother-in-law or Ned Hamlin. They had never owned slaves, had never had any reason to complain about the Federal government. And yet they supported the South in the war, and without any reason they could say except that they supported the rights of states to govern themselves.

Katie tugged at his arm, pulling his attention back to the clearing. "Where were you thinking of putting those windows?"

"Perhaps that was only an excuse to talk to you for a little while." He led her across the bridge to the clearing. "Summer is a busy time, and we don't get to spend the evenings together."

"I'm glad we came. It's cooler here, under the trees."

"What were you working on?"

Her cheeks turned red. "Something for our new house."

"What are you making?" He pressed her for an answer, stepping close.

"Something." Her entire face was red, and she dropped her voice to a whisper. "It's a sheet for our bed."

Jonas let go of Katie's hand as they sat on the bench in the cool shade. Knowing Katie was preparing for their lives together, and in such an intimate way, made him long for the months to pass quickly.

"What if I don't finish the house in time for the wedding?"

"Then we'll set up a tent and live in that."

"The mosquitoes will be terrible in August."

She grinned. "Then it looks like you'll need to finish that house."

Jonas looked at the stacks of lumber. "The planks aren't seasoned yet. I can't start building until September, at least."

"Then we'll have to ask our families to help."

"I don't want any more help than necessary." He glanced at her. She was beautiful with the sunlight filtering through the leaves, dappling her with shadows, and she was his. "I want to make this house for you, Katie. It's my gift to you."

She scooted closer to him and laid her head on his shoulder.

After a few minutes, he asked, "What are you thinking about?"

Sitting up, she smoothed her apron. "It was sad. Are you sure you want to hear?"

"I want to hear everything that you think about."

Katie smiled at that, then her smile disappeared as she looked at the stacks of lumber. "I was thinking about Elizabeth. If Reuben goes off to join the army, what will happen to her? And what if—" She bit her lip, as if saying the words would make them come true.

"What if he never comes home?"

She nodded.

"She has family here, and we'll take care of her."

"Ja, ja, ja. But that isn't the same as having her husband here. Do you think she'll miss him if he goes?"

Jonas didn't say what he was thinking, that it would be better for Elizabeth if her husband left and never returned, for whatever reason. Maybe then the haunted, sad look would finally disappear from her eyes.

"Of course, she'll miss him. But she'll get used to not having him around."

Katie laid her hand on his knee. "I would never, ever, get used to not having you around."

He looked into her eyes, deep brown and welling with tears. "I don't intend to give you the opportunity. I'll be around so much that you'll get sick of me."

"I'm serious. When you were gone to Smithville for those days, I nearly died."

"Now you're exaggerating."

"All right. Maybe I didn't come close to dying, but it felt like it by the end. I don't want to live without you, Jonas."

"You won't have to." He grinned at her and pointed at the piles of lumber. "Now tell me, just how many rooms do you want in this house?"

"Enough for our family." Her mood had lightened with his question, as he hoped it would. "We need a bedroom for us, one for the girls, and one for the boys."

"I thought we'd have our bedroom downstairs, and then put a partition in the loft for the children."

She turned toward him. "How many children do you think we're going to have?"

"We'll start with three boys, and then go from there."

Katie shook her head. "We need girls first. I need help with the housework if you're going to have boys."

"Hallo!" The call came from the road. "Jonas! Are you there?"

Jonas stood. Levi Beiler was at the bridge. "Ja, Levi. Come into the shade."

Levi stopped at the creek to splash water over his bright red face, then came toward them, looking all around at the clearing and the piles of lumber. "I stopped by the house, and your mother said you were here. When will you start building?"

"In September, I hope."

"That's a lot of work," Levi said. He grabbed a handkerchief and wiped his face, dripping with water and sweat. "It sure is hot today, isn't it?" He didn't wait for an answer, but waved a hand in Katie's direction. "Hello, Katie. What are you doing here?"

"Just visiting with Jonas."

Levi grinned. "You're not helping him build his house, are you?"

Katie didn't laugh at the suggestion. "We were just talking."

"What brings you by?" Jonas said, pulling Levi's attention away from Katie.

"I have news from Millersburg, and Father thought everyone in the community should know."

"What news?"

"There is going to be a military draft soon. Ohio needs to send seventeen more regiments to the army, so they're going to conscript soldiers. Father thought the men of our church should meet to discuss how we should respond."

A military draft. Jonas sighed. He wasn't surprised it had come to this. "I know how the church will respond. We won't fight."

"But we will be breaking the law if we don't. And I don't want to go to war."

"You won't have to. I heard that we'll be allowed to pay a fee instead."

"That's only a rumor." Fear crept into Levi's voice. "What will we do if it isn't true? Or if it's only for church members?" He wiped at his brow. "Now I'm glad I joined the church last year instead of waiting."

"We'll figure out something." Jonas didn't know what they would do, but the church had faced times like this in the past and had survived. "When did your father think we should have this meeting?"

"He suggested this Sunday, after church."

"That's a good idea. The entire congregation will be together then."

Levi's pale eyebrows met in the middle of his forehead.

"What about you, Jonas? What if they force you to join the army? What will you do?"

Jonas glanced at Katie's worried face, then faced Levi again. "I don't know." The memory of the casualty lists in the newspaper flashed in his mind. "I hope I never have to make that decision."

# 7

While the morning was still cool, Abraham walked with Lydia, Jonas, and Ruby to the Beilers' farm for church. They would arrive early, but he had no desire to make the two-mile journey after the sun started beating down on them. When they arrived, families stood in the shade of the trees talking quietly with one another. He hadn't been the only one with the idea to avoid the heat.

Gustav welcomed him with a wave and pulled him over to the shade of the barn. "Did you hear what Lemuel did last Sunday at the Walnut Creek church?"

Since building their meetinghouse last year, the Walnut Creek congregation had started meeting on a weekly basis like the Mennonites did, rather than every other Sunday. Abraham wondered if the members of the church missed the fellowship and close family ties they had enjoyed during the off-church Sundays.

"I haven't heard anything," Abraham said. "I don't listen to gossip."

"This isn't gossip."

Gustav looked indignant and Abraham patted his shoulder. "I'm sorry. What were you going to tell me?"

"Bishop Lemuel encouraged his members to vote in the election in October."

"We knew he would do that. He has admitted that he thinks we should make our voice heard in politics."

"But he said it during a sermon." Gustav emphasized the last word, his nose turning red. "He is now mixing Scripture and worldly events. How far will he go?"

Abraham smoothed his beard. "As far as his congregation lets him, I suppose."

"It doesn't upset you?"

"It bothers me more than you can know," Abraham said. "But this is Sunday morning and time to worship. I'll not let another man's actions rob me of that peace."

But Gustav's news had done its work, Abraham thought to himself a few hours later as the service ended and folks started making preparations for the meal. It had intruded on his thoughts all morning, as much as he had tried to prevent it. As he helped carry the benches to set up the tables in the shady yard, he noticed Gustav talking to Preacher Amos, his hands gesturing as he spoke. He joined them, along with a few other men.

"We have to do something about it," Gustav said. "He can't be allowed to carry on like this without some sort of protest from the other churches."

"Do about what?" Peter Lehman asked.

Gustav told the group what he had told Abraham before church. "We have to do something about it," he said again.

Preacher Amos fingered his beard, rocking back on his heels. "What would you suggest?"

Gustav glared. "I don't know what we can do. The man is out of control."

"This is a bishop you're talking about," Amos said, his voice calm. "We need to speak with respect."

Gustav frowned at the mild rebuke.

"We could write a letter from our congregation to his, talking about our concerns," Peter said. "Bishop or not, he and his congregation need to know that we feel they are wrong in pursuing this direction. This isn't the first time they have participated in elections."

"Did he try to tell people how to cast their vote?" asked Wilhelm Stuckey, one of Gustav's sons.

"Bishop Lemuel has never made a secret of supporting the Democrats. He says he's a 'Peace Democrat' because he supports ending the war." Gustav's temper seemed to be more under control as he spoke. "And I heard he was supporting Vallandigham for congress."

"Who?" asked Simeon Keck.

Preacher Amos nodded. "I heard that too. Mr. Vallandigham is the one who proposed the scheme we're going to be discussing after dinner, so we'll wait until then to talk about it. But do others think Peter is right? That we should write to him regarding our feelings about his actions?"

The call for dinner sounded as the men in the circle nodded their agreement. They made their way to the tables filled with sandwiches and various salads. After the prayer for the meal, Abraham and Gustav took seats at one end of the table.

"What do you think?" Gustav asked, taking a sandwich and passing the plate to Abraham. "You were very quiet during that discussion."

"I agree with you that Bishop Lemuel was wrong in taking this step, but I'm not sure a letter will be effective."

Gustav nodded. "They have a way of ignoring what we say."

"You're turning this issue into an 'us' and 'them' problem again. This issue is bigger than who is wrong and who is right. The issue is whether our church, the Amish church, is following Scripture or not. We aren't responsible to make sure the Walnut Creek congregation follows what we believe God's Word is saying. We're only responsible for ourselves."

"But as long as we're in fellowship with the other Amish churches—"

Abraham raised his hand to interrupt Gustav. "Ja, ja, ja. We have a responsibility to point out error where we see it. The question that remains is what the best way is to do that."

Gustav finished his sandwich. "Another thing I wanted to talk to you about is our children."

"Jonas and Katie?"

His friend's eyebrows raised in surprise. "Who else?"

Abraham chuckled. "They're the only ones. All of your other children are married."

"Ja, ja, ja," Gustav said. "That is true." He took a bite of potatoes and swallowed. "Now we find out that your Jonas wants to marry my Katie."

"We've known this was coming for a long time."

"You might have known, but our Katie is so young. We hadn't expected them to talk about it so soon."

"Have you heard what their plans are?"

"Katie said they wanted to be married in November, after taking the membership class."

"That soon?" Abraham speared a potato slice with his fork. That would mean Jonas would be joining church this fall, but would he join out of love for the Lord and for the church? Or was it only to be able to marry?

"Don't worry. Margaretta and I told them they had to wait until after Katie turns eighteen next year, and after they've both joined the church. The last time I spoke to them about it, they agreed to an August wedding. Next August."

"That sets my mind at ease." Abraham looked across the table at his friend. "I suppose that means we'll finally be related, you old German."

Gustav showed his teeth in the grimace he liked to call a smile. "I suppose so, you old Yankee."

Abraham chuckled and went back to his potato salad.

---

Katie wiped a drip of sweat from the end of her nose with her forearm. Washing dishes was a hot chore on a warm day like this, but she was nearly at the end. After these plates were washed, she and the other girls could have their dinner.

Rosie Keck dried the dishes as Millie Beiler, Levi's sister, rinsed them in a dishpan of clear water.

"I'm so hungry," Rosie said, taking the next dish from Millie. "You'd think they'd let us eat first, and then start washing the dishes."

"This is our opportunity to serve," Millie said.

Rosie and Katie exchanged glances behind Millie's back.

"That sounds like something I've heard your father say," Katie said. "Wasn't it in his sermon this morning?"

Millie beamed, her face as pink and round as her brother's. "It was. Father was talking about it at supper last night too. Every chore that we dislike is our opportunity to serve. Isn't that wonderful?"

"I don't know about you," Rosie said, wiping another plate, "but I think I'm about done serving today. Wasn't there going to be a meeting this afternoon? And is it for everyone, or only those of us who are members of the church?"

"I think everyone is invited," Katie said, handing the last dish to Millie. "From what Levi said when he brought the news, it's something that affects everyone."

Katie dried her dishwater-wrinkled hands and filled one of the plates with a ham sandwich, pickles, and potato salad. The girls found a bench at the edge of the assembled crowd just in time to bow their heads as Preacher Amos Beiler started the opening prayer.

As the prayer ended, Rosie leaned toward Katie. "I thought my stomach would start growling before he finished."

Katie smothered a giggle, then took a bite of her sandwich.

The meeting started with some remarks from Preacher Amos about the war, and then he said, "We have received word that Ohio is being asked to send seventeen additional regiments to the army. In the last fifteen months, the quotas have been met by volunteers, but the governor believes that all of the volunteers have already joined other regiments. So he has called for the legislature to authorize conscription, which they have done."

Rosie leaned toward Katie again. "What does that mean?"

For once, Katie was glad she had listened when Jonas had read his newspapers to her. "It means the government can force men to join the army."

"What if they don't want to go?"

Katie shushed Rosie as Preacher Amos started talking again.

He held up a letter for everyone to see. "We, that is, all of the nonresistant churches in the state, have received assurance that our men will not be forced to fight. Instead, we will be allowed to pay a fee of two hundred dollars. Or the draftee will be allowed to hire a substitute."

Simeon Keck, Rosie's father, stood. "What does that mean, to hire a substitute?"

"It means that the man whose name appeared on the list of draftees could pay someone to take his place."

"So this substitute would be doing the fighting, and killing, in place of me?" Simeon asked.

Preacher Amos nodded. "That's right."

"And this man could potentially be killed?"

Preacher Amos nodded again.

"I will not be part of that kind of scheme." Simeon turned to the men and women sitting behind him. "If my substitute is acting for me, then I would feel that I'm guilty of murder with every man he kills while fighting in the war. And if he is killed, his blood would also be on my head. I am glad for the alternative of only paying a fee. Two hundred dollars is a lot of money, but I'd rather pay that than suffer the guilt I would feel by hiring a substitute."

Many of the folks lining the benches nodded their agreement to Simeon's words, but then Papa stood up.

"Does this letter give any conditions to the option of paying the fee?"

Preacher Amos scanned the letter. "It only says that members of nonresistant churches are eligible."

"What about sons of members?" Papa said. "We have many young men in our church who are not yet the age to consider baptism and membership in the church, yet are eligible to be drafted. Would they be able to do this?"

As Preacher Amos read the letter to himself, the gathered men and women talked among themselves.

Rosie yawned. "I wish they would just end this meeting. I need to be home before suppertime."

"Why?" Millie asked. She was sitting on the other side of Rosie.

"Oh, no reason." Rosie smiled.

Millie covered her mouth. "Is your beau coming to visit you?"

"I didn't say that." Rosie's smile grew.

"What else would it be?"

Katie leaned forward to hear how Rosie was going to answer Millie's question, but just then Preacher Amos started talking again.

"I see nothing here that stipulates that the young man himself needs to be a member. The wording states 'part of the congregation,' with no mention of membership."

"What would these two hundred dollars be used for?" Samuel Weaver stood up. "Will it be used to support the war? To hire substitutes whether we want them or not?"

"We have no information on that," Preacher Amos said.

"I don't speak for any of you," Samuel said, looking around at the gathered men, "but I will not contribute any money to support the war, and I will not hire a substitute."

"What if you have no choice?" Simeon Keck asked. "What if it's either that or fight in the army?"

Samuel didn't answer at first but only looked at the ground.

Abraham Weaver, who was sitting next to him, stood and motioned for Samuel to take his seat.

"We need to remember that our members do not fight in wars. The government has given us an alternative, but some may not wish to accept it. But any member who willingly joins the army, regardless of the situation, would be in danger of shunning." He looked toward Bishop and Preacher Amos for confirmation.

In the silence that followed Abraham's statement, Rosie started to whisper something to Katie, but she shushed her. "I want to hear what they're going to say."

At Bishop's nod, Amos sighed. "That is right, Brother Abraham. Of course, each man's actions would be examined, and his reasons, but he would be subject to discipline from the church, and perhaps shunning."

"Then the only answer I see is prayer." Abraham looked at the congregation, finally resting his gaze on his sons. "We must be in prayer that none of our number is selected in this draft, or any in the future."

"And if names from our body do come up in the draft?" Simeon asked.

"Then we pray for guidance in how to proceed."

Katie glanced at Jonas, sitting next to Samuel on the bench. His head was bowed, just like his brother's, and she bowed her head also, silently praying that the Good Lord would spare them.

As the sun drifted toward the western horizon on Sunday evening, a breeze helped the weather mellow. Jonas wandered to the woodlot after a cold supper, enjoying the quiet. The meeting after church had been an eye-opener with news of the draft. What would he do if his name appeared on the list?

"Jonas?" Katie had been sitting on the bench, waiting for him. "I hoped you would come here tonight."

"I wouldn't miss an opportunity to see you." He took her hands in his and gave her a kiss. Nothing was better than spending time with Katie.

They sat on the bench again, and Jonas was glad that the breeze had found its way into the clearing.

"What did you think of the meeting?" Katie asked. "It's the only thing Papa has talked about since then."

"I was happy to see that some people in the government have a respect for our religion."

"It sounded like Samuel wouldn't pay the fee or hire a substitute, though. What will he do if his name comes up?"

Jonas shook his head. "I wish he would just pay the two hundred dollars. The church is asking everyone to contribute to a fund so that anyone whose name is on the list won't have to bear the expense alone."

Katie turned toward him. "What will you do if your name comes up?"

"I've been trying to figure that out all afternoon."

"You'll pay the fee, won't you?"

Jonas didn't answer right away. The smart thing to do would be to pay the fee. But he still remembered the look on Tom Porter's face as he talked about the war. He had been scared, but anxious to get into the action. Jonas knew what he believed. War was wrong, and killing another person would be horrible. But would he ever know what he really believed if his convictions were never tested?

"I think so," he said. Katie's eyes glittered at his words.

"I believe I would. But it's easy to talk about it when we're still weeks away from seeing which names will be chosen. Mine may never appear on the lists." He stroked the soft skin on the back of her hand. "The same goes for Samuel. If it came down to it, I don't think he knows what he would do."

They sat in silence for a while, listening to the evening sounds in the forest. A mourning dove called from a stand of pine trees near the road, and another answered from deep in the trees. The sun was fading, and it would soon be twilight.

Jonas leaned back, ready to tease Katie. She was so cute when she was angry. "If I went off to war, you'd have to find someone else to marry."

Her temper exploded, just like he knew it would. "You wouldn't. You couldn't." She jumped off the bench, facing him. "If you went off to war, Jonas Weaver, you better not come back here. You'll have to find yourself another wife."

He rose and grabbed her in his arms, tightening his embrace as she struggled to get away. Once she was quiet in his arms, he loosened his grip. "Who else would you want to marry besides me?" he asked, whispering in her ear.

She turned to face him and put her arms around his neck. "Hmm. Maybe Levi Beiler."

Jonas dropped his arms and took a step back. "Levi Beiler? He's . . . he's . . ."

"A nice boy and a minister's son. I like Levi."

She couldn't be serious. She had to be teasing him, just as he had been teasing her. Levi Beiler? Levi's round pink face flashed through his mind. She couldn't like him.

Katie giggled. "You're turning red." She grabbed his

hands. "I like Levi, and Millie is a good friend. But I wouldn't want to marry him. I don't want to marry anyone but you."

He pulled her close again, drawn by her very kissable lips. "You won't get a chance to marry anyone else. It's nearly the end of August already."

"It's going to be a long year." She stood on her toes and gave him a kiss on the cheek. "But then we'll never have to be apart again."

He nodded, thinking only of returning her kiss, but not on her cheek. He sat down again, and she sat next to him.

Katie gave a happy sigh and leaned closer to him. The mourning doves called again, and deep in the woods an owl hooted. A chipmunk ran along one of the boards in the pile of lumber, then jumped to the ground. It rustled through the grass and last year's leaves, looking for food, and not noticing them. Jonas stayed still, watching the little creature until it was nearly touching his toe. Suddenly, it sat up, looking at them for a long minute before leaping away and scampering toward the lumber again.

"I know they can be pests," Katie said, sitting up, "but they are so cute. I love the way their tails stick straight up." She stretched and yawned.

"It's time to go home." Jonas stood and took her hand, pulling her up with him. "Tomorrow is a busy day with all the work that needs to be done."

"The washing for me."

"And we're going to start harvesting the oats."

They walked together to the end of the Stuckeys' lane, where Jonas finally got the kiss he had been waiting for.

## AUGUST 25

Lydia Weaver put the last clean dish away from Monday's dinner and slipped onto the washing porch to sit a spell.

For thirty-five years this had been her routine. When the children were small, she had waited for this moment of peace until they were taking their naps, looking forward to it through the long mornings. But now that they were all grown, she still gave herself this few minutes of quiet time before tackling the next task. A moment to pause and to pray.

This August afternoon was hot and getting hotter. The heat turned the air into waves shimmering on the barn roof, and the leaves of the maple tree curled in on themselves. Lydia scooted to a more comfortable spot on her stool and leaned against the wall, crossing her ankles in front. She patted her face with the damp cloth she brought and sighed.

Everything was quiet. Even the cardinals nesting in the spruce tree next to the outhouse were silent. The team of horses stood under the branches of the grove of trees in the pasture where Abraham had put them after their morning's work. Their heads were down. An occasional tail swished, but even the horses were drowsing in the heavy air.

Abraham and Jonas had gone to work on the house Jonas was building in the woodlot, and Ruby was . . . Lydia wiped the back of her neck with the cool cloth. Ruby had gone somewhere after dinner. Perhaps to see Elizabeth. Lydia closed her eyes. Ruby went where she pleased. That girl needed to find a husband. Although, at twenty-six, some would say she was past the marrying age.

Thinking of Ruby brought the other children to mind,

and Lydia brought each one before the Lord as she often did during the quiet times of the day. Samuel and Anna and their four children. Miriam and Jacob with their two boys. Rachel and Mose and their three little ones. She said a special prayer for Rachel's two daughters and Samuel's little Dorcas. After all the grandsons, she was so blessed to have granddaughters. All three were young yet, but she looked forward to the time when they could come for a long visit.

She smiled at the plans she had for those granddaughters. She would teach them to bake and to sew. And she would take the time she never had to spend with her own daughters as they grew. What a privilege it was to be a grandmother! Even if Abraham did say the boys in the family were the most important.

Her thoughts landed on Elizabeth next. How different would her life be if she had never married Reuben? Still, she was close and often dropped by in the afternoon to visit with her and Ruby.

Last was Jonas. The youngest son. She felt she had hardly gotten him out of diapers when he was off, following behind Abraham and Samuel. Growing up all too soon but becoming a fine man. The only worry that intruded was this talk of the war and possible conscription. She brought prayers for the protection of her sons to the Lord.

At the sound of approaching footsteps, Lydia opened her eyes. Elizabeth and Ruby were walking toward the house, arm in arm with their heads bent together. Lydia rose to her feet, stretching her back. The girls wanted something, that was for sure.

She patted her little stool. "I'll be back tomorrow, for sure and certain. You can count on me."

"Mamm," Ruby said as she reached the porch steps, "are you talking to yourself again?"

Lydia gave Elizabeth a quick hug, not sure if she should say anything about the tears standing in her younger daughter's eyes. "You know better than that. Come into the kitchen and have some buttermilk. The stove is out and it's cooling down in there."

Ruby fetched the pail of buttermilk from the springhouse, where it had been sitting in the cold running water. Lydia dipped the refreshing drink into three glasses, her mouth watering for the treat. Sitting at the table with the girls, she took a drink before looking at Ruby's face, expectant and waiting. Elizabeth only stared at the table.

"You look like you've been planning something."

Ruby glanced at her sister, then back to Lydia. "Reuben is gone."

The buttermilk turned in Lydia's stomach. "Gone?" She took Elizabeth's hand. "You mean he left you?"

"Not exactly." Elizabeth squirmed in her chair.

In all the years she and Reuben had been married, Elizabeth had never said anything against her husband, but Lydia knew how unhappy she was.

"What do you mean?"

"He's gone away to fight in the war."

If Elizabeth had said Reuben had sprouted wings and flown to the moon, Lydia couldn't have been more surprised. "To the war? Why?"

"He and Ned Hamlin have been talking about it for weeks, and two days ago, Reuben finally said he wasn't going to wait any longer. He packed a few things and went south to join up." Elizabeth looked dazed, as if she still couldn't believe what she was saying. "He said he was going to fight for states' rights, whatever those are."

"When will he be back?"

Elizabeth shrugged. "He said he'd be gone for a couple months at the most, and he'll be back in time to harvest the corn."

"And he's left you alone to take care of the farm?"

Catching her lower lip between her teeth, Elizabeth glanced at Ruby, who leaned forward to speak for her sister.

"That's the problem, Mamm. He asked Ned to look in on Elizabeth for him, and to take care of whatever needs taking care of. But Ned . . . Well, we don't trust him."

Lydia had only seen Ned from a distance, but she knew him and his father. Shiftless, lazy men who hunted and did odd jobs for their living. She wouldn't trust Ned to take care of her daughter, either.

"You must come here to stay until Reuben gets back."

"I can't." Elizabeth's tears were close to running down her cheeks. "I have to take care of the cow and the chickens. And the garden is just coming on. If Reuben comes home and finds that I've neglected them . . ." She bit her lip again, unwilling to say what outcome that could bring.

"So I thought I would live with Elizabeth and help her on the farm until Reuben comes back." Ruby picked up her sister's line of thought with a smile. "What do you think of the plan?"

"Two women alone?"

"Better than one." Ruby's voice was strong and confident. Her red hair had frizzed in the heat and humidity, making a halo of fire around her face in the sunlight coming through the window. She took Lydia's hands in her own. "We will be fine, Mamm. I'll help Elizabeth with the farmwork, and Ned Hamlin wouldn't dare try anything improper with two of us there."

"You need to talk to your father about the idea, but I do feel better at the thought of Elizabeth having someone around she can trust."

Ruby grabbed Elizabeth's arm as she rose from the table. "Let's go find Datt. He's in the woodlot helping Jonas with his house."

As the girls left, Lydia drained her glass of buttermilk. Reuben was gone. So quickly. How many other young men from the area would follow the call to war? And how many would never return?

And what of Jonas? He wasn't baptized yet, so he was free to make his own choice. If his name was chosen in the draft, what choice would he make?

Lydia gathered the glasses and took them to the sink, rinsing them out as she stared through the window. The war shouldn't touch them here. Not in Weaver's Creek. But it already had.

# 8

The next few weeks went quickly as Jonas worked on the house. Every afternoon, after putting in a full day's work with Datt, he added to the house. By the beginning of September, the foundation was laid and ready for the framing. In the middle of the month, the lumber was seasoned enough that Datt judged it ready to use, so Jonas started building the walls.

In the evenings, Katie often sat and watched him work. Their time was shortened as the month passed the first day of autumn, but the hours were pleasant as they dreamed of their lives together.

"Which way will the front door face?" Katie asked one evening.

Jonas dropped onto the bench next to her. "Which way do you want it to be?"

"If it looked toward the road, we would be able to see people as they came across the bridge." Katie sat with her chin in her hand. "But that's toward the north, and could be cold in the winter."

Leaning against the back of the bench, Jonas lifted his hat and ran his hand through his hair. The cool September evening was a welcome relief from the heat of summer. "I could build an entryway there, or a lean-to to break the wind."

"Or we could have the door face the lane leading to your parents' farm. You'll be going that way nearly every day to work with your father and Samuel."

"Ja, that's true. But you'll be heading over the bridge and down the road to see your family almost as often."

Katie was silent, looking toward the bridge, and then toward the lane, and then back again. Jonas caught her kapp string in his fingers and tugged on it.

"What if I make both? The one facing the bridge can come out of the front room, and the other one can lead off the kitchen. I can build a porch on that side of the house."

She smiled at him. "Two front doors? Can you afford to build another door? You had already planned to put one facing the woods, in the back."

"Ja, ja, ja." Jonas melted under her smile. He would build five doors if she wanted them. "I will only need another set of hinges and a latch."

"Do you think you'll finish it by next summer?"

"For sure. I want to have all four walls and the roof on by December. Then in the spring I can start working on the inside. We'll order your stove next summer, after we harvest the wheat in July. I'll sell some of my share of the crop to pay for it."

"And by next August . . ." Katie's voice trailed off, her eyes soft as she stared at the partially built wall on the east side of the house.

Jonas took her hand. "By next August, this will be our home. You and I." He stood and pulled her up with him. "It's getting late. I'll walk you back."

They started across the bridge.

"I'm making a trip to Millersburg tomorrow, and I'll pick up the hardware I need for the doors."

"All the way to Millersburg? Can't you buy it closer?"

"The only place that carries nails and hinges is the hardware store. Plus, I'm going to buy windowpanes too."

Katie stopped, pulling him around to face her. "Do you think I could go with you? I have some things I need to buy too."

She looked so eager that he laughed. "We'll ask your father. If it's all right with him, I would enjoy your company. It's a long ride, though, and we have to leave early in the morning."

"What else can we do there?"

"I need to pick up a newspaper for Elizabeth. She tries to keep up with the war news."

"Has she heard from Reuben since he left?"

Jonas tucked her hand in his elbow as he shook his head. "Not a word. She doesn't even know which division he's in. All she knows is that he's in the Confederate army."

"Has anyone asked Ned if he knows?"

"Ned is gone too. He left soon after Reuben did, and they're probably together." Jonas started walking toward the Stuckeys' house again, bringing Katie along with him. "Elizabeth hasn't said so, but I know she worries about Reuben. Ruby thinks she's better off without him. No matter how unhappy she was when he was home, she seems sadder now."

"I'm sure she loves him."

Jonas watched Katie's profile as they walked. Did Elizabeth love Reuben as much as he loved his Katie? Whatever happened in the future, he would make sure his love for Katie didn't die, the way Reuben's seemed to have. He couldn't imagine leaving Katie and then never getting word to her. He pulled her hand closer to his side. He couldn't imagine leaving her at all.

Before sunrise the next morning, Jonas had Nan hitched to the spring wagon. He ate a quick breakfast, then drove to the Stuckeys' house to meet Katie. She was waiting on the porch and climbed into the wagon as soon as he had stopped.

She set her basket on the floor between them and pulled her shawl around her shoulders. "I didn't know it was going to be so chilly this morning."

"Datt thought it might frost last night, but it didn't get that cold." Jonas drove down the lane toward the road. "Once the sun is up, we'll be warmer. It's going to be a clear day."

Katie moved closer to him on the wagon seat and leaned her head on his shoulder. Once they climbed the hill out of the valley, and passed Elizabeth's cabin, Jonas let Nan move along at a comfortable trot. They rode in silence as Jonas watched the sky lighten from soft gray to blue streaked with yellow as the sun came over the horizon. By the time they turned onto the Walnut Creek road heading toward Berlin, Nan had settled down to a walk.

"Where are we?" Katie asked, sitting up and stretching.

"We have a couple hours to go. This is a good road, but we're not in a hurry. Nan will get us there by midmorning."

"I haven't been to Millersburg since last year, when I went

with Mama and Papa to trade for winter supplies. Mama sent a list with me today. She was glad that she didn't need to make the trip." Katie watched some cattle grazing in a field as they passed. "I don't understand that. Why wouldn't she want to go to town?"

"My mamm is the same way. She would rather stay home than spend a day driving to town and back."

"Will we be that way when we're old?"

Jonas grinned at the thought of growing old with Katie by his side. "Probably."

"Then I'm glad it will be a long time from now." She turned in her seat to watch a flock of passenger pigeons fly above a cornfield, wheeling and turning in on themselves. "The birds are gathering for their flight south."

"If I had my shotgun, we could have pigeon pie for supper."

"I'm glad you didn't bring it," Katie said, her voice soft. "I like to watch them fly. If you started shooting them, they would scatter."

"There will be another chance. They'll be gathering all month, and soon the flocks will be large enough to blot out the sun, and that means as much pigeon pie as we can eat."

"Do you like pigeon pie?"

"Doesn't everyone?" Jonas grinned at her. "It's much better than chicken pie."

"Then I'll make you one for supper sometime." Katie looked at him with a little shudder. "You have to clean them, though. It takes so many to make a pie, and cleaning them is a never-ending job. I can do one or two, but then I start feeling sick."

"I can clean the pigeons for you." The job made him sick too, but it was the price of enjoying the pigeon pie. He put his arm around her and drew her close. "Are there any other jobs I'll need to do for you?"

Katie snuggled next to him. "I'll think of more as the years go by."

"Then make a list. I'll do anything that you want me to."

As they neared Millersburg, the haze Katie had seen in the sky soon after they left Berlin turned into a pillar reaching toward the gathering clouds.

"Look at that smoke. Could it be from one of the factories in town?"

Jonas stood to get a better look. "I don't think so. It doesn't look like it's near the railroad tracks." He sat again and urged the horse into a trot.

Katie gripped the wooden back of the wagon seat as it swayed. They were passing the outskirts of town now, and Jonas had to slow his horse again because of the people crowding the road.

"What's going on?" he asked a man hurrying toward town.

"There's trouble at the newspaper office." The man held onto his hat as he ran.

"What kind of trouble?" Jonas called after him, but the man was gone.

Jonas pulled his horse to a halt next to a dressmaker's shop at the edge of the downtown area. Two blocks ahead, the burning building was obscured by a mass of people, and the noise was tremendous. Katie held her shawl in front of her nose to filter the smell of the smoke.

"Can you tell what happened?" she asked Jonas.

He had stood up again, trying to get a better view. "It looks like there's a fight going on in the middle of the crowd." Suddenly, he handed the reins to her and jumped down. "That's Mr. Cabot in the middle of it. I need to see if he needs help." He looked into Katie's eyes. "Stay here. I'll be right back."

Then he was gone. As much as Katie tried to see where he had gone, he had been swallowed up by the crowd. The spring wagon was jostled by the men running past on the street, and the horse was getting frightened.

Katie climbed out of the wagon and went to Nan's head. "It's all right," she said, trying to soothe her, but the horse's eyes rolled wide and she pulled her head back, fighting Katie's grip on the reins.

Grabbing the bridle, she led Nan off to the side of the dressmaker's shop, where an alley offered more protection. Away from the shouting crowd, Nan quieted down. Katie tied her to a post next to the building, then went back to the main street. Jonas had told her to stay with the wagon, but there must be some way she could find out what was going on.

A woman had come out of the shop and was standing on the boardwalk in front. When she saw Katie come out of the alley, she beckoned to her.

"Come stand with me." The woman was dressed in a rich brown skirt and white shirtwaist. "I don't want to be alone, but I can't see anything from inside."

"Do you know what is happening?" Katie asked as she joined the woman outside the door of the shop.

"I heard that some men threw dynamite through the window of the newspaper office. When it exploded, everything inside caught on fire."

"Was anyone hurt?"

The woman twisted her hands together. "I don't know. I don't know. It's terrible to have something like this happen here."

Clanging bells sounded from the direction of the fire, and the crowd scattered to let the fire engine through. Men formed a line and passed buckets from one hand to another, filling the tub of the engine with water, while others pumped the handles on either side.

As they watched, the fire was extinguished, and the crowd began to disperse.

"I saw your husband leave you and the wagon," the woman said as the noise died down.

"He said he'd be right back," Katie said, not bothering to correct the woman's assumption.

"If he got entangled in that fight, he might be a while. Do you want to come into the shop? I could use a strong cup of tea after all that."

Katie looked through the doorway to the shop full of fabric, with a comfortable seating area near the front window. "I had better wait here. Jonas won't know where to look for me if I go inside."

The other woman patted her arm. "I understand. I'll wait with you so you don't need to be alone. My name is Miss Watson. I'm the dressmaker."

"I'm Katie Stuckey."

"You're one of the Amish, aren't you? I don't see any of your kind come into my shop."

"We make our own clothes," Katie said, looking at the fancy cut of Miss Watson's skirt.

Miss Watson's eyebrows rose. "Yes. I can see that. I could help you find a more stylish pattern, if you'd like."

Katie shook her head. "We wear plain clothing. It's part of what we do to remain separate from the world."

"Oh." Miss Watson shifted from one foot to the other, as if she didn't know how to continue the conversation.

"You don't have to wait out here with me. I'll be fine until Jonas comes, and I'm sure you have things you need to do."

The other woman blushed at that, but smiled. "Yes, I do." She stepped toward the shop door. "It was nice to meet you." Then she disappeared.

Katie moved to the alley opening, where she could watch the wagon, but where Jonas would still be able to see her when he came. Miss Watson reminded her of the other Englisch people she had met. They didn't understand the Amish way of life, something that was so simple for Katie. What Katie didn't understand was why the Englisch women wore such wide skirts, almost like a bell. How could Miss Watson work in an outfit like that?

Before too much time had passed, Jonas appeared out of the thinning crowd of people, and she ran to meet him. His face was black with soot, and blood oozed out of a cut over his eye.

"You're hurt!"

Jonas shook his head. "It's nothing. I got in the way of someone's fist." He saw the wagon in the alley and led her to it. "But Mr. Cabot is badly hurt. He had been in the newspaper office when someone threw a stick of dynamite through the window."

Katie's fingers chilled. "You mean they threw it on purpose? Did they know he was in there?"

Jonas nodded, leaning against the wagon's tailgate. "Some

people don't like what he prints in his paper, so they did this to try to stop him, I suppose."

"We need to get you cleaned up, and it's after lunchtime. Is there a place where we can get some water?"

"We'll go to the public square by the courthouse. There is water there, and we might find a quiet spot to sit to eat our lunch."

Jonas drove behind the buildings along the main street. As they passed the back of the newspaper office, Katie could see the scorched false front standing black and broken against the partly cloudy sky.

"Was anyone besides Mr. Cabot injured?"

"He was the only one in the building. Someone said he had just sent his clerk out on an errand."

Pulling Nan to a halt at the horse trough in the square, Jonas jumped down, then helped Katie with her basket. She carried it to a bench nearby while Jonas splashed water over his head, washing away as much of the soot and mud as he could.

Setting out the lunch she had packed for them, Katie watched the other people in the square. Today's events made her want to run home and forget about going to town ever again. She longed for the quiet routine of her mornings, helping Mama with housework and the garden. Even though the tumult around the fire and the crowd of men had quieted down, the square was noisy with groups of people gathered, some of them talking loudly as they conversed. From the main street, the traffic that had been held up because of the fire was now making its way through. Heavy freight wagons, light buggies, and carriages filled the road. Every driver seemed to be angry with the other drivers and shouted at them and their horses.

Jonas finally joined her, his hair and shirt soaking wet.

"I'm hungry." He reached for her hand. "Are you ready to eat?"

Katie nodded, curling her fingers between his. He didn't seem to be bothered by the noisy town at all. After their silent prayer, he reached for a sandwich.

"After we eat, we'll make our purchases. Then before we start for home, I would like to stop in at Mr. Cabot's to see how he is doing." He took a bite of his bread-and-butter sandwich, then looked at her. "Are you all right? You look pale."

Leaving her sandwich on the napkin she had spread on her lap, she looked around at the strangers on all sides. "I'm just not very hungry."

As Jonas chewed, he frowned, following her gaze to the other men in the square. "You're not enjoying yourself."

"I thought I would." Katie shrugged, staring at her lap. "But it's all so noisy and rough." She forced a smile and looked at him. "I guess I'll be glad when we get home."

"I like the farm better too, but there's something exciting about being among all these people."

"Do . . . do things like this happen often in towns?" Katie looked toward the newspaper office.

Jonas was quiet until he finished his sandwich. "The war has brought out the worst in people, so that even here, away from the fighting, men still wage their battles." He brushed crumbs off his knee. "Are you sorry you came with me?"

"I wouldn't have wanted to miss this day with you, but I'll be happy to leave the town behind."

"I guess you'll be content to wait at home for me the next time."

Katie smiled. "Ja, I'll be content at home."

By the time Jonas and Katie had finished their lunch, the main street of town was quiet, with an occasional freight wagon or buggy passing by. Jonas left Nan tied in the shade along the town square and walked with Katie to the dry goods store for the first items on her list.

"Mama wants me to buy a bolt of muslin," Katie said, "and a spool of cotton thread."

"I'm not sure you'll be able to buy either of those things."

"Why not?"

"Because cotton is grown in the South, using slave labor. I promised myself I wouldn't buy cotton until slavery is abolished."

She stopped in the middle of the board sidewalk. "How can we sew the things we need, then?"

"We have to make do with linen and wool, like our grandparents did. They didn't have cotton, and got along just fine."

"But I didn't make that promise, and it's on Mama's list."

Jonas led her to the side of the walk, out of the way of the folks trying to get past them. "You can't buy something that people have suffered to provide for you."

"But Jonas, it's only cotton fabric."

"Cotton most likely picked by the hands of slaves, working under horrible conditions. Torn from their families at the whim of their masters and forced to do whatever work he decides." He glanced at the passing crowd, not wanting to start another riot, but no one paid attention to them.

"What difference will one bolt of fabric make? Whether I buy it or not won't influence those slave owners."

"It's a matter of principle."

Katie fingered his sleeve. "But you wear cotton."

Jonas scrubbed the back of his neck. "I've had this shirt for a long time."

"It's still made of cotton, and the principle still applies."

"We have to choose someplace to make a stand."

Katie stared at him, then looked down at her list. "I hope Mama isn't too disappointed."

"Let's see what they say at the store. Perhaps the other women in town are using something else."

As they opened the door, a bell rang. Other customers were ahead of them, so Katie went to the display of bolts of cloth.

"Here's muslin, Jonas." She lifted the tag attached to the bolt. "This says it was produced with free labor, to the standards of the American Free Produce Association."

While Jonas read the tag, a young woman approached them. "May I help you?"

"This cloth is cotton?"

"Yes, sir." She unrolled the bolt to display a yard of the fabric.

"And produced without slave labor?"

The clerk smiled. "That's right."

"How much is it?" Katie asked.

The clerk named a price that would have been enough to supply the materials for his entire house.

Katie turned away from the cloth with a little shake of her head. "I don't think we'll get any today." She handed her list to the clerk. "Here are the other items I need, though."

While the clerk filled their order, Katie drew a hand across the muslin fabric. "I can't believe it's so expensive."

"That's one of the problems with a war."

"And another reason not to like it."

Katie paid for her package and they went on to the hardware store. Jonas chose hinges and latches for three doors, and enough windowpanes for five windows, arranging to pick up the purchases on their way out of town. As they headed back to the wagon, Jonas looked down the block to where the riot had taken place. Mr. Cabot, his head bandaged, stood in the street, looking at his burned-out office.

Jonas shifted Katie's package. "Let's go this way. I want to see if Mr. Cabot is all right."

As they came closer, Jonas saw that his friend was bruised, but not too badly hurt. He turned to greet them as they came closer.

"Hello, Jonas." He nodded to Katie. "Thank you for stepping in earlier."

"I'm glad I wasn't too late. Will you be able to open the paper again?"

Mr. Cabot shook his head. "I don't have the heart for it anymore. Today's fire was the last in a series of incidents. One time they broke in and spilled ink all around the floors and counters. Last week they stole the papers I had stacked to take to the post office and set fire to the pile in the middle of the street." He kicked a piece of burned wood with his boot. "I get the message. I'm not wanted around here, and I don't feel like fighting anymore. At least, not here."

"What will happen to the paper?"

"The press wasn't damaged in the fire. It was in the back room and can still function. There's a fellow from Cincinnati who's been wanting to buy the business. I'll sell it to him and head west. Now that the years of Bleeding Kansas are done, my son wants me to join him in Lawrence. There is still much work to be done for the abolition movement, he says. And I can publish a newspaper there as well as here."

Jonas gazed at the burned office, the printing press visible in the back room. He was going to miss this man.

"What about you, Jonas?" The older man turned his penetrating blue eyes toward him.

"What about me?"

"We're in a war. We didn't want it, but it's here. No one can remain untouched by it. And you're not one to remain at home while others fight for a cause you believe in."

Jonas felt Katie step closer, leaning in to hear Mr. Cabot's words.

"Have you forgotten that I'm Amish? We don't fight."

"But this is a fight to defend others. To take care of those who are helpless under the rule of government." His voice strengthened. "Every man should work to help their brothers in need. Slavery must be abolished, and now."

A coarse laugh came from behind Jonas. A crowd had gathered, including some young men who had been drinking.

"Hey, old man. Didn't you get the message earlier? We don't want you spouting your antislavery speeches around here. It's time for you to leave town."

Mr. Cabot faced the crowd and held up his hand as Jonas moved Katie out of the way.

"You boys don't have anything to worry about. I'm leaving tomorrow." As they cheered, he waited quietly. Once the noise died away, he continued. "But that doesn't mean you've silenced me. I'll still write, and I'll still champion the abolitionist cause until I'm in the grave."

Someone threw a rock that landed at the editor's feet. "We can make sure you won't have to wait long for that."

"Mr. Cabot, you need to go home," Jonas said, pulling the man away. "You can't fight all of them."

"You're right," he said, letting Jonas lead him away from the main street. "One man can't fight a mob like that. But together, we're unstoppable."

"Fighting isn't the answer."

"No, not always. In fact, it's probably rarely the answer." Mr. Cabot stopped as he reached his house behind the newspaper office. "But sometimes, it's the only way to quickly stop evil from continuing." He laid his hand on Jonas's shoulder. "I told you once before that the Lord may have a place for you in this fight. I fight with my pen, battling evil with words. You need to find your calling."

After leaving Mr. Cabot, Jonas's mind was filled with questions. He had thought that to fight meant to carry a gun and serve on the front lines. But the editor was right. There was more than one way to fight against evil.

"What are you thinking about?" Katie asked. "You're awfully quiet."

They had reached the wagon and she put her package in the back.

"About fighting this war. There must be something I can do to help."

Katie's brows knit together. "You're not going to volunteer to join the army, are you?"

Jonas helped her onto the wagon seat, then checked Nan's harness. "I wouldn't do that." He led Nan to the horse trough and let her drink. He leaned on the wagon wheel, feeling the familiar tug that came whenever he talked with Mr. Cabot.

He was being called, but to what? And who was doing the calling?

In front of the courthouse, a drum started beating out a peppy rhythm and a fife joined in, playing a tune he had never heard before, but it pulled at him. If God was calling him to do something, he must answer.

But what about his plans with Katie? He glanced up at her and she smiled. She had liked his answer, that he wouldn't volunteer. But as much as he loved Katie, he would have to obey if he received clear direction from the Lord.

Nan finished drinking and Jonas climbed onto the wagon seat next to Katie.

"I have a question for you," he said as he turned Nan toward the street leading behind the hardware store. "Do you think God gives direction to people?"

Katie was quiet for a moment. "He did in the Good Book. The Scriptures are full of people being called by God and being told what to do."

"But what about now? Does God speak to people today?"

"It would be prideful to think that God speaks directly to a person, wouldn't it?"

"What about a feeling that won't go away. An impression that you're supposed to do something."

Katie shook her head. "I don't know what you mean. I know what I'm supposed to do."

"Maybe that's my problem." Jonas sighed as he pulled Nan to a stop behind the hardware store. His packages were on the step, waiting for him. "I don't know what I'm supposed to do."

"I can help you with that," Katie said, slipping her hand

into his elbow. "You're supposed to marry me so we can raise our family together."

Jonas squeezed her hand, then jumped off the seat to load the hardware and window glass. If only he could be as certain about the rest of his life as he was about his future with Katie.

# 9

## OCTOBER 3

An hour before dawn on the first Friday of October, Levi buried his face in the muffler Mother had convinced him to wear. He was glad of it too. Fog was thick in the creek bottom, and even on the rise where he waited, mist swirled around him in the pale light.

According to the newspaper Jonas had brought home from Millersburg last week, the draft office would be drawing the names for the Holmes County draftees today, the third of October. Once Father had heard that news, he consulted with the bishop, and the two of them decided that two men from their church should be in Millersburg that day and bring home the list of men who had been selected from their township. Jonas had volunteered to go and asked Levi to go with him.

So this morning Levi was to meet Jonas at the top of the hill, near Reuben Kaufman's place, where the Weaver's Creek road met the road to Berlin. His knees shivered, and Levi hoped it was only from the cold. Traveling to Millersburg was something he tried to avoid, and with the announcement of the draft lists today, the city streets could be crowded. There was always the possibility his name would be on the list, even though he had prayed for the Good Lord to prevent that. Paying the fee to keep from serving in the army would take time and energy, and he would much rather spend his time working on the quiet farm or studying. He had set himself the task of memorizing the hymns in the *Ausbund*, which wasn't hard, but it did take time and daily work.

Levi started singing one of the hymns under his breath, concentrating to remember the words of the many verses. His voice was low and echoed in his own ears as he pulled his face down into his muffler. After four verses, he caught sight of some movement on his left as Jonas appeared out of the foggy creek bottom like some sort of specter.

"I didn't hear you coming," Levi said as Jonas climbed into the wagon. "The fog muffled your footsteps."

"You knew I wouldn't be late. I want to be in Millersburg in time for the draft. Last week when I was there, some fellows made trouble. They set fire to the newspaper office."

Levi held the reins, keeping the horse from starting. "Do you think there will be violence today?"

"It's hard to tell. The least thing can set them off. Mr. Cabot, the newspaper editor, often said he thought they were being goaded by someone who wants to keep things in Ohio agitated."

Levi clicked his tongue and Pacer shook his head as he started off at a steady trot. "Why would they do that?"

"There are quite a few in Holmes County and the counties around who want Ohio to join the Confederates. The worst part is that because we don't vote, they've claimed that the Amish and Mennonites are on their side."

"We're not on anyone's side, except that we don't want to have a war."

Jonas drew his coat more tightly around himself. "That's just it. They don't want a war either. They want the Federal government to let the Confederate states leave peacefully."

"That sounds good to me." Levi glanced at his friend. "Why do you know so much about this?"

Jonas shrugged, his breath making a cloud in the pale predawn light. "I'm interested. I want to know what is going on in the world. That's one reason why I volunteered to go to get the draft results."

"So you must side with these . . . what would you call them?"

"One of the newspapers started calling them Copperheads a while back, and the name stuck. They're Democrats, trying to work against the republican government. But no, I don't side with them. My sympathies are with the abolitionists, and they're Republicans."

Levi laughed. "Copperheads? Democrats? Republicans? It sounds like you're speaking a foreign language."

"I know you aren't all that concerned, and it's complicated."

"You're right. I'm more concerned with the things of the church than the things of the world." Levi paused as he guided Pacer around a mud hole. "You should be too. A good Amishman doesn't get involved in worldly things."

"I'm not sure that's the right way, though." Jonas's voice was thoughtful. "By knowing what is going on in the world, we know how to act when something happens that could affect us, like this draft."

"Perhaps you're right. Part of what I love about our church is that even though we take pains not to stand out from one another, we encourage people to pursue ideas that interest them. The church considers new ideas all the time, contrary to what those folks in Walnut Creek believe. But we consider the ideas and then come to an agreement on whether they are good for the church, or ill. Your interest in this war has made us aware of how we can legally avoid military service, and that's a good thing."

"I think we should be wise in the ways of the world. Or at least a few should be."

"The Good Book says that God gives gifts to people, and those gifts should be used for the church."

Jonas chuckled. "Now you sound like a real minister."

By the time they reached Millersburg, the sun had been up for hours. Jonas directed Levi to park the wagon near the courthouse away from the draft office where people were already beginning to gather.

"It's almost nine o'clock," Jonas said, checking the time on the courthouse tower. "Let's find a spot to wait."

He led the way to the boardwalk and stopped in front of a lawyer's office. Across the street was a storefront with a hand-painted sign declaring it to be the draft office for Holmes County. The crowd in front was quiet, standing in groups of three or four, talking quietly.

"It looks like we're here in time," Levi said. "And I don't see any signs of trouble."

"That would be great. All they need to do is draw the names, then we'll wait for them to print the list."

The clock on the courthouse struck nine, the long notes

sounding over the crowd. Still, long minutes passed without any movement from the draft office.

"When are you going to get started?" A man in the crowd had shouted, and others joined in.

Levi backed against the wall of the lawyer's office. "Are they getting violent already?"

Jonas grinned at him. "They're just being noisy. If violence breaks out, we'll get out of here and come back later."

Just then, the door of the office opened, and four men emerged, two of them carrying a large wooden box between them. The box had legs and stood just below shoulder height. One of the men held up his hand for silence.

"This is how we're going to proceed. The name of every eligible man in the county has been written on a list and assigned a number. In this box are tokens with the numbers. After we draw the numbers, we will write down the names and townships of the men corresponding to that number."

"How many are you drawing today?" shouted a man standing near Levi.

"The state has received enough new recruits since the draft was announced that the earlier numbers have been greatly reduced. Holmes County will need to supply three hundred men for our quota."

The process of drawing the numbers began, but the men from the draft office did their work in silence and the crowd waited. More people showed up, and the street was blocked. Still they waited. Finally, the numbers had all been drawn, and the list handed to a man standing nearby, who took it to the newspaper office.

Levi watched his progress, just like every other person

standing in the street. "I thought you said that building had burned."

"Only the front office," Jonas said. "The press survived, and the paper is being sold."

Jonas and Levi found a place to sit on the edge of the boardwalk while they waited.

"What will you do if your name is on the list?" Jonas asked.

"I'll pay the fee. I have no intention to be part of the army, and I'm thankful that the government has made this way for us." He glanced at Jonas's profile. "What about you? Have you thought what you would do?"

"I might go ahead and join the army."

Levi let his shock at Jonas's words subside before answering. "You want to fight?"

"I want to do something to free the slaves. I don't want to fight." Jonas picked up a stone from between his feet and rolled it in his fingers. "I certainly don't want to kill a man." The stone dropped. "But I feel like I need to do something. Perhaps my presence in a battle can make a difference for good."

"How?"

Jonas shook his head. "I don't know. But it's like something inside me says to go. I guess I'll know if I'm supposed to or not if my name ends up on the list."

"Then you won't volunteer if it isn't?"

"I told you, it isn't something I want. But it's something I would do if I was forced to."

Levi had no answer for that. Sometimes Jonas was like a brother, but other times it was as if they were complete strangers.

Jonas shifted. "Will you do something for me, though?"

"For sure I will. Anything."

"If I do end up going to war . . ." Jonas leaned forward and picked up the stone again. "If I do, will you look after Katie for me? She'll be fine with her family, but I think it would do her good to be able to have someone close to her who can check on her occasionally. See if she needs anything."

"I can do that." Levi's answer was automatic, but his thoughts raced. He would do anything for Jonas, but he would also do anything for Katie. If things happened the way Jonas described, he would be hard put to keep his feelings for her in check. But Jonas trusted him and he wouldn't do anything to betray that trust.

The sun had passed the meridian when the printer emerged with a stack of papers in his hand. Various bystanders reached for one, but he trotted across the street and delivered the stack to the draft officials. The crowd surged forward as they were handed out, and Jonas and Levi joined them. When they finally got their copies, they made their way back to the wagon.

Levi held his sheet in trembling hands. The type was small, and the names were divided by township. Levi found German Township, and scanned the names. He sat on the edge of the watering trough when he realized his name wasn't there, wiping the drops of sweat from his forehead.

"This can't be," Jonas said. He peered at the list, reading it over again.

"What is it? Did you find your name?"

Jonas sat next to him at the edge of the trough. "Not mine, but my brother's. Samuel's name is on the list."

The sun soared in the afternoon sky, leaning toward the southern horizon on this early October day. Abraham placed the last stalks on the shock of corn and let his gaze drift up the road, to the rise where Jonas would appear on his way home from Millersburg.

Last week, when he went to purchase hardware for his house, Jonas had been delayed, and he had arrived home with Katie after dark. But this trip should take no longer than the time it took for a horse to travel the twelve miles there and then return. On top of that, he had gone with Levi Beiler. Levi had a steady head on his shoulders and would keep Jonas's mind where it needed to be, which was on getting the news from the draft office and bringing it home.

Samuel finished his shock of corn two rows over and took a moment to look in the same direction.

"Waiting for news is the longest wait there is." Abraham lifted his hat, letting the cool breeze through his hair before setting it in place again. "Are you anxious to see who is on the draft list?"

Samuel shook his head. "Not anxious. The Good Lord is in control of which names are drawn. But still, I wonder what impact it will have on our community."

"You know we've been raising funds to pay the fees for any man on the list."

"But will it be enough? I heard that enough had been donated for thirty men, but what if there are more names than we have the money for?"

"What if only a dozen names are chosen? If so, then we can share with any neighboring congregation that needs it."

Abraham glanced at his oldest son's face again. "But you say you're not anxious."

Samuel shrugged. "I suppose I am."

"You've decided what you will do if your name is drawn?"

"I don't want to pay the fee, and I don't want to fight." Samuel stooped to gather stalks to start building his next shock. "And I certainly don't want to hire a substitute. I've been thinking about what Simeon Keck said, how the substitute would be acting in my place. I don't want to feel guilty of murder every time that man killed another soldier."

"So you would end up in the army?" Abraham stepped closer to Samuel, letting a handful of cornstalks fall to the ground. "You would go to war?"

Samuel's mouth pressed into a hard line above his beard. "I would go to Canada, if it wasn't against the law." He shook his head. "I don't know what I'll do. I just keep praying that my name won't be on that list."

Abraham stroked his beard. Samuel was frightened, and he didn't blame him. If he wasn't too old for his name to be included in the draft, he would feel the same way. But what decision would he make?

"What about Jonas?" Abraham asked as he started building his next shock. "What will your brother do if his name is called?"

"I don't know. He hasn't spoken to me about it."

"He hasn't talked to me, either, except that I know he supports the abolitionists."

"Jonas is an impetuous boy and likely to join the army just to be able to free the slaves." Samuel laid the last cornstalks on the top of his shock to protect it from rain. "Or for the adventure."

"But he isn't a boy any longer." Abraham stopped his work, looking toward the north again. "He's a man with thoughts of his own."

"And you're thinking his thoughts may lead him away from us?"

Abraham tied a bundle of stalks and leaned them against two others. "I wish he had already joined the church. Then that commitment would keep him where he needs to be."

"You mean at home, and safe."

"I mean not being trained to shoot at another man." Abraham finished his shock and moved on to the next one. "His life is precious to me, but his eternal soul is what hangs in the balance."

They worked in silence until they got to the end of the row, Abraham praying the entire time. His sons, his sons-in-law, his neighbors, the other men in the church. They were all at the mercy of a government bent on war.

Abraham shook his head at himself as he reached the last shock. They were not at the mercy of the government. They were at the mercy of their loving Lord and Savior. There was no reason to worry.

"There he is."

Up on the rise, where the road passed Reuben and Elizabeth's place, Jonas appeared. He was walking. Levi must have let him off at the fork in the road.

Abraham finished his shock and joined Samuel. They walked to the stone bridge and met Jonas. The young man walked slowly, a paper in his hand.

"You were successful?" Abraham asked, watching his son. Jonas's shoulders slumped, and the closer he got, the slower he walked.

He stopped in the middle of the bridge and held the paper out to Abraham. "Twenty-two Amish men from Holmes County are on the list, six from our district."

Abraham unfolded the page, scanning the list. Names he knew. Men he had watched grow from young boys. Fathers, husbands, sons . . .

"Samuel?" Abraham nearly dropped the paper at the shock of seeing Samuel's name on the list.

"What?" Samuel reached for the paper. "What did you see?"

Abraham knew when Samuel saw his own name. His son's face grew pale and he staggered to the side of the bridge. He sat on the stone wall, crumpling the page in his hands.

"I never thought it would be there," Samuel whispered. "I never thought . . ." He looked at Abraham, the reality of what that list meant growing by the minute. His eyes grew wide. "Datt, what am I going to do?"

The answer was clear in Abraham's mind. "We will pay the fee."

"But I said I wouldn't. I said it at the meeting, in front of the entire church."

"No one will blame you for changing your mind."

Samuel stood and looked from Abraham to Jonas, then back. "But I haven't changed my mind."

"If you go to join the army, you'll face the discipline of the church. You risk being shunned."

"I know." With a shaking hand, he handed the paper back to Jonas. "I know."

"Come to the house," Abraham said. He felt weak and helpless. "Come to the house and we'll talk about this."

Samuel shook his head. "I need to go home. I need to tell Anna before she hears from anyone else."

"Do you want me to go with you?" Jonas held out a hand, as if he would support his brother.

"I must do this alone."

Jonas stood beside Abraham as they watched Samuel trudge across the road and up the lane to his own house. Jonas was silent, kicking at the gravel on the bridge with the toe of his shoe.

"How are things in Millersburg?" Abraham asked. He put an arm around Jonas's broad shoulders and turned him toward the house.

"There was a riot of sorts outside the draft office, just before they pulled the names. Some were saying that they should have waited until after the election to have the draft."

"An election?" The election Bishop Lemuel had urged his church to vote in.

Jonas nodded. "For the state legislature. The election is a week from Tuesday, in eleven days."

"What difference would that make?"

"The Democrats think that most of the names pulled in the draft would be from their party, and then they would be off to war and not able to vote in the election."

"The drafted men are to leave home so quickly?"

Jonas nodded, stopping as they reached the porch step. Abraham looked for Lydia, not wanting her to overhear the talk of what happened, but she was in the kitchen with the door closed.

"Samuel is supposed to report to the draft office in Millersburg on Wednesday. In five days. From there, they will go to Camp Mansfield for training."

The strength that had been draining from his knees gave out completely, and Abraham sank to the porch step. Five days? That wasn't enough time for the drafted men to get their farms or businesses in order, and barely enough time for the church to pay the fees. Or if a man wanted to hire a substitute, would five days give him enough time to do that?

Jonas sat beside him. "Do you think Samuel will really join the army?"

"I don't know." Abraham took off his hat and buried his hand in his hair. If only this hadn't happened. If only another name had been chosen. He had prayed for protection, but where was that protection now?

Datt told Mamm about Samuel's name being on the draft list as soon as they entered the house. She had sunk down onto one of the kitchen chairs, her hands shaking. As Datt sat beside her, holding her, Jonas slipped back out the door, stopping only long enough to pick up his hunting rifle. He needed time alone. Time to think.

All the way home from Millersburg, he had considered what this news would mean to the family. Levi had been in a cheerful mood, and he could afford to be. Jonas strode toward the clearing in the woods, remembering how his friend had tried to keep his face sober. But Levi couldn't hide his relief that his name hadn't been chosen by the draft committee. The war hadn't touched the Beiler family.

It had reached into the Weaver family, though, and plucked Samuel, as if a hand had picked him from a grapevine. Samuel, who was a husband and a father. He had children at home, a farm to manage, parents who depended on him.

He was a member of the church. Samuel, who had reacted to the news with shock and fear. Why did his name have to appear on that list?

Jonas reached the clearing. The sight of his house, the two finished walls standing silent against the background of red, orange, and yellow leaves, failed to bring the satisfaction it normally did. Today, they seemed to be the remnant of a dream.

He sat on the threshold of the doorway, his rifle between his knees. Samuel would never back down from the words he had spoken at the church meeting. Rash words, as it turned out, because Samuel had backed himself into a corner. With his call to the draft, he had given himself one choice, and that was to join the army. In only five days, Samuel would be a soldier in the Union army, unless the Good Lord intervened.

They could hope that Samuel would change his mind and agree to pay the fee, but Jonas knew his brother. He was just stubborn enough to keep his word, even if it killed him. And it might.

Jonas loaded his gun slowly, taking care with the powder and ball. The afternoon was waning, and by dusk the deer would show up at the salt lick at the southern end of the woodlot. With the cool evenings and frosty mornings, it was time to start hunting the game that would make up a large part of the family's meat supply for the winter. But Jonas knew hunting was only an excuse. He needed to think through this problem, and his mind worked better if he was deep in the woods, with no distractions.

Following the trail the deer had made from the creek to the salt lick, Jonas felt his weariness slip away with every step. Birds called in the treetops, hidden by the leaves still remaining on the branches. Beneath his feet he trod on a carpet of bright colors, the leaves not yet dry and crisp. Ja, for sure and certain, it was a good day for hunting.

He reached the salt lick before the light changed from afternoon to evening. The sky was still a bright blue, and the leaves all around reflected the bright October sun. Finding the tree branch he always used, an oak limb growing parallel to the ground about six feet up, he scrambled up to his seat. He took a deep breath and settled in. All that was left to do was wait. Wait and not think.

Jonas let his mind clear, holding his memories of the past closed in their corner. Thoughts of war and of Samuel tried to grasp his attention, but he pushed them away. Time passed, and he let his mind drift to thoughts of Katie and their future together. By the time they married, perhaps the war would be ended. There couldn't be another draft. From the violent shouts outside the draft office in Millersburg this morning, folks wouldn't stand for the government to do this again. And the war couldn't last much longer. So many men had died already.

Impatient with the direction of his thoughts, Jonas shifted, scowling. He wasn't going to think about the war.

As the light began to change, Jonas saw movement between the trees on the far side of the clearing. He swallowed, licking his dry lips, but as he watched the cautious figure step into the clearing, he let out a long breath and let the hammer down slowly on his rifle. Gentry Hamlin, Ned's father, waved to him and started making his way toward him around the salt lick. Jonas jumped down from his seat. No deer would be coming to the lick while Gentry was out in the open.

"Jonas Weaver?" Gentry said as he drew close. "I couldn't tell if it was you or your brother from across the way."

"It's me." Jonas had never had much to say to Ned's father, who kept himself buried in the woods as much as possible, and Gentry had never spoken directly to him before.

"Any luck?"

"Still early. I was hoping to find a deer coming to the lick."

Gentry spit into the grass at the base of the tree, then wiped his mouth with the back of his hand.

"I heard from Ned." He thrust his hand inside his shirt and drew out a folded paper. "The store clerk in Farmerstown give this to me, and said it was from my boy." He turned it over. "I'm not so sure about that, seein' as Ned can't write, and I don't read. But when I seed you sittin' over here, I thought maybe you could do the readin' for me."

Jonas took the paper from him and broke the seal, opening it. He scanned the scrawling handwriting and read the signature.

"This isn't from Ned." Glancing over the first sentence, he swallowed a sudden lump that appeared. "It appears to be bad news. Do you want me to read it to you?"

Gentry widened his stance, as if bracing for a blow. He held his hunting rifle across his chest and bowed his head, waiting.

*Dear Mr. Hamlin,*

*I regret to inform you that your son, Edward, died this morning, September 5, 1862. He did not suffer long, but succumbed to typhoid fever within a day of contracting it. He died in the presence of myself, the camp physician, and his friend, Reuben Kaufman. We buried his earthly remains in a grave near the camp in Vicksburg, alongside other victims of the fever.*

> *Sincerely,*
> *Lieutenant William*
> *Spencer, CSA*

Jonas glanced up, waiting for Gentry's reaction, but the man remained as he had been until he extended one hand. Jonas folded the letter and gave it back to him.

"Thank you," Gentry said, his voice full of gravel. "I'll take my leave now, and good hunting to you."

Without another word, Gentry walked back into the forest and disappeared. Jonas leaned against the oak tree and looked up into the deep blue sky, streaked with orange and pink clouds. Ned Hamlin was dead. He had been a part of Jonas's life at Weaver's Creek, even though they had never been friends. And Ned hadn't even been killed in battle but in camp. In bed.

A deer stepped out of the trees to Jonas's right. A buck, with ten points on his antlers. He took another step, then stopped, his nose searching the air. Behind him came his does. Three of them, and their half-grown fawns, walked past the buck, grazing on bits of grass. Jonas didn't move.

Finally, the buck urged his does toward the salt lick, keeping watch as they alternated between grazing and licking the salty ground. He stood twenty feet away, upwind from Jonas. After a few minutes, he also grazed, but that magnificent head rose as he chewed, keeping watch over the others. Another buck appeared across the clearing, and the two looked at each other.

A dog barked in the distance, startling both bucks, and the first one moved toward his does, pushing them toward the cover of the trees. The second one disappeared.

The dog barked again. Jonas looked at the rifle in his hands and at the stars beginning to appear in the sky. He had forgotten that he had come here to hunt. The peaceful scene had been a long way from his thoughts of Ned and the grave in Mississippi. Far from the specter of war.

# 10

OCTOBER 4

"Samuel Weaver's name is on the draft list," Papa said as he sat down to dinner on Saturday. His clothes were dusty from working in the field, shocking the corn. The weather was warm and dry.

Katie had a dish of potatoes in her hand, and when Papa mentioned Samuel's name, she dropped the dish onto the table, nearly spilling it.

"Be careful, Daughter," Mama said. She reached behind Katie to put the plate of ham slices next to the potatoes. Mama scanned the table, then nodded, satisfied that all was ready for the meal. As she sat in her chair, she said, "Were there any other names that we know?"

"Ja, ja, ja," Papa said. "Twenty-two Amish boys and men from Holmes County alone." He sighed, then closed his eyes for the silent prayer.

Katie prayed a quick blessing for her meal, then waited for

Papa to signal that he was done. Her mind raced. Who else was on the list? He would have told her if Jonas was one.

Papa reached for the potatoes, filling his plate, then Mama's, then Katie's. He did the same with the ham, and then the sauerkraut. He laid Katie's plate in front of her before he continued.

"Samuel Weaver is the closest one to us. Both Gingerich boys and the oldest Hochstetler."

"Amos? But he has a family to support."

Papa nodded. "Ja, ja, ja. But the draft committee doesn't care about that. They only draw names." He glanced at Katie and smiled. "Jonas's name wasn't on the list, so you can stop looking so worried."

Mama buttered a slice of bread. "Did the church collect enough to pay the fees for that many?"

"And more, if needed. None of the ones on the list will need to go to war. I am thankful that the government recognizes our stand against war. That would not have happened in the Old Country."

Papa ate in silence until his plate was clean. "Some more news. Jonas said that Gentry Hamlin got a letter saying that Ned has passed away."

Katie stopped cutting her ham. "Ned Hamlin was killed?"

"Not killed in the war. He died of typhoid in the camp. Jonas said that Reuben Kaufman had been there when it happened."

"Elizabeth will be glad to get word of her husband." Mama rose from the table to get the pie for dessert. "Katie, after dinner, you can take the other pie to Elizabeth and Ruby. Tell Elizabeth we're thinking of her at this trying time."

"Ja, Mama." Katie stared at the piece of pie Mama had

put on her plate. It was still warm, and fragrant with the aroma of apples, cinnamon, and cloves, but Katie couldn't bring herself to eat it. Ned Hamlin was dead. She began to tremble.

"I . . . I need to be excused." Katie started toward the door. "I'll be back to clear up from dinner . . ."

She ran to the privy, the only place she could be assured of privacy. Ignoring the odors and the flies, she closed the door behind her and leaned on it.

Ned Hamlin was dead.

And then she was sick.

Afterward, she sat on the bench, her head in her hands. She hadn't seen Ned since that time in the woods last spring, but several times she had thought someone was watching her. He had sinned when he had accosted her, and now he had paid for that sin. But she was the one who had tempted him. How many more had to die because of her?

When the sick feeling finally passed, she returned to the house and her work. Once she had cleared away the dinner dishes and washed them, she wrapped the second pie in a towel and walked up the road to Elizabeth's house. Clouds were beginning to gather in the west, and Papa had said that a storm was coming when he had come in from the corn-field for dinner. As she passed the trail leading to the sturdy bridge across the creek, she saw the two walls of the house that Jonas had finished. Two walls standing straight and true against the trees, reminding her of his promise to her.

A breeze blew by carrying a rustling wave of brown leaves along the road, brushing against her ankles. Jonas would not die. His love was pure, not evil. They belonged together. He would not die. Papa had said Jonas's name wasn't on the list, so he wouldn't even be tempted to go to war. He would stay here in Weaver's Creek, finish the house, and next year they would be married. He would be safe. She continued down the road, against the gusting breeze.

The wind had strengthened by the time she reached Elizabeth's cabin, and Katie paused to look toward the west again. The clouds were building into thunderheads, but they weren't a threat. Not yet.

"Katie? Is that you?" Ruby Weaver called to her from the chicken house behind the log cabin. "Come back here. We're giving the henhouse its fall cleaning."

Katie put the pie on a small table outside the door of the cabin. Through the open door, she could see that the little building was cleaner than she had ever seen it before. Without Reuben here, perhaps Elizabeth had more time to care for the place. She heard laughter coming from the back of the cabin, and found Ruby and Elizabeth enjoying the dirtiest chore Katie could imagine. She had to laugh with them, in spite of the smell and mess. Feathers covered both of them from head to foot, and every time one of them looked at the other, they would start laughing again.

Trying to stay out of the cloud of flying feathers, Katie found a shovel and helped load the wheelbarrow with the litter from the henhouse. In a short time, they had the little building emptied and Ruby dumped the soiled bedding onto the compost pile.

"Let's take a rest before washing the walls," Ruby said, breathless. "Did I see a pie in your hands?"

"Ja, for sure. Mama sent it." Katie shifted her gaze to Elizabeth. "She wanted to let you know we're thinking of you."

"*Denki*," she answered. Elizabeth was the opposite of

her sister. Short and slim where Ruby was tall, and her soft brown hair contrasting with Ruby's curly red hair that was escaping from the kerchief she had tied around her head. "Come to the house. Ruby put a pitcher of mint tea in the springhouse, and we can sit for a spell and visit."

Katie followed the sisters to the washbasin outside the cabin, then to the little table set in the grass.

Ruby brushed a stray leaf off the wooden surface. "The weather has been so fine that we moved the table out here. No use crowding the cabin more than we need to." She went into the house and came out with plates and glasses.

"We'll have to take it inside soon, though," Elizabeth said, watching the gathering clouds. "It looks like a storm is coming."

The three sat for a while, listening to the sounds of the afternoon as they ate their pie. In such good company, Katie's second piece tasted better than her first one had.

Elizabeth took a couple bites, then laid her fork down. Ruby leaned toward her.

"Aren't you hungry?"

"It's good pie," Elizabeth said, smiling at Katie, "but I'll save the rest of my piece for later."

Ruby shook her head. "She's worried about Reuben and has been ever since last night when Jonas told us about Ned."

"Aren't I right to be worried about him? He's my husband."

"If he acted more like a husband, I would say you are." Ruby took a long drink of her mint tea, as blunt as ever. "But you know you've been happier since he's been away."

Elizabeth blushed. "He's still my husband. I worry that perhaps he became ill also and died."

"They would have sent a letter to you," Katie said, putting her hand over Elizabeth's. "They sent a letter to Gentry Hamlin, so they would send one to you, for sure."

"That's right," Ruby said. "He would have told them to write to you, and you know folks always do what Reuben tells them."

Elizabeth smiled again. "You're so good to me, Ruby. How would I get by without you?"

"I'm just glad you took me in." Ruby leaned across the table so they could both hear her as she whispered, "And you don't keep asking me when I'm going to find a husband and get married."

"Ach, Ruby, you know Mamm means well."

"For sure she does. But I don't need to be reminded of it every day." Ruby laughed then. "And she should be happy that Jonas is getting married. She can pester him all day long and he won't mind. Will he, Katie?"

Elizabeth looked from her sister to Katie. "Jonas and Katie are getting married? When?"

"Not until next summer," Katie said. "Only our folks know about our plans. And now, I guess you do too."

"I'm so glad you told me! But why wait so long?"

Katie wrinkled her nose. "Papa thinks I'm too young to get married. He thinks a girl should be older, even though I know I won't marry anyone but Jonas."

"Your father is right." Elizabeth's face was solemn. "I wish I had waited until I was older." A cloud's shadow passed over the table, and when the sunshine came back, so did Elizabeth's smile. "But you're marrying our brother, so now we'll be sisters. You'll have to come over often when winter arrives so that Ruby and I don't get too tired of each other's company."

"And you'll have to visit me too." Katie smiled at both of them. "I'm making a quilt, and I'll need plenty of help to finish it."

Ruby grinned back. "That's a wonderful plan. Every time we get tired of our cabin, we'll spend the afternoon with you and our needles."

"I haven't quilted since I got married." Elizabeth's eyes were shining. "I wish it was winter already."

## OCTOBER 5

Every time Lydia thought of Samuel's name on the draft list, her stomach turned with a sickening twist. She was glad there was no church today, because she wasn't sure she could answer questions from the other women. Those same questions swirled in her head and were on the tip of her tongue whenever she could corner Abraham to talk, but he spent the days in silence.

"There is no sense in worrying about something you have no control over," he had said yesterday, wrapping her in his strong embrace. "Until Samuel changes his mind about paying the fee, we can only pray that he will."

Lydia scrubbed the table after clearing up from their cold dinner. Men never could understand what mothers felt for their sons. She worried, for sure, more than she ever told Abraham. But one thing she took comfort in was that Jonas's name wasn't on the list along with Samuel's. She also took comfort in the provision of the alternatives for her son, but at that thought, her worries started all over again. She sat on the closest chair, holding her aching head in her hands.

What if the unthinkable happened and Samuel ended up as a soldier in the army?

Voices in the yard broke through her thoughts. Samuel and his family were here. They had walked over in spite of the rain. Lydia rose to take Dorcas from Anna as they came in the door.

"What a wet day!" Lydia snuggled Dorcas against her while Anna hung her shawl near the stove. She had kept Dorcas under it, and both stayed dry in the light rain.

"For sure, it is." Anna stood in front of the stove shivering. "And chilly too."

Lydia patted Dorcas's back. "Are you cold, little one?"

The two-year-old shook her head.

"Samuel and the boys must have gone to the barn." Lydia set a chair near the stove for Anna, then sat in her chair with Dorcas on her lap.

"I don't know what men find to do in the barn on a Sunday afternoon," Anna said. "But look at us. Sitting in the kitchen, where we spend every day."

"It's where we're comfortable, I suppose." Lydia held her granddaughter's cold fingers to warm them.

"I want to ask you something before they come in." Anna leaned closer. "What does Abraham think about Samuel's decision not to pay the fee?"

"He hopes Samuel will change his mind."

"I wish Abraham will tell him to do just that." Anna hunched on the chair, hugging herself. "I'm so worried that Samuel is just being stubborn because his pride won't let him change his mind."

Lydia sighed. "Abraham will give Samuel advice if he's asked, but he won't say anything otherwise. Samuel is a grown man and needs to make his own decisions."

"I just want to do what's right," Anna said. "But he won't give an inch. He says it's a matter of principle. But what will he do when the time comes for him to report for training? He can't join the army if he's going to stick by his principles."

"I know my son. He likes to wait and let a problem resolve itself, but sometimes they don't."

"There isn't enough time. We need to leave early on Wednesday morning to get to the draft office by nine o'clock."

"The ministers are taking the fees for the men on the list to the draft office tomorrow." Lydia shifted Dorcas on her lap. The little girl had fallen asleep.

"Are all the others paying the fee, then?"

"Abraham said that Michael Kuhns has hired a substitute, but the others from our district are paying. The families in the congregation donated enough money so all who need it can use it."

"How did they come by that much?"

"Some sold things, others had money saved." Lydia tried not to think of the promising colt Abraham had sold to raise cash.

At the sound of footsteps on the back porch, Lydia took Dorcas into the bedroom and laid her down, covering her with the quilt. By the time she returned, the rest of the family had gathered in the front room. Abraham had brought out the corn popper, and Jonas helped thirteen-year-old Bram get it started over the fire. Lydia sat in her chair and rested her feet on the small footstool. How fine it was to have them all here, talking together. The only thing that would be better was if the other children and their families would come, but that was too much to expect on a rainy afternoon.

After the corn was popped and bowls passed around, the

conversation turned to the war. Lydia listened, but she would rather talk of other things. This war continued, in spite of the many folks who wanted it to end. Why couldn't men just stop fighting? Was that too much to ask?

"Jonas," Abraham said, "you keep up on the war news. Is there any hope of it being over soon?"

"I thought it would have been over months ago. The Federals are close to Richmond, but they don't seem to be able to reach the city and take it over."

"Is the other side too strong for them?" Bram asked. He leaned forward, interested. Lydia shook her head. He was too interested.

"One newspaper article I read said that the South has better generals than the North, and that's why the Federal troops can't win."

Abraham tapped his foot on the floor, a sign that he was getting angry. But Lydia knew her husband would control his anger. He always did. He leaned forward as he spoke. "And meanwhile, battles are fought that give neither side a victory, and men are killed who will never see their homes again."

Lydia was looking at Samuel as Abraham said this. Her oldest son stared at the floor.

"What are you thinking about, Samuel?" she asked.

He looked at her, his eyes dark. "I'm thinking about how I'd rather talk about anything else but this war. I'm tired of hearing about it, I'm tired of knowing that it's going on out there." He stared at the floor again. "And I can't help thinking about poor Ned Hamlin. How many more men need to die?"

They were silent after Samuel's comment. Anna reached out to take her husband's hand.

Jonas stared into the fire as if he hadn't heard his brother. What was going through his mind?

## October 7

Tuesday morning was still overcast, but the rain stopped while Jonas was eating breakfast after the morning chores. Datt and Mamm were quieter than normal, passing meaningful looks between themselves. He knew what those looks were about, or he thought he knew.

"You don't need to wait for me to leave the house before you talk about it," he said, helping himself to another stack of pancakes. "You're still wondering what Samuel is going to do tomorrow."

Datt cleared his throat and pushed his plate away. "You're right. I'm worried that he didn't want to talk about it on Sunday."

"I don't think he wants to face the truth." Jonas paused, his fork full of pancakes and dripping syrup. "He doesn't want to take any of the choices in front of him, so he's waiting for another one to come along."

"But there isn't another choice."

"So tomorrow, he'll be on his way to the draft office in Millersburg, and whatever awaits him there."

Mamm made a small sound and covered her mouth.

"I'm sorry, Mamm. I meant that he doesn't know what he'll find when he gets there. Maybe he's hoping to be sent west, to one of the frontier forts instead of into combat. There are more things for soldiers to do than fight on the front lines." Jonas put the waiting pancake bite in his mouth, savoring the sweet buttery flavor. It wasn't that he didn't care about Samuel. He just didn't understand his brother's hesitation to make a decision.

"I'm glad we got to spend the afternoon with the family yesterday." Mamm began clearing the plates. "I do wish he would accept the offer of the church to pay his fee, though."

Rain drummed on the roof in a sudden sweep. Datt got up to look out the window, then poured himself another cup of coffee.

"No fieldwork today, and I finally have time to oil the harnesses."

"I think I'll go over to Samuel's." Jonas met Datt's eyes. "Maybe he'll talk to me if it's just us."

Datt nodded his agreement. "Let us know what he says."

Jonas's coat was made from oiled canvas, and his hat was felted, so the rain sluiced off as he skirted the puddles on the way to Samuel's house. But his feet were still soaked by the time he reached the back porch. Anna saw him coming and opened the door. Her kitchen floor was covered with laundry and he heard the boys playing in the loft.

"Samuel is in the barn." She stepped out onto the porch, closing the door behind her. "Are you here to talk some sense into him?"

"He's decided to go, then?"

Anna's eyes filled. "He told me to pack a bag for him and put in his winter coat. Don't let him go, Jonas. Make him see what this is doing to us. To his children."

"I'll talk to him."

Jonas ran to the barn, ignoring the puddles, since his feet were wet already. Samuel stood at the back door, looking out into the pasture. He hadn't heard Jonas come in over the sound of the rain on the roof. Thunder cracked and the rain fell harder.

Samuel didn't move. Jonas joined him in the doorway.

"It's a good rain."

Samuel turned his head. "What?"

"It's a good rain. This will fill up the ponds before winter sets in."

"I suppose."

As his brother looked out into the pasture again, Jonas leaned back on the doorframe, facing him.

"Tomorrow is Wednesday. You need to set out for Millersburg early in the morning, unless you're going to pay your two hundred dollars at the draft office."

Samuel didn't move. The rain let up as a roll of thunder sounded again, farther away this time.

"Mamm and Datt are worried about you. So is Anna. They want to know if you've made a decision."

"There's no way around this one, Jonas."

"Is it your pride that's keeping you from paying the fee?"

He shook his head. "I admit, it would be a sting to go back on my word and pay, but the principle of the matter is still there. That money will be used to continue the war, and I won't be part of that."

"The alternative is to be part of the war yourself."

"Or be arrested."

"But you can't do either one. Your family needs you here. Anna needs you."

Samuel shot him a look, his eyes smoldering. "You think I don't know that? It's tearing me apart. My responsibility is here. But what example would I be giving to my boys?"

"If you pay the fee, you're showing them that you refuse to fight in the army."

"If I pay the fee, I'm showing them that my life is more important to me than another man's."

Jonas didn't have an answer to that. He tried a different tactic.

"If you report to the camp in Mansfield, you'll also be turning your back on your vows to the church. Have you thought of that?"

Samuel's shoulders slumped. "I can only hope I'll be forgiven once I confess my sin."

"But you're taking this action knowing full well that you're breaking those vows. What if . . ." Jonas searched his mind for an example to use. "What if you married another woman in another town and live with her for a year. Do you think Anna would take you back just because you said you were sorry?"

Samuel stiffened. "That isn't the same thing."

"You pledged to support the teachings and the regulations of the church. Part of that is submitting to nonresistance. When you purposefully turn your back on that promise, you turn your back on the church and its teachings, just like you would turn your back on Anna if you took up with another woman."

No answer came from Samuel. The rain had stopped, and sunshine was breaking through the clouds. The scene outside the barn door was fresh and clean, as if God had given the world a fall cleaning.

"You're right," Samuel finally said. "I'm sacrificing my life in the church, my marriage, and my home." He took off his hat, running one hand through his hair. "But I can't . . . I can't pay that fee."

Watching his brother's face, Jonas had a sudden thought, as clear as a vision, that he would never see him alive after today. He had to do something to prevent Samuel from sacrificing everything.

"I'll go." As he said the words, the thought of his own sacrifices flashed through his mind. But it would be a temporary sacrifice. Not permanent. Not like Samuel's would be.

Samuel looked at him. "You can't go. I was the one who was drafted."

"I'll be your substitute."

"*Ne*. I won't let you. You have your whole life ahead of you."

"But I haven't joined the church yet. I don't have a wife or family. I wouldn't be breaking any vows."

Samuel ran his hand through his hair again and Jonas's hopes grew. He was considering the idea.

"This is the way around your problem, Samuel."

"I can't ask you to do this."

"You're not asking. I'm telling you. This is the only way."

"Mamm and Datt won't let you go."

"They won't know until I'm already gone."

Samuel shook his head. "You won't do this. It isn't an option."

His brother's face was set in the expression Jonas knew too well. He wasn't going to change his mind. But being stubborn ran in the family.

⁓

Katie laid the piece of navy blue cotton on the table and applied the iron, straightening the wrinkles. Her sisters and sisters-in-law had given her piles of fabric scraps and remnants, and with the rain this morning and the continuing threat of showers this afternoon, she finally had the chance to start preparing them for her quilt top. The kitchen was pleasant with the tantalizing aroma of a dish of sausages and cabbage roasting in the oven for supper, and the sight of the irons lined up on the stove top created a warm, satisfied feeling.

Papa was working at Wilhelm's and Mama had gone with him to visit with Esther and their four little boys, and Katie loved having the quiet house to herself, knowing that she had the freedom to do whatever she wanted.

She laid the navy fabric aside and took the last scrap. This task was nearly done, and then she could start cutting the scraps to fit her blocks. As she ironed the green material, Katie turned it around, trying to see it in the quilt top. Should she make a crazy quilt? Mama said they were the best, since they used every scrap of fabric. But Katie wanted this quilt to be special. Crazy quilts were for every day. She had seen a pieced quilt at Millie Beiler's house one time. Her mother had made it from squares of fabric arranged in a diamond pattern. The colors had blended together beautifully, turning an everyday bedcover into a work of art.

After taking the irons off the stove to cool, Katie laid the stack of ironed scraps back in the box where she stored them. After supper she could start cutting them. Squares. Her chin lifted as she made her decision. Even if Mama did think it was wasteful, this quilt would be pieced in squares, and it would be beautiful. She fingered the green piece on the top. She would have a lifetime of making do, of using every scrap, of making things last. This one quilt could be made for beauty as well as function, couldn't it?

A knock at the door startled her. "Katie?"

Opening the door to Jonas, she greeted him with a hug, right on the doorstep. "I was thinking about you."

He pulled her arms from around his neck, looking past her into the house. "Your parents must not be at home."

"They're spending the afternoon at Wilhelm and Esther's."

"Get your shawl, and we'll sit out here. I have something to tell you."

By the time Katie returned, Jonas was sitting on the washing bench. With the cooler weather, the washtub and towel had been put away, so it made a good place to sit. She wrapped her shawl closer and sat next to him. As she glanced at his face, Katie's joy at seeing him turned to worry.

"Is something wrong?" She moved closer to him, partly for warmth, and partly for assurance that his solemn expression didn't mean there had been an accident.

"What I'm going to tell you, you need to keep secret. At least for a few days."

Katie nodded, taking his hand in hers.

"You know that Samuel's name was on the draft list." He didn't look at her but stared into the woodlot across the road. "He can't join the army, and he won't pay the fee."

"What is he going to do?"

Jonas grasped her hand in both of his, pulling it even closer to him. "Nothing. Samuel is going to stay home, work on his farm, and raise his family."

"But won't he be breaking the law if he does that?"

"Not if he has a substitute."

"I heard him say he wouldn't hire someone to fight for him."

"Katie—" His voice cracked and he paused. "I'm going to be his substitute."

Her breath stopped as if a weight pressed on her lungs. But no, it couldn't be true.

"That isn't something to tease me about, Jonas." She tried to laugh at how ridiculous the idea was.

"I'm not teasing."

"Samuel would never allow you to take his place." She shook her head. Jonas was serious. Too serious.

"He doesn't want me to, but I'm going to do it anyway. It's the only thing to do. Samuel has responsibilities, where I have none—"

"What am I?" Heat rose in Katie's cheeks and her stomach swirled. "What about our plans? Our dreams?"

"I won't be gone forever." Jonas smiled, but his reassurance didn't change anything. "This war can't last much longer. I may not even reach the front lines before we're all sent home." He moved closer, leaning his forehead against hers. "I'll be back in time for our wedding next summer. I wouldn't leave if I thought I'd be gone longer than that."

A slow dripping from the house eave told Katie that it was raining, a light shower that she could barely see in the air. But the clouds had gathered again, blotting out the late-afternoon sun. She turned away from him, pulling her hand out of his grasp, and walked to the edge of the porch. Down the road, toward the partially built house nestled in the woods on the other side of the creek, her view was obscured by the misty rain. The drops increased until they were a steady downpour.

She couldn't think. Not past the pounding in her mind. Jonas couldn't leave. He couldn't. He was supposed to stay here. He would be safe here.

Her face was wet. She couldn't cry. Not in front of him. She wiped the corner of her shawl across her eyes, just as he came up behind her. He grasped her shoulders in his warm hands, then slipped his arms around her so that he was holding her, his hands clasped around her waist. Closing her eyes, Katie leaned back against him.

"I'll write to you." His voice was muffled. Strained.

"If you tell me where to send the letters, I'll write to you too." She turned around, clinging to him. "When do you leave?"

"Tonight. After dark, so that I reach Millersburg before Samuel gets there. I'll leave my parents a note to keep them from worrying. But I don't want anyone else to know what I've done. I don't want anyone to come after me, trying to stop me."

Hope rose. "Could that happen?" Katie saw herself running down the long road to Millersburg, pleading with him to come home.

"Nothing is going to change my mind, Katie. There would only be arguing and heartbreak, and I don't want to leave that way. It's better to do it quietly."

Katie nodded. If these were going to be her last moments with him, she didn't want to disagree, as much as she wanted to keep him from going. But she couldn't let him go without telling him . . .

"You know that you're sacrificing everything, don't you?"

"Not everything." Jonas tightened his hold. "I'm not giving you up."

"But you're leaving me behind. You chose this, Jonas, but I didn't. You're asking me to wait and to worry while you're off—" Anger rose, even though she tried to tamp it down.

She bit her lip, keeping back the terrible words she wanted to say. Her entire body ached. She had to tell him.

"If you go, you won't come home."

"For sure I will, just as soon as I can. I love you, Katie."

No, you don't, she wanted to say. But she didn't.

"I mean it, Jonas. Don't go. Please don't go. If you do, something terrible will happen." Movement on the path leading to Wilhelm's caught her eye. "Mama and Papa are coming home."

"The rain shower has stopped. Walk with me, at least to the road."

She let him take her hand and lead her down the lane. Water ran along the gravel, running toward the creek. When they reached the road, Jonas continued until they were hidden from the house by a grove of sumac. They were at the opening to the lane leading to the clearing and their house.

Katie stopped when he did. She closed her eyes, hoping that somehow she would wake from this nightmare. Jonas kissed her then, his lips soft and warm against hers. Kissing her longer, deeper, and more desperately than he ever had before. Kissing her as if he would never get the chance again.

# 11

Jonas woke to the sound of low, rolling thunder and a steady rain on the roof above his head. The thunder had echoed his dreams. Confused dreams of Katie, their half-built house, and the sound of hunting rifles in the woods.

Sitting up, he reached for his shoes. He hadn't meant to sleep at all, but only wait until the house was quiet. He had written a note for Mamm and Datt, and as he passed through the kitchen on his way to the back porch, he laid the note on the table. He hoped that would keep them from worrying too much until he could send his first letter to them.

He took his hat and coat from the hook by the back door and let himself out onto the covered porch. The rain had stopped, but the wind had picked up, moving the rolling thunder off to the east. The full moon drifted between the broken clouds, sending a cold light shining on the farm buildings and the road. Even though he had slept, the moon showed that the time was still early. Pulling his jacket close, Jonas started toward the stone bridge. When he reached the end of the lane, he turned back for one last look. The clouds had moved on, and the white house stood out against the dark fields behind it. The creek splashed, swollen from the autumn rains, and he turned back toward the road.

There was no use in being sentimental. Like he told Katie, it wouldn't be long before he would be home. The president had issued a proclamation saying that all slaves would be freed by January 1 unless the Confederate states ceased their rebellion. Once the South realized the impact of that proclamation, the war would be over for sure. He would be home soon, maybe even by Christmas.

He paused again at the top of the valley and looked back. All was dark and quiet. He could see all the houses along Weaver's Creek from here, except his own half-finished house in the woods. He turned and left the valley behind.

Reaching Millersburg before dawn, Jonas stopped for a rest in the courthouse square while he ate the apple and bread he had brought with him. The moon had set, and the eastern sky was turning from gray to pale blue. He had forty miles to go to Mansfield. First though, he needed to stop at the draft office and inform them that he was taking Samuel's place.

From his seat in the square, Jonas could see the draft office. As the morning light grew stronger, the door swung open and a man walked to the edge of the boardwalk and nodded at the crowd. Jonas adjusted his pack and went across the street. Other folks were gathering, including men who were heading toward the draft office, the same as he was. Jonas walked in, taking his place at the end of the line. When it was his turn, he stepped up to the counter.

"Good morning," said the man behind the counter. "The draftees are meeting in front of the office. We leave for Mansfield in fifteen minutes."

"I'm not on the list." The man looked at him for the first time. "I'm here to take someone else's place."

The man drew a pen from an inkwell. "The name of the other man?"

"Samuel Weaver."

"Township?"

"German."

He shuffled some papers, then drew a line through Samuel's name. "And your name?"

"Jonas Weaver."

The man paused, looking at him over wire-rimmed spectacles. "Related?"

"Ja, I'm his brother."

After writing Jonas's name in the blank space next to Samuel's, the man indicated where Jonas should sign his name. "The train will be leaving shortly." He pointed to the door. "That way and wait for the captain."

The group waiting in front of the draft office had swelled to fifty or more, with men coming by twos and threes, and even wagonloads. Jonas took his place next to another man who stood alone, looking ill at ease. He nodded to Jonas.

"You're goin' to Mansfield too?" The fellow looked to be about Jonas's age, with red hair that reminded him of Ruby.

"Ja, with all these others also, I expect."

"Are you Mennonite?"

"Amish."

The redhead nodded. "I thought you must be, the way you talked. My neighbor back in Mechanicsburg is Mennonite. He was called up, but he paid a fee." He looked Jonas up and down. "It must be nice to be rich enough to be able to buy your way out of fighting."

Before Jonas could think of an answer to that, the rat-a-tat of a drum sounded from the direction of the railroad station. The crowd, now numbering at least a hundred, turned and looked toward the sound. A group of men in uniform marched toward them, led by an officer on a horse. A boy kept time on the drum. When they reached the waiting crowd, they stopped at a signal from the leader.

"I am Captain Wentworth of the 261st Ohio Regiment. You men have been assigned to my command, and I'm here to escort you to Camp Mansfield."

A voice shouted from the middle of the crowd. "When do we get our guns and uniforms? I want to go kill some Rebs."

Captain Wentworth gazed into the crowd, searching for the man who had called out. "You'll get your chance. Although if you are this eager, I thought you would have volunteered instead of being conscripted into the army."

Without waiting for further comments, the captain stood in his stirrups. "We are going to march from here to the railroad station, where we will board the waiting train. We will arrive in Mansfield this afternoon." He nodded to the man beside him. "The sergeant will form you into ranks."

Jonas took a place on the end of a row, behind the red-headed man and next to a friendly boy who grinned at him.

At the sound of the drum, the column walked down the street, past the newspaper office and the courthouse, and on to the railroad station. When they passed the grain mill, the memory of the day he and Samuel had bought the seed corn flashed into his mind. His stride broke and he lost step with the boy beside him until someone from the rear shoved him back in line.

He tightened his sweaty grip on his sack. The monstrous locomotive hissed and puffed as they marched along the train to the cars behind. Another train stood on a track just feet away, enclosing them all in a darkened, steaming canyon. The somber idea came to him that they were marching through the gates of hell.

### OCTOBER 8

Lydia came into the kitchen, following her usual routine, lighting the lamp on this chilly October morning. She urged the stove into life, expertly stirring the hot coals and tossing some wood shavings and kindling on them before laying some split pine logs on top. Then she turned back to the table and saw a note. She picked it up and her hands began to tremble.

*October 7, 1862*

*To my dear parents,*

*I know this will be a grievous thing for you, but I have gone to join the army in Samuel's stead. Do not think that I am chasing after whatever glory War may hold, or that I wish to do this. But it is the only sensible thing to do. Samuel is a family man, and a man of principles that he will not ignore. This is the only*

189

*way I can prevent him from having to make the terrible choice between two tightly held beliefs.*

*Your loving son,*
*Jonas*

Sinking into the chair, she clasped her hand over her mouth. It couldn't be true. She set the page back on the table and nearly laughed with relief. Of course it couldn't be true. Jonas was out in the barn with Abraham doing chores. She had heard her husband calling him from his bed before going out to the barn.

Abraham and Jonas would be wanting their breakfast when they came in. Lydia's hands trembled as she took the frying pan from its shelf. She set it on the stove, then glanced at the note again. It was still there.

When she came back into the kitchen after fetching a ball of sausage from the cellar, the paper still lay there. Right where she had left it. In the center of the circle of lantern light.

Turning her back to the table, she dumped the sausage into the skillet and smashed it with her spoon, stirring the bits of crumbled meat until the aroma of frying herbs and pork filled the room. She cracked eggs into a bowl, scrambling them until they were a solid mass of yellow while the sky outside the window slowly lightened.

Stirring the sausage again, she looked out the window. Chores should be done by now. Abraham and Jonas were late. But Abraham would take longer doing the chores alone if Jonas had really gone. She pushed the thought out of her head, peeling the potatoes with quick, hard strokes. Jonas hadn't gone anywhere. The note from him was a practical joke.

Lydia removed the crumbled, browned sausage from the skillet, then added the potatoes. Hot grease spattered and popped. She stirred them, then covered the pan and moved it to the back of the stove, where the lower heat would cook the potatoes slowly. Just before serving them, she'd move the pan to the higher heat again and brown the potatoes to a satisfying crunch, just the way Jonas liked them.

The spatula dropped from her fingers, clattering on the floor. Lydia leaned against the kitchen counter. She closed her eyes as Abraham emerged from the barn. Alone.

Her voice was little more than a moan. "Jonas, what have you done?" She rubbed her throbbing forehead.

Abraham came in the kitchen door without a word. The muted sizzle of the potatoes cooking echoed in the comforting thump as her husband shut the door tightly against the autumn chill.

"Jonas didn't get up in time to do the chores this morning." Abraham hung his hat and coat on the hook by the door. "Did you wake him?"

Lydia set a cup at Abraham's place and poured him some coffee, not spilling a drop, in spite of her trembling hands. "Jonas isn't here."

She slid the note across the table and stirred the potatoes while Abraham sat in his chair. He read the note, then read it again.

"What is the boy thinking?" Abraham's voice rose as he dropped the paper onto the table. "He can't be serious about doing this."

After dishing the potatoes and sausage mixture into a

bowl, Lydia poured the beaten eggs into the hot pan. Her stomach turned.

"It appears he is."

"He left without saying anything to us."

"Maybe he talked with Samuel."

"Ja, ja, ja. Maybe." Abraham took a sip of his coffee as Lydia set the bowl of potatoes on the table. "He couldn't have gotten all the way to Millersburg already. I'll go to Samuel's after breakfast and we'll go after him."

Lydia set the plates on the table with two sharp thuds. "And then what?" Her voice had risen also, and she took a deep breath. "Then what, Abraham? You bring Jonas home, but Samuel goes on to report for duty? The state will claim one of our boys, won't it?"

"I'll take the money along with me to pay for Samuel."

"He's already decided that he won't let you do that."

Abraham watched her for a long minute, then took her hand. "Let's pray for our meal and then talk."

Lydia bowed her head and ran through a short, perfunctory prayer in her head, one she had memorized as a child, but Abraham's head remained bowed. She brought her thoughts back and centered on God. Her Lord. The Provider of all blessings. Her heart filled with thanksgiving as Abraham squeezed her hand to signal the end of his prayer.

Abraham served her and then himself. "This is what we should have expected of our Jonas."

Lydia nodded, staring at the steaming food on her plate. What was Jonas eating this morning? Was he still on the road, or had he already arrived in Millersburg?

"Samuel sits back, hoping for a solution to his predicament." Abraham took a bite of his eggs, his expression thoughtful. "But Jonas has always been the one to take a problem head-on, not worrying about the outcome of his actions until afterward."

"What do you think will happen to him?"

"He'll make his way, but it will be hard." Abraham took her hand again. "But it would be harder for Samuel. He would have to be away from his wife and family. And then to come back and repent of his actions before the church would be the most difficult of all."

They ate in silence. Abraham's frown told Lydia that he was deep in thought. Her own thoughts went back into her memories of Jonas as a little boy. Back to the time when he was still hers, before he entered the world of men. She saw the bright spring sunshine on his hair, his grin turned toward her, his apple-red cheeks. He was always getting into mischief and always able to find a way out of it again.

"What if . . ." Lydia stopped. She hadn't meant to let the thought escape, but Abraham waited for her to continue. "What if he isn't able to get himself out of this scrape? What if . . . he doesn't come home?"

Her husband sighed deeply, squeezing his eyes shut. "We must leave him to the Lord."

Lydia stood, dumping her breakfast into the hog's bucket. She hadn't eaten a bite and couldn't with her stomach turning in on itself. Men died in battle, and that thought frightened her. But the most dreadful thought was that he would fall into the company of men who would lead him astray, onto paths that would steer him away from the church.

She could trust the Good Lord with his life, and always had. But this? Lydia trembled at the thought of the snares that might be waiting for their boy.

Katie did her morning chores, but her mind was on Jonas. She had to know if he had really gone to Millersburg last night, but how could she find out?

Mama thumped furniture, muttering to herself as she dusted the front room and then moved into the downstairs bedroom. Katie swept the kitchen floor and took the dish towels out to hang on the line. The morning was breezy, but the rain had moved on. The sky was filled with wisps of white clouds. Looking up the valley, she could see the roof of the Weavers' home, with a steady stream of gray smoke caught by the wind as it came from the chimney.

She chewed on her bottom lip, watching the light gray line. She could pay a visit to Lydia. A good excuse could be that she wanted to copy a recipe. Lydia made the best cream pie, better than Mama's, and no one would think twice about Katie asking about it. And while she was there, she would find out if Jonas followed through with his plans.

Katie found Mama in her bedroom, making the bed after letting it air all morning.

"May I go visit Lydia?"

Mama didn't look at her but ran her hand over the woven coverlet she had brought from Germany so many years ago. "Why would you do that?"

"I want to ask if I can copy her recipe for cream pie. It's different than yours, and I want to see why."

"Your chores are finished?"

"Ja, for sure. I have some sewing to do, but I can do that this afternoon."

"It's all right with me. But be home in plenty of time to help with dinner."

Katie didn't give Mama an opportunity to change her mind but threw her shawl over her shoulders and hurried down the road. When she reached the lane leading to Lydia's house, she saw Samuel going into the barn. How much did he know of Jonas's plans to be his substitute?

Lydia had seen her coming and opened the kitchen door for her. The room was warm and smelled of onions and sausage. Katie took a deep breath of the homey fragrance and smiled at Jonas's mother.

"I hoped you were at home this morning." She stopped as she noticed Lydia's eyes, red and watery as if she had been crying. On the table was a note in Jonas's handwriting. "I . . . I wanted to borrow . . ." She couldn't go on with the excuse she had given Mama. Katie followed Lydia farther into the kitchen and stroked the paper that Jonas had touched so recently. "So he's gone? He said he would leave a note for you."

Lydia poured a cup of coffee for herself and one for Katie and they sat at the table. "I should have guessed he would have told you."

"He came and talked to me about it last night, but I couldn't believe he would leave. I hoped he hadn't."

The older woman rubbed one finger along a crease in the paper. "He must have left sometime during the night."

"Are you going to go after him? You can't let him join the army."

Lydia shook her head. "Abraham and I talked about it, but we know that once Jonas has made up his mind, nothing can dissuade him. And the alternative is exactly what Jonas wanted to avoid. Samuel would have to go or break the law."

She rubbed the crease again. "In a way, I'm glad Jonas acted. I wouldn't have been able to decide between the two."

Katie leaned on the table, her coffee forgotten. "It was never our choice anyway."

Lydia's smile was sad. "That's the way it is for women. The men make the decisions and we make do with the results."

Staring at the stiff, straight letters that formed Jonas's words, Katie felt the despair in Lydia's voice. He had made his decision, and there was nothing they could do but wait for the news that he had been killed.

Then Lydia straightened her back, taking Katie's hand in hers. "Now listen to me going on. Don't mind me. I'm just an old woman who's feeling sorry for herself. We'll leave Jonas in the Good Lord's care. He'll be safe there."

Katie shook her head, her temples throbbing. "He won't be safe. He's going to die."

"What makes you say that?"

Biting her lip, Katie looked at Jonas's mother. She had known Lydia since she was born, and could trust her, but she had never told anyone about the curse Teacher Robinson had laid on her.

"It's what happens to men who are around me."

Lydia pushed her coffee cup to the side and leaned toward Katie. "What do you mean? There are men all around you who haven't died. Your father, your brothers. The church is full of men. Why do you think that?"

Katie pulled her hand back, her heart pounding. "It isn't all men. Only men who . . . want to be . . . romantic with me. It's a curse."

Sunlight fell through the window, landing on the table.

Dust motes danced before Katie's eyes. How much could she tell Lydia about Teacher Robinson? She had never told anyone about the curse, but now that Jonas was in danger, maybe Lydia could help her save him.

"Katie"—Lydia's voice was firm—"what are you talking about?"

Katie closed her eyes, trying to shut away the memory of those hot afternoons after the other students had gone home the summer when she turned thirteen. The private lessons in arithmetic, and the poetry he taught her to love. He said she was intelligent and beautiful. He said she was a pleasure to teach because her mind was so quick. She had thought of him as a kind grandfather, opening doors to a world she had never seen before.

"Teacher Robinson put a curse on me."

"Teacher Robinson? You mean the man who taught school for you children?"

Katie nodded, shuddering as his fat, puffy face appeared in her memory. His friendly smile turning to a leer as his fingers pressed against her knees. His red face, scowling as she pulled away from his heavy body leaning against hers. The flash of anger in his eyes as she wrenched away from his groping hands. And the agony that twisted his features as he fell to the floor, gasping in pain and cursing her with his last breath.

Lydia paused, frowning. "When he died, it was a terrible thing, but that has to be four, maybe five years ago. What does his death have to do with you?"

"I killed him. He . . . he tried to . . . touch me, and when I pulled away from him he grew so angry. He tried to come after me, but he fell on the floor, like he had some kind of attack, and he cursed me. He said that I was a . . . a Siren. That I lure men to their death."

Lydia drew back. Repulsed, just as Katie feared. But once she understood, then she would make sure Jonas came home.

But Lydia laid her hand on Katie's. "There is no curse powerful enough to harm one of God's people."

Katie chewed on her bottom lip. Somehow Lydia must understand. "But the curse is true. Teacher died, and Ned died. I thought Jonas was safe, but he isn't. Not if he's gone into danger." She shivered as ice crept up her fingers to her aching arms. She pulled her hand back and clasped her elbows, hugging her arms close.

"Ach, Katie." Lydia's red-rimmed eyes brimmed with tears. "Ned died far away in the South."

"But before he left he said he . . . he wanted to kiss me." Katie leaned toward her. "Don't you see? Every man who thinks he has romantic feelings for me ends up dying."

"Mr. Robinson's words have no power over you. His death wasn't your fault, and neither was Ned's. If Jonas—" She stopped, tears spilling down her cheeks. "If Jonas should die, it won't be because of you."

The sunbeam fell off the edge of the table like a stream of water. Katie gripped her arms more tightly as she considered Lydia's words.

"I wish what you are saying was true."

"It is true. A curse has no power over us."

"I'm not a member of the church."

"It has nothing to do with being a church member. It all has to do with whether you believe that Christ's sacrifice is your only hope. God has provided the way for you to belong to him."

Katie pressed her knees together as the cold crept up her legs.

Lydia moved around the table to sit in the chair next to her and folded her in her arms. "What Mr. Robinson tried to do to you wasn't love. It wasn't romantic. A true love doesn't bring fear, but safety and joy. I know Jonas loves you, and he will never willingly hurt you."

Tears stung in Katie's eyes as she melted into Lydia's embrace. The aching stiffness eased. She wanted to believe Lydia, but Teacher's voice still echoed in her ears.

"Datt?"

High in the barn loft, forking hay into the horses' mangers, Abraham heard Samuel's voice but didn't answer right away. First thing after breakfast, he had gone to Samuel's to tell him of Jonas's action. But when Anna had answered the door, Dorcas on her hip and eyes red, she said she didn't know where Samuel was. She had said she was afraid he had gone off to report for duty with the army, but he had left his bag behind.

Abraham had gone back to work, his emotions seething. He rarely gave in to anger, but he was ready to give full vent to it now. One son had taken his pride off to war while the other son, in his own pride, had done nothing until his hand was forced. Had Samuel gone to report to the army, as Anna had feared? Or had he given in to fear, and was trying to escape to the Canadian border? Until he heard Samuel's voice calling him in the barn, he was thinking the worst thoughts of his oldest son and regretted every minute.

"Datt?" The call came again.

"Ja, Samuel. I'll be right down."

Filling the last manger, Abraham thrust the hayfork into the loose pile and headed down the ladder. Samuel waited for him in the center of the barn, next to the patch of sunlight that streamed through the eastern door. It looked like the rain of the past few days had finally cleared away.

Abraham faced his son. "You heard about Jonas?"

Samuel nodded, his arms crossed in front of him. He pushed a stray piece of straw with the toe of his shoe. "Anna told me." There was no hint of surprise in his voice or his features.

"You knew he was planning this?"

"He suggested it yesterday, but I told him not to do it."

"You know you can't tell Jonas not to do something once he's made up his mind."

Samuel didn't answer but pushed at the straw again.

"What did you intend to do today? Were you planning to go to Mansfield yourself?"

"I did not intend to give myself to the army." Samuel finally looked him in the eye. "I've been praying, and thinking about nonresistance and what it means. I had determined to do nothing."

"But Jonas acted instead."

"I told him not to. I don't want him involved in this war or thinking that he has to take my place." Samuel scrubbed the back of his neck and paced toward the horse stalls and back. "But you know Jonas. Better than I do. He got this notion in his head that I was sacrificing too much by either going to war or being arrested for not reporting. I know what I choose to sacrifice, but he thinks he's saving me by going to war in my place."

Abraham rubbed his temple. This problem wasn't something he could wish away. If it was, the war would never have started.

"Are you certain that you've counted the cost of your actions? The whole cost?"

Samuel ticked the list off on his fingers. "If I am arrested for being nonresistant, I leave my wife and family alone. I would be risking my life, as I could be convicted of treason. I would risk being forced into the army in spite of my resistance. I risk losing . . . everything." His hands dropped at his sides.

"Have you considered the rest of your family? Your mother and me? Your brothers and sisters? And Jonas? What have your choices cost him?"

Samuel ran one hand over his face. "I didn't ask him to take my place. What could I have done differently?"

"I don't know. Perhaps you could have taken one of the options the government provided for us." He hated the sound of his own voice as his anger and frustration ground out. Sarcasm wasn't his best choice.

"And compromise my principles?"

Abraham's temper roared, making his head throb. Jonas's life was forfeit because of his brother's principles. He slammed the heel of his hand against the huge support beam in the middle of the barn. Dust sifted through the sunbeam, the millions of motes reflecting the light like broken shards of glass. As he leaned on the beam, he heard Samuel's footsteps go out of the barn.

How had his family come to this point in only a few days? It was as if some force from outside had reached into the center of his home and snatched away the peace. Was it his

201

fault? Had he done something that he was being punished for? Something so terrible that it affected his family in such a devastating way?

He searched his memory but came up with nothing. A verse from the Psalms came to his mind, and he prayed it out loud. "'Search me, O God, and know my heart: try me, and know my thoughts: and see if there be any wicked way in me . . .'" His voice failed. He brought things he knew were sins into his mind. Pride. Hatred. Foolish thoughts. Murder.

Pride. Had he been overly proud of his family? If anyone would ask, he would say that he was content rather than prideful.

Hatred. Did he harbor hatred toward the change-minded leaders who would pull the church apart? The only feeling he was aware of was sorrow. A deep sorrow.

Foolish thoughts? Not that he remembered. Murder? Not in action . . . and not in thought.

Abraham lifted his head as a thought came to him. Had he been so proud that he assumed his family was safe from the troubles that were part of this world? There was no reason to think they would be immune from the effects of this war only because they lived in this valley that had known nothing but peace since the time his father had settled here so long ago.

"Have mercy, dear Lord, have mercy on us." Then the last words of the Psalm came to his mind. "And lead me in the way everlasting."

The sun had shifted and the dust motes had settled, but the light coming through the barn door was still clear and bright. The sky was the clean blue of October, with the red and gold leaves blazing at the tops of the trees in the woodlot.

Abraham drank in the sight. It was as if he was viewing

God on his throne, just as Isaiah had, and the train of his robe filled the temple, and the whole world was filled with his glory.

He needed to make amends with Samuel. He couldn't let his sin of anger become a wedge between them. His work could wait until after he found his son and talked with him.

The solid beam had held fast once more. Abraham let a smile come as he ran a hand along the worn wood. Solid and strong, just as God's faithfulness had proved to be once more.

# 12

**OCTOBER 13**

On Monday afternoon, Katie sat at the kitchen table with her scissors and fabric. She had brought out her fabric scraps to cut into squares as soon as the dinner dishes were done, to the accompaniment of many tongue clicks from Mama. But Mama had gone to Lena's and now Katie could work in peace.

She needed peace. Her thoughts swirled in her head like storm clouds on a summer's day. She still expected Jonas to walk up to the porch with the smile reserved just for her, but he was gone. Yesterday had been Sunday, and normally she would have spent the afternoon with him, talking and making plans for their future. But the time after church had been empty, relieved only by a visit to Wilhelm and Esther's house. The rest of the family had been there too, and as the cousins played, the adults talked of every subject Katie could think of, except the war. Except the news that Jonas was off somewhere, possibly even now being shot at by another soldier.

Katie finished cutting a piece of light green fabric into squares and counted them. Putting the pile into the basket, she noted the thirty-two squares on a scrap of paper. Once she knew how many squares she had of each color, she would plan the design of the quilt. Laying her pencil down, she sighed and picked up the next piece of fabric. She hoped the complex pattern would help the time pass through the coming winter.

Footsteps sounded on the wooden porch, followed by a sharp knock that made Katie jump. When she opened the door, Ruby greeted her with a smile, her hair windblown and escaping her kapp as usual. Elizabeth was next to her.

"We thought you might be at home," Ruby said, walking into the warm kitchen. "We've been to Farmerstown to buy a few things at the dry goods store there, and they had a letter for you."

Katie took the envelope, recognizing Jonas's handwriting on the front.

"I've never gotten a letter before." She turned it over.

"Ruby and I got one too, and there's one for Levi Beiler." Elizabeth said. "See on the front where it says, 'Soldier's Letter'? The postmaster said that means that Jonas can send his letters without having to pay. We pay the postage when we pick them up."

"We won't stay to visit," Ruby said. "You'll want to read your letter. Jonas said that he is lonesome already and wants news from home whenever someone can write. We can take turns going to the post office to mail the letters and pick up the ones he writes."

Katie ran her finger over her name on the envelope, then remembered Elizabeth. "Did you get a letter from Reuben?"

She shook her head. "Very few letters get through from the Confederate soldiers. I haven't heard a word since he left. But it is a joy to hear from Jonas, isn't it?" She reached into the basket she carried and pulled out a second envelope. "Will you be seeing Levi soon? Ruby thought you might, since you're friends with his sister."

"Ja, for sure. I can take the letter. It will give me an excuse to stop in to see Millie."

As Katie closed the door behind her friends, she put the letter to Levi in her sewing basket and turned her envelope over again. The postmark was Mansfield, so that meant he was still in Ohio. She had to read the letter, but not here, where Mama might walk in at any minute. She added wood to the fire and adjusted the damper, so it would burn slowly but not go out, then put on her shawl and bonnet.

She ran down the lane to the road, and then to the wooden bridge that crossed the creek to the house. The two walls provided a bit of shelter from the gusty autumn wind. She settled down on a log against one wall and opened the letter.

*Camp Mansfield, October 11, 1862*

*My dearest sweet Katie,*

*I think of you every hour of every day, and hope to receive a letter from you soon. We will be located here for another week before moving east to join the Army of the Potomac. When you write, address the letter to me, Company C, 261st Ohio Regiment. That will get your letter to me no matter where we are.*

*I pray that you are well and that all at home are also. I worry that Mamm and Datt have not taken my leaving well but pray that they will come to understand. I have written to them also, and to others in my family. Even though our days are long, the evenings are empty unless one wishes to participate in idle entertainments, which I don't, so I have time to think about you and to write.*

*We trained hard today. Many of the men are from farms and used to hard labor, but some are from the cities where they are not required to walk many miles every day. That is what we did. If we marched in a straight line, I suppose I would be nearly home again by now. But our marching was confined to the camp. We have been issued uniforms and guns, but no ammunition except what is doled out during practice. We shoot at straw targets, which is fine with me. The straw bales are fitted with cloth that is decorated with an outline of a man's body on it. Some men took great joy in hitting the center of their "man." I take no such joy, but the officers were satisfied with my aim.*

*We get no war news here, only rumors. But as all rumor has a thread of truth in it, we listen and sift, trying to know what will happen tomorrow, the next day, and next week. You will be glad to know that I have found a comrade, a fellow from Darke County by the name of George Watson. We often talk about the homes we left behind—could it only be three days ago? It seems that I have been parted from you for a month.*

*Write soon, dearest one. I want to know that you are well. I am well, and eating good food. I have blankets*

*and a tent, companionship, and even some fun times.*
*But all this is a poor substitute for the sight of your*
*sweet face.*

*Goodbye until another day,*

*Jonas*

Katie read the letter through, and then again. She could almost hear Jonas's voice as she read the words, sitting here in the shelter of the house he was building for her. As she folded the letter and placed it back in its envelope, she knew she had to write back to him immediately. If she wrote today, the letter might reach him while he was in Mansfield.

Holding the letter close, she ran back to the house to find some paper and a pen.

---

## OCTOBER 15

Levi straightened, brushing the chaff off his clothes and trying to catch his breath. Father didn't look at him, but Levi knew what he was thinking. Father had made two corn shocks for every one Levi had made, no matter how quickly he tried to work. But Father's tall lean form was made for this kind of work and every movement was effortless, while Levi puffed as he picked up a bundle of stalks from the ground. By the time he reached the end of his row, Father had finished his half of the field and gone back to the barn without a word, leaving Levi to finish.

Reaching for the next handful of stalks, Levi could feel the frown creasing his forehead. Resentment could build quickly if he let it, so he had to stop it. Better to put that energy into constructive work, as he had read somewhere. Life was filled with work from the beginning to the end, but the work didn't have to be tiresome. Man was made for work, from the first day in the Garden of Eden. Smiling to himself, Levi tied the next corn shock. Only one more row to go.

He should write his own book someday. What should he call it? Another corn shock was done as he thought of possible titles.

"The Writings of Levi Beiler," he said aloud, listening to the rhythm and sound of the words. "In My Youth." That one sounded good too. He could write about all the things a young man needed to know as he was coming of age and ready to start his own family.

Levi finished another row while he thought of the topics he would address in his book. Work should be included. And courtship should be a subject also. Finding a wife.

Taking off his hat, Levi wiped his sweating brow with the back of his sleeve. Finding a wife. That was his challenge. A fellow like Jonas seemed to have no problem, but Levi couldn't get any girls to look at him.

Voices from the direction of the house caught his attention, and when he saw Katie Stuckey in the yard talking to Millie, he almost dropped the bundle of cornstalks he was twisting together. Katie . . . He caught his thoughts and brought them around to their proper place. Katie was here to see Millie, of course. But he couldn't stop himself from watching her.

Then Millie pointed toward the cornfield and Katie started walking toward him, waving when she saw him watching her.

Panic set in. Even though the day was cool, he had been

sweating and he could feel a film of mud covering his face. Chaff from the cornstalks covered his clothes, and he was tired. He didn't want Katie to see him this way, but here she came, striding along the lane between the fields.

"I see you're working hard," Katie said when she got close. "Papa is shocking his corn too."

Levi tried to wipe his face with his hand, but one look at his palm told him he hadn't helped his appearance at all. "It's a fine day for the harvest."

Katie held out an envelope. "Jonas has written letters, and one is for you."

Levi took the letter from her. The handwriting was Jonas's, for sure, and it was postmarked from Mansfield. The rumors he had heard at the church meeting on Sunday had been true. A sudden thought crossed his mind. "Did he go voluntarily? Or was he forced to go?"

Katie looked at the corn stubble at her feet. "He chose to take Samuel's place. No one forced him, but he felt like he had to do this. He was afraid for his brother."

Jonas in the army. Levi's mind went through the consequences he would face on his return, going against the Ordnung this way. Of course, since he wasn't baptized yet, the results of his actions might not be too serious. But if something happened to him—

"Are you all right?" Katie's words broke into his thoughts. "I wish he had told you what he was planning to do. Perhaps you could have changed his mind. You're his best friend."

Levi's heart swelled a bit at that. Katie was right. They were best friends. "Ja, ja, ja. I am only worried about him, away from us and off in the world."

"I must get home. Mama is expecting me to help with the string beans."

He watched her walk back down the lane and out to the road. He swallowed. He would have asked her to stay longer, to talk about . . . what? She was concerned about Jonas, not him.

Looking at the remainder of the field, he guessed he had six or seven more shocks of corn to go. Then he looked at the letter. The corn could wait while he took a short rest. He found a grassy spot to sit on at the edge of the cornfield and slit open the letter.

*Camp Mansfield, October 10, 1862*

*Dear Levi,*

*I hope the news of my joining the army hasn't taken you by surprise. I hope you would have heard by now that I am part of a company of soldiers. So far, I am doing well and feeling good. We leave for Virginia to-morrow, to join the Army of the Potomac. I am ready to leave Ohio, but I don't think I will ever be ready to go into the area of the bitterest fighting.*

*I am writing to remind you of your promise. Do you remember it? It seems like such a long time ago, but was it only last week that we sat together in Millersburg waiting to find out the results of the draft? You promised to look after Katie for me. It has torn my heart in two to leave her, even though I tried to hide that from her. I worry that she will become morose and her bright spirit quenched while I am away. She needs her friends by her side, and I am counting on you to be there.*

> *Keep me in your prayers, and write often to tell me how things are at home.*
> *Your friend,*

*Jonas*
*Company C,*
*261st Ohio Regiment*

Levi let the letter drop to the ground. Jonas trusted him to watch over Katie, and he must live up to that trust, no matter how painful it would be.

～⌒

## OCTOBER 27

Jonas woke as the train pulled into the station at Harper's Ferry and grabbed his gear. Captain Wentworth was the first one on the platform, shouting orders as the men jumped off the train steps and into formation in front of him. Once he was in place, Jonas looked around, trying to get his bearings.

He had read about Harper's Ferry and the battles that had been fought there, including the skirmish with John Brown and his supporters back in 1859. The more recent battle, fought just six weeks before between the Army of the Potomac and General Lee's Confederate forces, was all the newly formed regiment on the train had talked about. The Union had lost the battle but gained back ground at Antietam a week later, then recaptured Harper's Ferry. Rumors about the battle at Antietam reported horrible losses for both sides in the battle, but most of the regiment had been jubilant at the news of the Union victories under General McClellan.

The train had pulled into the station at dawn, tendrils

of fog from the river bottoms mingling with the smoke and steam from the engine. Jonas glanced at George Watson, standing next to him with his eyes closed.

"George," Jonas said, nudging his elbow. "Don't fall asleep. The captain hasn't given orders yet and you'll miss them."

George yawned. "When are they going to let us sleep? That train was too noisy with all the talking."

"You just have to ignore it and sleep when you can. Forget about the noise."

At the order of "Attention!" called out by a corporal, Jonas snapped his head to the front and straightened his shoulders.

"Men, we will be starting our march south to join the Army of the Potomac at noon." Captain Wentworth paced back and forth in front of the rows of men. "We will make camp in the churchyard, yonder. Sleep while you can. After I dismiss you, the corporal will conduct mail call."

After dismissal, George turned to Jonas. "Let's stake out our campsite before the others get there."

"What about the mail?"

"I don't expect to get any. Do you?"

Jonas wavered. He had sent letters to Katie and the family more than three weeks ago but had not received any replies. "I'm due to get a letter or two. I'll stay for mail call and pick up yours if there is any."

George yawned again. "Look for me on the high ground of the churchyard. No swampy bedrolls this morning."

As George disappeared into the mist, Jonas joined the crowd around Corporal Miller. The corporal had the difficult task of handling mail call. The men were overjoyed when they received letters and morose when they didn't. Jonas had heard some threaten the poor man when their names weren't called. But Miller was efficient and called the names quickly and clearly. Jonas was glad he stayed. George received a letter, and Jonas had three. He stuffed them into his shirt front and went to find his friend.

The high ground George had claimed turned out to be against a vault in the graveyard, in a spot overlooking the confluence of the Shenandoah and Potomac rivers. George was sound asleep, so Jonas tucked his friend's letter inside his coat and settled in next to him.

One of the blankets was permeated with rubber, and this one Jonas folded so that it covered him both above and below his wool blanket. Tucked in this way, he expected he would be warm enough as well as protected from the damp. Before turning over to succumb to his weariness though, he looked at his letters in the growing morning light. The first was in Datt's handwriting and the second was in Ruby's sharp script. When he saw that the third was from Katie, he couldn't wait until later to read it. Stuffing the other letters back in his shirt front, he pulled the blanket up over his shoulder and opened the letter.

*October 13, 1862*

*My dear Jonas,*

*I was pleased to get your letter and hear that you were safe.*

*Things at home have not changed much, since you left only a few days ago.*

*Papa and the boys are still working to get all the corn in. The bottom field took an extra week to dry. Mama*

214

*and I have the last of the garden produce to harvest. We haven't had a frost yet, so the beans are giving us another crop.*

*At church yesterday, a few folks wondered where you were. I think your father told the ministers what had happened, but the rest of the people had to be content with rumors. I didn't say anything. Your parting is much too recent to speak of it to others.*

*But I had determined that this letter was going to be filled with happy news!*

*Rosie Schrock and her new husband visited church yesterday. It seems funny to think of her as Rosie Schrock rather than Keck. It makes me wonder if I will have trouble getting used to being called Katie Weaver. Her husband didn't look happy after the service. Rosie told me he thinks our church is old-fashioned and should make changes. It isn't his church though, is it? Rosie said they have a large meetinghouse in Oak Grove, but she misses her friends from Weaver's Creek. She also said they are living with his parents in an addition that the folks built onto their house. After talking with her, I am so glad that we will have our own house when we are married.*

*Elizabeth and Ruby are going to come over next week to help me piece our quilt top. They are such good company. They were the ones who brought your letter to me today, along with the one for Levi. I will take it to him on Thursday, if the weather is fine.*

*Keep yourself safe, and know that I will always love you,*

*Your Katie*

Jonas read through the letter twice before folding it back into its envelope and tucking it inside his shirt with the others. The sun had risen above the eastern mountains and the fog was burning off as he closed his eyes. If he was lucky, he might get a few hours' sleep before they were rousted awake for the march to join the great army somewhere south and east of them.

# 13

October 30

Katie sat at the kitchen table long after dinner was cleared, her fabric squares in piles while she tried to arrange the complex quilt pattern she had chosen. After drawing the pattern out on a piece of paper, Katie counted the number of squares she needed of each color. But none of the amounts she needed matched the number of squares she had. She needed to find more fabric scraps.

Who would have scraps they would be willing to part with? Millie would, if she had any, but the walk to her house would take too long and Katie wouldn't be home before dark. She thought of Elizabeth and Ruby, but there wasn't any place to store an unnecessary item like fabric scraps in Elizabeth's little cabin. Then she thought of the Weavers' big farmhouse. Lydia would have plenty to share with her.

With that thought came the sudden urge to see Jonas's mother. No letters had arrived from Jonas since the first one came more than two weeks ago and waiting for news from him filled her with worry. Had he gotten ill? Was he wounded? Perhaps Lydia and Abraham had received a letter. Katie started stacking the fabric squares back in her box. Now she had two reasons to visit Lydia.

"Are you still working on that quilt?" Mama lumbered into the kitchen, moving slowly. She had complained of not feeling well again today. She often felt like this during the cooler weather of autumn. In the winter, Mama suffered enough on some days to stay confined to her bed.

"I'm just putting it away for now. I need more fabric, and I thought I'd run over to Lydia's to see if she had some scraps I could use."

Mama sat in her chair and pulled the paper pattern toward herself. "This is what you're making? It's a bit fancy."

Katie tried not to let it show, but the biting tone in Mama's voice wrenched her heart. Again. She dreaded the coming fall rains and winter snows when she and Mama would be alone in the house together all day. Once she had her quilt top ready to put in the big quilting frame, then Elizabeth and Ruby could come over for an afternoon sometimes, and that would help relieve the tedium. But every autumn Mama acted like this, making Katie long for spring.

"I want to make this quilt special, since it's for my wedding."

"Don't take up too much of Lydia's time, and be back in time for supper."

"Ja, ja, ja," Katie said. She picked up the box to take up to her bedroom and glanced at Mama. Her expression was sad, as if she was lonely. "Mama, do you want to come with me? We can visit with Lydia together. We'll take a loaf of the bread you made this morning."

"I don't want to go anywhere." Mama leaned on the table, rubbing her forehead.

"Do you feel all right?"

"Ja, for sure. I feel fine. I think I'll take a nap while you're gone."

But when Katie came back downstairs, Mama still sat at the kitchen table.

"Do you want me to make a cup of tea for you? Or some coffee?"

Mama shook her head, her mouth set in a bitter line. "I'm fine. I told you that. Now go on to the Weavers'."

Katie took her shawl from the hook and settled it around her shoulders. Mama hadn't moved. She put her bonnet over her kapp and lifted the door latch. Mama ignored her. She slipped out the door and started down the lane to the road.

The ache in her heart only grew stronger when she reached the half-built house. Since Jonas had gone, she was the only one who came here, and the place was already looking neglected. She stopped to pull some weeds away from the foundation near the front door. Or where the front door would be. She looked through the empty doorframe that led nowhere. Jonas had propped the two walls up with the beams he would later use for the roof, but until then the house looked more like it was falling down instead of being built into a place where they could live and raise their family.

She took the trail Jonas had worn between their house and the Weavers' farm. Smoke poured from the chimney of the house, and the sight cheered her. When she knocked on the door, Lydia opened it immediately, as if she had seen her coming.

"I'm so glad to see you, dear Katie." Lydia helped her

take off her shawl and hung it on a hook by the door. "I am making cookies from a recipe my sister sent me, and I need someone to taste them to let me know if they're any good."

Lydia winked at her and Katie laughed. The Weaver kitchen was bright and warm, with the fragrance of spices and warm cookies.

"I'd love to try one," she said. "What can I do to help?"

"That baking sheet is ready for more cookies. If you could drop some of the cookie dough on it, then it can go in the oven as soon as these are done." Lydia opened the oven to check the baking cookies, then closed it again. "A couple more minutes should do it."

By the time the second sheet of cookies was done baking, Lydia had hot tea made and they sat at the table.

Lydia picked up one of the cookies and inspected it. "Naomi said these were her family's favorite, so I thought I'd try them. They're made with molasses and ginger, plus an ingredient that might be a surprise." She took a small bite while Katie broke hers in half. "What do you think?"

"They smell wonderful." Katie ate one half slowly, making the flavor last. "They taste a little bit like the Pfeffernusse cookies Mama makes but different."

"You're right. Pfeffernusse cookies have more spices than just ginger. These are more like gingerbread."

"What else is in them? They almost taste like pumpkin pie."

Lydia nodded. "That's what Naomi calls them. Pumpkin pie cookies. I had never thought of putting pumpkin in a cookie."

"Does Naomi live around here?"

"She's in Illinois, near Arthur. A large Amish settlement

is there, and that's where her husband lived when they met." Lydia brushed cookie crumbs from her fingers. "He came from Germany about the same time your parents did, and the crossing was just as hard for him as it had been for them."

"Mama doesn't talk about their trip across the ocean." Katie finished her cookie and pulled her cup of tea closer. "Do you know what it was like?"

"You should ask your mother. I don't intend to be a gossip."

"Mama doesn't talk to me, not like you do. If I asked her about it, she would just tell me to feed the chickens or something. Especially today. For some reason, she always gets sad this time of year."

Lydia watched her for a long minute. "Your mother has never spoken to you about their trip?"

Katie shook her head. "No one mentions it, or their lives in Germany before they came."

"I'll tell you, but only because it will help you understand your parents better." Lydia sipped her tea, then set the cup down. "The crossing was difficult. It was late in the year and many storms made the crossing take longer than they expected. The ship had also been delayed in England for some reason, so they didn't leave Europe until September was nearly over. The conditions on the ship were terrible, according to what your mother told me when they first got here. They were crowded into the hold, and many people were ill. Your brother and a baby sister both died on the voyage, nearly on the same day. They were buried at sea, and I don't think she has ever gotten over it. This is about the time of year that they would have died."

Katie sat back in her chair. "I had another brother and sister? Mama has never mentioned them to me."

"It's a very painful memory for her. I think she has tried to put the past behind her. I heard her say several times that a new country was a new start, and she meant it."

"Mama seems to be happy here, except in the fall."

"When you came along, you were a complete surprise to everyone." Lydia rested her chin in her hand and smiled at Katie. "You were such a beautiful baby, and I've seen a lot of babies."

Katie took another cookie. "But I don't think I've made her very happy. I've always felt like, well, like I was in the way."

"I think your mother was afraid to love you. That happens sometimes when we've loved so deeply and then lost the person we've loved. It's hard to open our hearts to another." Lydia sighed, her eyes taking on a faraway look. "You were a beautiful baby, but also very fragile. You were often sick during your first two years, and we all thought you might not live to see your third birthday."

She shook her head a little and went to the stove to put more wood on the fire. When she came back to the table, she smiled at Katie again. "Don't be afraid to love your mother just because she might be afraid to love you. You're her daughter, but you can also be her friend."

Katie finished her cookie, thinking about Mama. For years she had wished Mama could be more like Lydia or some of the other women in the church. She would love to be able to talk with Mama the way Millie talked with her mother or the way Ruby and Elizabeth did when they dropped in to see Lydia.

Perhaps if she tried, she might be able to change the way Mama felt about her after all these years.

～◦

## November 4

It took nearly three weeks for Levi to find the courage to drop in on Katie after reading Jonas's letter. He tried to tell himself that catching a glimpse of her at church on Sundays would be enough to keep his promise to Jonas, but he knew better.

If he faced the truth, the problem wasn't that he didn't want to see Katie but that he longed to see her. That was the problem. Jonas expected him to act toward Katie as a friend. A brother. But his feelings were much deeper.

As he headed down the road leading toward Weaver's Creek, he argued with himself.

"You can't disappoint Jonas. He's counting on you."

"But you know you're giving in to temptation. Just seeing Katie will start you thinking about her again."

"She's Jonas's girl, not yours."

Ja, ja, ja. He could talk to himself until he was arguing in circles, but that didn't quiet the thought that reached like a tendril into his mind . . . that if Jonas didn't come home from the war . . .

He clucked to Pacer, urging the horse into his rocking gait as he passed the Weavers' farm. Searching through his memory for the verse from Second Corinthians he recited every time that thought tried to worm its way into his consciousness. "And bringing into captivity every thought to the obedience of Christ." Every thought.

The temptation to wish Katie was his was strong, but not

stronger than the Good Lord himself. Jonas deserved more than a friend courting his girl behind his back, so he would stop at the Stuckeys', exchange a few words with Katie, then be on his way. Then he could write to Jonas with an easy heart.

When he reached Katie's house, all was quiet. Levi sat on the wagon seat, watching the kitchen door. The news on Sunday had been that Hans and Lena had welcomed a new baby to their home last week, and it could be possible that Katie and her mother were there. If so, he could make his way home again and put off this chore until another day.

But it could also be that Katie was inside the house, watching him and wondering why he wasn't approaching the door. His palms grew clammy at this thought. He climbed down from the wagon seat and trudged up the two steps to the porch. Just as he lifted his hand to knock, the door opened.

"Levi Beiler." Katie eyes were pink and puffy, but she smiled at him. "What brings you this way?"

"I told Jonas I would stop and check on you while he was gone." Levi took a deep breath. He had inherited his father's ability to talk, whether he knew what he was going to say or not.

Katie grabbed his arm and pulled him into the warm kitchen. "Have you heard from Jonas again? Is he all right?"

"I haven't gotten a letter since the one you brought me."

Her face fell. "I had hoped you had gone to the post office. Mama and Papa won't let me go alone."

"I can take you." Levi smiled with relief. Here was something Katie needed. Something he could do.

"Could you? I can't tell you how wonderful that would be."

The expression on Katie's face was enough to make him want to take her to Farmerstown every day if he needed to. "I have time to go this afternoon, if it's all right with your parents."

Katie grinned. "I'll leave a note for Mama."

While Levi waited for Katie to write her note and take care of the fire so she could leave it, he thought about his impetuous offer. He never did anything like this without thought and planning. What was it about Katie that made him feel so reckless?

She came down the stairs with a reticule and a letter in her hand. "I have a letter to post while we're there." She glanced at Levi. "I need to get some things at the store too, if we have time. Mama mentioned that we're almost out of salt, and I need a needle."

Her brown eyes were wide and trusting, and Levi found himself nodding in agreement. "Whatever you need to do."

The drive to the little village was short, but it seemed to take forever. Levi was aware of every time Katie's arm brushed against his. Every time she laughed at a story he told her. Every comment she made.

The day was one of those that held a hint of summer, but with the full knowledge of the coming winter. The leaves glowed with a fire that burned against a deep blue sky, making a last glorious effort at life before they passed into drab obscurity. Levi shook his head at his fancies, but shared them with Katie anyway.

"Look at those trees," he said, pointing to a stand of maples. "It's almost as if the leaves are glowing with a light of their own."

Katie gazed at them as they drove by. "I don't know which

color of leaves I like better. The orange ones are pretty." She glanced at him. "But calling them pretty isn't quite enough, is it? I like the way you put it better. You have a way of making words say exactly the right thing."

Levi shrugged. Her comment pleased him more than he wanted to admit, and he didn't want to seem proud. "I read a lot."

"More than the Good Book?"

"Ja, much more. I like to read poetry."

"Poetry? I haven't read poetry since—" A sad expression flitted across her face but disappeared before Levi could rightly say that it had been there. "Since I left school. Can you recite any?"

"One I read this morning is about a snowstorm. James Greenleaf Whittier is the poet's name, and it starts, 'The sun that brief December day rose cheerless over hills of gray.'"

Katie shivered. "I can see it in my mind. We've had many December days that have started that same way. But I would never think to put the feelings into words like that." She turned to him. "Do you think I could borrow one of your books to read?"

"For sure you may."

"I might not understand all the words."

"We could discuss them after you've read them, and that might help."

Katie nodded. "And it might help the time pass more quickly."

"Is time heavy on your hands?"

"Without Jonas here, every day seems like it lasts for a week."

Levi tried to steer the conversation back onto easier ground. "Farmerstown is around this bend."

Katie was silent as they drove past a grove of trees and the tall general store came into view. Levi tied the horse to the hitching rail and helped Katie climb down from the wagon seat.

"I want to post my letter first, and see if there is a letter from Jonas."

"For sure."

He led her to the post office desk at the back of the store. There were six letters from Jonas to the folks at Weaver's Creek. Katie blushed when she saw that three of them were addressed to her. She paid the postage, then purchased the items on her list while Levi waited.

As she looked through the different size needles available, he found a shelf with books. Longfellow, Harriet Beecher Stowe, Emerson, Browning, and Walt Whitman. At the end of the shelf were two slim copies of poems by William Wordsworth, one of his favorite poets. He picked one up, leafing through it. He could buy one as a present for Katie, rather than loan her a book from Datt's collection. He asked the storekeeper the price and paid for it, asking the man to wrap it in plain paper while Katie was busy making her purchases from the man's wife.

Imagining her reaction to the gift, he helped Katie into the wagon and untied the horse. He would present it to her as they left Farmerstown, and the trip home would pass quickly as she read the poems aloud to him. But he had forgotten the letters from Jonas. Before he was in his seat, she had opened the first one.

Not looking at him, she held the unread letter close, a

smile on her face that had never been directed at him. "I hope you don't mind, but I've been so hungry for news from Jonas. I have to read these right away."

"For sure, read your letters. You can share his news with me . . ."

His voice trailed off. She wasn't listening. Her cheeks were tinted pink as she read the first letter to herself, her lips moving slightly.

Levi tucked the book under his seat and slapped the horse lightly with the reins, preparing himself for a long and quiet ride home.

## NOVEMBER 11

Katie read the three letters from Jonas over and over through the next week, every time she had a few minutes alone. The weather had turned gray and cloudy, with a chilly wind from the north and frost every morning. Since it was too damp and cold to spend her time where she felt closest to Jonas, in the shelter of the house he was building for her, she made herself content in her room. From the window, she could see the ridgepole and the top of the walls he had gotten done before leaving.

On Tuesday morning, a week after she had received the letters, she sat on her new blanket chest. Papa had made it to fit under the windowsill, and it had become her favorite spot in the house. Up here, away from Mama and out of the weather, she could read Jonas's letters in private. Her morning chores were done and she had a few minutes before she needed to start on dinner. She opened the one he had written most recently and ran her fingers along the words.

*October 28, 1862*

*Dear one,*

    *I have no words to say to you this evening except to tell you how much I miss you. I was thinking today of the hours we spent in the clearing where our house will someday be, and how sweet those times were with you by my side, dreaming of the future. How I wish that future was now!*

    *Our company is on the march, somewhere south of Harper's Ferry and west of Washington City. We are with our regiment, all made up of draftees from Ohio. When I think of the marching we did back at the training camp in Mansfield, I long for those days. The captain tells us we must cover nearly a hundred miles in the next week, which sounds dreadful at this point. But I am certain we will achieve this goal, only because the captain has ordered it and we must follow orders.*

    *The men are in good spirits, even though we are on our way to certain fighting with the enemy. The Federals have claimed the victory at the battle called Antietam, but at heartbreaking cost. Even so, the men are cheering for "Little Mac," as they call General McClellan. They give him the credit for the victory, but do not lay the blame of the casualties on him. I, on the other hand, cannot forget those poor men. Soldiers who were at the battle have told of the sights they saw, and while I will not burden you with their gruesome descriptions, I will tell you that it is something that should give great grief to all who beheld it.*

We do not expect such battles in our future, however. The Federals now have the upper hand, and we are on our way to Richmond, the capital city of the Confederacy. Once that city is taken, then the war will be over. Pray that this will happen quickly and with little loss of life.

You will be glad to hear that I have made friends here so far from home. I have told you about George Watson in another letter. I have also come to know the fellows who camp near us, Hiram Long and Bill Jenkins from Cleveland. Their description of life in the city holds sway over George, as he wishes to live there one day. I listen to their stories with feelings between disbelief and longing for our quiet Weaver's Creek. City life may be exciting for some, but I will be content to see the farms, woods, and streams of my home once more.

There is a chaplain assigned to our company who conducts services on Sunday mornings, even if we have no more time than to pray and sing a hymn. He always starts each day with a Scripture reading, also, for those who are within earshot of him. I make it my duty to be close to him at that time. The words from the Good Book are a healing balm to the soul, as the chaplain says, and a fine way to start the day.

This is one good thing I have learned in the army, that a man does not need to be Amish to love the Good Lord and serve him. The Christian men I am with are devout and manly, seeking to follow the teachings of Scripture. While I can differ with them on the interpretation of some passages, as indeed, they differ among themselves, I can say that they are good companions.

*I must close, as it is growing too dark to see what
I am writing and I am weary to the bone. Keep me in
your prayers, dear Katie, as I keep you in mine.*

*Yours,*
*Jonas*

Katie ran her finger along the final words once more. So far, he was safe. She shivered, cold air creeping up her legs, but she wasn't ready to go downstairs to the kitchen yet.

Leaning her head against the window frame, she could see the Weavers' chimney, with the line of light gray smoke rising from it to disappear against the gray sky. When she had her own kitchen, it would be bright and warm like Lydia's. In Mama's kitchen, the fire was small and frugal, keeping the house from freezing, but not really providing any warmth.

In the winter, Mama rarely made bread or anything else that required effort, and the season always felt tired and heavy. Long enough to make one wish for a year full of hot summer days. After Lydia had told her of the tragic crossing from Germany her parents had made so many years ago, Katie had tried to talk to Mama, to let her know that she could talk to Katie about anything, but Mama had only told her to keep doing her chores.

If Mama didn't want to talk, though, perhaps Katie could do something to bring warmth to the house. She could make something warm and filling for dinner, even if Mama usually did the cooking herself. Maybe Mama would see that fall and winter didn't need to be so dark if Katie helped make it light and warm.

The kitchen was empty, it being only midmorning. Mama

had gone to visit Lena and the new baby again, so Katie was free to make dinner the way she wanted rather than the chicken soup Mama had planned. Soup was warm, but hardly filling with just thin broth and a few vegetables. Katie would make a pot pie instead, with flaky crust and rich gravy. Papa would like it, and it would be a warm and satisfying meal.

Katie built the fire up to bring the oven to the right temperature, then made the pie crust. She made enough for a pie also. The extra crust could wait until this afternoon, and then she would try the recipe Lydia gave her for cream pie. The chicken was already cooked and waiting in the cellar, cooled in its own gelatin. Katie warmed the gelled broth on the stove, and cooked peeled carrots and potatoes in it. By the time she had thickened the broth into gravy, the kitchen was toasty and warm.

She put the chicken pie in the oven, and looked around. What did Lydia's kitchen have that Mama's lacked? What made her kitchen inviting while Mama's felt cold? Closing her eyes, she imagined herself in Lydia's house. Light filled every room. Katie opened her eyes again, the one small window over the sink glaring at her. The size of the window couldn't change, but it hadn't been washed in weeks.

While the chicken pie baked, Katie cleaned. The window was first, and she worked to clean the panes until they were clear. Mama had put geraniums in pots on the windowsill, but they had become leggy and ragged. Katie trimmed them back and discarded the dead and shriveled leaves. She polished the lamp chimney and refilled the lamp oil and dusted the stove chimney and cleaned the soot off the wall behind the stove. Looking at the results, she shook her head. It was a beginning, but the clean windows showed the shabbiness of the rag rugs. New ones could be made, but these would have to do for now.

She took the pie out of the oven and checked the clock. Nearly dinnertime. She set the table, putting the last plate on just as Mama opened the door.

"How is little Trina this morning?"

Mama smiled. "She is growing just as she should. The other children love to play with her and hold her, and that helps Lena get along better. There's nothing like a happy and contented baby to make a happy home."

Katie thought back to what Lydia had said about how sickly she had been as a baby. "Was I a contented baby?"

The smile disappeared. "You were always crying, and I was ill for most of the winter after you were born. It was a hard time for all of us."

"So our home wasn't very happy then."

Mama didn't deny it. Katie set the chicken pie on the table, ready to serve as soon as Papa walked in.

Mama looked at the table. "You didn't make the soup I had planned."

"I had time to make chicken pie, and I thought it would be more satisfying on such a chilly day."

As Mama hung her bonnet and shawl on the hook by the door, she said, "I thought you could follow my directions."

Katie held back the retort that sprang to her mind. Instead, she thought of Lydia's home, and the way she and her daughters talked and laughed together. She wouldn't have that kind of home if she let her feelings rule her actions.

Walking over to the sink, Mama touched the leaves of the geranium plants on the sill. "What did you do to my flowers?"

"I cut away the dead leaves and some stems that were overgrown. I saw a bud on one of them. You may have flowers before too long."

"Flowers in the dead of winter?" Mama's voice was wistful, as if she couldn't believe such a thing.

"Lydia Weaver has geraniums on her windowsill too, and the last time I was there, I asked her how she got them to be so pretty."

"I only bring them into the house to keep them alive until spring."

Katie joined her at the sink, and pointed out the bud she had found. "There's more to life than just being alive, Mama."

Mama stared at the plants. "Ja, perhaps there is."

Papa came out of the barn, his shoulders hunched inside his coat as he made his way to the house.

"Why don't you get a jar of peaches from the cellar?" Mama stroked the geranium leaf again. "They would look pretty on the table, wouldn't they?"

Katie ran to get the jar of peaches. She could already see the bright, golden peach halves in the glass dish Mama had brought from Germany, adding their beautiful glow to the dinner table.

⁓

Even though the weather was unpleasant on Tuesday afternoon, Levi hitched the horse to the wagon. He had determined to take Katie to the post office once a week, and tomorrow's weather could be worse than today's. At least today was dry, even if the wind had a bite to it.

He tucked the book he had purchased last week in the

box under the seat, still in its paper wrapping. He would give it to Katie today.

Waving to Mother as he passed the house, Levi pulled his hat down snug against the wind. Ja, ja, ja, she would like the book. The poems were easy to read and simple in their descriptions, but deep in their meanings at the same time. But he had to admit to himself that he had a different reason for giving it to her. He wanted an excuse to talk to her, to discuss the poems. Perhaps discuss the sermons they heard at church. Talk about the meaningful things of life. Things to keep her from brooding over Jonas's absence.

He would give her the book before they reached the post office, because if there was another letter from Jonas, that would take all her attention on the trip home. The day brightened a little at the thought of her face when she opened the package. Would she feel joy? Anticipation? Maybe she would open the book immediately and begin reading to him from it. Levi smiled as he imagined the scene.

When he arrived at the Stuckeys' house, Katie was on the back porch, shaking the rag rugs.

"Hallo, Levi. What brings you by this afternoon?"

"I thought you might want to go to the post office again."

She smiled, warming him inside and out. "For sure, I do. Come in the kitchen while I finish up, then I'll be ready to go."

The Stuckey kitchen was warm, but in disarray. Margaretta stood on a chair, wiping off the shelves, while all the dishes, pans, and other items cluttered the table.

"You've caught us in the middle of cleaning." Katie took his hat and hung it by the door, while he removed his coat. "Sit down. It won't take long."

Margaretta finished the last shelf, and climbed off the chair, breathless and smiling. "We weren't expecting company this afternoon, or we wouldn't have started this project."

"I thought I'd take Katie to Farmerstown," Levi said. He tried not to stare at the change in Katie's mother. He had never seen her this way, interested in what she and Katie were doing. He had always thought of her as being gray and quiet, like a mourning dove on a November day.

"To see if there are any letters from Jonas," Katie finished for him. "Is there anything you need from the store, Mama?"

Margaretta thought, tapping a forefinger on her lips. "What do you think about getting a new can of stove black? That will make the stove look cleaner, won't it? I was going to wait until it was time for spring cleaning."

"Stove black is just what we need. And don't wait for spring."

Katie had been right, they were nearly finished. Soon the kitchen was back to normal and Katie was tying her bonnet on.

"I just checked the pie," she said. "It isn't quite done yet. Will you be able to take it out when it is, Mama?"

"For sure, I can. You just go on and have fun." Margaretta smiled at Katie. "The pie will be good to have with our supper. Denki, Katie."

As they climbed into the wagon, Katie shook her head.

"What's wrong?" Levi asked, spreading the lap robe over Katie.

"Nothing is wrong, it's just that I don't ever remember Mama saying thank you to me before."

"Your mother seems different today."

"She spent the morning visiting Lena and the new baby."

Levi turned the horse toward the road. "A new baby isn't that special, is it?"

As soon as the words were out of his mouth, Levi regretted them. He never understood the fascination babies held for women, but he knew it was there. Millie and Mother both forgot about everything else if someone brought a baby to the house.

"A new baby changes everything." Katie didn't seem to mind his thoughtless comment as she watched the trees go by the wagon. She shifted in her seat, bringing her attention back to him. "I appreciate you driving me to the post office, but you don't really need to. Someone from the neighborhood makes the trip to Farmerstown at least once a month. They would get any mail for us that might be waiting there."

Levi smiled at her. "Do you really want to wait a month between letters?"

She smiled back. "For sure, I don't. You're being a good friend."

Turning onto the Hyattsville Pike, he pretended to concentrate on his driving to hide his disappointment at her words. A good friend? He wanted to be more than a good friend. Reaching under the wagon seat he pulled out the slim package wrapped in brown paper.

"I thought you might like this."

Katie unwrapped the book and leafed through the pages. "It's a book of poetry?"

"William Wordsworth. One of my favorites."

"Will your father mind if you loan this to me?"

Levi felt his cheeks grow hot. "It isn't a loan. It's a gift. For you."

"I can't accept it." She held the book out, waiting for him to take it. "It isn't right." Her eyes were wide, almost as if she was frightened.

His stomach twisting, Levi forced a laugh. "It's only a gift between friends."

"I . . . I can't. And you shouldn't even offer it."

Levi's face grew hotter. He was making a fool of himself. "I didn't mean anything by it. Jonas wouldn't mind."

"It isn't Jonas I'm worried about." Her face was pale. "You shouldn't . . . you can't think of me as anything but a friend. Like Jonas. Or as a sister."

He glanced at her. She wasn't embarrassed or angry. She was frightened, but of what?

"For sure, we're friends. I don't think of you any differently than I think of Jonas, or Millie. I like you, Katie, but I know you're promised to Jonas. I wouldn't do anything to get in the way."

She looked at him, her eyes searching his face. "Are you sure?"

"Ja, ja, ja." He shrugged as if his stomach didn't feel like he had dropped it over a cliff. "If you don't want the book as a gift, then call it a loan. You can return it to me after you're done reading it." He made himself smile. "But don't hurry through it. Take your time and enjoy the poems."

Opening the book again, Katie turned to the first poem.

"Why don't you read it aloud?" Levi's smile turned genuine as she relaxed. "That way we can both enjoy it."

The rest of the trip to Farmerstown went quickly as Katie read the poems. The little town was quiet on the cloudy afternoon. There were two letters for Katie from Jonas and two more for Abraham and Lydia Weaver. A fifth envelope was addressed to Levi.

As Katie posted her letters and purchased a can of stove black, Levi read the postmark on his letter. It had been sent from somewhere in Virginia, on the first of November, almost two weeks earlier. He slit the envelope open.

*Buffersville, Virginia*
*October 27, 1862*

*Dear Levi,*

*I take pen in hand to bring you greetings. I am well, if a little underfed. I can't tell you how much I would enjoy an apple pie right now, even one of your sister Millie's creations.*

*I don't complain, though. Our food may be plain, but it is not full of worms or other such unmentionables as I have heard of from other units. I'm sure we will have our share of those victuals eventually.*

*You will be glad to hear that marching has been my chief occupation. We have not been near the enemy and have seen no action. The other fellows in my camp complain of boredom, but I am well content to march with no opportunity to use my rifle.*

*I pray that you are well and all is carrying on at home as usual. I should like to help with the corn harvest, if I could. Perhaps next year. I see the corn shocks in the valleys here as we march along. There are farms here in the midst of war, but I am afraid that with two armies competing for the same ground, the farmers won't have much crop to take into their barns. I would say that the farmers won't have corn to feed their livestock, but most of the cattle, horses, and hogs have also been taken by the armies. I do hope they are left with enough victuals for their families, though.*

*Write to me. I miss our conversations about the things you have been studying. George, my tent mate, has no greater interests than the size of the deer he shot last fall. He doesn't read and has no interest in religion or history. Even politics, which affects him greatly, is beyond his scope of interest. Even with all that, he is pleasant to be around and has become a good friend.*

*I hope to receive letters from home in the mail every day but am often disappointed. So write! Please!*

*Take care of Katie for me.*

*Yours,*
*Jonas*

Levi folded the letter and returned it to the envelope as Katie joined him.

"You read your letter already?" She climbed onto the wagon seat. "Is there any news? Is he well?"

Levi spread the robe over her skirt and turned the horse toward home. "Ja, ja, ja. He is well. But I'm sure your letters will tell you that."

She smiled at him, happier than she had been before they had arrived in town. Levi hunched his shoulders against the chilly wind and hurried Pacer along. With two letters to read, Katie would be occupied all the way home.

As he drove, he mulled over Jonas's letter to him. When Jonas mentioned the talks they used to have, it was as if he had shined a light on an empty spot in his life. He missed Jonas more than he thought could be possible, and not having the opportunity to say goodbye to him when he left made his absence even harder to bear. Who else had the patience to listen to his ramblings about the ideas he discovered as he read through the hymns of the *Ausbund* or studied the Dordrecht Confession?

The wind picked up, cold and sharp from the north. Levi urged Pacer into his rocking gait that ate up the ground. There was a storm coming, and he wanted to get Katie home before it arrived. As she tucked her letters away inside her shawl, she shivered.

"Were the letters good ones? Everything you hoped for?"

She nodded. "He's well. The most recent one was from a week ago. I just hope he gets the letters I've written to him."

"Keep writing them. In my letter, he sounded like he was a bit lonely." Levi turned the horse up the lane to the Stuckeys' house. "Expect me next Tuesday afternoon. I'll plan on taking you to Farmerstown every week. That way we'll make sure Jonas is getting regular mail."

"For sure, he'll like that."

Katie held on to her bonnet as Levi stopped Pacer in front of the house. A gust of wind had nearly blown it off in spite of the tightly tied strings. The horse was restless, even after the drive to Farmerstown and back.

"Be careful getting down. I can't keep Pacer still in this wind and I don't want you to get caught in the wagon wheels."

"Don't worry." Katie jumped clear of the wheels and then turned with a wave. "I'll see you at church meeting Sunday."

He waved back and let the horse have his head. The wind carried sleet with it and the icy pellets stung. The horse was in as much of a hurry to get home as he was.

# 14

The wind increased through the night, driving the pellets of rain and sleet against Katie's bedroom window until midnight, when the sleet turned to snow. By the time she woke the next morning, a thick layer of ice obscured the view from the window and all she could see was white and gray.

She dressed quickly and ran down to the kitchen. Mama had built up the fire in the stove, but Katie could still see her breath in the cold room. The storm battered the north side of the house.

"This is some wind, isn't it?" she said, but Mama didn't answer. It was as if yesterday's good mood had disappeared.

"Should I cut some ham for breakfast?"

"For sure. Some ham. It's down in the cellar." Mama gazed out the kitchen window at the snowflakes dancing against the window. "We'll make pancakes too."

Katie fetched the ham and sliced it while the stove heated

242

up. Mama hadn't moved. It was as if she was captured by the swirling snow.

"The snow is pretty, isn't it?" Katie was determined to make things bright and cheery, no matter what Mama's mood was. "I love the way it makes everything so clean and white."

Mama shivered, hugging her elbows. Katie checked the fire in the stove and added a couple more sticks.

"The flower buds on the geraniums look a little larger today."

Mama sat at the table while Katie got the mixing bowl down from the shelf.

"And it is nice to have clean and orderly shelves. I should have cleaned them earlier, but now they look so pretty."

Leaning her head in her hand, Mama closed her eyes. "Stop your chatter. It's just . . . too much."

Katie sat in the chair next to Mama's. "What is wrong?"

Her mother shook her head. "It's nothing you can help with."

"I know what happened on the voyage from the old country. Maybe you'd feel better if you talked to me about it."

Mama stared at her, eyes narrowed. "What do you know? Has Lydia Weaver been talking to you about me?"

Katie's eyes grew damp at the sharp tone of Mama's voice. "She cares about you, and thought I should know . . . about when you came to America."

"Ach, Katie." Mama looked toward the window again, the view beyond it now hidden by the built-up snow and ice. "Sometimes it weighs on me. During a storm like this, it's as if it is happening now instead of twenty-two years ago." She clasped her hands together in front of her as if she was trying to hold on to something. "I don't think I'll ever forget." Her voice had dropped to a whisper.

Katie couldn't imagine that something that had happened so long ago could still affect Mama like this, but she seemed to be reliving the memories of the ocean crossing. Something that had happened even before Katie had been born.

"Maybe you're not supposed to forget." Katie took Mama's cold hand in her own. "Maybe you're supposed to remember until it stops hurting so much."

Mama closed her eyes, shutting everything out. "But remembering . . . brings all the pain back."

"You've never told me about them, my brother and sister." Katie scooted her chair closer to her mother and put one arm around her narrow shoulders. "What were their names?"

"Christian, my darling boy. He was three years old." Mama shuddered. "Nina was only a baby. I can see their faces, cold and gray. Whenever I think of them, that's all I see."

Katie could picture them in her mind, such little children, like her nieces and nephews. "What were they like before? Perhaps if you remembered the good times instead—"

Mama shook her head and stood, shaking off Katie's embrace. "I don't want to dwell on this. Your papa will be in soon and will want his breakfast. The stove is hot, so you can fry the ham while I make the pancakes."

Katie started her task, responding to Mama's orders as usual. If the storm let up, she would visit Lydia later today and take the letters Jonas had sent to his parents. The Weavers' warm kitchen would be a welcome relief from Mama's bad mood.

But the storm kept its strength until almost noon. After

breakfast, Katie cleaned up the kitchen and added leftover ham from breakfast to the pot of bean soup in the oven. She rubbed the stovetop, polishing it as well as she could. Blacking the stove would have to wait until the weather warmed. She sighed as she rubbed at the dull finish. That job might have to wait for spring after all.

Mama had gone into the cold front room and sat in her chair, watching the snow through the front window. It faced south and showed a clear view of Weaver's Creek and the woods beyond it. When Katie looked in at her, she hadn't moved, but only stared. In her lap was the old Bible Papa had brought from Germany, but she hadn't opened it.

Katie huddled next to the stove and looked around the kitchen. It was better after the work she and Mama had done yesterday, but with snow covering the window, the room was dim and gray. Even with the lamp lit, the kitchen didn't have that warm glow she had hoped for. She closed her eyes, picturing Lydia's kitchen in her mind. Lydia's table always had something on it between meals. Sometimes a plant, sometimes a glass with flowers from the garden. She also put a cloth on the table, a bright red square that cheered up the whole room.

Running upstairs, Katie dropped to her knees in front of her blanket chest. Inside were the scraps of fabric Lydia had given her. She hadn't sorted through them yet, since she was still cutting out squares from the fabric she had gotten from the girls. Katie pulled out the bundle, looking for a scrap the right size. She found a dark green piece. It wasn't as bright as Lydia's, but the green was the color of the pine trees in the woods and would look nice. She took it, her scissors, and her needle and thread back to the kitchen and started working.

The cloth would only cover the center of the table, but that would be all right. She hemmed the edges, then pressed it with the iron. She spread it on the table, then put one of the geranium plants in the center, the one with the flower buds. When they bloomed, they would show nicely against the green cloth. She put her sewing things away and mixed up a corn cake to have with the soup.

By noon, the wind had died down. Papa came in from working in the barn looking more cheerful than he had at breakfast.

"The sun is breaking through the clouds," he said as he took his boots off by the door.

"Did we get much snow?" Katie asked as she set the table. The center cloth was small enough that it didn't interfere with the dishes.

"Only an inch or so on top of the ice we got last night. It's slippery in places, so be careful if you go out."

Mama ladled the soup into bowls. "Is it getting warmer?"

"Ja, ja, ja." Papa sat at the table and lifted his bowl up, breathing in the scent of the bean soup. "With the sun shining, the ice will soon be gone."

Mama stared at the table. "What did you do, Katie? Where did these things come from?"

"I thought they would make the kitchen look pretty."

When Mama frowned, Papa put a restraining hand on her arm. "Leave the girl be, Mama. The table looks nice."

Her frown softened as she looked at Papa. "You don't think it's too fancy?"

"Not at all. It's a bit of cheer on a snowy day."

Papa smiled at Katie, giving her a wink, and Katie smiled as she took the corn cake out of the oven. The red flower buds glowed in the light filtering through the window, and as she cut the cake, she looked toward the woods beyond the creek where she could see the top edge of the house Jonas was building.

She looked again. It was gone. Her house was gone.

"Katie, come sit down," Mama said, taking the pan of corn cake from her and setting it on the table. "What's wrong with you?"

"The house," Katie said, standing on her tiptoes. Maybe the trees were in the way. "I can't see the house Jonas is building."

"Sit down and eat," Papa said. "The storm probably knocked it down, but that isn't a problem. It can be built again."

Katie obeyed Papa, sitting and bowing her head for the silent prayer, but her thoughts were far away. Of all the things surrounding her day in and day out, the house was the one thing that held the greatest memories of Jonas. The hours they had spent planning it and their future together. The days and weeks Jonas had spent clearing the land, preparing the lumber, building the walls. And now they were gone.

The house could be built again, like Papa said, but with it gone . . . Katie sighed, pushing down the lump that was rising in her throat. With the house gone, where could she be close to Jonas and her memories of him?

Papa moved his plate, the signal that the silent prayer was over, and reached for a piece of corn cake. "The storm did more damage than to Jonas's house. It blew some shingles off the chicken house and one of the trees on the lane to Karl's was blown down." He cut his piece of cake in half and let a pat of butter melt into the hot slice. "I'll replace the shingles this afternoon, but I'll have to get the boys to help me with the tree."

"Do you think they could repair Jonas's house too?" Katie asked. "Maybe we could rebuild the walls."

Papa watched her as he chewed his cornbread, his beard moving up and down as he considered her question. "We'll leave it be, I think. We have an entire winter to get through, and another storm could knock it down just as easily as this one did. Wait until Jonas comes back, and then we'll help him rebuild."

Katie stirred her bean soup, watching the pieces of ham disappear beneath the surface and then rise again. As long as the house had been standing, she could believe that Jonas was still standing too. But with the house gone . . . She stopped her thoughts. Jonas would be all right. His letters told that he was well and ready to come home. It was silly to think that the fate of the house would also be Jonas's fate. She stirred her soup again. If only she could see into the future. If only she could know he was going to come home to her.

⌒‿⌒

**NOVEMBER 13**

The day after the storm, Lydia rejoiced in the bright sunshine. The storm had been a foretaste of the coming winter's dark days, and she wasn't ready for it. Not yet. Taking advantage of the reprieve, Lydia was spending the afternoon cleaning the chicken house and filling it with a deep blanket of fresh straw.

"Lydia?" Katie stuck her head in the open doorway. "Are you in here?"

"Ja, for sure." Lydia leaned the pitchfork against the wall. "I'm just making the hens' winter bed." She went out into the sunshine but stopped when she saw Katie's expression. "What's wrong?" Lydia took a step back. "Has something happened to Jonas?"

Katie shook her head. "I've brought some letters from him that were at the post office Tuesday."

Relief flooded through Lydia so strongly that she had to sit down on the chopping block nearby. "I'm so glad to hear that. When I saw your face, I thought something terrible had happened."

"It has," Katie said, handing her the letters she had brought. She sat on another log by the woodpile. "The storm blew down the walls Jonas had built before he left."

"That's too bad." Lydia crinkled the envelopes between her fingers. Two letters. "But Jonas can rebuild it when he comes home."

"If he comes home."

Katie looked miserable, leaning her chin on one hand and gazing toward the woods. Lydia tucked the letters into the waistband of her apron.

"Let's go inside. I have a pot of coffee on the stove."

Lydia placed the precious letters on the shelf where Abraham kept the Good Book and pulled the coffeepot to the front of the stove, where it would heat quickly. She took down two cups and set them on the table before sitting across from Katie.

"You know that Jonas is in the Good Lord's hands. We've talked about this."

"Ja, ja, ja. But that doesn't keep me from worrying about

him." Katie leaned on the table. "Don't you worry about him too?"

Lydia started to deny Katie's question, but then remembered her reaction when she thought Katie was bringing bad news.

"Worrying is something we do, whether we should or not. But that doesn't mean we need to. We need to keep Jonas in our prayers and commit him to the Lord."

"But the house . . ." Katie shook her head. "I know it's just lumber and walls and nails, but Jonas worked so hard on it."

Lydia got the hot coffee from the stove and poured some into each cup. "And it's a reminder, isn't it?"

"A reminder?"

Blowing across the hot surface of her cup, Lydia thought about how to say what she meant.

"Upstairs, in Jonas's room, I have reminders of his past. The quilt I made for him when he was a little boy, and some of the toys he played with. The house he is building for you is a reminder of his future. The dreams of the two of you living there together and raising your family there."

Katie nodded. "For sure, that's what it is. When I'm there—" She stopped. "When I used to go there, I would remember our plans. It was as if he was there, dreaming along with me. But now, I don't have anything."

"You still have your dreams. They aren't gone."

"But I can't help thinking that it's a sign. He might not come home to finish the house."

"We don't have any reason to believe that. We must continue to pray for him and trust the Good Lord for his safety."

Katie chewed her lower lip, her coffee forgotten. "I don't know . . ."

"You don't still think about that curse, do you?"

Katie shook her head, then nodded. "I don't know what to believe. I want to forget that it ever happened, but Jonas is in such danger."

"Not all of the time. He's written about some of the things that happen in camp, and the long hours of marching, day after day." Lydia smiled, thinking of some of the fun times Jonas had written about, and waited until Katie smiled too. "He will be in danger at times, but that's where we need to place our trust in God, not in superstition."

"Do you really think he's going to come home?"

A cold chill ran through Lydia. "I don't know. Sometimes I'm afraid he won't. But whatever happens, I know that we can rely on the Good Lord to keep us strong and hope for the best outcome."

After Katie left, Lydia took the letters from the shelf and leafed through them. She should wait for Abraham to read them, but she had to know how Jonas was doing. She opened the letter with the most recent postmark and unfolded the paper.

*Warrenton, Virginia*
*November 5, 1862*

*Dear Mamm and Datt,*

*I take my pen in hand today to let you know that I am well. My health is good, and most days I am warm and fed.*

*Some ladies from a church in Washington City took it upon themselves to knit stockings for the troops, and our company received some of their handiwork. My new stockings are not pretty, and one is much larger than the other, but they are thick and warm. I am grateful to the young knitter who made them. The note that accompanied the stockings said that she is twelve years old, and these were the first stockings she has knitted by herself. It brings to memory the first pair of stockings Elizabeth made for me all those many years ago. A labor of love is not quickly forgotten.*

*Our captain has informed us that we will be camping here in Warrenton for a number of days, perhaps as long as two weeks, so George and I have made a tent out of our rubber blankets. The two together make a warm and waterproof dwelling, and we are happy with it. Our friends from Cleveland have made a similar shelter, so we are ready, no matter what weather November throws our way.*

*Camp life can be boring, but our prayer group is using the opportunity to meet together every evening, while many of the rest of our company entertain themselves with more sordid pursuits. One of the boys, Peter Williams, was a seminary student in Pittsburgh before he was called up and brings many subjects up for discussion. There can be quite a debate between the Methodists and the Lutherans and the Presbyterians about certain subjects, but I don't enter the debates. I only listen and learn. I do miss the discussions Levi and I used to have, though. I look forward to seeing what he thinks of these ideas from other denominations.*

*We sing together at the end of these discussions, and the hymns unite us, just as singing from the Ausbund does in our worship services at home. I am learning new songs, of course, since none of these fellows know the hymns we Amish sing. A favorite of mine is "Nearer, My God, to Thee." When the boys sing it, gathered 'round the fire in the evening, I feel as if I see the sky itself cleaved in two and angels beckoning me to come to my Lord. Even though that is only a fancy of mine, it gives me great comfort as we come closer to the time of engaging in battle. The Lord is watching over his people, and if my time to die should come, I am as confident as I can be that he will care for my soul in his own way.*

*I don't mean to be so maudlin, dearest parents, but I only wish to give you hope and joy, no matter the outcome of my time in this army. I am deeply content, except that I wish with all my heart to be at home with all of you. Pray for a speedy end to this war.*

*Yours at all times, and especially at the present,*

*Your son, Jonas*

## NOVEMBER 16

Rain and cold. Jonas had heard that the farther south one traveled, the milder the weather became. But this northern Virginia weather was more miserable than any Ohio November he remembered.

After marching for three days, the regiment had made camp in a field somewhere northeast of Winchester, and Jonas had little hope that this torture would ever end. George let him know his feelings on a daily basis.

"This isn't what we signed up for," he said on their second day in camp.

Jonas put another stick on the fire. He was trying to heat up their supper of beans before the rain started again. "You didn't sign up. You were drafted."

George shifted his hat forward so the brim covered his face as he stretched out on the soggy ground. "Even so, if we're going to be in the army, I'd like to see some action. The Rebs are right over that hill, according to what I heard." He waved his arm in a direction that might have been to the west.

"You can't believe camp rumors. The Rebs are always over the next hill. But I'm sure we'll see our share of fighting before long, and I doubt if you're going to like that."

"It would be better than dying of boredom."

Jonas took the pot off the fire and stirred it. The beans steamed in the chilly air. "Your dinner is done."

He dished the mess onto two plates and took his under the cover of the tent as a light drizzle began to fall. But he had only taken his second bite when a bugle call sounded for assembly.

George stuck his hat back on his head and took a bite of the beans as he grabbed his rifle. Jonas poured the pot of coffee he had just made over the fire to douse it and took his rifle. The bugle call continued as the camp all around them sprang to life. Jonas and George reached the assembly ground and slid into line while Jonas was still fastening his coat. He couldn't seem to get used to the buttons.

Captain Wentworth started speaking as soon as the last stragglers got into line. "A regiment of rebel soldiers has been spotted by our scouts some two miles to our northwest. We assume they know our position and are maneuvering to cut us off from the main body of the army along the Rappahannock River. Our company will be joining the rest of the regiment in an effort to dissuade them from their objective." The captain paused, surveying the lines of soldiers in front of him with a frown. "You men have not yet been tried. None of you has seen a battle, and few, if any, of you have ever fired a rifle at another man. Remember your training. Remember your objective. Once the enemy has been routed, we are under orders not to pursue him."

The next hour was a jumble of confusion to Jonas. First, the order came to march, and then to stop. Silence was to be maintained, and then a few minutes later, orders were shouted. He stayed close to George and the rest of his company, but as they marched over the uneven ground, the lines straggled and disappeared. Then they came to a road and were ordered to line up along it.

Captain Wentworth passed along the line, instructing the men. "Load your weapons, but hold your fire until given the order. Do not, under any circumstances, fire blindly. If you don't see your target, you could easily be shooting at one of our own men. The enemy will come along this road, and our job is to stop him." He paused, chewing on the cigar he always had with him but never lit. "Do you understand?"

At the assent from his men, Wentworth took his position and they waited. Jonas checked his gun. He had fired it enough during training to know that it pulled slightly to the left and had adjusted the sights to compensate. Hitting the target was easy. He never missed. But that was when his target was made of straw.

"Are you nervous?" George whispered the question, his eyes on the road.

"A little. Are you?"

"A bit. It'll be different, shooting a man."

"Ja, for sure it will."

A soldier Jonas didn't know was on the other side of George. "This your first fight?"

George nodded.

"Just remember that if you don't shoot the Rebs, they're going to be shooting you. And they won't hesitate to kill you dead, or the man next to you. So shoot the enemy. The man you may save might be me." He gave them a grin and went back to watching the road.

In the distance they could hear the tramp of feet on the packed dirt. Jonas felt the familiar turn of his stomach that came when he had to hunt deer back home. He shut his eyes as the metallic smell of blood flooded his memory. This was it. This was the test of whether he was a coward or not. He loosened the tight grip on his gun that made his hands ache and grasped it again. He went through the motions of firing his rifle in his mind. Lift, aim, shoot. He didn't have to kill his man, he only had to wound him. But he knew how devastating a wound could be.

He had been twelve that day, hunting alone for the first time, wanting to surprise Datt with venison for the smokehouse. But the doe he shot had only been wounded. His shot had broken its back, and it had struggled, bleating in fear and pain. Jonas's eyes flew open, trying to banish the sight from his memory. He had put the doe out of her misery with his knife, but the memory repulsed him. His failure to kill with the first shot. His fear of the doe's pain. The smell of the blood.

His hands were trembling. If they trembled when he fired his rifle, his aim wouldn't be true.

Jonas pulled away from the line as he retched. He vomited behind a tree, then heard the first shots and pivoted back to his position.

George was on one knee, firing, reloading, and firing again. The soldier who had spoken to them lay on the ground, a bloom of dark red blood on the back of his uniform. Jonas's feet wouldn't move. He couldn't move. He willed his arms to raise his rifle into position, but they didn't move. He watched the scene unfold in front of him, the noise deafening. Then a man wearing a uniform of brown charged from the road directly toward George, a bayonet fixed to the end of his rifle. George was looking down the road, away from him, but the man fell back, his shoulder red with blood. Jonas looked at the smoking rifle in his hands. His training had taken over and he reloaded. A bugle sounded, and the fighting slowed.

Jonas rushed to the soldier he had shot. Pain twisted the man's face and he looked at Jonas with pure fear.

"Don't kill me, mister."

Jonas dropped to his knees, laying his rifle next to him. A vision of the doe flashed through his mind again, but he pushed it away. "I'm not going to kill you. Our orders were to stop you, and I've done that." He looked at the wound. "It isn't too bad."

"The bone ain't gone? Those Minié balls will do that."

"It doesn't look like it."

Jonas looked around. The battle had moved on down the road. This rebel was behind enemy lines.

"It looks like I'll have to take you to our medical tent, but they'll give you good care."

The man's eyes narrowed. "That shows how little you

know. I'm the enemy. Billy Yank will always come first to them."

"I'll look in on you myself."

"Why?"

Jonas took a kerchief out of his pocket and wrapped it around the man's shoulder, hoping to stop the blood. "Because you're a man, just like me."

The man's look of fear was replaced with hatred. "Don't do me no favors. You and I are nothing alike. Nothing."

"You don't want me to help you?"

"Take your help somewheres else. I'd rather be dead than be beholden to the likes of you." Jonas backed away from him as the man tried to struggle to his feet, but loss of blood was making him weak. "I'll take my chances getting through the lines and back to my unit."

"You won't do that." Jonas might be inexperienced, but he knew letting this man go back to his unit could mean the death of more troops and his own court-martial. "You'll stay here until I can get you to the medical tent."

He tied the man's hands together behind him, trying not to injure the shoulder more than it was. Then he tied the man's feet, using the last of the cord he carried in his pack.

"Stay here until someone can get you."

He spat at Jonas's feet. "You're a fool, Billy Yank. You should just shoot me and be done with it. No wonder we're gonna win this war."

Jonas left the man, picking up his gun as he walked down the road, heading toward the sounds of the battle. His grip on the gun stock slipped and he looked at his hands, covered with blood. He wiped them on his trousers and kept walking.

A bullet whined past his ears and he dropped to one knee in the center of the muddy road. A body lay to his left, wearing a gray uniform. Jonas didn't have to look closely to see that he was beyond help. To his right lay a man in blue. His foot twitched, and he moaned. Jonas crawled to him and turned him over.

"Water?" The man gasped, his face pale. "Do you have water?"

Jonas held his canteen up to the man's lips and he drank as if he was parched.

"Are you shot?" he asked. "Where are you hurt?"

The man's head moved as if it was too heavy for him. "I don't know. I'm just cold. So cold."

Jonas felt his arms, his legs, then opened his coat and had to look away. This man was beyond help also, but not beyond comfort.

"Try to rest." Jonas gave him another drink, then took off his coat and rolled it into a bundle to put behind the man's head. As he did, the whine of a Minié ball sounded next to his ear and the slug hit the dirt just beyond where the soldier was lying. Jonas flinched, then looked into the man's eyes, burning with a light that had nothing to do with his wound.

"Ma, help me," he whispered, looking beyond Jonas's shoulder. He shuddered once, and then the light was gone.

Another ball went past Jonas, and he realized the sounds of the battle were coming close again. He crawled off the road and back into the trees, waiting for the fighting to reach him.

## NOVEMBER 25

With the return of fine weather after the early November storm, Levi continued taking Katie to Farmerstown on Tuesday afternoons. Katie enjoyed the company, especially since Levi had changed in his attitude toward her. For a couple weeks, she had been worried that he was sweet on her. But lately he had acted no more caring than any other friend, and she was grateful.

On the last week of November when Levi drove to the house in his spring wagon, Katie was waiting for him on the porch. She was surprised to see Millie with him.

"I'm so glad you could come with Levi today," Katie said as she climbed onto the seat. "I don't know why I haven't thought of asking you to come along before."

Millie gave her a funny look before glancing at her brother. "Levi said you didn't want anyone else to go with you."

"Never mind, Millie," Levi said, spreading the lap robe over both of the girls. "It's a nice day for a drive, isn't it?"

The sky was blue, but the brightly colored leaves were gone. Dark brown leaves clung to the oak trees, but the rest of the trees held bare branches toward the sun. As Levi drove, Katie and Millie talked about their friends at church and the quilts each of them were making over the winter. By the time they got to Farmerstown, Katie was ready for a bit of quiet. Levi enjoyed talking, but he wasn't as chatty as his sister.

Katie went straight to the post office window in the general store.

"Good afternoon," Mrs. Lawrence, the postmistress, said. "I have three letters for Weaver's Creek folks today. That will be nine cents' postage."

"And I have two to mail," Katie said, handing her the envelopes. She counted out the pennies to pay for the letters.

"Your young man certainly likes to write, doesn't he?" Mrs. Lawrence reached into a drawer to get the stamps for Katie's letters. "All the boys that are off to war do."

"I'm glad he writes as much as he does," Katie said. "It's good to hear from him."

"It will be even better when he comes home, won't it?" The elderly woman smiled at Katie as she glued the stamp onto her letters and dropped them in the mailbag.

Millie purchased some thread and a box of cream of tartar and then they were ready to go. Katie wished she could read her letter from Jonas on the way home, as she usually did, but Millie insisted on talking.

"I read in the newspaper that cream of tartar is the latest thing in making cake," she said, reading the instructions on the box.

"What is it supposed to do?" Katie asked. She had never heard of the product before.

Levi sighed heavily, but Millie ignored him. "It's supposed to make cakes much lighter than relying on the eggs alone to make them rise. Mother said we could try it, but she didn't think it could make much of a difference."

"I'm sure I will continue to use eggs," Katie said. "I don't want to add anything unnatural to my cakes."

"It isn't unnatural," Millie said, then she wrinkled her nose. "At least, I don't think it is."

Katie laughed. "You might want to learn more about it before you use it."

Levi grunted. "You and your new ideas are going to land

you in trouble one day, Millie. You know what Father says about new ideas."

"Ja, ja, ja, I know. But it isn't all that new. We just haven't seen it here, yet. Besides, the storekeeper wouldn't carry it if it was dangerous, would he?"

The rest of the way home, Millie talked about a new dress made of soft gray wool that her mother was making for winter until they reached the lane leading to the Stuckeys' house.

"Stop here, Levi," Katie said when they reached the bottom of the lane. "I'll walk the rest of the way."

After Levi and Millie drove on, Katie ran down the road to the log bridge. Once under the leaning wall of the ruined house, Katie sat on the log she had dragged there after the snow had melted and opened her letter. Jonas's straight handwriting greeted her.

*November 16, 1862*

*Dear Katie,*

*I hope you keep me in your prayers as continuously as you are in mine. I often close my eyes and dream of your sweet face, the peace of the home place, and the touch of your hand on mine. Those memories are so real that when I open my eyes again, I am dismayed that I am not with you.*

*We are in Virginia, and our company has taken part in its first battle. I will not describe it to you, dear one, except to say that I came through it with no hurt to myself. I was forced to shoot my weapon, and I know I hit at least two men, but I pray that the wounds are not mortal. I take comfort in the fact that by wound-*

*ing those men, I saved lives. That is the only thing that keeps me from total despair.*

*Good things have come out of that battle, however. I've learned that the soldier's greatest enemy is boredom. My friend George even wishes for a battle to commence sometimes because he is ready for action. I wish for no battles, so I have looked for other ways to occupy my time.*

*I have made my way to the hospital tent, where they are always in need of an extra pair of hands. I fetch water, change dressings, bathe fevered faces, read the Good Book, write letters, and generally make myself useful. The doctor has taught me some simple skills, such as binding a wound, but don't fear that I will take up doctoring. Bringing comfort to the sick and wounded seems to be a balm for my own soul. A battle wounds a man in ways that can't be seen, but helping others has great healing power.*

*I pray that you continue to be well. In the last letter I received, you gave me the good news about the new little dishwasher in Hans and Lena's family. I pray the babe continues to grow well and is healthy. When I see death all around me, news of a new life brings much joy.*

*Continue to pray for me, my dearest Katie. I remain confident that I will soon be by your side once more, never to part again until we are in our old age and are bound for heaven.*

*Always yours,*
*Jonas*

Katie folded the letter with care and put it back in the envelope. She leaned against the wall of her little shelter.

She looked forward to each letter, but at the same time, reading Jonas's letters was a torture she never expected. To read his words and to feel so close to him was comforting, but when the letter ended, she felt bereft, as if she had just said her farewells again. Each letter heightened her longings for him and at the same time was like the stab of a knife in her heart.

Each letter might be the last she ever received.

# 15

*Weaver's Creek*
*November 18, 1862*

*My Dearest Jonas,*
   *I received your letter of November third and am glad
to hear that you are well.*
   *You are missed here at home, more than you can
know. I visit your mother often, and I think we give each
other comfort as we share the news from your letters
with each other. She is happy to hear of the prayer group
you mentioned. I think one of her greatest concerns is
that you may be led away from our Lord and Savior
during your time away, so she is comforted to hear the
news of the good friends you have made.*
   *Levi has told me that you have asked him to make
sure I have everything I need while you are gone, and
I am happy to report that he is following your wishes.*

*He has made it his duty to accompany me to the post office in Farmerstown each Tuesday afternoon where I mail my letters to you, as well as letters from others in Weaver's Creek. I am always overjoyed when there are letters from you waiting for me when I arrive. The postmistress, Mrs. Lawrence, knows of you and watches as eagerly for your letters as I do, it seems.*

*We had an early winter storm here last week, with a strong wind. I must tell you the sad news that one of the walls of our house has blown down. Papa says he and the boys will help you repair it when you come home, but for now the last wall stands bleak and lonely as a silent testament to our dreams. But, as your mother has reminded me, our dreams continue. The house can be repaired.*

*I am still working on the quilt I am making for our home. Elizabeth and Ruby come nearly every Thursday afternoon to ply their needles to the task. We have become very friendly, and your sisters refer to me as their sister also, because of your love for me. Elizabeth is happier than I've ever known her, in spite of her worry about Reuben. As you know, letters from the South rarely make their way north, so she has had no news. I think of her as a rose that struggled to survive in the shadow of a dark pine tree, but now the pine tree has fallen, and the rose can grow toward the sun.*

*I must close, as Levi will be coming soon, and I must get this letter ready to be mailed.*

*Every stitch I make on our quilt holds your name,*

*and every breath I take breathes a prayer for you. Stay*
*safe, dear Jonas.*

> *Your loving sweetheart,*
> *Katie*

As Jonas finished reading the letter, he folded it with care
and tucked it inside his jacket. He settled back against a tree,
thinking of Katie. The news of their house was disappoint-
ing, but it seemed that Katie was taking it well. He would
rebuild it when he returned home. He would write back to
her this afternoon and tell her of the hulled corn they had
eaten for dinner and the long hours spent waiting.

He had plenty of time to write to her, now that their regiment had reached the main body of the army a week ago.
Thousands of men filled the bluffs above the Rappahannock
River, with a view of Fredericksburg across the way. And they
lingered there, useless. Rumor was that General Burnside desired to cross the river before the rebel forces gathered on the
opposite bluffs, but they were waiting for pontoon bridges
to achieve this. Until they arrived, the army was stuck.

As the dull thunder of cannon drifted from the north, up
the river, George rushed into camp, grabbing his gear.

"What's going on?" Jonas rose to his feet. The artillery
sounded again, the thunder that meant death.

"Our turn for patrol, I guess." Hiram shoved his foot in
his boot as the regimental bugle call sounded assembly. "And
it sounds like we'd better hurry."

Jonas grabbed his own gear and trotted to the center of
the camp where Company C gathered and took his place in
line, just in time to face the captain as he gave the orders.

"Men, our regiment will be meeting with the enemy on the north end of the line, where they are attempting to cross the river in a flanking maneuver. Two Union regiments are already engaged in the battle. Our regiment will march double-time down the bluffs to the river and the battle."

Jonas swallowed. A battle. The skirmish they had fought a few weeks ago had been minor, according to the seasoned soldiers in the unit, and didn't compare to a full battle.

"Make sure you have ammunition and your rifles are ready." Captain Wentworth rode his horse up and down the line, searching the faces of the men. "I expect no less than your best effort, men. If we fail in this battle, we leave the entire Army of the Potomac open to attack from the north."

A bugle call sounded, and Captain Wentworth drew his sword. "Double-time, men. Follow me."

Lieutenant Wilson kept the formation together as the company moved to a quick jog. Jonas followed the man in front of him, his face sweating even though the weather was nearly freezing. They went on this way for a mile, while the sounds of the artillery grew closer. By the time they came to a halt, the air was filled with shouting and gunfire. An artillery shell struck the ground a few feet away from Jonas and bounced into the trees.

"Here, men. This is our line." Captain Wentworth pointed along a small ridge leading from the river up the bluff. "We hold this line. Lieutenants, keep your men engaged at all times. We will not retreat."

Lieutenant Wilson led Jonas and the rest of his squad down the slope to a point where the trees ended, just yards from the river. "This is our spot, men." The sound of firing increased, and he glanced behind him toward the enemy forces. "Get ready as best you can. Pile up rocks or driftwood for shelter and stay down. Wait for the order to shoot and take your time. You want to make every shot count."

He might have said more, but his voice was swallowed up in the sounds of the battle. Fifty yards away, a group of ragged men started running toward them.

"They're trying to flank the line," Wilson yelled, jumping behind Jonas and the other men as he drew his pistol. "Hold your fire . . ."

Jonas checked his rifle. All was ready. The charging enemy soldiers turned into a sea of gray and brown. The bayonets fixed on the ends of their rifles flashed in the sun.

"Ready, men," Wilson said.

Jonas lifted his rifle to his shoulder. The smoke grew thicker as the enemy discharged their guns. Minié balls hit their targets with sickening thuds. Lieutenant Wilson fell against Jonas, and he turned to see what the man wanted from him, but staring eyes looked toward the cold blue sky.

George, crouching next to Jonas, saw what had happened and looked at Jonas with panic on his face.

Then his face hardened as he gave the order Wilson couldn't. "Fire!"

Jonas lifted his rifle as he had been trained and shot in the direction of the smoky cloud. He reloaded and fired again, tears blurring his vision. Had he hit anyone? Was his aim true? He shot again, the roar of the weapons nonstop in his ears. He couldn't see any men. Couldn't see anyone beyond George on his right. The man on his left had been hit and groaned as he rolled on the ground.

The shooting lessened and Jonas laid down his gun, turning to the wounded man beside him. He recognized him but didn't know his name. The man held his thigh, and below the knee his leg was mangled. Jonas used the man's belt for a tourniquet, and the bleeding slowed.

George grabbed Jonas's shoulder. "We fought them off! They're retreating!"

A man down the line heard George. "They're only getting ready for another charge. They'll be coming back, so stay on your toes!"

"Jonas, check to see if any of the other men around us are wounded." George turned back to the line. "Make sure your rifles are loaded, men. Be ready."

Jonas crawled along the ridge, from man to man. Their squad was all accounted for, except the lieutenant and the man with the wounded leg. The squadron next to them had one casualty, a man who had taken a bullet in the arm and was lying behind the line, unconscious. Jonas bound his wound the best he could but had no idea if the man would ever wake up again.

Three times the enemy charged and was repulsed, until Jonas finally heard the thin bugle call of retreat from across the river. The artillery fire ended, and then the gunshots lessened and finally died away. Quiet descended before anyone on their line moved. Jonas checked his cartridge box. He had used eighteen out of his sixty rounds of ammunition.

Eighteen shots fired at the enemy.

As the smoke cleared, the dead and wounded could be seen lying on the battlefield. A man out on the mud flats along the river lifted an arm toward the heavens, and then it dropped. Jonas leaned over the pile of driftwood George had piled up for a shelter and got sick. Groans and cries for help rose all around him, but he huddled behind the barrier, his hands over his ears.

He couldn't pray. He couldn't breathe. He couldn't stand. His hands trembled as he wiped his eyes.

"Jonas, the captain is coming," George said, pulling him to his feet. "Stand at attention."

George's prodding worked, and Jonas stood as the captain rode toward them. The officer's left hand was bandaged, and his hat was gone, but he had a smile on his face. "Good job, boys. Good work there." He encouraged each of the men as he came down the line. He pulled his horse to a halt in front of George and Jonas.

"Private Watson, I hear you took over command of your squad after Lieutenant Wilson's death."

George saluted. "Yes, sir. Someone needed to, sir."

"That is very true. You are now a sergeant, Watson. Your squad will report to you."

"Yes, sir."

"And you, Weaver."

Jonas tried to straighten his shoulders.

"Your bravery speaks well of you. I saw you administering aid to the wounded, even in the midst of battle."

Jonas swallowed. "I wouldn't call it bravery, sir. It's only what I felt I needed to do."

The captain chewed on the end of his cigar, watching him for a long minute, then moved on.

Hiram slapped George on the back. "Congratulations, Sergeant. We should celebrate your promotion."

George grinned at him. "Maybe after we get back to our tents." George hopped up on a log so the men could hear him better. "Time to form up, men, and be ready for the march back to camp."

As the others got into formation, Jonas went to Lieutenant

Wilson's body. He felt in his pockets and found the letter he knew would be there. A letter addressed to his parents, to be sent in the event of his death. Another letter was with it, addressed to the lieutenant in a woman's handwriting. A sweetheart, perhaps? Or a wife?

Jonas hadn't known the young lieutenant well, but he had joined in the prayer group gatherings sometimes. He would be remembered, Jonas was sure. But when he looked up from the lieutenant's body and saw a dozen more lying motionless on both sides of the battle line, he shuddered, retching again. This had only been a small battle, one that might not even be recorded in the regiment's log, and yet so many had lost their lives. And in their homes, all over the country, this day would be remembered only for the grief and heartache it brought.

He would give the letters to Captain Wentworth, to be sent to the lieutenant's home along with a letter from the captain. He could only pray that someone would do the same for him when his turn came.

***

**DECEMBER 7**

Levi sat in his usual place on Sunday morning, on the bench directly behind the ministers and deacons, next to the aisle. Church was at the Beiler house on this first Sunday of December, and Levi glanced around at the gleaming wood floors and clean walls with approval. Mother kept the house spotless at all times, but they had turned the place inside out this week preparing for the worship service. Both Levi and Millie had been happy to help. They hosted the worship service twice a year, and it was the opportunity to show the community how a minister's family should live, as Mother always said.

While Father was sequestered in an upstairs bedroom, praying with the other ministers during the singing, Levi let his mind wander, as he often did, to the time when he would be sitting in the front row of the congregation. He sang with his gaze on the bench in front of him. That was his seat. Or it would be one day. First a minister, then a bishop. Levi was content with his future plans.

And the future was unrolling before him. This winter, church was different with Jonas gone and Rosie Keck off and married. The group of young people was shrinking. Even Henry Keck was absent today, having gone to the services at the Berlin church. They were growing up, Levi thought with satisfaction. No longer too young to be considered one of the men, now that they were marrying age.

Although that line still stood between them and true adulthood. Unmarried men were rarely nominated to be minister when the selection time came around. Folks thought unmarried men were less mature than their fellows, but Levi knew they were wrong. Being married was good for a minister or bishop, for sure, but the apostle Paul had advised against marriage, if one could keep from it without sinning. Still, marriage would be a good step for him to take, and soon.

He didn't glance behind him, but he knew where Katie was sitting, next to her mother and the Weavers. Keeping his mind on the sermons was harder with each week that went by. Sometimes he wished Jonas had never asked him to look after Katie, not when doing so had placed such temptation before him. But at other times he felt that marrying Katie was as much a part of his future as becoming bishop. For sure and for certain.

Thinking of Katie reminded him of Mother, sitting in her normal place, on the second row of the women's side, with Millie next to her. Ever since he was old enough to sit through church alone, the Beiler family had sat in these seats, and Mother saw to it that they followed the pattern Father had set. She was the perfect minister's wife, dedicated to making sure her husband's physical needs were met so that he could focus on his calling. Levi would have a wife just like her someday.

After the fellowship meal at noon, Levi stood by the front room window, watching the snow fall. Folks would start heading for home soon, since the house was crowded. Some of the men had gone to the barn, but it was too cold for him out there. Katie found him and handed him an envelope.

"I have something for you," she said. "A letter from Jonas."

Levi smiled, even though a flash of disappointment caught him off guard. "You went to the post office without me?"

"Elizabeth and Ruby went on Friday and asked me to go along. Even though I had gotten a letter from Jonas on Tuesday, there was another one there already."

Her smile made Levi warm and comfortable. He could spend a lifetime with that smile. "Do you still want to go on Tuesday, then?"

She nodded. "For sure. I don't want to miss a chance to find a letter."

Katie went to talk to Lydia Weaver and left him by the window. He turned the envelope over. The postmark was from Washington City. He opened it and unfolded the letter.

*Fredericksburg, Virginia*
*November 24, 1862*

*Dear Levi,*

It is Monday, and another Sunday has gone by without my presence in church with you and the others. Although, by my reckoning, yesterday was a non-church Sunday. Still, even though I attend services every time they are held, the worship in camp is different from our sedate gathering at home. I do long to talk with you about the different Christian churches represented in our regiment. Nearly every nationality and religion are represented here, and you would enjoy the exchange of ideas. When I come home, you and I will sit down and have a long talk about it.

We ended our long march yesterday, arriving in position on the bluffs across the Rappahannock River from Fredericksburg. The town is occupied by Confederates. From here, it looks to be a fine city, and well kept. I pray it will look the same during the Yankee occupation to come. The word is that we are to wait here until we are able to cross the river on pontoon bridges. I think we could swim across, but I suppose that isn't the army way. And the river is cold, with ice along the edges. Being nearly December, the weather is becoming wintry.

George and I have gotten better at constructing our tent to keep out the worst of the weather. It even gets warm inside, if we remember to keep the flap closed. Although, I must say that my "warm" is a bit colder than George's idea of it. He complains constantly about *the cold. I remind him that it is better than sleeping without a tent, as we hear the rebel soldiers are forced to do.*

*As far as action is concerned, we have only had one small skirmish, as the veteran soldiers are calling it. I consider that it was a battle, since men were shooting at each other, and some were killed or captured. I received commendation for capturing a rebel soldier, although I would rather that it not be counted. I had wounded the man, and only captured him so he wouldn't return to the opposite army and start shooting at us again.*

*I pray every day that we can march from here to Richmond without fighting another battle, but I am sure that is too much to hope for. It seems that I am to pass through fire before this war is done. My greatest prayer, though, is that I will not kill any man, while all around me soldiers are praying that they will "get their man" before they go home. If you never thought so before, dear brother Levi, know that war is evil, and it does evil things to men.*

*The home folks are always in my thoughts and prayers, also. Letters come, but not often enough for my voracious appetite for news. I wonder how my dear Katie is doing. Her letters to me are heartening and comforting, but I wonder if she is telling me the entire truth in them. I am glad to hear that you gave her an outing the other week, taking her to the post office. She wrote to me of how much she enjoyed it, and how she found my letters there. You are my eyes and ears while I am gone. Report to me the truth of her health and well-being, and I will be forever grateful.*

*Take care of yourself also. I trust you with the one
closest to my heart.*

*Best wishes to all,*
*Jonas*

Levi folded the letter and returned it to the envelope, his
stomach sick. He was betraying Jonas by his thoughts of
Katie, and Jonas's trust was misplaced, at best. He must
bring every thought captive, as Paul said in the letter to the
Corinthians. Every thought.

Across the room, Katie laughed, attracting his attention.
She was beautiful, her smile lighting her face, and she was
popular among the other women in the church. Again, the
thought of how perfectly she would fit into his future plans
flitted through his mind.

Disgusted with himself, he turned toward the window
again, the envelope crumpling in his hand. Every thought
captive. He leaned his head against the cold glass. He had
no idea where to start.

## December 12

On the west bank of the Rappahannock River, just south of
the center of Fredericksburg, Jonas shivered in his blankets.
Their regiment had crossed the river earlier in the day under
the constant fire of artillery from the Confederate positions
on the heights west of the city, and they had marched to the
southern end of the city to camp for the night. Temperatures
had fallen below freezing on that December evening, and he
was unable to sleep, in spite of being bundled in both of his

blankets. The artillery had stopped once darkness fell, and Captain Wentworth had told the men to prepare to attack the enemy in the morning.

The word from their commanding officer had been whispered, flying through the regiment from company to company, along with rumors. The fight on Marye's Heights, to their north, had been a bloodbath. The Confederates held their position along a stone wall at the top of a long slope, and the Union soldiers had launched charge after charge up the bloody slope all through the previous day, but to no avail. Even through the night, the poor men caught on the slopes as darkness fell were under the watchful eyes of snipers, and Jonas heard the intermittent rifle fire as they had shot at any movement.

Finally, morning came, with George fidgeting next to Jonas, his face shining with perspiration. "I hate waiting like this. I hate it."

"I don't like it any better than you, but it's no good worrying about it." Jonas gripped his rifle in his own damp hands. As the sun rose, the sounds of the renewed battle on Marye's Heights drifted toward them. Nonstop artillery punctuated with sharp pops of rifles, and underneath it all, the echoes of the rebel yell and the shouts of the Union soldiers. The battle for the heights was in its second day.

Jonas checked his rifle. The Minié ball was loaded, the powder was dry. His ammunition pouch was filled with paper cartridges. The only thing that would keep him from shooting was his own fear. He would have to shoot, if he was ordered to, because the alternative was to be shot for cowardice. So he would shoot and pray that his bullets would cause no harm. The metallic taste of his own blood filled his senses and he forced himself to relax. He whooshed out a deep breath, not even aware that he had been holding it.

"At least we won't be heading up the heights," George said. He hunched his shoulders against the cold wind blowing from the northeast. "Whoever is waiting for us along that line up there won't have the advantage of a stone fence for cover."

"I heard it was Stonewall Jackson, himself, up there," the soldier on the other side of George said. "Word is that he's fearless in battle, sitting on his horse while the bullets swerve to miss him."

"We won't be fighting old Stonewall," George said. "Just the men who consider it a privilege to die under his command."

Captain Wentworth signaled his company to be ready and Jonas checked his rifle again. Once the charge started, only God knew what would happen next. He reached inside his jacket, feeling the comforting envelope holding Katie's most recent letter. All he wanted to do was to return to her.

When the order came, Jonas followed the man in front of him. They ran at a steady pace for nearly a quarter mile before the gunfire started. The man in front of him went down and Jonas tripped over his body. Turning him over, Jonas could tell the man was already gone. He backed away from him and stumbled to his feet.

While he had been checking the dead soldier, the rest of the regiment had left him behind. A copse of trees appeared in front of him, obscured by the haze of smoke rising from the guns. He stopped behind one to catch his breath.

"George!"

His voice was lost in the overwhelming roar of gunfire. He moved to another tree. A shadowy group of men ran past a dozen yards away and he lifted his gun to shoot, then lowered it. He couldn't tell which side they were on in the smoky air.

He climbed on a rock to get his bearings. There, ahead of him, was the company flag, floating above a gray haze. He ducked down and ran toward it, dodging bodies on the ground. He topped a small rise and stumbled again, rolling to the bottom of a small ravine. Feeling pain on the side of his head, he touched it and his hand came away bloody. Either a bullet had grazed him, or he had hit a rock. No matter. He had to keep going. He wasn't a coward.

The ravine provided some shelter from stray bullets and the fighting was still ahead of him, so he followed the fold up toward the sounds of the gunfire. When he came to a tangle of brambles, he had no choice but to turn to the left, up the ravine. At the top, he had a better view of the battle off to his right, and in the middle was the company flag.

Somehow, he had dropped to his knees, but now he struggled up, heading for the flag. He stumbled again, this time falling over a body that grunted as he fell. Shaking his head to clear his vision, he saw a Confederate officer, dressed in a fancy gray uniform that would have been something to see that morning. But now it was torn and bloody, the left sleeve in rags, and the arm it should have covered a bloody mess. The man's face was gray, his lips a pale blue under his blond mustache. The man was still alive, but he wouldn't be for long without help.

Jonas took the man's belt and made a tourniquet around his upper left arm, the way the medic had shown him, then untied a yellow scarf that the man wore around his waist and used it to bind the wounded arm against his body. As he lifted the captain to pass the scarf behind his shoulders, the man's eyes opened. His face was calm as he watched Jonas.

"I thank you, sir, for your help."

The man's voice was gentle, in spite of the chaos around them. Jonas ducked as a Minié ball whined past his head, his vision going dark at the sudden movement, then clearing. He turned back to the wounded man.

"Are you thirsty?"

"Oh, my, I certainly am. Do you have any water?"

Jonas's canteen was full. He lifted the man's head to drink, cradling his head, careful not to disturb the wounded arm.

"I thank you, again, sir."

Jonas moved him so he could recline against a tree root.

"Will you be all right here? I need to find my company."

The captain, as weak as he was, struggled to look toward the sounds of the battle. The gunfire had slowed and had moved back toward the city. Back to the area where the Union regiment's charge had started this morning.

"It appears that they've left you, and you are now behind the Confederate lines." The captain fumbled with his jacket, pulling out a pistol that he pointed toward Jonas. "And I am afraid, sir, that you are my prisoner."

Jonas looked for his rifle, but the captain stopped him. "Don't think about trying to escape. I would hate to have to shoot you after you've been so kind to me. Besides, with that head wound you have, I don't think you'll be able to get far after all."

Lifting his fingers to the bloody spot on his head, Jonas felt a sudden weakness. Blood had matted his hair, dripping onto his shoulder and down his sleeve. Until now, he had felt no pain. But he sank to his knees, suddenly weak, then the ground rushed up to meet him as everything went black.

# 16

## December 23

With six inches of snow covering the ground, Katie didn't expect Levi to come by for their weekly trip to the post office, but when he pulled up the lane driving a sleigh, she ran for her bonnet and cloak.

"I'm going to Farmerstown to the post office," she said, looking in the front room where Mama sat with her sewing. "Do you need anything from the store?"

Mama shook her head. "I can't think of anything."

"I'll be back before supper, but it might be dark."

"I'm sure Levi will take good care of you." Mama held the seam she was working on up to the light coming in the window. After the sad days of November passed, Mama seemed to be better, but was still quiet and withdrawn most days.

Levi pulled up to the porch steps just as Katie closed the door.

"Are you ready for a quick ride?" He held up the lap robe for her and she slid underneath. A hot brick was under the robe to warm her toes. "I'm driving Champ today, and this cold weather makes him want to trot at a good pace."

"Ja, for sure." Katie snuggled under the robe. The afternoon was colder than she had anticipated.

Levi was right about the horse. The landscape flew by as he trotted along the road, the sleigh skimming across the snow behind him. Levi held the reins with both hands and laughed as Champ's hooves threw chunks of snow at them. Katie tried to laugh with him, but a nagging worry wouldn't leave her alone. There had been no letter from Jonas last week, but this week there surely would be. Perhaps several would be waiting for her.

"It's almost Christmas day," Levi said. "Have you gotten your presents ready?"

"For sure. They're all done. I made dolls for my nieces and wooden horses for my nephews. Papa carved them, and I colored them with ink."

"You make me wish we had young children in our family to make toys for."

"It is a lot of fun." Katie smiled, thinking of the excited children on Christmas day. "I knitted wool mittens for the grown-ups. I feel like I've been knitting for weeks." She pushed her toes closer to the brick. "Did you make any gifts for Christmas?"

"I purchased gifts for Mother and Millie. I bought wool fabric so they could make new dresses."

"That was a good idea. What about your father?"

"I always buy a book for him. Mother and I traveled to Millersburg last week to pick it up. Mother had ordered it from Ephrata, Pennsylvania. It's a copy of the *Martyr's Mirror*, to replace the one Father sent to my oldest brother last year."

"Is he the one who lives in Illinois?"

Levi nodded. "He had sent the book to Hosea, but then Father said he wanted a new copy for his library. I'm glad he did, because it isn't easy to find books that he would like to have."

Katie rode for a while, watching the roof of the Farmerstown General Store coming closer. Even though money wasn't scarce for her family, she had always enjoyed making the gifts for her family and receiving them too. Purchased gifts just didn't seem as much fun.

The store was crowded on this Tuesday afternoon. With Christmas only two days away, folks were buying curious things like decorated cards and tiny candles to put on trees. Katie hurried to the post office window to mail her letter and had to wait for two customers who were in line ahead of her.

When her turn came, she smiled at Mrs. Lawrence. "Your store is very busy today."

The older woman returned her smile. "Yes, isn't it wonderful? It's always this way just before Christmas."

"Are there any letters for Weaver's Creek folks?" Katie slid the letter for Jonas under the wire enclosure along with three pennies to pay for postage.

Mrs. Lawrence looked in the cubbyhole where she kept the sorted mail, but it was empty. Then she looked in a basket that held letters she hadn't sorted yet. She came back to the window shaking her head.

"No letters today." She smiled. "But I'm sure there will be. Sometimes the war mail gets delayed for a few days, but then we'll get several letters in one day."

Katie turned from the post office window to make room for the next customer and walked to the door. None of the fancy Christmas things caught her attention as she tried not to worry. Mrs. Lawrence would know about the mail from the soldiers, and she must be right. Often on Katie's weekly visits she would find more than one letter from Jonas. The mail had been delayed, that was all. She hugged herself in the chilly air as she waited for Levi.

But this delay had lasted two weeks already. If he had been killed—

Katie shook her head to stop her thoughts from going that direction. If anything had happened to him, surely Lydia and Abraham would be notified.

Levi came out of the store carrying a package. "Are you ready to go home?" He put the package under the wagon seat and held her hand as she climbed up. "How many letters were there?"

She sat, pulling the lap robe up and pressing her toes against the warm brick. "None. Mrs. Lawrence said that the soldiers' letters are delayed sometimes."

"She would know the truth of it," he said. "Don't worry. There will be plenty next week."

"But what if there aren't?"

He nudged her shoulder with his. "Then we'll come back the next week, and the one after that, until we do hear from him again. Don't worry about something that might not have happened."

Katie nodded her agreement but heard Levi's worry behind his assurances. He admitted that something might have gone wrong for Jonas.

The drive home was cold. Champ didn't trot as briskly, and as the sun dropped toward the horizon, the air grew frigid. Levi and Katie both buried their chins in their wraps and didn't talk. When they finally reached Katie's home,

Levi reached under the seat and pulled out the package he had stowed there. He held it out to her.

"This is for you from Jonas. He asked me to buy it for you in his last letter." His words were muffled in his scarf, but his eyes reflected the same worry she felt.

"Denki, Levi." She took the package from him. The box was large enough to hold a mixing bowl but felt too light to be something like that.

"Have a happy Christmas, Katie."

Katie watched from the porch as he drove away into the growing dusk, then let herself into the house. Mama was setting the table for supper.

"Did you have a good time?" Mama asked, glancing up as Katie closed the door behind her. "Were there many letters today?"

Katie hung her bonnet and cape on the hook, then set her package on her chair as she moved to the stove to stir the pot of soup.

"No letters." The soup was rich and thick, full of potatoes, ham, and corn. Her favorite chowder.

"What do you have there?"

Katie looked at the package on the table. It was wrapped in brown paper, tied with string, but nothing written on it.

"Levi got it at the store. He said it was something Jonas asked him to buy for me for Christmas."

"It seems that Levi might have rather given you his own present," Mama said, slicing a loaf of bread.

"Why would he do that?"

"Haven't you noticed that he goes out of his way to spend time with you? Why do you think he takes you to Farmerstown every week?"

Katie ignored the sinking sensation in her stomach. "He takes me to the post office to send my letters to Jonas and to get the mail."

"Ja, ja, ja. And he has to take you with him? He could go to Farmerstown alone."

"He's Jonas's friend. He's only doing what Jonas would want him to do."

"And how long has it been since Jonas wrote to you?"

Katie bit her lip. The last letter had been dated December 5. "Not that long ago. Just over two weeks."

"I'm only saying that you shouldn't discount Levi and his feelings. If something happens—"

"Don't even mention that possibility," Katie said, interrupting Mama for the first time in her life. "Nothing is going to happen. Jonas will come home, we will be married, and everything will be fine."

"Ja, for sure." Mama's voice was soothing, as if she was speaking to one of her grandchildren. "Jonas will come home. But Levi would make a fine husband—"

"Not for me." Katie pressed her lips together, holding back the biting response she wanted to make, holding in her fears that Mama's words were true. "I'm going to marry Jonas and no one else."

She ran up to her room, tripping on the steps on the way. She pressed her hand against the pain in her knee and stumbled to her bed. She buried her face in her pillow, her eyes dry and hot, her head aching. She was tired of fighting against the fears that tore at her. All the possibilities of what could happen to him. And the certainty . . . Katie's stomach wrenched with a pain that had no name. She was going to lose him. He was going to die on a battlefield somewhere in the East, or from disease. The curse was going to haunt her forever.

When she woke, her room was dark. Someone . . . Mama . . . had covered her with a blanket. Katie sat up, clutching the blanket around her as she got ready for bed. She felt drained and alone. Where was Jonas tonight? What was he doing? Was he even now, at this minute, in the midst of a battle? Was he wounded? Or worse . . .

She lit the candle by her bed and got Jonas's letters from her blanket chest. She sorted through the envelopes until she found the one she was looking for. His most recent letter . . . his last letter. Katie sat on her bed, legs crossed, and her feet tucked under her blanket. She opened the letter and tilted it toward the candle.

*Fredericksburg, Virginia*
*December 5, 1862*

*Dear one,*

*I take my pen in hand to open my heart to you. When I so quickly chose to take Samuel's place in fighting this war, I was naive and foolish. I thought I would sacrifice a few months of my life to help my brother, but I am afraid that I underestimated the devastation this war would rain down upon my soul.*

*We fought in a battle yesterday, against a group of rebel soldiers who were trying to attack us by flanking our northern end. We had fought in a skirmish before, and that had been bad enough. The battle . . . what a small word to name this horrible evil. For it is evil, dear Katie. Have no doubt of that. There is no glory*

*in men lying wounded, drowning in their own blood.
No glory in pulling the trigger on a rifle, knowing that
each pull may take another man's life. No glory in the
smells, the putrid smells of blood and death.*

*Before yesterday's battle, I dreamed of you. We were
having a picnic supper at our house, like we did so
many times last summer. The light was golden, but in
the distance we heard the thunder of a coming storm.
Do you remember, dear one, how I once told you I
liked to hear the thunder? No more. I've grown to hate
thunder. It is the sound of death.*

*I must end so this can go in the next post. I love you,
dear Katie, and long for the day when I can tell you
those words from my own lips. Although sometimes I
wonder if that world will ever exist again.*

*Yours, always,
Jonas*

Katie returned the letter to its envelope, her headache
beginning again. As she turned to slide her feet under the
covers, she noticed the forgotten package Levi had bought
in Farmerstown.

She put it on the bed and untied the string. Opening the box,
she found a lamp chimney, a bowl, a wick, and a glass shade
decorated with green and blue flowers. Setting the bowl on the
bedside table, she ran downstairs for some lamp oil. Carefully
filling the lamp, she set the wick in place and lit it. Then she
set the chimney over the flame and set the shade on its brass
supports. The flame sputtered a little as the new wick took
time to draw the oil, but soon it was burning with a clear light.

Katie turned the wick down and watched as the lamplight glowed behind the painted flowers on the shade. Curling up on her bed, she smiled as she gazed at the beautiful gift. She knew the perfect place for this lamp. It would sit in the center of the kitchen table in her house. Imagining the hundreds of wintertime suppers her family would enjoy around this lamp, she sighed. Jonas had chosen the perfect present for her Christmas.

A sudden thought chilled her, dimming her joy. Had Jonas asked Levi to buy this for her, as Levi had claimed? Or had he purchased it for her himself, and only said it was from Jonas? She sat up, dismissing the idea. Levi was a friend, not a beau. The gift had to be from Jonas.

She blew the lamp out and settled down under the covers. Only Jonas would think of such a beautiful present.

---

### DECEMBER 30

On the Tuesday after Christmas, the coldest and darkest afternoon of the year, Levi Beiler stood in the kitchen of Abraham and Lydia's house, bringing news that was no news. Abraham had invited the young man to sit down, but Levi had refused, shaking his head.

"There were no letters again today."

Lydia lowered herself into her chair as if her knees didn't have the strength to support her. "For sure, there must have been a letter for Katie, even if there wasn't one for us."

Levi shook his head once more, placing his hat back on his head. "Not even for Katie. I don't know what this means, but Mrs. Lawrence, at the post office, said that sometimes whole bags of letters are delayed. She seems to think that we will eventually hear from him."

"Denki, Levi, for stopping by and telling us." Abraham stood behind Lydia, gripping her shoulders. "It's a cold day to be out."

"Ja, for sure it is. I can't leave Champ standing any longer. Katie and I will go to the post office again next Tuesday."

As Levi left, Lydia trembled, then stood. "We'll just have to wait and see what happens next week."

She wouldn't look at Abraham, and he knew she was working to hold back her tears. He gathered her into his arms and held her for a long minute.

"He's all right."

"How can you be sure?" Lydia's voice was muffled against his chest.

"Because he's in the Good Lord's hands. Even if he's wounded, or something worse, he's still all right."

Lydia drew back, her face composed. "You're right." She forced a smile. "You should get out to the barn. Samuel is waiting for you."

"I'll be back in for supper." He kissed her cheek.

As Abraham left the house, he knew what Lydia would do next. Whenever something worried her, she waited until she was alone in the house, and then she would talk to God about it. Early on in their marriage she had told him that there were times when she just needed to release all of her feelings and worries to the Good Lord. If she did that by crying out to the heavens, then that was all right with him. By the time he returned to the house for supper, she would be at peace.

After nearly forty years of marriage, Abraham was beginning

to understand that women were different than men. It used to weigh on him that he couldn't stop Lydia's tears, but now he accepted that they were part of her life. An occasional time of weeping was to be expected, like the Good Book said. A time to weep and a time to laugh.

Abraham approached his worries as he reckoned most men did. He knew the Good Lord's ways were not always what he would choose, but they were always right. He would trust the Lord and wait.

Samuel was working in the wood shop on the south side of the barn. Abraham had installed a small stove in the shop to make it warm enough to work there during the winter months, but even though the cast iron was almost red-hot, the edges of the room were still freezing. Standing with his back to the door, Samuel stood at the long workbench, sanding the new handle he had made for the scythe. Two glass windows provided light to work by on most days, but today the sunshine was dimmed by low-hanging clouds and Samuel had lit the lamp that hung over the bench.

"Levi had no letters for us," Abraham said, joining Samuel at the workbench.

Samuel watched the scythe handle, rubbing the wood free of splinters. "What does that mean? Is Jonas all right?"

"We don't know, but the Good Lord does."

"You mean he might have been killed." Samuel's hands stilled. "You mean he could be one of those thousands of men that are killed in every battle in this war." His words bit the air, hard and clipped. He looked at Abraham. "If he dies, I'll be the one to blame." He turned back to his sanding, rubbing furiously.

"It wouldn't be your fault," Abraham leaned on the bench, looking out the window. It seemed that Samuel was finally ready to talk about his brother. "Jonas chose to go, even though he knew we would stop him if we knew he was contemplating this." A sigh escaped. Jonas. Always so hardheaded and determined.

"That's the problem." Samuel dropped his sanding block and picked up a rag to wipe down the handle. "I should have done something to stop him."

Abraham ran his hand through his beard, taking a deep breath. "You knew he was thinking about doing this, but I don't think anything you could have said would have changed his mind."

"I told him not to go." Samuel rubbed his forehead. "I should have been more forceful with him. I know how stubborn he is, and how he'll decide on things without thinking them through. But I let him go anyway. I thought . . . I don't know what I thought. Maybe that he'd change his mind, or that once he got to the draft office, they'd refuse him."

"Meanwhile, you thought you'd find a way around your problem."

Samuel gave him a quick look, as if Abraham had discovered a closely held secret. "I suppose I did."

"But it didn't happen that way, and now he's in the Union forces, fighting this war."

"He accused me of letting my pride stand in the way of paying that fee."

"Did you?"

"I didn't think so at the time. But Datt, what if it was pride that made me say those things? And what if my pride destroys my brother's life?" Samuel gave up trying to work and turned toward him. "I don't think I could ever forgive myself for that."

"There's a reason why some call pride the soul-destroyer. It is the source of never-ending grief when we let it have its way."

"But I didn't think I was being prideful. I thought I was following what Christ would do." Samuel shook his head. "I don't know how I can tell the difference. And if I can't distinguish between the two, how can I keep from sinning?"

Abraham nearly smiled, thinking of his own years of questioning God on the same subject. "We can't keep from sinning. It's part of our nature. But a man who trusts in the Lord learns to ask for guidance and forgiveness."

"But Jonas—"

"Don't blame yourself for your brother's actions. He took this upon himself and made his own choices. And for a reason I can't fathom, the Good Lord can use Jonas's actions to work in his plan. Leave your brother's welfare to the One who knows him best."

"But I feel like I need to do something, anything, to make things right." Samuel clenched his fists. "Sometimes I feel like I should travel to Virginia and bring him home by his ear, just to save him from himself. Who knows what kind of trouble he'll get into out there?"

Abraham grabbed Samuel's shoulder. "The Lord knows, Son. And as for what we can do, we can pray. Always keep Jonas in your prayers."

# 17

JANUARY 6, 1863

The weather was fine on Old Christmas morning. Later the family would be coming to the house to break the morning fast with a big dinner, but before she started helping Mama with the preparations, Katie had to take some time alone.

She made her way to her house . . . at least, what was left of her house after the November storm had blown down the wall. The east wall still stood, but only because it was leaning against the ruins of the north wall that the storm left behind. Snow covered every flat surface, making the place look like a cake with frosting. Katie stepped carefully through the sticks and debris surrounding it, searching for firm places under the snow. She finally reached her spot beneath the leaning wall. Sheltered from the wind and snow, it was dry. But most important, it was private. The only place where she could be certain of not being interrupted.

Another week had come with no letters from Jonas, but instead, when Katie and Levi had made the trip to Farmerstown last Tuesday, the general store had been filled with news of another major battle in Virginia, and the Union Army had been defeated again. Katie rested her chin in her hands and propped her elbows on her knees. That was the battle Jonas had written that he hoped they wouldn't have to fight. If it hadn't been for that battle in the place called Fredericksburg, the war might be over by now. Jonas and all the other soldiers could have returned home to their families.

The thought that the battle in Fredericksburg had been fought about the time Jonas had written his last letter floated through her mind once more, but she banished it. That was only a coincidence. The reason why his letters hadn't been coming was because the Union had lost that battle, and things like the mail were in disarray.

Instead of dwelling on the war, Katie closed her eyes, willing her memories of Jonas to fill her mind. Memories of his happy grin as he set these walls in place. Memories of that special look he gave her as they parted at the end of the day. The promise that one day, they would never be parted. But a different thought crept in, that the curse was working against them. That Jonas was lying dead in a field in Virginia, or in a shallow grave, unmarked and forgotten. Her eyes flew open. If she didn't keep busy, that vision would stay with her all day long and into the night, as it often had during the last week.

She went home, following her footsteps from earlier that morning. Mama would be wondering where she was.

By noon, the families had arrived, and the house was filled with noise. Even Katie's sisters had come with their families. Everyone was hungry after the morning's fast, and the table was filled with special dishes Mama had learned to make as a young girl in Germany. Papa had butchered the hogs earlier in December, so fresh sausage had a place in nearly every part of the feast, including the delicious mincemeat pie. Katie always thought Mama's mincemeat was tastier than others she had tried because she used sausage instead of plain ground meat.

After dinner, Katie gave gave presents to the nieces and nephews who lived farthest away, since they had spent Christmas with their other grandparents. All six little girls, except for Margaret, who considered herself too old for dolls, ran upstairs to Katie's bedroom to play. The little boys went out to the barn with their fathers to help Papa with the afternoon chores, and the women settled in the front room, watching the babies play.

"I hear your friend Jonas is off to war," Susanna said, her little Barbli asleep on her lap. "You must miss him."

"Ja, for sure I do." Katie didn't want to talk about Jonas. Not today. "Did I see that Barbli has a new tooth?"

But the effort to change the subject was unsuccessful.

"He was in that awful battle in Virginia, wasn't he?" Karl's wife, Mary, asked. "It was all Salome Beiler would talk about yesterday when she dropped by our house."

Katie wasn't sure why Levi's mother would be talking about Jonas.

"Does Salome know something about Jonas that we don't?" Lena asked. Mama was holding baby Trina while Lena entertained little Ruth with some blocks. "I know that Levi and Jonas are good friends."

Mary leaned forward, ready to gossip. "Salome said that Levi brought home a newspaper, and Jonas's name was in the list of soldiers who were missing from the battle."

Katie's stomach clenched, but Mary went on.

"You know that means he's probably been killed, poor boy." She turned her attention to Katie. "It's a good thing you didn't marry him before he left, or you'd be a widow now."

Katie stared at her sister-in-law, too shocked to say anything, but then Susanna tried to soothe her feelings by saying, "Losing a beau is easier than losing a husband. Mary's right."

Running from the room, Katie ignored the exclamations of her family and headed for the door, stopping only long enough to find her bonnet and cape under the piles of wraps in the washing porch. Lena had followed her, and now grabbed her arm. Katie tried to tug away, but Lena's grip was firm.

"Are you going to let a couple thoughtless comments drive you out of the house?"

Katie's eyes blurred. "I have to see Levi. I have to ask him if what they said is true."

"Levi didn't tell you?"

Shaking her head, Katie leaned into Lena's embrace. "I need to see the newspaper. I need to know for sure."

Lena folded Katie in her strong arms. "No matter what the news is, you'll be all right. Do you understand?"

Katie sniffed, and Lena put a finger under her chin, lifting it as if Katie was one of her children. "I know what I'm talking about. Before I met Hans, I was planning to marry a young man."

"What happened?"

"He died when a cholera epidemic went through our area. The same epidemic that killed my parents."

"I didn't know that."

"I don't talk about it. It's part of the past, not the present. But I want you to know that the Good Lord was with me every step of the way during that dark time. And he'll be with you, no matter what has happened to Jonas."

"He must be dead, don't you think?"

"I don't know, and neither do you. All you know is what Mary told you. Perhaps she misunderstood what Salome said, or Salome could have been mistaken."

The sharp cry of a baby came from the front room. "That's my Trina, hungry again." Lena gave Katie another hug. "Whatever you do, don't act rashly. Learn the facts first."

While Lena went to take care of the baby, Katie went out into the afternoon. The sun had shone all day, and the air wasn't as bitter as it had been during the last couple weeks. The boys had started a game of catch out by the barn, with Karl and Wilhelm organizing it. Papa and the other men were standing to the side, watching the game and talking. Katie looked down the lane toward the road, traveling the route to the Beilers' house in her mind. It would take nearly an hour to walk there, and by the time she reached the house, it would be dark. She pressed her lips together, not liking the thought of the long walk alone when she was already tired after a long day.

Her oldest brother Hans walked across the yard to where she stood.

"It's a little cold out here. Why aren't you inside with the rest of the girls?" Hans's tone was conversational, as if Katie's world wasn't falling in.

"I . . . Mary said something, and I need to ask Levi Beiler if it's true." She took a step toward the farm lane.

"Wait," Hans said. "It's late and it's a long walk to the Beilers'. What do you need to ask him?"

"Mary said that Jonas's name was on the list of soldiers who were missing." She looked toward the road again. "I need to see the newspaper for myself, to make sure it is Jonas."

"Will it change anything if you see the list or not?"

Katie dug her toe into the snow. "Probably not."

Hans was quiet for a moment, and then stepped closer. "You're my littlest sister, Katie. I was twenty-one years old and starting to farm on my own when you showed up, so will you listen to some advice?"

Katie sniffed, now cold as well as tired. The afternoon light was bright, but the sun was lowering toward the horizon. "I'll listen."

"I understand that you want to see the list in the newspaper. You won't quite believe what you heard is true until you see it for yourself, ja?"

Katie nodded.

"But you're upset right now. And it's a holiday. Are you sure you want to talk to Levi when you're feeling like this? After all, you won't only be seeing Levi, but his family too. They're all gathered to celebrate Old Christmas just like we are."

The cold air made Katie shiver. "You're trying to tell me that this isn't a good time to talk to Levi."

"That's what I think."

"But how will I know—"

"What? If Jonas is really missing?" Hans watched the boys at their game. "You have to leave some things in the Lord's hands."

"You're right, and that's just what Lydia says." Through the bare tree branches, she could see lights glowing in the windows of the Weavers' house. The sun had dipped below the hills in the west and the world was turning to twilight.

"I've never known Lydia Weaver to be mistaken about something like that."

Her brother was right. She could learn a lot from Lydia.

"If you still want to talk to Levi tomorrow, I'll take you to see him then."

"I don't want to take you from your work. I'll walk over after my morning chores are done."

Hans put his arm around her shoulders and kissed the top of her head. "Don't go alone. If it is bad news, you won't want to be by yourself."

Katie nodded. "You're right. I'll ask Ruby and Elizabeth to go with me."

He hugged her again and went back to the barn and the other men. Katie went back to the house, hoping the others had moved their conversation on to other things. Just before she opened the door, she looked back through the bare trees to the Weavers' home. Jonas's home. She would give anything to have him back and safe again. If only this war had never started.

⌒

## January 7

Levi stood at the door of Father's library. No other family he knew had a room like this. It only had one use, and that was to give Father a quiet place to study the Scriptures and to prepare his sermon. Even Bishop worked in a corner of his family's front room, with a small shelf nearby for his books. But Father's collection of books was too valuable, he said, to leave them in the open where anything could happen to them.

Looking over his shoulder to make sure he was alone in the house, Levi stepped over to the bookcase. Touching the spine of each book, he read the titles. The Holy Bible, the first American printing from 1743. The *Ausbund*, the hymnal of the Amish. A slim copy of the Dordrecht Confession. The new copy of the *Martyr's Mirror* he had given Father for Christmas.

Levi moved to the lower shelf and selected a thick volume covered with black leather, a collection of Martin Luther's sermons. He shifted the other books on the lower shelf so that the empty space wouldn't be noticeable. Father didn't know how many of his books Levi had borrowed in the past few years. The first time, Levi had asked for permission, but the only answer he had received was a stern look. Since then, Levi hadn't bothered to ask and Father had never missed them.

Tucking the book under his arm, he ran up the steps to his room, and just in time. The kitchen door opened, and he heard Mother's voice in the kitchen. He slid the book under his bed, then heard a different voice. Someone was with Mother. He opened his door slightly and the voices drifted up the stairs. His throat went dry when he recognized Katie's voice.

"My sister-in-law told me that Levi had purchased a newspaper, and that it had Jonas's name in it."

"That's right," Mother said. Levi could imagine her quick movements as she hung her wool cape on a hook by the kitchen door. "The poor boy. Missing. We can only wonder what that means, can't we? Levi seems to think it means that Jonas has been killed and they haven't yet found his remains. But I have to wonder—"

Levi clattered down the stairs, interrupting Mother's speculations. He had heard her theories about Jonas being lost in the wild forests of Virginia or captured by the enemy often enough. Katie didn't need to hear them too.

"I have the newspaper here, Katie, if you wish to read it." Katie, her cheeks pink from the chilly air outside, stood just inside the kitchen door. "Come with me to the front room."

Katie looked down at her feet. "I really shouldn't. My shoes are muddy from the walk over here, and Ruby and Elizabeth are waiting for me outside."

"Ach, I forgot," Mother said. "They must come in. You must all have something hot to drink after your long walk." She clucked her tongue. "Go back to the mud porch, Katie dear, and take off your shoes. Call your friends, and tell them the same. I'll fix some hot chocolate for us all, and we have a cake Millie made this morning. Come in, come in."

As Katie and the others took off their shoes and outer wraps, Levi got out the cups and dishes. Mother measured the chocolate for the hot drink.

As they came into the kitchen, Levi fetched a chair from the front room, and the newspaper he had purchased in Berlin on Friday. He had planned to tell Katie about Jonas when they were alone, so he could comfort her while she leaned on his shoulder and cried. He had the entire scene planned in his mind, but somehow Katie knew already. How did she find out?

As Katie sat at the table, she reached for the newspaper. "I have to see if what I heard is true."

Katie's brow peaked in the middle in a worried frown that Levi thought was beautiful. "I'll show you where it is."

As Jonas's sisters looked on, Levi turned to the second

page of the paper and turned it so the page faced out, as he had seen Jonas do. He folded it in half, and then quarters, so the list of names was in the center of the page, and handed it to Katie.

"See, right here." He pointed with his finger as he leaned close to Katie. "His name is at the end of this list."

Katie looked at the name for a long minute as her face turned white, then she passed the paper to Ruby, who showed it to Elizabeth.

"Do you want cream in your chocolate?" Mother held a small pitcher in her hand.

"Not right now, Mother," Levi said, embarrassed by her insensitivity.

Mother pressed her lips together but put the cream down and was silent.

Ruby put her arm around Elizabeth. "May we take this notice with us?" she asked. "Our parents will want to see it."

Levi nodded his head. "For sure. It won't give them any comfort, though."

"It's probably just as well that this happened," Mother said. "At least this way Jonas is no longer with the army."

"Mother," Levi said, his face burning. "Please don't say any more."

Katie stood, her hands shaking. "We must go."

"But you haven't eaten your cake," Mother said.

Katie glanced at Elizabeth, whose tears were spilling down her cheeks. "We're not hungry. Really. We must get home."

The three girls went out into the mud porch where they stopped to put on their shoes and wraps.

Levi turned to Mother. "I'm going to walk them home. This news has upset them."

Mother looked at the table, the cups of chocolate that hadn't been touched and the cake in the center, ready to serve. "I can see that." She started stacking the clean plates together. "Levi, I'm so glad you are a kind and thoughtful son, and not one who would run off to war because of some ideal, or duty, or whatever." She frowned as she stood to place the plates back into the cupboard. "Jonas was very thoughtless to do this to his family."

"He didn't intend for this to happen." Levi had his hand on the door latch, afraid the girls would leave without him.

"It doesn't matter what he intended, does it?" Mother took a drink of her chocolate. "What matters is that the boy is missing, and now his family has to pay for his impetuous actions."

"Jonas is my friend, but you don't seem to care that he might be injured, or worse. Don't you wonder where he is?"

Mother frowned. "For sure I do, but don't lose sight of what is important. Jonas joined the army, which is against everything Scripture teaches. His life is in God's hands, of course, but I think that when you turn your back on God, nothing good will come of it."

Levi stared at her. "Scripture also teaches compassion, Mother, and love. Whether Jonas has turned his back on God or not isn't for us to decide. The Good Lord knows his heart, just as he knows yours and mine."

He grabbed his coat and hat and shut the door behind him. Sliding his feet into his shoes, he ran to catch up with Katie and the others.

"Let me walk home with you," he said as he reached them.

Katie slipped in a pile of snow and he reached for her arm, but she pulled away.

Levi watched her walk on. She acted as if she was angry with him.

"Katie, what is wrong?"

Ruby glared at him. "You don't know? Why did we have to come here to find out about our brother? Why didn't you let us know as soon as you heard the news?"

The snow was soft, and mud showed at the bottom of their footprints. "I wanted to tell you myself."

Ruby and Katie turned and walked on, catching up to Elizabeth who hadn't stopped her determined steps, following a wheel track in the road. He ran to catch up to them again, and Katie faced him, her eyes red and her cheeks splotchy.

"I had to hear about Jonas from my sister-in-law, Levi. She heard the news from your mother." She wiped at her cheek as a tear spilled, tracing a path toward her chin. "What else have you learned about him that you're keeping from me?"

"I . . ." Levi shrugged. He had no excuse. "I wanted to spare your feelings. I was going to tell you."

"When? In the spring? Or after he . . . he appeared on the casualty list?"

Levi shook his head and took a step closer to her. Ruby and Elizabeth had stopped and were watching them. "I wanted to tell you sometime when we were alone. So that you wouldn't have to go through something like this." He glanced over his shoulder at the house behind him. Mother's reaction to the news had been embarrassing, but she wouldn't be the only one in the church with that opinion. Turning back to Katie, he took her hand, and she let him. "I only wanted to do what I thought would be best for you. That's what friends do."

Katie's expression hardened, her cheeks red with cold. Levi longed to wrap her in his arms so she could cry on his shoulder as long as she needed to, but she turned from him and continued the long walk home. She didn't want his comfort. She didn't need him. He sighed and turned back toward the house.

_____

## JANUARY 10

A month after the Battle of Fredericksburg, Jonas had recovered from his wound but was still a captive.

In the first confused days, he lay in a hospital tent in the Confederate camp outside of Fredericksburg, where General Stonewall Jackson's brigade had their winter camp. Once he had recovered from his wound, he was put to work as an aide in the hospital. He was assigned to see to the comfort of his captor, Major MacGregor, who was recovering from the amputation of his left arm. By the first week in January, the major was moved to his own quarters in the care of Jonas and the major's aide, Captain Charles Meredith, and their cook, Private Hiram Norris.

On this Saturday morning, Jonas was changing the bandages on the major's wound while Hiram prepared their breakfast in the little fireplace on one end of the cabin where they had set up housekeeping only two days earlier.

"Captain Meredith, you still haven't told me why we have this spacious cabin to live in," the major said, grunting as he shifted to a sitting position with Jonas's help.

The captain looked up from the report he was writing. "General Jackson selected this cabin for you. It is a former slave's quarters on the grounds of the plantation."

"It is because of your wound, sir." Hiram turned a spit

with slices of bacon skewered on it. "General Jackson wanted you to have the best care." He muttered to himself as he turned back to the fireplace.

"What did you say, Private?" The major pulled the blanket up and Jonas draped it over the shoulder of his missing arm.

Hiram looked pointedly at Jonas. "I said that if General Jackson wanted you to have the best care, he would not have allowed a Yankee to be your attendant."

Major MacGregor caught Jonas's eye and gave him a solemn wink. "I suppose, Private, that General Jackson's opinion of the best care must come into question doubly then, since he has allowed you to continue to prepare my meals for me."

"I'm a good cook, Major," said the private, pulling his short, slender body to its full height. "The best in the outfit, excepting General Jackson's own cook. And I can make a tasty meal out of any of the victuals the army provides, whether it's pork, beef, or shoe leather. Can't say the same for the other officers' cooks, now, can you?" He took a step closer to the major, who continued to regard him with an amused expression. Jonas hid his smile as he prepared a mug of shaving soap. "And those victuals may be sparse and wormy, but I can turn them into something fit to eat. You have to admit that, don't you?"

"Of course, I do, Hiram. I will agree that you are the best cook in the regiment. Possibly even the brigade." He held up a finger. "Excepting, of course, General Jackson's own cook, as you said."

As the captain chuckled from his seat at the table, Private Norris calmed down a bit at this compliment, but he still pointed a meat fork in Jonas's direction. "I ask you, though, sir, what do you think you are doing with this Yankee? He might just cut your throat with that there razor, he might."

"I trust Jonas with my life, private. He and I became friends the first day we met." He tilted his head to look at Jonas.

"Ja, for sure we did. We saved each other's lives that day." Jonas draped a cloth around the major's shoulders. "I kept him from bleeding to death, and when the major took me captive, I was no longer in danger of getting shot for being behind enemy lines."

Norris turned back to the sizzling bacon. "It's your neck, Major, but don't come to me when he's stabbed you in the back."

After breakfast, Norris went to scrounge some food for their dinner. Captain Meredith also went out, needing to file his reports while the major rested.

Before leaving, the captain had stood before the major. "You're certain you'll be all right, sir? I feel uneasy leaving you with only this Yankee to care for you."

"Don't worry, Captain," the major answered. "He isn't your typical Union prisoner."

The captain bowed slightly. "As you say, sir."

Once they were alone, Major MacGregor's expression drooped. "I'm weary to the bone, Jonas," he said, pulling at his blankets, "and cold too."

Jonas took the blanket from his bed in the other corner of the cabin and added it to the major's coverings. "You've had a serious wound and it takes time to heal. I'm glad that we're not marching every day. This winter camp is just what you need to recover."

"You're a born doctor. Have you had any training?"

"My father taught me to care for the animals at home,

and the medic in our regiment taught me a few things to do to take care of wounds on the battlefield. He saw I was interested."

The major waved his hand toward the stool near the fireplace. "Bring that over here and sit for a while. Tell me about your people."

As the morning stretched toward noon, Jonas told the major about Weaver's Creek, his family, the house he was building, and the farm, but he couldn't bring himself to say anything about Katie. He didn't want to share her with anyone.

The major yawned as Jonas ended. "Your descriptions remind me of my home."

"Is your family similar?"

"In some ways. My mother is a strong woman and loves my sisters. I have no brothers. My father passed away in the last war, when I was just about your age. He fought alongside some of your Yankee generals down in Mexico."

"Do you . . ." Jonas wasn't sure how to phrase his question. "Do you own slaves?"

The major nodded. "We have a few slaves. Not like the cotton plantations farther west, but we have a family who has been working for us for two generations. My grandfather bought Seth's grandfather when he first came to America from Scotland. Servant and master worked together to build Tall Pines. They both married, had families, and their descendants and ours still work to keep Tall Pines the place it was, and we hope will always be."

"You speak of your slaves as if they are part of your family. I thought . . . I had heard that slaves are all mistreated."

"That is a lie the abolitionists tell to bring supporters to their side. A responsible slave master would no more mistreat his slaves than he would his horses." The major looked at him steadily. "But you are coming near to the main problem of our peculiar institution, as I see it. We in the South are all enslaved, in a way. The slaves belong to the land, but so do the slave owners. We are bound to it, imprisoned by it, and love it as part of our own flesh." He paused, rubbing his shoulder. "As a Christian man, I would like to set Seth and his family free. But then what would they do with their lives? The only work they know is farming, and the only place they've lived is Tall Pines. Part of my responsibility as the owner of Tall Pines is to care for those who call it home."

"But home is a place where you choose to belong. Your slaves don't have that choice."

"You suggest that I should turn them out into the world?"

"Yes. If they were free, they would be their own masters. They could make their own choices. They could live where they want to live and work at the jobs that suit them. They could raise their children in freedom, not slavery. Free to seek an education, if they wish, or to learn a trade. Free to travel, or to remain at home." Jonas looked into the major's eyes and wondered if the other man understood what he was try-ing to say. "They are men and women, not horses, or dogs, or cattle who need you to look after them."

Major MacGregor watched the fire for a long minute. "I think I understand what you are saying, Jonas. I know that my people aren't the same as livestock. But they are people who are in my care as much as you are, or the soldiers in our regiment. According to your government, as of January first, my people are already free. I pray for their safety and well-being as this war continues. If—and I pray that this may not be so—if the Federals win this war and the emancipation

311

proclamation stands, I hope that some of my people would choose to remain at Tall Pines so that it doesn't fall into ruin. But you have given me much to consider." He turned his gaze back to Jonas. "In the world's eyes, you and I are enemies. We have different ideals and different ways of life. But as Christian men, we are also brothers."

He reached his right hand to Jonas, who took it in his. "I pledge to you that when this war is over, I will do my best to see that any of Seth's family who are still with me have the means to leave if they wish or stay with us if that is their choice. I will also pledge that I will seek an exchange for you, so that you are returned to your home. That may not happen until spring, but until then, are you content to stay with me?"

Jonas shook the major's hand. "Until then, I am content."

---

### JANUARY 30

Katie lit her new lamp. Her usual time to rise in the morning was long before dawn, and before she got Jonas's gift, she would dress by the light of her candle. But now, every morning and evening, her small dark room was filled with light. Katie traced one of the painted flowers with her finger. Beautiful light, warming her with the reminder of Jonas's love.

But nearly two months had gone by since his last letter. As much as she tried to remember Lydia's encouragement that Teacher's curse had no power over her, there were times in the middle of the night that she could only believe she would never see Jonas again. He was gone, lost to her forever.

She traced the flower again, then started her day.

By midmorning, all of the indoor chores were done, and

Katie took the opportunity to sit at the big quilting frame in the front room. Elizabeth and Ruby would be over later in the afternoon to quilt with her, and Lydia would be joining them. Mama hadn't seemed very happy when Katie told her that they were having company in the afternoon, but then she shrugged in agreement. The day was cloudy, with snow threatening, which made the house dim and Mama morose.

Just as Katie was thinking it was time to start fixing dinner, Hans opened the kitchen door, calling for Mama, his voice sharp. When they got to the kitchen, Hans grabbed Mama's shoulders, forcing her to sit at the table.

"Hans, what's wrong?" Katie asked.

"You sit, also." Hans, who never showed emotion, was trembling. He knelt in front of Mama. "I have something to tell you."

"What is it?" Mama started to stand. "Is something wrong with one of the children?"

Hans shook his head. "Papa . . ." His head dropped as Katie's fingers grew cold.

"What about Papa?"

"He had an attack." He looked at Mama, and now Katie saw tears on his cheeks. "He's gone, Mama. He just fell, and he was gone."

Katie sat back in the chair, stunned. Mama covered her mouth with one hand, seeming to shrink as she turned away from Hans.

"Ne," Mama said, whispering. "Ne, it can't be true. Not Gustav."

"Where, Hans?" Katie said. "How did it happen?"

"We were working in my barn. Papa was helping me build a new pen for the cow. I was working on one side and he was on the other. I heard him make a sound, and I turned. He . . . was just lying there."

"Did he say anything?" Mama asked, clutching Hans's arm.

He shook his head. "He was already gone. It happened so fast . . ."

Katie was numb. Papa was gone?

"Take me to him," Mama said, rising to her feet. "I must see him."

While Hans helped Mama put on her outdoor wraps, Katie still sat in her chair. They were gone then, leaving Katie alone in the house.

Papa was gone.

Suddenly Katie couldn't remain there any longer. She grabbed her cloak and ran out the door, down the lane, and all the way to the Weavers' house. She pounded on the door until Lydia answered.

She caught Katie in her arms and brought her into the warm, bright kitchen. "Katie, what has happened?"

Wrapped in Lydia's strong arms, Katie told Lydia about Papa. At some point, she realized Abraham was in the kitchen also, but she didn't care. She clung to Lydia, her head throbbing and her eyes burning. Papa was gone. Jonas was gone. Everyone had abandoned her and left her alone, so alone.

Lydia sat her down on a chair and brought a cool wet cloth. Katie held it against her forehead, and then her cheeks. Abraham left the house, on his way to spread the news.

"I'm so sorry, Katie," Lydia said. "I wish there was something I could do to help you."

"You're here," Katie said, her voice catching. "I c-couldn't be alone any longer."

"I understand." Lydia patted her arm. "We all need to be with our loved ones at a time like this. Our church will gather around and help your family in any way we need to." She gathered Katie into her arms once more. "Your poor mother. Her heart must be broken. Gustav was a good man, and we will miss him."

Katie stayed with Lydia for the rest of the day, and at suppertime, the two of them carried the dishes of food Lydia had prepared through the afternoon to the Stuckeys' house. Every member of the family was there, gathered in the kitchen or in the front room where Katie's quilt had been pushed to the side to lay Papa's body on a table.

She glanced into the room, but that figure wasn't Papa. Papa was warm and gentle. Big and sometimes noisy. Laughing, his cheeks red above his beard. His hug tight and strong. Papa was . . . life. Not that silent form with his hands folded on his breast.

Lydia took the dishes of food to the stove and set them at the back to keep warm. She had made chicken and noodles in one pot, and potato filling in the other, dishes that would keep well through the evening and be available whenever anyone was hungry. Katie looked around at the faces of her family. How could any of them be hungry again?

Mama sat in the front room, in her chair. Hans sat next to her, in Papa's chair, holding her hand. No one told him he didn't belong there. He was Mama's oldest son, so perhaps that was his place. Mama's face was stony and cold, watching Papa's body as if she could will him to rise up and ask for his dinner. But Hans only stared at the floor, his eyes wide and unseeing.

Lena and Mary got food for the children and sat them at

the kitchen table. The room was crowded, and Katie pressed against the walls.

"I'll leave you with your family," Lydia said, wrapping her cloak around her. "I've spoken to Margaretta, but I'm not sure she even realized I was here." Lydia glanced toward Mama in the front room, then turned to Katie with a reassuring smile. "Everything will be all right, even though it looks so bleak right now. I will be back in the morning with breakfast."

"Denki, Lydia." Katie grasped the older woman in a quick hug. She felt like Lydia was leaving her with a house full of strangers. "I'll see you in the morning."

Lydia pressed Katie's cheeks between her hands. "If you need anything, no matter what time of the night or day, you can always come to me. You know that's true, don't you?"

Katie nodded, and Lydia left. Slipping out the door after her, Katie stood on the porch watching as she hurried home in the cold twilight. Lydia waved to someone in a sleigh. Katie recognized the rig. It was Preacher Amos, and behind him was the bishop's sleigh. Abraham had gotten the word out to the church. Four figures were in Preacher Amos's sleigh. The Beiler family was coming to keep watch through the long night with Mama and the others.

Shrinking back into the shadows, Katie wished she could be anywhere else. Anywhere but in the house with Mama's grief, the family's pain, and Preacher Beiler taking over for Papa . . . She had to leave. She reached into the mud porch for her heavy cloak and wrapped it around her shoulders. Before the Beilers' sleigh turned into the farm lane from the road, Katie slipped around the corner of the house and waited.

She heard Preacher Amos's booming voice and Salome's

cheerful one, and shuddered. She heard Levi asking about her, and Millie talking to one of the children. Bishop finally came, and after he tied his horse, she heard his slow footsteps going to the door and then into the house.

Then leaving all the grief and pain behind, she ran down the lane, across the road, and over the bridge to her house. Jonas's house. She crept into the sheltered space and sat on the seat she had made for herself there. Here she could be alone, with no one watching her. Here she didn't have to speak to anyone, or think, or . . . see that silent form in the front room.

A shudder ran through her. Papa was dead. She pressed her lips together. If she let herself cry now, she was afraid that the tears would never end. The twilight was turning to darkness as the minutes passed. The end of this horrible day. She leaned against the wall behind her and looked up to where the two walls met as one had fallen crookedly against the other.

In a small gap between them, she saw a star. One star. Could Jonas see that star too? Was he out there, somewhere, thinking of her?

"Come home, Jonas."

No one heard. No one answered.

# 18

In the three weeks since Gustav's passing, Levi couldn't stop thinking about Katie. When he saw her at church, she acknowledged him with a slight smile, but the life in her was gone. He had been to Farmerstown twice to see if there might be a letter from Jonas, but both times she had refused to go with him. Today she had met him at the door, the kitchen behind her dark and shadowed.

"I can't go with you." Katie had glanced behind her. "Mama's not well, and I can't leave her. Besides, do you really think you'll find a letter from Jonas after all these weeks?"

Then she had shut the door without a farewell.

"It hasn't been that long," he told Champ as the horse trotted down the familiar road to Farmerstown. "She's given up hope. She doesn't know what she's saying. We'll hear from Jonas again. I'm sure of it."

But when he got to the general store, Mrs. Lawrence saw

318

him come in the door. She caught his eye and beckoned him to follow her to the post office window.

"There's a letter here for the Weaver's Creek folks, but it isn't from your friend. It looks official."

She passed it to him through the opening in the wire gate. It was addressed to Abraham, and the return address was from Washington City. Levi took it, trying to stop his hand from trembling. This could only be bad news. The worst news.

On the way home, he let Champ choose his own pace, but the horse had no reason to dread getting to their destination, and he covered the few miles to the Weavers' farm before Levi was ready. Abraham saw him driving over the bridge and met him at the house.

"Have you been to Farmerstown? Is there a letter?"

Levi pulled the envelope from inside his coat and handed it to Jonas's father. "It isn't from Jonas."

Abraham's face paled. He took the letter, then glanced at the kitchen door. Lydia had opened it with a welcoming smile, but it disappeared when she saw her husband's expression.

Abraham ripped open the envelope and pulled out the letter. He read it silently, then looked at Lydia. "He isn't coming home. The letter says he was buried at Fredericksburg."

Lydia closed her eyes and leaned against the doorframe.

"Denki, Levi, for bringing the letter." Abraham took a step toward his wife, then looked back. "If you could spread the word, I would appreciate it. We need the support of our church at a time like this."

"For sure," Levi said. "I'll tell your family first, then Father."

Abraham nodded, then took Lydia inside the house.

Levi did as Abraham asked, making the rounds to Samuel's house, then to Elizabeth and Ruby at the top of the hill. Next were Jonas's married sisters, and by the time Levi left Miriam and Jacob Blank's home, he was exhausted. His news had been met with grief from Jonas's sisters, but Samuel had looked angry, and then frightened. It would be a sad evening in the Weavers' home tonight.

As he reached the crossroads after leaving the Blanks' farm, he pulled Champ to a stop. The next person to tell was Father. As the minister, he would take the news to the rest of the congregation. But Katie needed to hear the news from Levi, not anyone else. He turned Champ toward Weaver's Creek again, and the Stuckey farm.

Levi knocked on the door, waited, then knocked again when there was no answer. Finally, the door opened, and Katie invited him in.

"What brings you back?" she said as he hung his coat and hat next to the door. Gustav's coat and hat still hung on their hook.

"There was a letter."

Her eyes widened, and her fingers flew to her mouth. "From Jonas?"

He shook his head and sat at the kitchen table. Katie took the chair next to his. "It was from the army."

"Why would the army—" Her voice broke as she realized the truth. "Jonas is dead, isn't he?" Her voice was flat. Strained.

"Abraham said it told that he was buried at Fredericksburg."

Katie sat, silent and still.

Levi had expected her to cry. To become angry with him. To deny that the news he brought could be true. But her silence broke his heart. He took her hand in his. "We will always remember him."

She turned toward him. "For sure." She stood, pushing her chair back. "I haven't offered you anything to eat. I can make some tea . . ." Her voice drifted off as she stared at the stove.

"Katie, are you all right?" He rose and stood behind her, not knowing what to do. He should comfort her, but how? What did she need?

Suddenly, as if he had thrown an icicle on the fire, her knees gave way and he caught her in his arms. She was as light as a child. He turned her toward him, and she buried her face in his chest, trembling, but making no sound.

"I can't do this," she whispered after a long minute. "I . . . I can't."

"Do you want me to take you to the Weavers'? It's good to grieve together, don't you think?"

She shook her head. "I can't leave Mama."

"I can get someone to stay with her."

Katie shook her head again. "I'll be all right."

Levi looked around the kitchen. A pot of soup stood on the stove and a partial loaf of bread was on the table. A row of dead geraniums filled the windowsill. "Have any of your sisters-in-law been here to help you with your mother?"

"Mary and Esther have sick children, so they can't come. And Lena is busy with her children . . ."

"And you told them you didn't need them."

Katie pushed away from him and sat at the table again. "I don't need them. Only Mama and I are here, and Mama doesn't eat much."

She didn't look at him. Any other time, he would leave now, but he couldn't. He couldn't leave her like this. He pressed on.

"How much does Margaretta eat? What did she have for dinner today?"

Katie looked at him. "I made some soup, but she didn't want any."

"Did she eat breakfast?"

Katie shook her head, still not looking at him.

"Do you have any bread in the house?"

"Lena brought some last week, and Lydia brought a loaf yesterday. I was going to make some more tomorrow."

"Do you have any eggs?"

"The chickens aren't laying in this cold weather."

Levi sat, listening to the dry cough that came from the downstairs bedroom. "You've told everyone you're doing all right, haven't you?"

"For sure." Katie ran her finger along the edge of the table. "Mama was doing fine until she got sick a couple days ago. It's been hard . . ." She looked at him again, her eyes wide, as if she suddenly remembered why he was there. "Ach, Levi, what will we do? Jonas—"

"I'll take care of you. Don't worry." He stood up and took his hat and coat from the hook. "I'm going home to fetch Mother. She will know how to fix meals Margaretta needs to eat, and you won't be alone."

Katie nodded, still sitting at the table. Levi untied Champ and started toward home. Filled with awe and sorrow at the news about Jonas and the grief that filled the Stuckey home, he still had to admit that he felt a little bit of satisfaction. Katie needed him. Finally, she needed him.

## FEBRUARY 19

The first signs of spring creeping into northern Virginia brought new life to Major MacGregor. He had been the victim of an infection through January and into the first days of February, but as the middle of February had approached, he regained his strength.

"I reckon it's your good cooking that has helped the major," Jonas told Hiram one day as they cleaned up from the noon meal. Major MacGregor rested on his bed, reading a book. "You've provided him with plenty of good chicken broth and spring greens, although I don't know where you have found such items."

Hiram scrubbed the plate in the dishpan. "Victuals are always available for those as know where to look, Billy Yank."

"Where did you find the greens, though? The weather is still chilly, although the sun is growing warmer."

"That's a secret my granny taught me years ago." Hiram looked up at him, squinting his eyes. "I'm not sure she'd be wanting me to share it with any blue-belly."

Jonas shrugged, knowing Hiram couldn't keep a secret to save his life. "It's up to you, for sure. But for all I know, you might have purchased those greens from some other fellow."

Hiram glared at him as he thrust the plate into the tub of rinse water. "The secret is knowin' where to look. Cow pastures is good places, on the south side of trees and fenceposts. That's where the first dandelions will grow. Waterleaf and nettles too. There's plenty of food if you know what you're looking for."

"And the chicken for the broth? I thought all the chickens in the area were gone by the end of December."

"It ain't chicken."

"Do I want to know what it is?"

Hiram grunted. "It's edible. That's all you need to know."

"Whatever it was, it has helped the major gain his strength back."

Captain Meredith came into the cabin. "I have your papers, sir. We can leave as soon as you are able."

"Leave?" Hiram asked. "Where are we going?"

Major MacGregor looked up from the book he had been reading. "You are staying here, Private. The three of us are going to Manassas." He put down his book. "I didn't want to say anything about the situation earlier, since I didn't want to raise false hopes, but now that everything is arranged, there is no need to keep things quiet." He looked at Jonas. "You're going home."

Jonas wiped the last dish dry as the major's words sunk in. Home? "How did this happen?"

"I had word that my brother-in-law was taken captive at the battle of Stones River, near Nashville. The officer who captured him requested a ransom, and I asked if we could effect an exchange." He chuckled. "He wasn't willing to exchange a captain for a private, but I was able to persuade him with some cash thrown in. We will leave in the morning. Once you're exchanged, the Yankees will decide what to do with you."

Jonas swallowed down the rush of emotions. If he teared up, Hiram wouldn't let him hear the end of it. "Thank you, sir. You are most kind."

The major shook his hand. "I'm glad to do it. Now, pack my things."

"For how long of a trip?"

"Four or five days, depending on the weather. We are to meet with the Yankees two days from now."

The next morning was overcast and dreary, but the weather didn't dampen Jonas's spirits. He rode a fine gray horse, one of the major's own animals, and the three of them made good time. Captain Meredith reckoned that they had covered twenty-five miles by nightfall, when they reached an inn near the crossroads where they would turn north toward Manassas in the morning.

Major MacGregor spent a restless night, and Jonas woke often to give him a drink and powders to relieve the pain. He was glad to see there was no fever, however, and the night passed.

Captain Meredith had brought a white flag with them, and as they neared the old battlefield, he unfurled it. Jonas rode between the two men, and their mood was somber.

"Did you fight in the battle that was here last year?" Jonas asked the major.

"I did. I did, and it was a bloody affair. We won the day, but at great cost." He pointed to a hilltop a half mile away. "The boys of the Virginia Military Institute fought there, and I'll never forget it. The flower of Southern youth."

Ahead of them waited three men on horseback. Major MacGregor halted his horse about fifty feet away. While the captain went through the formalities of the prisoner exchange with the Union lieutenant, Jonas watched the man in the gray uniform opposite him. This was the major's brother-in-law, returning to his own world. Jonas had learned so much about Major MacGregor and his family that he felt this man was a friend also.

The major handed him a sack, small, but heavy with clinking coins. "This is for the lieutenant yonder," he said, then reached to shake Jonas's hand. "You've become a friend. I will always remember our time together."

"Yes, sir." Jonas gripped the major's hand in his own, glad to feel the strength in it. "I will too. You have taught me much about the South. Whenever I think of Virginia, I will always remember my enemy who became my friend."

Major MacGregor smiled. "And when the Yankees lose this war, as they surely will, you know where to turn if you ever need help. But I'm sure you'll be fine in your Weaver's Creek valley in Ohio. Give your parents my regards when you see them."

Jonas shook the captain's hand also, then dismounted. Walking across the field toward the man who walked toward him, he looked beyond him to the Union officers waiting on the other side. On the home side. He walked faster. When he reached the lieutenant and his aide, he stopped and saluted, just as if the two months in captivity had never happened.

"It's good to see you, Private."

The lieutenant reached for the sack and opened it, spilling the coins into his gloved hand. He counted silently, then nodded to his aide. Jonas stood at attention, aware that the three rebel soldiers were riding away, back to Fredericksburg. For some reason he felt as if he was among strangers.

"Your first duty when we return to Washington will be to report to General Hooker's staff at headquarters. They will need to be apprised of everything you were able to learn about the enemy during your captivity."

"General Hooker, sir? What happened to General Burnside?"

"He was relieved of command nearly a month ago. General Hooker is our man now." The lieutenant motioned for him to mount the waiting horse and they started the journey to Washington. "After you meet with them, you can return to your company. Where are they camped, Corporal?"

"Near Arlington, sir."

"Yes, that's right. I have signed the orders to give you a two-week leave. After you report to your unit, your leave will begin at the pleasure of your commanding officer."

Jonas's horse had lagged behind the others, but now he hurried to catch up. "A leave, sir?"

The lieutenant smiled. "Yes, Private. You have been the captive of an enemy army, and to me that deserves a few days to return home to see your loved ones."

---

## FEBRUARY 20

Within hours of Salome Beiler entering the Stuckeys' home, Katie finally felt some hope that Mama might recover from this illness.

The first thing Salome did was to make Katie a thick butter sandwich and heat up some milk, sweetening it with sugar. Katie ate what was set before her, somewhat afraid to disobey the minister's wife. Then Salome sent her to bed with orders to not come back downstairs until she didn't look so pale. So Katie went up to her room and dropped on her bed.

Salome's food had helped her feel sleepy and comfortable, but her head still ached. Ever since Levi had brought the news of Jonas's death, her temples had throbbed. After he had left, Mama had called to her, asking what he had wanted. When Katie told her the news, Mama had patted her hand.

"It's just as well that you know now. You have your life ahead of you. You'll find someone else." Then Mama had coughed until she could barely breathe.

Katie had been so thankful when Salome had arrived an hour later. Levi had brought in boxes of food, and Salome had taken charge.

"Jonas can't be dead," she said as she lay on her bed, whispering to the cold lamp beside her. "He can't be." She fell asleep and had strange dreams about thunder and children and Levi. But through them all, she saw Jonas's face in the background, smiling as he watched her.

When she woke, the sun was shining as if spring had come. Katie sat up in bed, ready to run downstairs, but then heard voices in the kitchen and remembered that Salome was there. She dressed slowly, putting on a clean dress. She couldn't remember the last time she had changed her dress. Couldn't remember the last time she had washed the laundry.

Salome's voice drifted up the stairway. "I'm glad you're doing better today, Margaretta. That cough can get you down, can't it?"

"I'm not sure what you gave me last night, but it helped the cough go away. I slept better than I have since . . . since we lost Gustav."

That was Mama's voice. Katie froze with her hair halfway up and a hairpin in her hand. She hadn't heard Mama mention Papa's name since the funeral.

"That elixir is an old family recipe. I'll write it down for you. It works as well on children as it does on adults too. You just give them less. No more than a teaspoon."

Katie finished putting her hair up and tied her shoes.

"Is it true, what Katie told me yesterday?" Mama said. "About Jonas Weaver?"

"Ach, ja, for sure and certain. Poor Lydia and Abraham, to lose their son to the war." Katie could see her in her mind, shaking her head. "And before he joined the church too. I guess that's what comes of turning away from the teachings of the Good Book."

"It is too bad. He was a bright and promising boy. I always thought he would make a good husband for Katie, and I should have told him so."

Katie bit her thumbnail. She should go downstairs and join the older women and stop eavesdropping, but she had never heard Mama confiding in anyone like this, not even Lydia. At least, she had never talked like this when Katie was around.

"Well, now that it has happened, Katie can go on with her life, ja? Maybe she'll even notice my Levi."

With that, Katie knew she had to go down to the kitchen. At least that would stop them from talking about her.

Salome had a big smile on her face as Katie joined them. "And here's our Katie. Sit down, dear. Dinner is almost ready. You must be hungry."

As soon as Katie had caught the aroma coming from the oven when she came down the steps, her stomach had started growling. "For sure, I am. What can I help with?"

"You can slice the bread." Salome put her hand on Mama's shoulder as she tried to stand. "Not you, Margaretta. You might be feeling better, but that cough will come back with a vengeance if you try to do too much. As soon as dinner is over, you're going back to bed for a nice long nap."

"All I've been doing is sleeping."

"And that's what will cure your ills, both your body and your heart." Salome opened the oven and took out a chicken pie. "That goes for you too, dear." She put the pie on the table and wrapped an arm around Katie's shoulders. "You have a heartache that only time can heal." She gave her a quick hug, then turned back to the stove. "I remember when my dear Amos lost his first wife, it took nearly two months for him to start thinking about love again."

Katie exchanged glances with Mama. Only two months?

Salome went on, not aware of them. "And his three little boys without a mother." She tsked her tongue as she took three plates from the shelf. "It was a good thing I was there for all four of them."

"This was before you lived in Ohio, wasn't it?" Mama asked.

"Ach, for sure. We lived in Pennsylvania. Amos was heartbroken when he lost his wife." Salome moved around the table, putting a fork and knife at each place. "He hired me to take care of his boys and the house, but it wasn't long before we knew we were made for each other." She gave both Katie and Mama a happy smile. "The same can happen for both of you too."

By the time dinner was finished and Mama was in bed for her nap, Katie's headache was back and throbbing. Salome liked to talk and had continued without a pause all through the meal.

"I'm going for a walk," she told Salome, "and I'll hang the dish towels on the line while I'm outside."

Salome was getting the big mixing bowl down from the shelf. "That's fine, dear. Don't catch cold, and don't go too far. I think Levi is going to stop by this afternoon."

Once Katie escaped from the house, she knew just where she was going. She hadn't been to her house . . . Jonas's house . . . since the day Papa died. The sun was causing the snow to soften, but it was still deep. Katie hadn't noticed that it had snowed during the last couple weeks, but then she hadn't noticed much at all. Her feet sank into the deep snow, and soon her shoes were wet with melting snow. She continued on until she had crossed the wooden bridge Jonas had built and crept into the safe corner. The log she used for a seat was dry on top, and Katie sat, enjoying the quiet. All around her melting snow dripped from the trees, and she could hear other sounds in the woods. The squirrels chattered to each other as they foraged for food in the afternoon sun, and chickadees cheeped in their endless quest for insects in the sun-warmed bark of the trees.

Here in this safe place, Jonas seemed to enfold her in his arms. Here, her dreams lived on, even if they were empty dreams.

She heard a wagon on the road, and then it stopped.

"Katie?"

Levi was calling her. He must have seen her footprints in the snow. She came out of her hiding place and walked back along the trail she had made. Now that Mama was feeling better, she could come here more often. Here, Jonas would live on.

"Katie, are you all right?" He was standing in the wagon box, watching her walk toward him. "Does Mother know you're out here?"

He helped her climb up beside him, then clicked his tongue to start Champ going toward her house again.

"For sure she does." Katie looked behind her, watching as

they drew away from the clearing. "I told her I was going for a walk." She felt better than she had, but she was still numb, as if part of her had died when she learned Jonas was missing. Ever since that day, she felt like nothing could touch her. Even the news of Jonas's death had only felt like a small bump.

Champ stopped by the back porch, but Levi didn't move.

"I've made a decision, Katie." He turned toward her and took her hand in his. "With Jonas . . . gone, and your father gone too, you need someone to take care of you."

She looked at his hand holding hers. Levi was capable, but soft. His hand was smooth, clinging, chapped red from the cold.

"I love you, Katie."

Katie looked into his face, which was hopeful and smiling. How could he smile?

"I like you too, Levi."

His smile grew broader. "I want to be the one to take care of you. I want you to be my wife. Say you'll marry me, Katie. Won't you say you will?"

Katie pulled her hand away from his. What other choice did she have?

She looked at the house in front of her, empty without Papa's presence. She missed his laugh. She even missed his fiery temper. Rubbing her forehead, she thought of her future. Karl and his family were planning to move into the big house as soon as the weather settled into spring, and she and Mama would move into the little house Karl had built when he and Mary set up housekeeping. In the trees, away from the road, Karl's house would be her home while she cared for Mama through the coming years. The thought made her head pound.

And then what? She would never love another man. Never.

But Levi had been a good friend, and the curse didn't seem to touch him. As a woman alone, she would always be dependent on her family. Never having her own home and children. At least with Levi, she would have a future.

She sighed, making the choice she loathed, but it was better than the alternative.

"Ja, Levi. I guess I'll marry you."

Levi enveloped her in a hug. "You've made me so happy."

She felt nothing.

"When can we have the wedding? Will next month be too soon?"

Katie heard Papa's voice, when she'd told him she was going to marry Jonas. She shook her head. "That's too soon. I'm too young, Papa said."

Levi looked disappointed, but then smiled again. "When?"

Climbing down from the wagon, Katie paused. Thinking. Not August. No, not August.

"May, I think. After my birthday. Papa would have liked that."

"Mother will be so happy for us. I'll tell her right away."

She walked onto the porch with Levi following her, carrying the box of groceries he was bringing to Salome. He held the box in one hand as he reached around her to open the door. As his hand grasped the doorknob, she looked into his face. His happy, pasty, doughy face. In her imagination, she saw Teacher Robinson's face instead. The leer, the double chin, the narrowed eyes. She started to tremble. She shook her head.

"I can't marry you. I'm sorry, Levi, but I can't." She stepped away from the door.

Levi let the door close and set the box on the bench. He reached for her hand, but she pulled away.

"But I thought—" He stopped and took a step back. "I thought you liked me."

Tears trickled down Katie's cheeks. She was finally crying, finally feeling something.

"I do like you, but I still love Jonas." A hard rock formed in her chest, a dam waiting to break. She took a deep breath and it ended up as a sob. "I still love Jonas, and I could never make a life with anyone else."

She left him, jumping off the porch. She ran all the way back to her hiding place in the ruined house and let the tears fall, groaning and sobbing until she was hoarse and spent. She would always love Jonas, and no one else. Only Jonas.

---

## February 24

Jonas paused as he reached the corner at the crossroads of the Hyattsville Pike and Weaver's Creek road. He was almost home. His uniform had turned some heads when he stopped at the store in Farmerstown to purchase some gifts.

"Where are you heading, soldier?" the storekeeper had asked.

"Weaver's Creek to see my folks."

The storekeeper and his wife exchanged glances as if they couldn't believe it. He supposed they were surprised to see an Amish man wearing a uniform. He could hardly wait to change into Plain clothes, but before that, he had to see Katie.

He walked faster after leaving the Hyattsville Pike and then started trotting up the hill toward the Stuckeys' farm. At the spot where the farm lane met the road, Jonas paused just long enough to drink in the sight of the home place in the distance. When he had returned to his unit last week, Captain Wentworth had been more surprised than anyone to see him and told how he had been reported dead.

And how the official letter had been sent to his family.

For nearly a month, they had thought he was dead. Not only his family, but Katie too. He ran the rest of the way to the Stuckeys' house, then came to a halt when he saw her.

She was at the clothesline, hanging up towels. Something he had seen her do so often in his memory over the last four months. He watched her as if she was another dream, but this was real. As Katie turned to go back into the house, she glanced his way. She stopped and stared, then ran toward him.

He met her, catching her in his arms and swinging her around. She clung to him, then pulled away.

"Put me down," she said, kicking her feet. He set her on the ground and she looked at him, holding his face between her hands. "Is it really you? Jonas? It's really you?"

"Ja, for sure and certain." He couldn't stop grinning. He kissed her, then kissed her again, pulling her close. "I'm here, Katie. I couldn't write to you, because I would get here sooner than any letter."

"Are you home for good?"

"Only a few days, but we'll make the most of them, won't we?"

"Do Abraham and Lydia know you're here?"

He shook his head. He couldn't take his eyes off her. She was thinner than he remembered.

"I need to see them next, but I'm not going without you. Tell your parents you'll be back later."

Her face fell. "You don't know . . . Papa passed away."

Jonas pulled her close, holding her tight. He had expected to see death, and he had seen much more than anyone should ever see in their lifetime . . . but Gustav? Dead?

"Ach, Katie. I'm so sorry."

Her voice was muffled in his jacket. "Somehow, hearing you say that makes it better." She pulled back to look at his face again. "I've missed you so much." Her fingers stroked his cheeks. "So much."

He kissed her yet again.

After breaking the news of his return to Margaretta, he took Katie's hand and they ran together down the road to the stone bridge. As they crossed the creek, Jonas looked at the house and barn with a new feeling of satisfaction. He had never seen such a beautiful sight.

Datt had seen them and came running from the house. Jonas met him with a big hug, then stood back, both of them grinning.

"Your mother!" Datt said, as if he had just remembered her. He called her. "Lydia!"

The rest of the afternoon was a joyous reunion as Datt told Samuel he was there, then young Bram went to tell the rest of the family. And through the entire time, he never let go of Katie's hand. He would have to leave her again soon enough, but not yet.

Mamm and the girls fixed a feast of ham, potatoes, biscuits, and gravy . . . Jonas lost track of all the food that covered the table. As they ate, Jonas told the story of his captivity and his time with the Confederates.

"You're still wearing your uniform," Datt said. "Do you have to return?"

Jonas squeezed Katie's hand. "Ja, in a few days."

Sounds of dismay went around the room. Samuel stared at the floor.

"But it won't be the same." He smiled at Katie. He hadn't even told her this news yet. "When I go back, I won't be in combat. There are many hospitals in and around Washington City to care for the sick and wounded soldiers. My captain recommended me for training as a medical officer, and I'll be working there." He held Datt's gaze. "I'll be healing instead of hurting. I'll be helping those who can to go home to their families, and I'll be there to comfort those who will never live to see their homes again. It's work that I know the Good Lord has prepared me for."

Jonas looked at Samuel. "It's why I was supposed to go to the army instead of Samuel, I think. This is what God was calling me to do."

Later, Samuel cornered him away from the rest of the family. "Jonas, I don't know what to say."

"Don't say anything. You don't need to."

"You forgive me, then?"

Jonas smiled. "Forgive you for what? Doing what God laid on your heart to do? For sure, if you need my forgiveness, you have it."

Taking a step back, Samuel looked at Jonas from head to toe. "I think you've grown some since you went away."

"I'm not any taller."

"There is more than one way to grow."

Jonas grinned at his brother and pulled him close for a hug. It felt good. So good.

When darkness fell, Jonas walked Katie home. "It's been a good day." He sighed, pulling Katie's hand into his elbow. He couldn't remember ever being more content than this minute.

"It's been a wonderful day." Katie leaned her head against his shoulder. "I know the next week will fly by, though."

"Ja, for sure it will. All too soon I'll need to leave for Washington again."

"But this time you'll write to me every day?"

He squeezed her hand. "For sure and certain I will. Maybe twice a day."

"I'm afraid you'll be too busy for that."

Jonas thought of the crowded hospitals he had seen while he had been in Washington. "You're right about that. What we need is an end to this war."

"How soon do you think it will happen?"

"Every day I think it can't last much longer. So many men have died, but the generals just keep throwing more soldiers into the battles. If the Union army can reach Richmond, then the war would be over, but the South is determined to win."

"What will happen when the winter is over?" Katie stopped walking as they reached her house and turned toward him.

Jonas encircled her in his arms and drew her close. "Only God knows that. But I know he hears our prayers." He bent his head to see into her eyes. "And one thing I do know is that I love you. And when this war is over, I will be coming home and marrying you without delay."

She flung her arms around his neck and clung to him as he kissed her. A kiss that held all his promises of their forever together.

Read on for an Excerpt of

# JAN DREXLER'S

Next Book in THE AMISH OF WEAVER'S CREEK Series

# 1

"How much farther, Daed?"

Gideon Fisher kept his eyes on his team's ears rather than answering his daughter immediately. At eight years old, Roseanna had taken on a burden much too heavy for her fragile shoulders but hearing him admit that he wasn't sure where they were wouldn't help ease her mind. Clearing his throat, hoping a bit of cheer would be conveyed through his voice, he turned and smiled at the children.

"It can't be too far now." His smile faltered when he saw Lovinia lying on her cot in the back of the wagon, her face pale. If he didn't find a safe place for his family soon, his wife might not survive this illness. He forced the smile to return. "The folks at the store back there said that we'd find quite a few Amish settlers up ahead, along Weaver's Creek."

Three-year-old Ezra stepped over his sisters in the wagon bed to join Gideon on the seat. Grasping his son's trousers, Gideon helped him climb up beside him. He smiled at

Sophia. At six years old, she worried more than the others about her mother's illness. While Roseanna cared for the baby, Sophia had kept Ezra occupied on the long journey from Maryland. But her little face showed the strain of the last few months with a pinching tension around her mouth that made her look much older than her years.

As Gideon urged the horses toward the crossroad ahead, he tucked Ezra close to his side. That must be the road the Englisch woman at the store in Farmerstown had spoken of. The ford through the small creek was just as she had described, and the road on the other side would take them to their destination. After crossing the ford and making the turn onto the smaller road, Gideon halted the exhausted team.

"Just resting the horses for a few minutes," Gideon told the children.

"Down?" Ezra asked, peering up at him.

At the same time, Sophia stood and plucked his sleeve. "There are flowers in the meadow, Daed. Can we pick some?"

Gideon wrapped the reins around the brake handle. "Ja, for sure. All of you should get out and run for a little. I'll stay with Mamm and the baby."

While the children ran through the meadow, Gideon sat next to Lovinia in the wagon bed, eight-month-old Daniel on his lap. His dear wife smiled at him and patted his arm.

"We're almost there?" Her voice was nearly a whisper.

When he clasped her hand, it was hot and dry. "I hope so. The woman who gave me the directions wasn't very clear about exactly where the Amish settlement is."

"Once we stop traveling—" She coughed, turning on her side as he supported her.

When the coughing spell ended, he finished her sentence.

"We'll find a place to stay and good food to eat. And then you'll get better."

The children's laughter made Lovinia smile. "You'll make a new home for us, husband."

He touched her cheek with the back of his hand. "We'll make a new home together, far from the war."

As Lovinia's eyes closed, Gideon stroked her cheek. How long could she go on like this, with every bit of her strength consumed by fever? Daniel fussed, rubbing his eyes. He was hungry again. They were all hungry.

*Dear Gott.* Gideon faltered. The words wouldn't come. What could he pray that he hadn't already said?

During the weeks he had been held captive by the Confederate army, forced to transport their supplies in his wagon, he had worried about the family and the church community he had left at home. But when the army had moved east, away from northwest Maryland, and had released him, he found that his family had fared worse than he had imagined. While their neighbors had moved on, away from the constant presence of the armies and their insatiable appetites, Lovinia had stayed on the farm, unwilling to leave until she knew what had happened to him. But with only a few supplies overlooked by the hungry soldiers, she had succumbed to worry and illness. By the time he had arrived home after six weeks away, there was nothing to hold them there, even if the scavenging soldiers had overlooked something they could survive on. All that was left was the worn-out team and his wagon.

Even his flock had scattered, leaving him a minister without a church.

*Dear Gott.*

Knowing that the army had intended to move north, into

Pennsylvania, Gideon had loaded his family and a few possessions into the wagon and set out for the west. To the large Amish communities in Ohio. There, they would be safe. There, Lovinia could recover from this sickness. There, they could be a family again.

But would he . . . could he . . . fulfill his calling as a minister again? Could Gott use a broken man?

Gideon rocked Daniel in his arms until the baby fell asleep and he laid him on the cot next to Lovinia.

Once the horses had rested, they set off again. Gideon walked to relieve some of the wagon's weight, leading the team as the road sloped upward away from the creek. They passed a lane leading to a house as they reached the crest of the slope, then Gideon stopped. In front of him, the valley spread out. The road they were on went down to meet the creek again, then followed it along the bottom of the valley. Beyond a wood, a large barn and farmhouse settled into the landscape on the far side of the creek. From there, the road swung to the right, away from the creek and past another farmhouse to disappear up the rise beyond.

Unbidden, a verse from the book of Matthew came to him: *For I was hungry, and ye gave me meat; I was thirsty and ye gave me drink; I was a stranger, and ye took me in.* Gideon bowed his head. Pride ate at him, rejecting that he and his family were in need. *Dear Gott, you are teaching me humility. Once more. Help me to humble myself before you.*

"Is this where we're going, Daed?" Roseanna's voice called, laced with longing.

*I was a stranger . . .*

"I hope so, Daughter." He climbed back on the wagon seat before driving down the slope to the creek.

As they passed another farm lane, one that disappeared into a stand of pine trees on the right, a young woman met them, striding down the lane with an unhurried gait that would fit better on a man. She wore a proper kapp, but no bonnet, and wild strands of red hair framed her face. Gideon's gaze met hers for a second, long enough to watch the coffee-brown eyes narrow and then shift to the wagon and the children watching her.

Gideon pulled the team to a halt, leaning on the brake handle. "We're trying to find the Weaver Creek settlement—"

"You've found it!" The red-haired woman broke into his question as she crossed her arms. "I'm Ruby Weaver, and my father's farm is across the stone bridge there."

A smile crept over her face as she looked back at the children and then at Gideon again. He blinked to keep himself from staring at her. So forward! Perhaps they shouldn't stop at Weaver's Creek, but go farther into Holmes County instead, where they might find a more conservative community where the women acted more like women than men.

Then he glanced at Lovinia, asleep with Ezra and Daniel napping on either side of her cot, her raspy breathing audible in the afternoon quiet. She couldn't travel any farther. They had to stop here, at least until Lovinia was better.

"Is there a place we could stay?" Gideon looked back at Ruby Weaver.

"Ja, for sure. If you drive on to the house, we can ask my father where he thinks would be best."

"Daed, can she ride with us?" Roseanna didn't stop staring at the stranger. "She doesn't have to walk if we're going the same way, does she?"

"Ach, ne." The woman's laugh bubbled, a sound Gideon

hadn't heard an adult utter in more months than he could count. The girls grinned. "I'll run on ahead and tell Mamm you're coming. She'll want to make sure you have a good supper."

Ruby Weaver ran toward the stone bridge as Gideon stared after her. When she had said she would run on ahead, he thought she had been using a figure of speech. But ne, she ran as if she was Roseanna's age rather than a grown woman. Roscanna and Sophia stood in the wagon bed, their heads on either side of him.

"I like her laugh," Sophia said.

"What do you think, Roscanna?" Gideon waited for his oldest daughter's answer.

Roseanna glanced down at Lovinia, then back at him. "I think she could make Mamm feel better just by smiling at her."

Gideon caught Roseanna's narrow chin in his hand and stroked her cheek with his thumb, thinking of the way the red-haired woman's presence had brightened the afternoon, even with her forward ways. "I think you're right, Daughter. Shall we go meet the rest of the Weavers?"

Both girls nodded as Gideon started the horses down the gentle slope. The road followed the creek at the bottom of the valley, then went to the right, while Gideon turned the horses into the farm lane on the left and across the stone bridge.

Ruby had disappeared into the large white farmhouse ahead of them, and as Gideon pulled the team to a halt by the porch, an older man stepped out.

"Welcome, stranger. Welcome." He tied the horses to the hitching rail. "I'm Abraham Weaver. My wife, Lydia, is inside.

She'll have a meal ready for you soon, but she's already pouring glasses of fresh buttermilk for the children."

"You don't have to—"

"For sure, we don't have to, but I can't stop Lydia when it comes to spoiling little ones." He lifted Sophia to the ground, then reached for Roseanna. "Ruby is making up the bed in Jonas's room." He peered over the side of the wagon where Lovinia and the boys slept. "We'll put your wife there and Lydia will take good care of her."

Gideon jumped from the wagon seat. "I'm Gideon Fisher, and my wife is Lovinia. I'm afraid she is quite ill. The trip has been hard on her."

Abraham glanced into the wagon, his face grim. Gideon knew what he saw. No supplies. A sick woman. Poverty.

"Where have you come from?" Abraham asked, turning his gaze back to Gideon.

"From Maryland, just south of the Mason-Dixon line."

"Did you see anything of the war?"

"That is why we left our home. The armies ravaged our farms, scattered our church, and left us with nothing." Gideon swallowed, pushing past the pride. "We need refuge. Just until we can get back on our feet. Then I can pay you back."

"'I was a stranger and ye took me in.'" Abraham smiled. "The Good Book only asks us to give, not to expect repayment. We have a place in our home for all of you, and you will stay with us as long as you need to. Perhaps you will find a new home here in Weaver's Creek."

Gideon pulled his girls close as he glanced around the Weavers' farm. "Perhaps we will."

# Acknowledgments

When a book comes to its completion, it isn't due to the efforts of only one person. I'm privileged to have my name on the front cover of this book, but many people have had a hand in it.

I'd like to thank my dear husband for being as passionate about history as I am and for concentrating on Civil War history several years ago. He is the one who dragged me to battlefield sites until I caught the bug too, and it hasn't let me go. I owe him a research trip to visit the Civil War battlefields we haven't seen yet.

I also want to thank the editors and staff at Revell and Baker Publishing Group for the fabulous behind-the-scenes work they do to take the story I send their way and turn it into the volume you hold in your hand. Special thanks go to my editor, Vicki Crumpton, who sees the "big picture" of the story. Her revision notes are always valuable.

As always, my agent Sarah Freese with WordServe Literary is indispensable. Thank you for your tireless work.

But most of all, I would like to thank my Lord for guiding every step I take and every word I write.

**Jan Drexler** brings a unique understanding of Amish traditions and beliefs to her writing. Her ancestors were among the first Amish, Mennonite, and Brethren immigrants to Pennsylvania in the 1700s, and their experiences are the inspiration for her stories. Jan lives in the Black Hills of South Dakota with her husband of thirty-five years, where she enjoys hiking in the Hills and spending time with their expanding family. She is the author of several books from Love Inspired, as well as *Hannah's Choice, Mattie's Pledge* (finalist for the 2017 Holt Medallion), and *Naomi's Hope*, all part of the Journey to Pleasant Prairie series from Revell.

"Jan Drexler's Amish family is so engaging that we're right there sitting down with them at their supper table, sharing their joys and sorrows as they embrace the adventure of life."

—Ann H. Gabhart, bestselling author of *The Innocent*

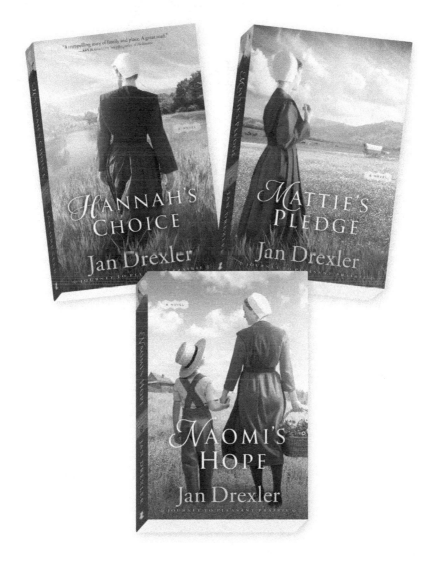

# Meet
# JAN DREXLER
www.jandrexler.com

---

Learn about the Amish

Find recipes, sewing, and quilting patterns

And more!

CPSIA information can be obtained
at www.ICGtesting.com
Printed in the USA
LVHW091703090419
613521LV00009B/130/P